WALLACE STEGNER'S
WEST

WALLACE STEGNER'S
WEST

Edited with an Introduction by Page Stegner

Santa Clara University, Santa Clara, California
Heyday Books, Berkeley, California

This book was made possible in part by a generous grant from the Book Club of California.

Library of Congress Cataloging-in-Publication Data

Stegner, Wallace Earle, 1909-1993.
  Wallace Stegner's West / edited with an introduction by Page Stegner.
      p. cm. -- (A California legacy book)
  Includes bibliographical references.
  ISBN 978-1-59714-111-6 (pbk. : alk. paper)
  I. Western stories. 2. West (U.S.)--Description and travel. 3. California--Description and travel. I. Stegner, Page. II. Title.
  PS3537.T316A6 2008
  813'.52--dc22
                        2008028609

Cover Photograph: *Calero Dusk*, © 2006 by G Dan Mitchell
Book Design: Lorraine Rath
Printing and Binding: Thomson-Shore, Dexter, MI

This California Legacy book was copublished by Santa Clara University and Heyday Books. Orders, inquiries, and correspondence should be addressed to:
      Heyday Books
      P. O. Box 9145, Berkeley, CA 94709
      (510) 549-3564, Fax (510) 549-1889
      www.heydaybooks.com

Printed on 30% consumer waste recycled paper. ♻

10 9 8 7 6 5 4 3 2 1

CONTENTS

Major Works By Wallace Stegner

Fiction

Remembering Laughter
The Potter's House
On a Darkling Plain
Fire and Ice
The Big Rock Candy Mountain
Second Growth
The Women on the Wall
The Preacher and the Slave
The City of the Living
A Shooting Star
All the Little Live Things
Angle of Repose
The Spectator Bird
Recapitulation
Crossing to Safety

Non-fiction

Mormon Country
One Nation
Beyond the Hundredth Meridian
Wolf Willow
The Gathering of Zion
The Sound of Mountain Water
The Uneasy Chair
American Places (with Page Stegner and Eliot Porter)
One Way to Spell Man
The American West as Living Space
Where the Bluebird Sings to the Lemonade Springs
Marking the Sparrow's Fall

INTRODUCTION

Wallace Stegner, the second of two sons born to George and Hilda Paulson Stegner, arrived in this world on February 18, 1909, on a farm owned by Hilda's father, Chris Paulson, in Lake Mills, Iowa. Paulson, a widower when Hilda was only twelve, was of Norwegian immigrant stock, English-speaking only when absolutely necessary, staunchly principled, hardworking, taciturn, rigidly Lutheran, and utterly patriarchal—the moral opposite in virtually every way of George Stegner, whom his daughter married at an early age, in spite of her father's vigorous protest.

George, whose origins and ancestry are obscure (beyond the fact that he grew up somewhere near Rock Island, Illinois, and fled from home at the age of fourteen never to look back), was, in the words of his son, "a husky, laughing, reckless, irreverent, storytelling charmer, a ballplayer, a fancy skater, a trapshooting champion, a pursuer of the main chance, a true believer in the American dream of something for nothing, a rolling stone who confidently expected to be eventually covered with moss." In short, a man who offended every piety Chris Paulson stood for—which was perhaps his major attraction to Paulson's "bond-servant," motherless daughter, and which very likely put the starch in her decision to run off. If she ever regretted her choice—and many times she must have—she kept it to herself.

Chasing the dream of getting rich quick, of finding some big rock candy mountain just over the horizon, kept the Stegner family drifting from pillar to post for nearly twelve years—from Iowa to North Dakota to Washington, back to Iowa, and eventually to Eastend, a frontier hamlet in the Cypress Hills of Saskatchewan. There they homesteaded a farm on the Canadian side of the U.S./Canada border and set about trying to raise wheat.

More pie in the sky. Six years and five busted crops later, they were on the move again, this time to Great Falls, Montana, where George made a furtive living running bootleg whiskey across the Canadian line into Prohibition-plagued America. But a year later restlessness overcame him once more and he packed up his reluctant entourage and headed southwest to Salt Lake City.

Miraculously, in the land of Zion they finally stuck. Wallace would attend high school in Salt Lake City, graduating from East High at the age of sixteen and immediately enrolling in the University of Utah, where, working part-time in a linoleum store to help make ends meet, he would complete his degree in five years. Encouraged by his professors to go on to graduate school, he went east to the University of Iowa, completing his Ph.D. in American Literature in 1935. After a brief teaching stint back at the University of Utah, he headed still further east to a position at the University of Wisconsin. A year later, and owing in part to a Little Brown Prize for his novelette *Remembering Laughter*, he was offered an appointment at Harvard.

So where does California fit into all this wandering? The California Legacy books are a showcase for distinguished "California" authors, and by this point Wallace Stegner has almost reached his forties without setting foot in the Golden State, except for one academic year at UC Berkeley (1933)—an adventure terminated, says Jackson Benson, because the "stodgy graduate curriculum in English, with its emphasis on philology—on Latin, Old French, Anglo-Saxon, and Middle English—was not really his cup of tea." As it would turn out for this deeply rooted Westerner, neither was teaching at Harvard, though Harvard would satisfy a provincial yearning for cultural respectability not intrinsic to the inter-mountain West, and would introduce him to at least two profoundly influential men with whom he would become lifelong friends, Robert Frost and Bernard DeVoto.

Nevertheless, "all my life I've been going away east and coming home west," Stegner once wrote. So when *Look* magazine offered him a job writing a series of articles on prejudice and the treatment of minorities in America, he left Harvard and moved to Santa Barbara, California, to be closer to the predominant sources of his investigation (Filipinos, Japanese, Chinese, Mexicans, American Indians), overshooting the true West by a few hundred miles, to be sure, but definitely headed in the right direction. And when a year later Stanford University offered him a half-time teaching job at a full-time salary, it was more than this child of the Depression could resist.

The rest, as they say, is history—nearly fifty years of it spent in the Palo Alto foothills behind Stanford, and more than enough to qualify him as an immigrant Californian. California, with its complex, pluralistic society, cultural diversification, and sheer worldliness, was precisely the environment for a man fleeing the provincial backwaters from whence he came but unable to find consoling habitat in the hills and hummocks east of the Mississippi.

In July of 1945 Stegner wrote an enthusiastic letter to his old friend and one-time University of Wisconsin colleague, Philip Gray:

> California, that is Palo Alto, is not wilderness, coming at three thousand an acre and selling altogether too fast at that price. It is very pleasant country, for all that: golden wild-oat hills dotted with marvelous old live oaks and bay trees, with a dark pine-covered ridge of the coast range behind, and in front the hills dropping down over orchards and town to the bay, and beyond the bay the barren gold ridge of the San Jose Mountains with Mount Diablo coming up in the midst of it.

It was the beginning of a long-term love/hate affair with a region he would describe in a *Saturday Review* essay (included in this volume, "The West Coast: Region with a View") as "America only more so," and it would remain his home for the rest of his life.

Perhaps love/hate is too strong. But Stegner's initial enthusiasm for this "region with a view" certainly tempered over time as those hillsides and orchards were transformed by development into an endless suburb stretching from San Francisco to San Jose, and as the home he built in 1949 in the Los Altos Hills became inexorably surrounded by mini-mansions and starter castles. A good deal of his time over the ensuing years was spent fighting that development and arguing for the preservation of open spaces. Asked by Richard Etulain (in *Conversations with Wallace Stegner on Western History and Literature*, University of Utah Press, Salt Lake, 1983) if he was optimistic about the future of the West, Stegner offered a qualified "no." The few things that had been done right in the West were belated, he said, inadequate, too little, too late, and while he was speaking specifically of the inter-mountain West, his opinion included California—only more so. Nevertheless, counting himself among its permanent inhabitants, he felt a moral responsibility to the place which he forevermore would call home, and while, as noted, he was no native son of the Golden West, over the years he did as much as any aboriginal toward the advancement of its cultural environment and the protection of its natural surroundings.

In must be said, however, that the "essential" Wallace Stegner was never so parochial or sub-regional in his literary output as to be categorized as a "California writer," unless that term refers only to living space. Relatively few of his 35 published books, 57 short stories, 242 articles, 164 forewords, afterwords, introductions, essays, chapters, and critical prefaces to other people's work are set in, or have anything to do with, that "terrestrial paradise" so named by our esteemed sixteenth-century composer of episodic novels, Garci Ordóñez Rodríguez de Montalvo. *All the Little Live Things, A Shooting Star*, two sections of *Angle of Repose*, and five short stories comprise the regional oeuvre—which seems remarkably little for so prolific a writer.

The *New York Times*, identifying him as "William" Stegner, went on to describe him as "the Dean of Western writers." That is perhaps closer to the truth, as most of his work was concerned with that much broader region, and as various localities west of the hundredth meridian claim him as one of their very own. The State of Utah counts him a native son, though he wasn't, quite, and the University of Utah's S. J. Quinney College of Law has created the Wallace Stegner Center for Land, Resources and the Environment in his honor. Montana, where he lived for one year when he was eleven, also argues for a piece of the action. Montana State University at

Bozeman has created the Wallace Stegner Chair in Western Studies to commemorate his passing through. The Eastend Arts Council in Eastend, Saskatchewan, where he attended grammar school and learned those frontier attitudes and cowboy codes of conduct he said he'd spent much of his life trying to escape (not altogether successfully), has restored the house his father built in the town in 1915 (now called the Wallace Stegner House), transforming it into quarters for artists in residence. And then there's the State of Vermont, the setting for two of his novels and five short stories, where he spent many summers of his life at his summer home on Baker Hill in the village of Greensboro, and where, in accordance with his written instructions, his ashes were scattered after his death.

But when the maples started to turn outside his "think house" on that hill and Vermonters started covering up their tomatoes in anticipation of an early frost, it was back to northern California, his home in Los Altos Hills, his duties as director of the Stanford Creative Writing Program. As much as anything it is that writing program that identifies him with the state and its contribution to literary culture. Founded by Stegner in 1946, it became, under the twenty-five years of his guidance, a virtual Who's Who of contemporary American writers—writers like Eugene Burdick, Tillie Olsen, Max Apple, Evan Connell, Steve Dixon, Larry McMurtry, Robert Stone, Ken Kesey, Ed McClanahan, Nancy Packer, Ernest Gaines, Merrill Joan Gerber, Scott Turow, Wendell Berry, Kenneth Fields, Robert Pinsky, Robert Hass, Edward Abbey, Al Young, James D. Houston, John Daniel, N. Scott Momaday, Thomas McGuane, Tobias Wolff, Ron Hansen, Ray Carver, William Kittredge. "Stegner Fellows" they were called. "Stegner Fellows" they are still called, fifteen years after his death, and in spite of the fact that not long after his retirement, furious with the Stanford English department for hiring a postmodern, avant-garde, experimental writer whose work was an insult to everything Stegner stood for artistically, he tried to have his name deleted from the program. Fortunately, cooler heads prevailed.

But he did retire early. As he explained to Richard Etulain:

I...was pretty fed up with the disruptions of the sixties. It was no fun teaching....So I decided I had other things to do, and it was getting on toward the time when I had only a few years to do them in...and I've managed to get three or four books into the years since.

Those few years turned out to be, in fact, twenty-one years (Stegner died in Santa Fe, New Mexico, in 1993 from injuries sustained in a car accident), and the books he turned out over that period included four more novels, *Angle of Repose* (which received the Pulitzer Prize in 1972), *The Spectator Bird* (which received the National Book Award in 1977), *Recapitulation*, and *Crossing to Safety*; a biography of Bernard DeVoto, *The Uneasy Chair* (along with an edition of his letters); and four collections of essays, *American Places* (with Page Stegner and Eliot Porter), *One Way to Spell Man* (for which he received the prestigious John Muir Award from the Sierra Club), *The American West as Living Space*, and *Where the Bluebird Sings to the Lemonade Springs*. A fifth collection, *Marking the Sparrow's Fall*, edited posthumously, was published five years after his death.

Betwixt and between this flurry of activity he wrote forewords and afterwords to a half-dozen books by other people, gave countless lectures and talks, traveled frequently to receive honorary doctorates from the University of Montana and Middlebury College, the first Robert Kirsh Award for Life Achievement from the *Los Angeles Times*, the John Muir Award for contributions to conservation from the Sierra Club, the Western History Association Prize, the Governor's Award for the Arts from the California Arts Council, the PEN USA West Lifetime Achievement Award, The Cyril Magnin Award for Outstanding Achievement in the Arts. Only when he was to receive a National Medal for the Arts Award from President George H. W. Bush did he stay home, declining the honor in protest over political controls imposed by the administration on the National Endowment for the Arts:

> I believe strongly in government support for the arts—believe, in fact, that a government that does not support the arts harms both itself and the nation. I also believe that support is meaningless, even harmful, if it restricts the imaginative freedom of those to whom it is given.

Asked why, in retirement, and fast approaching his seventy-fifth year, he continued taking on new projects, new assignments, new deadlines, he told Richard Etulain:

> It's like a beaver's teeth—he has to chew or else his jaws lock shut... You keep doing it because that's really what you're made to do, that's what you want to do, and everything that you do projects you one stone further...so you throw another rock, until you just wear out.

NON-FICTION

LITERARY BY ACCIDENT

Address to the Utah Libraries Association Convention, March 1975

It seems to me that every time I come back to Utah, I find myself talking in essentially regional terms. I find myself talking about regionalism as a literary movement, a historical movement; about local writing in relation to national writing or New York writing, or world writing; about cultural pluralism or New York provincialism; about Utah's coming of age; and topics of that kind. I find myself happily taking the side of local writers and local historians who promote regional culture, regional themes in literature, regional history, regional publishing, regional pride. And that's in spite of the fact that I have some real reservations about regionalism. It seems to me a stage, an inevitable stage, on the road to cultural self-confidence and maturity, and in that sense absolutely justifiable. But it sometimes leads us—and this I've observed in Canada; I've observed it in the literary history of the United States, among the Connecticut Wits; I've observed it in every region of the United States—it sometimes leads us to praise local writers not because they're good, but because they're local. (I even suspect that I'm often praised in Utah not because I'm good, but because I'm local. I don't like to think that, but it's a possibility.) It leads us sometimes to think that any adverse criticism of a local writer, or worse yet, any bland ignoring of his productions, is a conspiracy among Eastern snobs and esthetes. When we think that, I think our regionalism is tending to become something close to hysteria or paranoia, and that kind of regionalism

I don't espouse, or try not to. The fact remains that I have been writing about Utah and the West for about forty years. And the more I learn my trade, the more I comprehend how completely the West is my material, my knowledge. It's the kind of knowledge which is not merely knowledge but affiliation.

And so I didn't come here to knock Utah or the West or regionalism or Western readers and writers. I came here really to ruminate aloud, if you'll permit me, on the general question of how a writer of my generation, beginning in the twenties, found out who he was and what his job was. If I'm personal I hope you will think I'm local enough to be forgiven, also old enough to be indulged. The old is for sure. I just had a birthday. I agree with my friend Bruce Bliven, the former editor of the *New Republic*, who is about eighty-five and has a heart attack every year and writes a new book every year, and when he was asked, "Do you feel old?" said, "No, I don't feel like an old man, I feel like a young man with something the matter with him!" This is the way I'm beginning to feel. I'm sixty-six at this moment, and in a few months I'm going to be sixty-six and two thirds and that will make me an incommensurable case, and I'll start spitting out 6's like a stuck computer. And so I think I will take advantage of this not necessarily wanted anniversary to do some looking back.

Looking back from sixty-six isn't quite the same thing as looking forward from sixteen was. At sixteen, especially since I was sixteen in the homey, provincial city of Salt Lake, the view I had was pretty exhilarating. The whole world lay outside the immediate valley. We could look ahead to the day when we would achieve independence from our parents or the day when we'd get our driver's license or the day when we would graduate or the day when we would meet the girl we were going to marry or the day when we could go into a tavern and get a can of beer without a false mustache and an ID card. All kinds of little doors that one, according to the myth, passes through on the way to maturity and adulthood. The record is now, alas, behind me, not in front of me. I find I can't plant a tree anymore without thinking I'm endowing posterity more than I am my family or myself. I can't buy a pup without having E. B. White's kind of wry perception that the pup will probably outlive me.

We do learn, I think, by looking backward not forward. But looking backward comes pretty late sometimes, for some of us more than for others. If we didn't learn by looking backward, there would be no need of libraries or universities or history or any of the things which together make us custodians of the word and give us a cause for thinking that's a legitimate and honorable profession. "We get too soon oldt und too late schmart," as the old Dutchman said. And so the backward look is likely to be, if it isn't sentimental, depressing. Why look back? Well, precisely because I find myself here among what I conceive to be my own tribe, literary and Utahn. And having been blessed or cursed with a talent, I feel compelled to report to somebody on my stewardship of it. Moreover, both Utah and I have changed a whole lot since I was in high school and college here. Both of us are a lot more aware than we were then, and so what I'm going to be talking about will have more historical than contemporary relevance.

Let us say that I was born with a reasonable intelligence and with a certain gift for words. I'm not responsible for the endowment, but I am responsible for what I do with it. My parents weren't in much of a position to teach me anything, and so the responsibility for the direction I was given, the opportunities I was shown, the possibilities that were displayed to me, fell on the educational system, first in Saskatchewan in Canada and then in Montana and then more particularly in Utah. Of these three, Utah was incomparably the best because Utah had much more sense of its own history. The fact that I wasn't a member of the Church meant that it wasn't my history, but at least I knew some people who took their history seriously, which in other parts of the West I might not have. The difficulty was that I didn't take it that seriously and didn't know it that well. And because everybody around me was getting it through his church affiliation, it was not much taught in schools. So I didn't get much of it. I lived here without knowing exactly where I lived or what I was doing here.

It appalls me to realize really how much brute accident accounts for what became of me, perhaps of other people of my generation, perhaps even yet of people. Every significant movement in my life resulted from a conjunction between a lurking inclination, which was the talent undeveloped and raw, and opportunities that were not merely not taught to me or shown to me, but weren't sought for and often weren't recognized when they opened up. I didn't set out, in other words, to study the history and literature of my native region or to contribute to them. School never urged me to or taught me how to. I didn't even set out to become a writer. Very few people, I think, in the early stages of a regional civilization in this country do. Bernard DeVoto in pre-war Ogden had a red hot yearning to be a writer, but he's almost the only one I can think of. I suspect that now a lot of young people do get much better advice. There are writing classes in college. There are people who have some conception of what is possible to somebody in the wider world.

I became a writer because I had this little gift, which like a beaver's teeth kept growing and making me chew to wear them down or else they'd lock my mouth shut. I didn't chew to get trees down or to store bark or to build dams or to do anything intelligent. I just chewed because my teeth were growing, and I had to keep them worn down. And I didn't even know enough to do that at first. Let us say I knew I was good at words, better than some. I used to get good grades in English courses. When I got to the University of Utah, Vardis Fisher excused me from a couple of quarters of freshman English, because he thought I didn't need them. I took some writing courses with Fisher and L. A. Quivey, and I won a prize, and I sold a story to the Salt Lake *Telegram* and got ten dollars for it, and I edited *The Pen*, you know, that sort of thing. I was university-literary. It never occurred to me that I could become a writer. This was all something on the side. I had a job selling rugs and linoleum. I had it all through college, and I thought I was going to go on doing it. Very low horizons, I think you will grant—right on the floor. No ambitions, no imagination really. There were a few people in Salt Lake in the 1920s who were literary as I was, as a kind of game, and we all read Joyce and Hemingway and Havelock Ellis and Freud. We played at it part time in a collegiate sort of way. It wasn't a possibility in our coming adult world, which may account for the singular lack of volition and dedication I displayed.

I was about to graduate when the chairman of the Psychology Department, Professor Barlow, said to me, "Why don't you go on to graduate school?" And I said, "Uh, I don't know." "What if I got you a fellowship in psychology?" he said. "Would you like to come to graduate school?" "Sure," I said. "Fine. Great." So then I went and told Professor Neff of the English Department that I was going to graduate school in psychology, and he was very upset. He said, "You're an English major. What are you doing in psychology?" So why didn't he see if he could get me a fellowship somewhere? "Sure," I said. "Fine," surprised and pleased and everything. And shortly I found myself with a teaching assistantship at the University of Iowa and was off for what I then thought of as the East.

You could call it fate, but I would call it inertia. Pure inertia. I had no more volition than a chip on a big river. I knew no past whatever, and hence, I conceived of no future. I was really the existential boy. I was right here in the now generation a long time back.

Actually I had every reason to stay in Salt Lake. All my friends were here. I had that job, as before said, which could be expanded or contracted as I needed it, full-time or part-time. I had a girl, moreover, whom I had no desire to leave behind, and I might have looked forward to rising in the linoleum trade. Yet, when that absolutely unthumbed, unsolicited opportunity pulled up beside the road and opened its doors, I climbed in and said, "Where to?" He said, "The moon?" And I said, "Fine. Okay. Good. Let's go!" I wasn't going East to become a writer; I wasn't going East to become anything that I had thought of. I was going East to become an English teacher, something that a month before that had never entered my head. I was actually a piece of Silly Putty, I could be pushed into any shape that anybody wanted to push me into, and that I suspect was about as Western as anything else about me because I had grown up migratory, and I had grown up opportunistic, and when something showed, sure I followed that particular lead. And I don't think that tendency has changed entirely, here in the West, yet.

So I had a chance for more. I got to Iowa City, and I found that Norman Foerster had just instituted something that he called the school of letters, which would, among other things, give you an M.A. in writing with a creative thesis, with permission. I thought of myself as literary, so I applied for permission. Mr. Foerster read the two stories that I gave him, including the one the Salt Lake *Telegram* had paid me ten dollars for, and he didn't think I was good enough. I really didn't have any ambition to be a writer, but that made me mad, that hurt my pride. I was literary. Of course I was good enough. So I wheedled around and talked to a lot of people and finally got myself into the program with my confidence somewhat dashed.

I would like to say that at that point, having discovered my true bent, I neglected all my other courses and threw myself into writing the stories that I was supposed to write for my thesis. But I didn't. I did the stories just the way I did any other academic chores, and because I discovered that I didn't know anything, literally anything, about anything, I had to work my head off trying to catch up on things that it appeared all normally intelligent, educated people had known from childhood. So I found myself reading Chaucer, Shakespeare, Aristotle, Goethe, people whose names practically had not been familiar to me not too long before. It wasn't until the second year of graduate school that I began to feel half as confidently literary as I had been in Salt Lake.

By that time, I had discovered a role. I discovered that to those people in the middle, in a little college town in the middle of rural Iowa, I was a provincial from the West. I was a kind of romantic-looking character who lived out where things were bigger and better and noisier, higher and deeper. So all of a sudden I had a role. They sometimes made over me as if I were the janitor's bright child, you know. So without believing a word of it, literally, without thinking of it in any sense serious, I decided that I was a Western writer. Not only a writer, but a *Western* writer. I remember telling Stephen Vincent Benet when he came visiting on the campus that I was just about to set out on a three-decker peasant novel about Saskatchewan, a place so deprived, so culturally starved that Salt Lake City literally had looked like Rome to me when we came here.

Well, there I was with my three-decker novel project; this takes me up to maybe January 1932. I'd finished the creative thesis, and I'd taken the M.A. The banks were all closed, milk was 2¢ a quart, eggs were 6¢ a dozen, there wasn't a job in sight. I remember people fighting, literally fighting each other with fists—two graduate students—over who should be recommended for a job at the University of North Dakota at a yearly salary of $1600. There weren't any jobs. I might as well have said, "You can't teach, you might as well be a literary fella." But I didn't. I stayed in graduate school where it was warm. It wasn't *very* warm, but it was warmer than it was outside. And I went to studying, not writing; to American literature, because it became clear to me that if anybody ever did hire anybody again, the Ph.D. in a substantive field was more saleable than a vague literary aspiration and some unpublished manuscripts and an M.A. in a field that nobody considered academic.

Nevertheless, at this point I owe one professor two votes of thanks, Mr. Foerster for both of them; one because he encouraged writing among graduate students, and two, because when it became apparent that that was not a living, he steered me into American literature, which was a little closer than Aristotle and Goethe to what I knew and felt personally. And back at the University of Utah I owed another debt because, by pure accident again, I'd been taking a course as a freshman in geology from Frederick J. Pack. A friend of mine on examination day smashed his thumb in his car door, so I had to take him to the hospital to get his thumb patched up and splints put on it, and I missed the final exam. Mr. Pack, instead of giving me a make-up exam, made me read Clarence Edward Dutton's *The High Plateau of Utah*, one of the early geologic reports. And again by pure accident, we had a cottage down on the Fishlake Plateau, right in the middle of the high plateaus, and all of a sudden history crossed my trail. I found that when I went up Seven Mile I found I knew what had happened there sixty, seventy years before. I think that's the first time that my active, existential life happened to cross the track of history. And Dutton crops up later. As a matter of fact I did a very bad Ph.D. dissertation on Dutton, a most unlikely subject for a Ph.D. dissertation in English because he was a geologist examining the Southern Utah plateaus and the Grand Canyon. Accident had played three roles at that point.

Well, chance, chance, chance. My old friend Milton Cowan, who was just back from a mission in Germany, wanted to go to Berkeley on a fellowship and get a Ph.D. in German. "Why don't you come along?" he said to me. It never occurred to me to consider that American literature at Iowa and writing in Iowa were more up my alley than what I might be likely to get at Berkeley, so I said, "Sure, I'll go along with you!" So I transferred to Berkeley. Chance again. But if I was inert, at least I was beginning to be teachable, I think, about that time. In one year at Berkeley, I suffered through a year of Anglo-Saxon, a year of Old French, Arthurian romance, historical English grammar, and the Latin reading exams and other fossil remnants of George Lyman Kittredge. I decided at the end of that year that I didn't really need Old Norse and Gothic, which were also required for a Ph.D. in English, and that I much preferred Mr. Foerster's emphases to the emphases that were then in vogue at Berkeley. As for Cowan, he'd been taking Old High German and Mittelhochdeutsch and comparative philology and something else all at the same time, and he was beginning to babble the *Niebelungenlied* in his sleep. So I twisted his arm, and we went back to Iowa together.

On the road at last, you might think. But no, not quite. Still the deep Depression. I didn't have any money at all. About November a job turned up at Augustana College, a little Lutheran college in Rock Island—head of the department, no less, with a half-time teaching load. And let me explain that half-time teaching load: Anglo-Saxon, literary criticism, history of English literature, and one freshman English course. At a salary, as I recall, of $900, something like that. I would have weekends and Fridays off, they assured me, so that I could pursue my studies in Iowa City, which was about forty miles away. Also I could pursue a girl I had met in Iowa City. I did, too.

About May, Augustana offered me a full-time job for the next year, and I took it, turning down one that Mr. Neff had offered me here in Salt Lake because I wanted to be near Iowa City and that girl. And then just before the end of school the fundamentalists in Augustana College, the fundamentalists of the Augustana Synod of the Lutheran Church, seizing the chance to embarrass the evangelicals, who were charge of the college at the time, wrote me a letter—I'd been hired by one of the evangelicals, you see. I got the letter from the fundamentalist head of the board, asking me to answer charges that I was an atheist, an agnostic, a disbeliever in the Augsburg Confession, a disbeliever in the principles of higher Christian education, and something else that I forget. I could have replied that I was no such thing, that I was a Western boy being systematically educated out of his background, but I didn't really know that at the time. So I wrote cunningly back to them, saying that I couldn't see how I could be an agnostic and an atheist at the same time—that seemed to me philosophically difficult—and that as far the Augsburg Confession was concerned I never remembered ever reading it, and that the principles of higher Christian education were somewhat dark to me—I didn't know what they were. And then I rushed down to the Western Union office and wired Mr. Neff to see if the job in Salt Lake was still open, which it was. So quite by accident again it seemed necessary that my girl in Iowa City and I should get married and come West. These are the chances that move men's lives, I guess.

Do you begin to comprehend the life of the jellyfish? How little intelligent planning may go into a literary career, especially the career of a boy from the West? How accidental may be one's decision to return to his home town and home region to live and teach and write? And how little one may know about that home region after living in it for twenty-five years, knowing only the surface? I go on in that fashion for quite a while yet, if you can stand it. I'll try to cut it as painlessly short as possible.

Jump to the summer of 1935, to a little house on Princeton Avenue below 13th East. I didn't have anything driving me that summer, and I felt a vague sort of unrest. I didn't know it, but it was my teeth growing. So I sat down and started to write a story, something I hadn't done for three years since finishing my M.A. thesis. And it wasn't about *Beowulf*, it wasn't about Chaucer, it wasn't about Old French, it had nothing to do with the *chansons de geste*. It had to do with Saskatchewan, where I had spent my childhood; it was a little kind of counter-weighted idyll, a sort of prose poem which practically wrote itself, called "Bugle Song." It wasn't an especially good story, and it certainly wasn't a very complex one, but it felt good and it had written itself in about three hours. I sold it to somebody, moreover, the *Virginia Quarterly* as I remember, so this is almost the beginning of something. It also turned out to be the first words I wrote on that three-decker Saskatchewan peasant novel that I had threatened Stephen Benet with years before, which itself turned out not to be a three-decker and not to be especially about peasants, and not to be about Saskatchewan alone but to contain a good deal of the Northwest and Montana and Utah and other places where I had been. I published it five or six years later as *The Big Rock Candy Mountain,* and in it I made my first use of anything I knew about the West. All I knew about the West then was what I had lived of it, the places I had been, the people I had known.

Let me emphasize it again. I didn't choose a literary career and dedicate myself to it. I didn't choose the West as the place I would write about and from. They both chose me. It turned out that I had to chew, because I had those teeth, and it turned out that I had to chew cottonwoods because those were the trees I grew up among, the ones that I found handy for my chewing. My education didn't teach me who I was. It taught me primarily what I had derived from, many centuries back. This is common in new countries, that the education is geared for the old countries that we come from and not for the new countries that we live in. I wouldn't say, "Throw all of that out!" But I would say the emphasis was probably not in the right place for me.

Just one or two more autobioloquacious details. An awful lot of any career, in writing or anything else, is opportunity, which results most frequently from knowing people, knowing people who are in some way influential or powerful in whatever it is you're into. Inevitably ambition leads young Western writers eastward because that's where the opportunities are, still. That's also where people recognize the Western youngsters as a kind of different breed. That's also where the Western youngsters recognize themselves as, in the first place homesick, and in the second place, therefore, somehow becoming self-aware. But when we left Utah in 1937, we didn't go because I was mad at Utah or thought it was limited or because any clear opportunity lured us eastward. I was still accepting rides in any direction.

I happened to write a novelette about Iowa, a skeleton in my wife's family closet that won a prize, and made us a little money and emancipated us, as we thought, from academic drudgery. No more white man's burden—no more freshman English. There may be some people in this audience who remember the party we threw when that telegram announced that particular prize. My wife was so astonished she had a baby. But we were free, we thought, which we interpreted in a perfectly insane way as being free to get out of the West again. We were going to the Virgin Islands—why, God knows—live on the beach, eat coconuts and bananas, and write great books. We got about as far, we got exactly as far, as Dubuque, Iowa, where our child's grandmother persuaded us that we couldn't take that poor little baby down where they didn't have doctors even, probably nobody but witch doctors, and so she made us a proposal. She knew we weren't capable of taking care of that baby anyway, so she said, "Why don't I take him for a month and you go to France or somewhere and ride around on bicycles and have a nice vacation." So we did, and she did. And then we came back, and where did we find ourselves? Teaching at the University of Wisconsin, having blown our cash.

From Wisconsin by a series of contiguous jolts, the kind of jolts that move down a standing freight train when a switch engine backs into it, we moved from Wisconsin further eastward, by way of Yaddo and the Breadloaf Writer's Conference, to Harvard. By the time we arrived in Harvard in 1939 I was already a confirmed moonlighter. I had a profession which paid me wages, a living wage, and I had an avocation which demanded all my attention and time, which devoured them in fact. The talent which had, in a sense, liberated me and us had also imprisoned, at least me, and probably us. It told me where to go every morning from 8 to 12, seven days a week. It made me mine myself, fairly ruthlessly, exploiting the things that I found in myself; and those things which you find exploitable when you are a novelist turn out not to be the things you got out of books, but the things that you got out of living. Inevitably most of these things were Western. They were at least peripheral to my own experience. There's no depletion allowance, moreover. I don't get the break I would get if I were an oil well. Though my resources may be every bit as finite, I can't charge them off.

Well, from Harvard back to Stanford, finally. A very random life. Literary by accident, and with a kind of curve in and out, up and down, no perfect bell-shaped curve of finding the stuff that was mine properly to write about. You see, the first book was about Iowa, something I borrowed from my wife's family history. The second one was about Saskatchewan. The third one was about the University of Wisconsin and the Young Communist League. The fourth one, I guess, was *Mormon Country*, for by that time I was in Cambridge and homesick. There's nothing like Cambridge and Boston to make you in love with Utah, in spite of Harvard University. And the fifth book, I guess, was *The Big Rock Candy Mountain*. I was nudging up on Western subject matter. But then after *The Big Rock Candy Mountain* I did a book on racial and religious minorities in the United States for *Look* magazine. And then I did a book laid in Vermont. And so it went.

I was going up to Vermont to spend a semester off and finish *The Big Rock Candy Mountain* and do some other things. I had applied for a little grant from the Milton Fund, so called, of Harvard University. I couldn't think of anything that I wanted to do, and you had to have a project, so I quickly thought up a project. Out of the blue I thought up a project. I wanted to write a biography, I said, of John Wesley Powell, whom I had heard about from reading Dutton, whom I had read from the fact of my friend's smashing his thumb in a door.

It's like the loss of a horseshoe nail. There's a kind of inevitability in this accidental life. I found myself committed to a biography of John Wesley Powell and that committed me to the West. *Mormon Country* had made me begin to get an education. Reading for the vaguely conceived Powell book made me continue the process. I had to begin to know something. I hadn't yet got any very stringent sense of where I belonged in all this and what I thought about all this and what obligations I had in all this. I'd just been too busy writing to think.

I don't suppose I began to get any sense of obligation at all until about 1952, when I was at Stanford, teaching classes and seeing students in the afternoon, and running a program and reading papers and preparing lectures at night, and getting up in the morning to write from 8 to 12. Hot on the trail of whatever it was I was hot on the trail of, Ed Murrow tweaked my ear and said, "Write me a little piece" for that series of his called "This I Believe," which some of you may remember on the radio, little five-hundred-word credos. As usual, "Sure," I said, and I sat down that night to knock it off and clear the deck for whatever important thing I was going to do the next day. It took me a hard week. As soon as I started to think about it, I discovered that I knew very little about my own background and practically nothing about my own beliefs. What I finally read on the radio for Ed Murrow didn't satisfy me then, and it doesn't now, but there are certain things in it that I would still accept. Now and again you can say something halfway truthful without knowing what you're talking about. In the last sentence of that credo, for instance, I said, "For no right comes without a responsibility. In being born luckier than most of the world's millions, I am also born more obligated." That's a cliche, but I think that it's true. I felt that twenty years ago, though I didn't know what I was talking about. I feel it more now.

Nevertheless, you have to ask, "Obligated to whom?" To that abstraction, the reading public, which includes everybody from comic book collectors to graduate students poring over Aquinas, everybody from the disciples of Jacqueline Susann to the disciples of Søren Kierkegaard? I don't think so. You don't write for an audience, or you shouldn't. Even a fragment of an audience, even a regional audience, even an audience of your own family. You don't write for an audience at all, though unless you are fortunate enough to find one you might as well not have written.

You don't write to confirm the faiths or flatter the prejudices, or anything like that, of any group of people. There's nothing that a writer must do for any audience. And anyway the reading public seems to be a dying race. I was reading only a few weeks ago that more than half the entering freshmen at Berkeley can't read and write, and find bonehead freshman English a difficult voyage of discovery. So there soon may not be any reading public. If there isn't, then there's no obligation. Did I think that I owed an obligation to any set of ideas: religious, philosophical, esthetic, regional, fashionable, enduring, whatever? I hadn't been brought up to any such systematic belief, and I don't think I had adopted any. I didn't think I had to be a preacher, or a judge, or a propagandist. I knew that much even in 1952. But I knew I was lucky; I really was lucky. I didn't have any right to have got out of the furrow I was in, except that I was lucky. And I felt obligated not to any faith or audience or set of beliefs, but to my own talent, such as it was, big or little.

And beyond that, I suppose, to what I might call my constituents, or what I hope are my constituents. To the people who because of shared experience, shared sensation, shared affiliation, shared history, shared geography, are my most natural audience and at the same time are the principal force that shaped me, the lathe that put the crimps in me. If I seem to relate individual identity to a social group, I don't think that's so strange in Utah, and I think Utah taught it to me. If I suggest that Stegner is Stegner partly because he was for a long time in his formative years a part of Saskatchewan, Montana, and especially Utah, why that's precisely what I mean. I was shaped by the places and people among whom I grew, and they taught me ways of seeing and feeling. I learned from my elders' and my friends' attitudes folklore and all kinds of odds and ends, bits and pieces of experiences which have become part of me and therefore part of what I write, which have made me forever different from what I would be if I had grown up in Brooklyn or Queens, not better, not worse, just different.

The places where I grew up before I came to Utah were really culturally deprived: a few people culturally hungry, most people culturally anesthetized, no needs at all in that direction. Utah taught me at least a respect for history, though it wasn't my history, and though it and all other Western history was pretty dark to me. I had spent more time on Old French, literally, than I had spent studying the history of my own place and time. When it came to me that I wanted to write my way back into that history to learn more than my shallow personal experience had given me, to write my way back into it as an act of knowing, I had to get it up, practically from scratch. I had to add my personal history and to the little bit I knew from Dutton and to what I had got up from *Mormon Country*, an enormous amount more. And that, I suppose, is about where writing about the West became not an occasional but an essentially perpetual job. I haven't written about much but the West since. I finally put one book against another and began to, as they say, let one hand wash the other. From writing one book you learn enough to be able to conceive of writing another one. Eventually you begin to be by no means the master of a field, but at least halfway acquainted in it, and to know, therefore, who you are yourself and what it is you are trying to do. Personal Western experience and a *need* for a history in which I could belong lay around in me for forty years before I ever learned what to do about them, until quite by accident I arrived at an obligation both to my talent and (if you can bear the phrase) to my people.

The obligation I would like to detail because it isn't very complicated; it's only hard. The obligation is not to flatter, not to praise, certainly not to overpraise. The obligation is only to try to be honest, to try to be impartial, to try to be serious. That's not as simple as it sounds. Honesty is a virtue that is much asserted by writers, who very frequently confuse it with bad manners or with fashionable shock treatment. I was reading on the plane coming over this morning from San Francisco a piece in the San Francisco *Chronicle* about the new porn. And the new porn is going to be more honest than the old porn, it turns out. God bless. But I don't think you have to be garbage mouthed. I don't think you have to be sexually explicit or deviant or anything of the kind before you can be called honest. Honesty may involve any of those things, but it isn't necessarily limited to any of them. And only the critical intelligence of the person who is writing the book is ever going to be able to tell him what honesty is in that book that he is writing with that given material. I guess I'm afraid that a lot of our contemporary fiction is not so much honest, as it claims to be, but unbuttoned. That's not the sort of honesty I mean.

It seems to me that honesty consists in reporting what is there in approximately the proportions that it's there in. The minute you get your proportions wrong, you have begun to commit dishonesty. Also I don't think you can spend your time on what *should* be there without becoming dishonest, because then you are beginning to trace the shadows of dreams. It takes careful disciplining of yourself. Everybody who writes, and a lot of other people too, most people I hope, have to fight that battle all the time, because it involves being at once sympathetic with what you're writing about, understanding it as completely as possible, and, at the same time, standing one step back, stepping out of the culture, as the anthropologists say, in order to see yourself with something like an impartial camera eye.

Impartiality, the second element of this, what's that? I said I felt obligated to the Western society in which I grew up, which means I felt obligated to individuals, groups, attitudes, perhaps even myths, as being part of me. Some of them I wanted to eliminate by radical surgery; some of them I thought were limiting; others I thought were so incorrigibly myself that if I cut them out, I'd be dead. And I still think so. But I don't have to be, I think, a mouthpiece or a champion. I may turn out to be a foreordained critic like Bernard DeVoto, whose name is mud in Utah, but who said some very honest things about the West. Some things were not honest because he was neurotically involved in ways that he himself couldn't control, but a lot of things he said were honest, and he was disliked for this honesty. Nevertheless, I think it must be said of him that he loved what he was writing about. He castigated, as it were, within the family.

Permissiveness in certain situations, I think, is cowardice. Then here we come right straight into the problem that's raised by the doctrines of regionalism with which I began, problems which I'm sure I don't always solve. My friend Fred Manfred, that windmill of a man, he's a stout champion of everything Western. He thinks I'm not regional enough. You can read all about it in *Interviews with Fred Manfred*, which the University of Utah Press published recently, and for which I wrote an introduction getting even with him. He thinks I'm not regional enough. On the other hand, my friend Blair Fuller writes an article about me asking rather caustically why somebody who's familiar with the Campidoglio writes most of the time as if he were trapped in Temple Square. I would answer both of them at once: all I'm trying to do is to see through and around and into the material with which I am most familiar and sympathetic. I'm only trying, probably without too great success, to be true to my talent, to which, as Chekhov and Ibsen and a lot of other people have said, should not try to answer questions, but only to ask them correctly. All answers, I am afraid, are likely to be partial. But questions, if they are asked correctly, may be as impartial as the scrutiny of God.

Finally, what is it to be serious? Again, the obligation is two-ended;

it applies to the writer and to his material. The art of fiction is the art of human lives conceived in some contest of probability. The art of history is the art of recording human lives as they were in fact lived. Neither, I think, is to be handled frivolously by anyone who expects to be taken otherwise than frivolously. I don't mind persiflage, but I hate persiflage pretending profundity. Sympathy, which means literally feeling or suffering with, is the absolutely essential ingredient, as far as I see it, for the kind of history or fiction that I seem to want to write. And I have a great deal of trouble with those books which are written out of scorn and disgust. I won't say they shouldn't be written, and I certainly wouldn't censor them, but scorn seems to me relatively easy and relatively self-indulgent. It's moreover arrogant to a degree because it puts the scorner up here, shooting down upon, since he's shooting in print, people who haven't much defense against scorn. Laughter is supposed to cauterize, they tell me, and acid, I know, is used to etch. But scorn does have that superior stance, and I think only those without sin should cast the first stone. I don't know anybody without sin. I think scorn, in other words, falsifies experience in precisely the same degree but in the opposite way that sentimentality falsifies it. There is too much feeling for the circumstances or the wrong feeling for the circumstances. What I'm saying is that a writer of fiction ought to be as wise as he can be. Very easy prescription, very hard to follow. But virtue, I would guess, lies in trying, in not being sidetracked by trivia or subverted by the lowest forms of human taste and by the new porn, which have, I'm afraid, a Gresham's Law way of driving out higher levels of taste.

Because I am a Westerner, and, I suppose, therefore incorrigibly optimistic, I would prefer to say (if I were asked) that too much contemporary fiction does spring from disgust, from idealism gone sour. "Lilies that fester smell far worse than weeds." I remember once writing an essay on that subject in college, and I had the same feeling then that I have now, that somehow these soured books are not the books that say anything to me. I don't really want to repudiate the possibility, you see, of human decency and warmth and kindness and generosity and magnanimity, because I do see them, and I have seen them. The people that I grew up among, though they were by no means angelic or 100 percent virtuous, taught me at least the possibility.

There's another sentence in that credo that I wrote for Ed Murrow which might be pertinent in a confession or an apologia such as this one. I said there: "Everything potent is dangerous; it produces ill about as readily as good; it becomes good only through the control, discipline, and the wisdom with which we use it." By everything potent, I meant everything from human love to atomic fission. I certainly meant talent. By itself, as I said in the beginning, or maybe didn't say in the beginning but should have, talent is very common. It's as common as salmon eggs. And for the same reasons that millions of salmon eggs produce only a few salmon, millions of talents, through bad luck, ill health, poverty, bad social conditions, all sorts of causes, simply never come to anything. But talent is common. Everybody has a capacity for something, many people have a high capacity for something. That capacity is neither good nor evil. But it is quite often, I think, corrupt, corrupt as some of the tendencies in the society it reflects and the society that begot its author.

Literary people are sometimes inclined to take the book as something holy, and I know that I shouldn't say this to librarians, a horrible thing to say to a collection of librarians. And I am not advocating the burning of the books or the censoring of the books. Yet there is a Greek proverb, probably two and a half millennia old, which says, "mega biblion, mega kakon," "the bigger the book, the bigger the evil," which is just about as true as the opposite, that all books are good. I would prefer to steer between those two postures. I find myself, in fact, at the age of sixty-six a somewhat astonished Manichee, making my obeisance to God, but very aware of Lucifer over here. Paper, print, and covers don't make it good or bad by themselves. Regional loyalty isn't by itself good or bad. The quality is given by the writer, who is a person but who has affiliations, loyalties, roots, impartial judgment, a kind of a cultural matrix within which he lives. And who, let us hope, has a passionate openness to life, to the life of his own place and time as well as to the way in which that recedes backward in time. That writer knows that his own time is only the growing end of a tradition that comes to us from way back in the first dim aspirations of *Australopithecus*, from the making of the first crude tools, the asking of the first crude questions. It is the writer who keeps that sort of thing in mind who makes an enduring good out of his talent and out of the material that his talent chooses to work on, who makes something illuminating and enlarging out of it. And I don't mean goody-goody; I don't mean anything like that. I mean merely only seriously treated—however tragic, however bitter—seriously treated and treated with sympathy. He puts words on paper, I think, in the attempt to understand himself primarily, but he understands himself in relation to others and that makes all of the affiliation that I have been trying to talk about.

All of this, obviously, is not a report on what I did with the gift of words and modicum of intelligence that I discovered in myself and developed by accident, trial and error. It's a report on what, with the record essentially behind me, I wish I had done with it. So there's a little *mea culpa* in this apology too. You don't always make your books the way you want to; you make them as you can. With the growth of archives, with the growth of historical societies—county and state and national—literary societies, writing programs in the colleges, centennials and bicentennials, with the natural and inevitable accumulation, the accrual of comprehensible and comprehended local traditions, I don't think it should ever again be necessary for any young writer in Salt Lake City to be as accidental and as trial-and-errorish as I was. I think he can be shown what his talent is and what it can be geared into. I don't think it's necessary for any region, Western or otherwise, to be without self-knowledge and self-pride, and the determination to teach those things to its young. I wish we had the courage of our own traditions because the traditions are beginning to be there.

The Rediscovery of America: 1946

from *The Sound of Mountain Water*

Friday: I shall not begin where I probably should begin, with the preparations, with the maps spread all over the living-room rug, or with the late-afternoon start down the Santa Clara Valley and over Pacheco Pass into the San Joaquin, where after dark the power stations in the oilfields were jeweled clusters and the derricks were like a blasted forest on the hills. Those first hours of any trip are spent largely on the unprofitable pastime of remembering the things that have been left behind or neglected or forgotten. I shall not waste much space on how we drove until ten and then groped our way off the road into an "inner-spring wash" outside Coalinga and unrolled our sleeping bags in the sand; or how I awoke several times during the night to see the moon moving down the sky and feel the little cold wind that crept down the wash and into the neck of my bag. It is comparatively irrelevant how stiff-legged Orion looked, walking over the hills, or how I sleepily tried to find the Little Dipper by climbing up its tail from the Pole Star, but lost it in a sky too milky with moonlight.

These are things one might begin with, but I should rather begin with how it feels to be out on the road again, dry-camping in the desert, hitting the road after five years of rationing and restrictions, doing what a good third of America is doing this summer of 1946, if the polls and the prophecies mean anything. For many people—and I sympathize with them—one of the least-bearable wartime deprivations was the loss of their mobility. We are a wheeled people; it seems to me sometimes that I must have been born with a steering wheel in my hands, and I realize now that to lose the use of a car is practically equivalent to losing the use of my legs.

Returning to the road after a layoff of several years is like reestablishing intimacy with a wife or lover. There are a hundred things once known and long forgotten that crowd forward upon the senses, and there is the sharp thrill of recognition in all of them.

During war years I was luckier than most: I had had a 15,000-mile tour in 1941, and in 1944 I got to drive across the continent again and even to work in many side trips to Indian reservations, Japanese relocation centers, and other compounds where we keep the people we fear or dislike. But that trip was clouded by scarcities, rationing, the pressure of business. It had none of the fine loose-jointed feeling we get on this one, and it did not revive old acquaintance as this one does.

* * *

EVERY FIVE MINUTES I establish contact in a new area. The smell of wetted dust and wetted sagebrush in a desert thundershower is a fragrance more packed with associations than the most romantic of flowers. The signs that I have seen all my life on roadsides and weathered barn roofs are old friends well met, and I resolve that some day, not for health or enjoyment but for pure love, I shall try Dr. Pierce's Golden Medical Discovery, or Dr. Pierce's Pleasant Pellets. Some day I am going to chew Mailpouch tobacco, and treat myself to the best. Some day I am going to soak in Burma-Shave the whiskers that now are a pleasant untended roughness on my jaws. Some day I may even stop and ponder the signs that in staggering letters, in runny white paint, shout from the granite of dry canyons and the red sandstone of washes, "Jesus Saves," or "Christ Died for *You*." (I wonder who puts those messages up there, and when. Somehow I have a mental image of furtive little men clambering like monkeys after dark, daubing their messages, and then running barefooted and stealthy back to the caves where they must live.)

I have forgotten for too long how the tangled, twisted, warped and bent and bone-dry desert ranges lift out of their alluvial slopes, and how the road droops like a sagging rope from one dry pass to another. It is good to play the old game of guessing how far it is to that point, always foreshortened and looking deceptively close, where the road curves and disappears into the rock. It is good to get out of the monotonous green of tamed land and out among the changeable grays and browns and ochres and rusty reds and glaring whites of the desert. It is a fine and relaxing pleasure to sag into the corner of the seat and feel the hot sun on the bare left arm, the furnace-blast of wind from the flats. The wide sailing of buzzards is poetry.

I have forgotten—though I did not really forget, for how can one forget the things that at night in his childhood choked him with the sense of the wildness and strangeness of the world?—the way a car sounds on a lonely road when it comes fast in the dark, and you hear the growing hum, sometimes fading behind hills or down in washes, but coming on again, growing, and the lights pricking across the plain, until the glare bursts on sage and mesquite and the hum is a roar and a rush and the bushes bend and grass flattens, and light is darkness again and the rush is a roar, and now a hum, a diminishing buzz, a fading whisper, and then there is only the loneliness where it passed.

* * *

THE SHOCKS OF REMEMBRANCE and reminder are constant. The East does not provide the swift scuttling things that whip through the glare of the headlights on these night roads. There you would see a porcupine, perhaps, or a prowling cat gone wild, or a creeping opossum, but not this life that fills the lights with its variety and paves the highway with its rundown bodies. Here they move whitely and at skittering speed. Little high-tailed geckos, surely as fast as any footed creature, dart and are gone. A bigger lizard, looking huge and pleistocene but moving with that same lizard-speed, makes you jam your foot on the brake for fear of wrecking yourself. In the white glare he looks as big as a dog.

Jackrabbits seem not to be as numerous as they used to be, but on any night drive at least one will jerk into the magnetic beam and race and dodge ahead of the car, its ears up and then flat, its movements swift and scared. But it will not, or cannot, very often leap off into the dark and be safe. Eventually it will cut across under the wheels, and there will come the sodden thump and the tug of the steering wheel and the squeamish qualm. Geckos you can run over without feeling, tiny and harmless as they are. You can say, "He's wider than he used to be, but not so thick," and laugh. But being the number one natural enemy of the jackrabbit is a queasier business.

* * *

AS A MATTER OF FACT, the automobile is the natural enemy of dozens of small creatures—rabbits, gophers, snakes, mice, lizards, ground squirrels. The highways throughout the West are practically paved with flattened, crisped, sun-dried rabbits and ribboned snakes and wafered squirrels. By killing off the coyotes and wolves we let the rabbits and rodents multiply; by building highways we lure them to their death under our furious wheels. "Compensation," says Mr. Emerson. "It all evens up," echoes Mr. Hemingway. I wish I felt it possible to draw a moral about how it does not pay to be a predator in this brave new world, but all I can devise is that it doesn't pay to be anything except man. Maybe it doesn't pay to be man either.

Saturday: At four-thirty, at this date and latitude, the sky is full of light while the earth is still dusky. The horizons are ringed with pure, pale light without shadows; there is no wind or stir. Probably this is the same light Wordsworth saw on Westminster Bridge, but my associations with pre-dawn light have no cities in them. I grew up in the arid lands in close intimacy with grass and horizons and sky, and here they are again, as serene and grave as if they have been waiting for me. There is not a chance to sleep longer. This chilly wash, this air, this light, this brown grass and the gopher-dug dry earth are too like the homestead of my childhood and the mornings when I went up through the pasture after the horses. My rising wakes Dave and Miriam Bonner, sleeping thirty feet away, and then Mary and Page. On this first morning out we cook and break camp so briskly that we are on the road at six.

* * *

TECHNICALLY WE HAVE NOT begun this trip yet, but are merely on our way to it. At Bakersfield we gas up with the feeling that we are about to start. The service station attendant is full of admiration for our water-butt, which used to belong in a Navy lifeboat. He wishes he had one to age whiskey in, though he admits sadly that keeping-whiskey and keeping-money never seem to come his way. All he ever gets is the drinking or spending kind. But he fills our breaker with cold water and we leave his Oklahoma drawl behind and start up Tehachapi Pass, the lowest and southernmost of the Sierra crossings. Now the sense of freedom comes to us undiluted.

I doubt if there is any American with any of his country's history in his blood who is not excited at the crossing of a range. I had the feeling last night, crossing the Diablo Range by way of low, oak-dotted Pacheco Pass. I have it stronger now, on the spring-green slopes of Tehachapi. From Cumberland Gap to South Pass and Weber Canyon and the snowy passes of the Sierra, we have been a pass-surmounting people, fascinated by that newness on the other side, that land "vaguely realizing westward." We have misted our eyes with far-looking and stretched our minds on the high points of the continent. Like the bear who went over the mountain, we have got these crossings in our itchy bones, and perhaps always will have. The other side of the mountain is plenty to see, even if we have seen it before.

Tipping the summit of Tehachapi and rolling down the desert side we ran through acres and square miles of spring flowers, whole hillsides of lavender and white and yellow, and a pair of photographers were out, flattening their tripod almost to the ground to get a shot across the blowing flower-heads. Driving down this side was like discovery, and I kept thinking of other passes I had known and crossed.

There was Elbow Pass in the Canadian Rockies above Banff, and Snoqualmie Pass across the Cascades, looking down into the valley of the Cle Ellum; there was King's Hill Pass in the Little Belt Mountains in Montana, the place where for the first time the prairie child I used to be saw pines, and camped beside a mountain stream; there were Ute Pass and Trout Creek Pass and the Weminuche in Colorado, and the Spearfish Canyon road in the Black Hills; there was Sylvan

Pass opening up the whole forested lake-set Yellowstone Basin, and packhorse passes like Hades Canyon up into the permanent wilderness of the Granddaddy Lakes country in eastern Utah. There was the climb between Cheyenne and Laramie where the Lincoln Highway crawled up from the high plains to the Wyoming Plateau; there was San Marcos, switching across the Santa Ynez Mountains and breaking suddenly out high above the long lacy shoreline and peopled rivieras of Santa Barbara; there were little-known dirt-road passes like the Seven-Mile Canyon road over the Fish Lake Hightop to Salina, in south-central Utah—a pass that in the late mountain spring was so paved with flowers that a man could walk twenty miles and never set his foot down without trampling them.

They were fine passes to think of, and fine names to roll on the tongue. And ahead lay Mojave, and beyond Mojave the real desert. The stiff, cold wind blew us down the pass; the broken desert ahead was misted with dust beyond the scattered buildings of the town. But I was perfectly content. I knew that almost anyone in the United States would give his spare tire to be where we were, at the threshold of the dry country, with fifteen hundred miles of it ahead.

* * *

DAVE IS VERY MELLOW tonight. He is a back-road fiend, and is relatively unhappy on asphalt. But now we are out in what even he has to call happily the bald-assed desert. From Windmill Station, where we finally turned off Highway 91, we took a dirt road toward Cima, turned off that onto a still smaller road, and off that onto a trail that dwindled out in a wide wash. The wind was still blowing hard, and it was cold. To get the protection of a reef of sandstone, we lugged food boxes and water-butt and sleeping bags two hundred yards through the sand. The place was dense with joshua trees and cholla and barrel cactus. Every shrub we touched stabbed. Young Page stabbed himself on a yucca, which is not called Spanish bayonet for nothing, and then was clawed by a cholla. Only his discovery of the bleached and sutured shell of a desert tortoise consoled him for the cold and wind and thorns. The rest of us, trying to get camp set up before dark, and get some food going, fell back on the jug of heavy sweet wine which Dave insisted was the best of all desert giant-killers—swift and potable and uncomplex. Oddly enough, he was right.

Now about sunset there is a kind of miracle. The wind dies. Our blood lifts to the heavily-fortified wine. The steak we picked up in Barstow fills the little cross-wash with delirium, the dehydrated soup bubbles in the kettle. The sleeping bags, laid out in a row under a mesquite bush, look inviting and snug. It comes back to me that of all the places to camp, the desert is probably the friendliest. So far as I know, there are only three indispensable requirements for a campsite: wood, level ground to sleep on, and water. In the desert there is always wood, far more than you ever expect, yucca or sage or greasewood or mesquite, or sometimes the dry stalks of cholla, cleaned of thorns, hollow and bone-dry and perforated with neat surrealist holes, so that every stick looks like the cooling jacket of a machine gun. There is always some sandy wash where sleeping is not only level but soft. There is always water because you bring it with you. And you are pretty certain you won't get rained on.

From a disconsolate improvised shelter, the camp becomes a warm and jovial place. We wolf soup and steak and canned peas and bread and jam, wash the dishes and build up the fire and pull Page's sleeping bag close so that he can drowse in the warmth, and pass the jug again. Miriam declines: she says she has a low emetic threshold.

We sit up till midnight, until the talk has run down and the jug has run out. Up aloft the stars are scoured and glittering, and far down the valley the headlight of a train crawls along the Union Pacific's main line. The tracks probably pass within a dozen miles of our camp, and the main Salt Lake–Los Angeles highway is only another dozen back of us. Yet we are almost as remote as Frémont was in this desert a hundred years ago. The road we came in on won't see a half dozen cars a month, and the highway and the railroad will pour their thousands past without affecting this wash in the slightest.

Somehow the white casing of the turtle, sitting on a rock in the moonlight, is symbolic. Tortoises, like elephants, live a long time and die remotely. In this turtle's deathplace we have come directly and promptly to the ultimate isolation. Snuggled into our bags with the renewed wind in the mesquite over our heads, we do not rise up to watch the headlight creep down the valley, and if it whistles for the crossing at Cima we do not hear it for the wind.

* * *

SUNDAY: TWENTY YEARS AGO Searchlight had nothing to show but crumbling shanties with lizards on the sills, the sad open mouths of drifts and prospect holes, rusting machinery. Now it lies on a paved highway linking Boulder City and Needles. In the sprawling central square the false-fronts wear new paint, mostly orange. We count seven bar-and-casino joints, and even the cafe where we stop for a beer has a crap table, a twenty-one table, and a battery of slot machines. The population is variously reported at from twenty-nine to forty; the housing shortage is serious.

After one boom and a long decay and a flurry of renewed mining activity during the war, Searchlight is due for another boom as a recreation point for workers on the new Davis Dam. The old ghost town is full of drifters. On top of the most imposing of the casinos sits the buckboard in which a certain frontier lady brought in the bodies of two claim-jumpers back in that other boom. Everyone in town is dutifully repeating this story as part of the Searchlight build-up.

There is a curiously hectic metabolic rate about Nevada towns. It is as if, in the middle of the unwinking desert, man was forced into alternating periods of hibernation and hysteria. And the preparations for a boom are somehow less picturesque than the left-overs of one. We get off on a dirt road as fast as we can, heading for Boulder City by a roundabout way.

* * *

OUR MAP, THE MOJAVE and Colorado deserts map of the Automobile Club of Southern California, is the best of its kind, but it is several years old, and surprising things happen. As we come down El Dorado Wash past abandoned mines and caved-in drifts, new asphalt begins mysteriously in the middle of the gulch. At the mouth of the wash we find the wide clear river, see the ranks of trailers lined up hub to hub, hear the impatience of an Elto Twin as it rushes a boat downriver between the low red cliffs. This is the rainbow trout part of the

Boulder Dam Recreational Area. After the desert, it looks as populous as Market Street. Ghost towns with housing shortages, gulches which suddenly develop paved roads and trailer parks, confuse us. Obviously this back road we have been exploring with tourist zeal is familiar to every fisherman within five hundred miles. We give up the notion of a swim and head for Boulder City.

Here is another surprise, but a pleasant one. Ten years ago Boulder City was a temporary work town on the barren desert slope. Now it is as green as Ireland, palpitatingly and tenderly green, and over all the streets and the lush little park fast-growing locust trees, pink and white with blossom, spray the town with fragrance. Even the climate has been built from scratch. While the desert all around simmers and the heat waves beat up from sage, this emerald town blows cool in the face of the tourist, cooled by the evaporation from lawns and trees.

We have an invitation to go up the lake for two days as the guests of the Park Service. When I have called Superintendent Edwards and verified the date, we pull on down the long slope to the green patch of the camp ground, thick with tamarisks and trailers. Without unpacking we try a swim, which is cold, on the beach, which is rocky at this stage of low water. In a few weeks the lake will reach fifty feet higher and several hundred yards further up the shore. It is this annual rise and fall which prevents Lake Mead from developing vegetation along its littoral. The buff and pink and yellow and gray mountains rising up from the improbable cobalt water are as bald as when the water was a muddy red thread far down in the canyons.

Tonight we realize the full implications of being not in the wilderness-desert, but in the tourist-desert. In the wilderness, camping is casual and private. Here, a caretaker comes around to tell us that if we want electric plug-ins we'd better move down a few notches. We want no electric plug-ins, but evidently most of the campers here do, for they are standard equipment, along with camp stoves, water taps, tables, benches, clean washroom-toilets, and bath houses.

* * *

NEXT TO US AN ILLINOIS CAR and trailer pull in, and the man goes about plugging in his lights and blocking up his wheels. By the time we have finished our primitive and grubby meal our neighbor and his wife are outside with toothpicks in their mouths. The man brings out something white, and I see that it is a section of folding fence, which he sets up around the end of the trailer, and his wife comes out with two folding chairs, and in the dusk they sit within those palings on a spot of ground that is forever Peoria.

We run a course from amusement to irritation. We miss the freedom of last night's camp, and chafe against this crowded urbanism, and half contemplate breaking the rule against camping outside the designated sites. As sage-brushers, whiskery and with gritty ears, we grow bitter and witty at the regimentation of the tourist. Do Not Pick the Wild Flowers, Do Not Destroy or Injure Shrubs or Trees, Place Garbage in Containers, Park Here. Even the signs in the toilets: "Stand Close."

But by bed-time we have talked away our grouch. We remember the desert east of Mojave, every clump of greasewood or rabbit brush plastered with clinging papers, every stretch of sand strewn with cans and boxes and bottles and the débris of man. Wherever people come in any numbers, they spoil the land. Unsupervised campers, even such impeccable and responsible campers as we think we are, could spoil the whole desert, and without careful rules the campsites in parks and monuments would quickly become wheeled slums. This camp may be crowded, but it is no slum. It is as clean as a city park. We say goodnight fairly pleasantly to the pair sitting twenty feet away in Peoria.

Monday: In a way, camping by boat is more irresponsible than even sagebrushing in the bald desert. Making lunch in the galley of this ex-Coast-Guard patrol boat, we heave cans and scraps blithely overboard. Lake Mead, which could when full supply every person in the United States with 80,000 gallons of water (the Bureau of Reclamation pamphlets are emphatic on this point), is supposedly too big to be polluted.

We are nearing the upper end of the wide lower basin. Fortification Hill is behind us, and over the barren mountains back of Hemenway Wash the snow-peak of Charleston Mountain dreams in the high blue. Our hosts are Ray Poyser, the boatman, a Coast Guard veteran like his boat, and Wilbur Doudna, ex-Navy, a ranger-naturalist. Through the blue glass of the cabin, which deepens the color of the sky and water to postcard intensity, they point out a cluster of wild burros over on the south shore. The burros are so thick in the Recreational Area, Doudna says, that they sometimes have to be thinned out by slaughtering parties. It is hard to get volunteers. I should think it would be.

The shores begin to close in, and we cut into Boulder Canyon between nearly vertical walls. The rock is iron gray above, but from water's edge to high-water mark it is bleached white. We are seeing here what the birds used to see before Boulder Dam filled the canyon with water. On any natural lake this deep there would be legends of holes where no line could find bottom, and those holes would probably turn out to be exactly opposite similar holes in the Dead Sea in Palestine. It is nice to know that if we want to inspect the bottom of this lake we can do it on the pre-dam maps. We even know what the local lost Atlantis looks like: at the bottom of Boulder Canyon, undisturbed by the passage of our hull five hundred feet above it, lies the stone building that was once the Mormon river port of Callville.

* * *

AT THE END OF A HALF HOUR we break out of the pinching cliffs into what the maps call the Virgin Basin, and what Poyser calls Big Lake, or Middle Lake. History is with us here, as it was over the drowned port of Callville. On August 30, 1869, the remnants of Major John Wesley Powell's party, bearded and dirty and down to their last moldy pounds of provisions, met a party of Mormons seining here at the mouth of the Virgin. That day saw the completion of the first passage of the Colorado River canyons by boat, and ended the last major exploration within the continental United States. Because I have for several years been gathering materials for a biography of Powell, I look around here with interest, but where Powell saw low shores and placid muddy river and muddy banks, there is now an even spread of blue sweeping northward.

Neither Powell's journal nor the journal of Jacob Hamblin, who ran this stretch of river even before Powell, is of any use now except for an occasional identifying landmark like the Temple, opposite Temple Bar Wash, an hour upriver, where we meet a pair of fishing boats. The old road that used to come down to a ferry here lies on the cindery hills and hangs its tongue in the lake like a run dog.

The lake narrows into Virgin Canyon, widens out for a long run up Gregg Basin, then is squeezed into the slot of Iceberg Canyon, where high on the wall a Reclamation Service marker perches like an impossible highway sign. Now we are in Arizona.

There will not be for us the fun of sailing up under Emery Falls, which we can see in a side canyon across the bar, and filling our drinking cups from the fall. We won't see Rampart Cave, either. Ray feels his way until we have had a look, and that is all we will get. Here at the very threshold of the really stupendous scenery, under the lee of the first mighty walls, we have to turn back. I curse myself that I never got down here when the lake went deep into the cliffs, or when the river ran unimpeded.

Only Page, who has explored the boat from forecastle to propeller, looked out portholes and hung over the bow with his nose in the bow wave, who has had a hundred-mile boat ride and is tired of boat rides, is philosophical. "Now can we go fishing?" he says.

An hour before sunset we anchor in a side canyon and Dave, Ray, and Wilbur go off trolling in the skiff. Page fishes with a minnow off the stern of the big boat. It takes him ten minutes to get his first bass, about a one-pounder. Then he brings up a crappie. Miriam, Mary, and I have a highball with some of Ray's K-rations for canapes. In this still cove we can almost hear the rocks giving up their heat. I have a feeling I can even hear the evaporation (a quarter inch a day from the whole 227 square miles of lake) gradually slow up and stop as the sun goes. There is not a gurgle or a lap from the water, though along shore a carp jumps heavily. Down in the water around Page's lip-hooked minnow we can see the small bass chugging, interested but not excited.

I catch the pole, which Page has put down for a moment, and save it from going overboard. This time the fun is mine, two or two and a half pounds of big-mouthed bass. When our party returns with five small bass, we chase Page to bed belowdecks, clean fish, and set up cots on the deck. Miriam and Dave carry their sleeping bags ashore, determined not to miss a chance to sleep on the ground. Before we turn in we carry our last jug up on shore and make a fire up by high-water mark, where there is plenty of dry bleached wood snagged among the rocks.

The night, like the day, seems full of an intense purity of light and shadow. The driftwood burns hotly, almost without smoke, and the flames are clean. The moon rises full and round, chasing the dark out of our pocket except under the eastern cliff. Passing the bottle around, we get off on peace pipes, and I tell about Powell's experience with a Shivwits peacepipe, its stem broken and mended with sinew and buckskin rags, the whole making a mouthful oozy with old spittle and goodwill. But I do not seem to drive anyone away from the giant killer. All I get is a story from Doudna about a desert rat in the Panamints who had a little creek with minnows in it. Every night he put his false teeth in the stream to let the minnows clean them. "Did a good job, too," Doudna says.

We get talking of animals, which are Doudna's specialty. He and Dave, who is a micro-biologist, swap learning, but Dave cannot swap bear stories with Wilbur. Wilbur has known a man who killed a grizzly bear with a club. "What was the matter with his teeth?" I say.

"Well," Doudna says, "this fellow was pretty old. Teeth were all gone. He tried gumming the bear for a while, but he didn't seem to be getting anywhere, so he used the club."

I give up and crawl back to the foredeck to my cot. The stay from the bow to the boat's short mast is a black line across the narrow sky, and the sky itself is blue-and-silver with moonlight. Straight overhead the moon is molten, as if someone on the other side had burned a hole through the silver bowl with a blowtorch.

This is the fourth night in a row I have gone to sleep with the moon in my eyes.

* * *

TUESDAY: TWO DAYS on Lake Mead, and an afternoon and evening going through the dam and the powerhouses, have made boosters of us.* Nobody can visit Boulder Dam itself without getting that World's Fair feeling. It is certainly one of the world's wonders, that sweeping cliff of concrete, those impetuous elevators, the labyrinths of tunnels, the huge power stations. Everything about the dam is marked by the immense smooth efficient beauty that seems peculiarly American. Though no architect designed it and no one mind planned its masses and its details, it has the effect of great art. And the dam itself is only the beginning.

The tamed water of the Colorado is drunk in hundreds of thousands of southern California homes; it irrigates two million acres of desert land; it will generate, at full capacity, nearly six million kilowatt hours of electricity; it makes possible such big-time desert boomtowns as Henderson, between Boulder City and Las Vegas; it fructifies, instead of flooding, the Imperial, Coachella, Yuma, and Palo Verde valleys. And in addition to this it provides, in Lake Mead and Parker Lake and the clear river between them, a tourist attraction that will certainly draw a thousand times more people into the desert than ever the gold and silver leads did. Otherwise inaccessible country is opened; camping is possible along 550 miles of shoreline without the desert necessity of packing water; the bass fishing is probably not surpassed anywhere, and there is no closed season. It is no wonder that Las Vegas, the nearest supply point, has been on a red-hot boom ever since work began on the dam. It will continue to boom. Perhaps the Reclamation Service's seismological stations will record the enormous shifting weight of tourist travel, and prosperity be measured by the seriousness of the earth tremors.

* * *

WEDNESDAY: IF SEARCHLIGHT, on the brink of a boom, depressed us, Las Vegas in the midst of one depresses us worse. In the 1920s,

---

* The euphoria of 1946 has not lasted into the beginning of the 1980s. In the early 1950s, proposals by the Bureau of Reclamation to put dams in Dinosaur National Monument brought on a fight with environmental groups that led to a sharp revision of the Upper Colorado River Project, and affirmed that elements of the National Park system were safe from such intrusions. In the 1960s, similar attempts to site dams in Marble and Grand canyons were defeated. Up-river dams such as Flaming Gorge and Glen Canyon divide the available water with Lake Mead. There is seldom enough to fill them all. When we came down the Colorado by boat in 1968, Lake Powell, behind the Glen Canyon Dam, was being bled to keep up the power head in Lake Mead, and neither reservoir was anywhere near full.

when it was simply a way station on the Los Angeles–Salt Lake highway, Vegas was a pleasant little desert town. But now it has gone Hollywood, gone glitter and glass and chrome. The streets are full of slickers in Tom Mix shirts; every building is a casino, and you cannot walk past any door without a one-armed bandit reaching out to shake hands.*

We wander into the Golden Camel, which used to be a cool dark peekhole oasis in Prohibition times, but the charm isn't there. The only correct note is a desert rat with a sheep dog. The rat puts a nickel in the juke box and the dog begins to dance, but the proprietor shoulders out of his office and puts dog and prospector out. This is not as it was. Neither is the sign we see as we shake the dust of Las Vegas from our feet. "Restricted Area of Small Ranches," it says. All the spiders are busily spinning webs around this corner of the desert.

Off to our left, as we run for Death Valley Junction, we see the enticing snowfields of Charleston Peak. These too, we know, have been booby-trapped by the spiders, and contain an all-year lodge in the movie manner. It is so hot that we are tempted to turn off, but resist. Our only contact with the snow mountains is a golden eagle we meet in the desert, perhaps a refugee from the Hollywood characters upstairs. He is a very well-grown fowl indeed, as high as a hydrant on his feet, and as big as a Piper Cub when he takes off.

This is a country where distances mean as little to men as to the eagle. The postmaster of Death Valley Junction commutes seventy miles, from Furnace Creek Ranch. He tells us of the Star Route driver who serves Death Valley with mail. This driver covers four hundred miles a day, from Yermo to Stovepipe Wells and back. He puts in a new engine every two months; what he does to renew himself the postmaster does not say. To us he seems somewhat more heroic than the pony express riders, for the country he drives through is blistered under temperatures up to 125 degrees. Down in the valley yesterday it was 110. And it is 95 here today.

Dave and Miriam are already tired of paved roads. We inquire about the road up Greenwater Canyon, but nobody seems to know

---

* I read this passage with astonishment now. If 1946 needed this sort of description of Las Vegas, then 1946 was indeed the age of innocence.

much about it. The storekeeper guesses it is passable, and at two o'clock we pull out.

There is a line of stones across the entrance to the Greenwater trail, but they merely whet Dave's appetite. He assures us that those are probably put there for casual tourists unprepared for desert travel. For several miles we bounce across scrubby flats, past an abandoned borax mine, and on into a shallow canyon. By now the road is definitely not good. In fact, there is no road, but only the floodwashed gravel. There are tire tracks, however, and the wash has nothing alarming about it. We creak and warp and bounce and low-gear our way on and up.

* * *

SEVERAL TIMES WE STICK in deep sand and have to dig out. At 11.7 miles from the turn-off we get stuck again, just short of a sharp turn littered with boulders. We stop for twenty minutes to cool the motor, then shove out, swing wide, take the turn at a run, and crash over the bad spot. Nothing is broken, but it is blazing hot in the wash, the wind is behind us, and the radiator is already boiling again. Dave is very happy now, and full of admiration for the beauties of this scrubby little gulch. Everything on a back road always looks spectacular to him.

At 12.1 we meet our first native resident, a three-foot rattler under a mesquite bush. He strikes furiously at the stick I hold out, and when Page tosses gravel over him he goes into a continuous, hysterical rattle. The ladies screech from the car, so we leave the snake coiled in the midst of his own hysteria and go on.

At 12.4 we meet rattler number two, a joker who plays dead in the road so that I stop indecisively, afraid Dave, who is pushing behind, might step on him. He looks dead enough, but I toss gravel to see. He explodes into a tense coil and strikes in my direction. With pieces of greasewood I keep him from sliding up into a crevice, while Dave takes his picture. This is a sidewinder, a smaller snake than the first one, but just as mad. Eventually we let him slide up into his cranny, and go on.

The road now is totally gone. We strain and creak over bare shelf-rock, over ledges, plow with everybody pushing through deep sand. At 13.1 we stick again and stop to let the motor cool. Our map shows 16.2 miles of this road before we hit a summit trail leading to the Dante's View road. Only three miles to go. We start again.

At 14.3 the hot motor vapor-locks, and we stall. To our right a burro trail leads off, and a sign says, "Painted Rocks." We know there are petroglyphs in this canyon, and are tempted, but the road is steep, the temperature well over a hundred. And it is already five o'clock. We have been three hours making fourteen miles. We decide to get through this in daylight, and after long grinding on the starter I get the engine going. Its whole sound and action seem blown and winded. We take a run, get out of the sand, jerk off across the sagebrush to avoid some boulders. My shoulders are tired from wrangling through sand and rocks.

Ahead is a narrow slot between two big boulders, the slot itself deep with sand, and beyond it a high crown grown with rabbit brush. There is nothing to do but hit it. The wheels begin to chatter, the whole body shudders and shakes, the pushers grunt and strain. Then there is that sudden settling that says the bottom has gone out, Dave yells, and I quit feeding her. There we sit, high-centered and dug in to the hubs, and the motor vapor-locks again.

* * *

WE WAIT FIFTEEN MINUTES, a half hour, digging and brushing as we wait. Then I try the starter. Nothing happens. We wait some more and try again. Still nothing. Dave and I uncouple the gas line and blow through it. Bubbles in the gas tank, so the line is all right. I open the line at the carburetor and step on the starter. One feeble spurt, and then no more. Immediately I give up. I have been intimidated by too many mechanics about fuel pumps. Their automatic assumption is that a balky pump should be replaced. It would not occur to me, a baling-wire-and-string mechanic, to try fixing one. Instead I fill a couple of canteens from the butt, get the girls making sandwiches, and prepare for an eighteen-mile walk back to Death Valley Junction.

But less impetuous counsels prevail. If we have to walk, early in the morning would be a better time. And right now, after wrestling the car all afternoon, I am a little bushed. We repair to the giant-killer and start making camp. Dave, he of the curious scientific mind, takes out the fuel pump to see what makes it tick. If it will not serve as part of a high-compression engine, it will serve as educational equipment.

Between courses of dinner, he discovers how the pump works, isolates its principles, and concludes that nothing is wrong with this one. We put it on and try the starter. No go. Then I remember my last fuel-pump trouble, and vaguely recall something about length of stroke. This means nothing to me except that I heard the mechanic say it. To Dave it means everything. If the diaphragm isn't burst, then the length of stroke must be all that is wrong. Within five minutes I am cutting little circles of rubber from an old inner tube, and Dave is packing the connection where the pump hooks on to a rod that in turn hooks onto the cam shaft. When we put the packed pump back on, we discover a stripped setscrew, and wrap it with thread so it will hold.

Then I step on the starter. Nothing. We prime the carburetor. Before we try it now we take a prayerful pull on the jug. Then I press the button.

The engine practically blows me out of the seat. I grab for chokes and throttles, assuming that something must be pulled way out, but nothing is. In desperation I shut the ignition off. Cautiously, after a couple of minutes, I turn on the ignition again, and instantly, without my touching the starter, the motor almost leaps through the hood. Now it is clear: we have got too muscular a stroke altogether. Take out a couple layers of inner tube and we will be fixed. By eight-thirty we are sitting on the running board, while the motor purrs smoothly, and we drink a nightcap to the Scientific Mind before we roll into the bags.

This night I expect alarms from the girls, because I know that both have read about rattlesnakes that crawl into sleeping bags to get warm, and I have heard, from their screeches this afternoon, how little either likes snakes. I could show them, in the *Desert Magazine* (an authority whose weight is very great and completely deserved), that the danger from warmth-hunting sidewinders is statistically equal to that from falling meteors. I could demonstrate how much more danger we run any hour on any highway. But I remember the indignant reader who wrote in to the editor of *Desert* to say that he had had snakes in his covers three times during his life, and he did not like either the snakes or the people who said snakes never hunted warmth. It seems indiscreet, in the circumstances, to raise the subject. Everyone goes to sleep like an infant.

Quite late, the moon looks over the rim, and then I see it bridging the canyon, and then it is a luminousness over the western rim, and then I awake to find that the luminousness has shifted its ground, and it is morning. As I look around, I do not see any rattlesnakes, either on top of sleeping bags or in them. All I see is the gray, cindery canyon, the gray greasewood, the morning sky already hot with light, and the old station wagon, awkwardly high-centered and with her wheels deep in the sand, fifteen miles up a 16.2-mile canyon.

* * *

Thursday: Before breakfast, Dave and I take a walk up the canyon. The further we go the worse it gets. Eventually even Dave admits we had better go back down the way we came.

This is more easily said than done. From eight to nine we dig and brush our way out of the sand we are stuck in. From nine to ten-thirty we turn around. At a quarter of eleven, somewhat fagged, we start back down Greenwater, leaving our ruts full of greasewood brush for the next wayfarer to read.

In Death Valley Junction the mechanic tells us that only two days ago he went up in a towcar for a party stranded in the canyon. The stranded party walked in eighteen miles—exactly what I was going to do last night. What makes us feel better about our retreat from Everest is the mechanic's assertion that to his knowledge no one ever went *up* over the Greenwater road. His client of day before yesterday hadn't even been able to get down.

* * *

Friday: Into Rhyolite (pop. 3), most satisfactory of ghost towns. The metabolic rate was highest of all here. Rhyolite grew and matured and died in four years. And if one gets tired of the ghostly refrain among the ruins he can visit Bottle House, made of beer bottles laid in adobe, and buy rock samples or ultraviolet glass. Or he can go to the other intact building, the railroad station, once the grandest in Nevada, which now sits high and dry without rails to serve it. A gentleman named Westmoreland owns it now—bought the whole town at a tax sale—and has made it into the "Ghost Casino," patronized by tourists from the Valley. At eight in the morning it smells glumly of last night's revels. The barkeep is dourly cleaning up. On every square inch of wall photographs of nude ladies simper and coquette, but the hour and the hot morning sun are against them; we leave them for the bartender and the ghosts.

The Titus Canyon road is a steep, narrow succession of switchbacks. Twice, going up, we have occasion to comment on how miraculously a sidewinder can duck a car's wheels, even when he seems asleep. We have seen more than our quota of rattlers on this trip, and we guess that the lack of tourist travel during the war has let them multiply.

The road down loops in tortuous switchbacks through Leadfield, a very dead ghost rotting dryly in the gulch, and on between steep walls that at times pinch in so that we cannot open the car doors when we stop. Speculation on what it would be like to be caught in this slot during a flash flood hustles us out to the gateway. The whole north end of Death Valley opens up, with the unbroken barrier of the Panamints across the west, and Telescope Peak high and snowy. The interlocking alluvial fans of the Panamints are beautiful studies in clean line. Around us too is the patchwork poetry of our place-names. We have had it all the way: the Calicos, the Ivanpahs, the New York Mountains; Black Mountain and the McCullough Range and the El Dorados; Pahrump and the Funeral Range and the Bullfrog Hills; Muddy Mountains, the Grapevines, the Panamints, the Shadow Range. Most of the naming processes that George Stewart speaks of in *Names on the Land* are here.

For a while now we see sights again, winding up at the Hollywood Moorish pile of Scotty's Castle. This Page enjoys in spite of our superior airs. He is not annoyed by the transcribed commercial of the guide, nor by the tapestry which was woven by Don Quixote. He would be willing to buy the dollar postcards—not sold anywhere else—if we did not yank him away.

Except in wet weather, which is notably infrequent, a desert dry lake is the best of all possible roads, and the one we meet at the top of Grapevine Pass is smooth as concrete and hard as rock. Driving on it is like cutting didoes on ice skates. In the middle of the Sarcobatus Flats we meet Highway 95, and roll up over Stonewall Pass in a spattering thunder shower. Then a dusty graded road, and more passes—Lida Pass, through nutpines and drifts of snow, and down again into Fish Lake Valley, and then over Gilbert Pass into Deep Springs Valley. As we top the summit with the sun almost down, there is the Sierra across the west, white and pinnacled and filling the whole horizon. We see why it is called the Sierra Nevada, the snowy range, and when we make camp we pick a wash that will let us see the peaks when their snowfields are washed in rose at sunrise.

SATURDAY: WE SPEND THIS MORNING, visiting Deep Springs School, a private prep school conducted by the Telluride Association. Once, fifteen years ago, I was here for a few hours, and once twelve years ago I all but signed up to teach here, so I have a personal curiosity to see how education fares in the desert.

The school has not changed much. Students still work a half day on the ranch. The student body is still held down to about twenty. Masters are not quite as numerous as they used to be, but there is still one for every three or four students. The buildings look older.

Few of the boys are around now. The truck which passed our camp very early this morning contained about eighteen of them, bound on a nine-day trip to Death Valley, Boulder Dam, Grand Canyon, Zion, and Bryce. They make these annual trips unsupervised, packing camp equipment and armed only with letters from Simon Whitney, the director. The three boys who remain behind have voluntarily given up the trip so that the essential work around the ranch will get done.

Deep Springs is a friendly place. But it looks lonelier now than it did when I was twenty-four. The snow lies deep on Westgaard Pass in winter, isolating the valley for days at a time, and the nearest town is Big Pine, twenty-seven miles away. I am sure that the boys who spend three years at Deep Springs get something that they could get nowhere else, but I am just as glad that I am not a master here.

Deep Springs is our last desert port of call. From Big Pine up the Owens Valley and on north along the foot of the Sierra we are on Highway 395, which rolls behind us mile after mile. The passes rise and fall under our wheels: Sherwin Summit, Deadman's Pass, Devil's Gate. On all of them the snow remains in great drifts, with sometimes whole slopes covered. Skiers' cars are parked along the highway, and the slopes are cross-hatched with tracks. All afternoon we peg north, at times down in the hot valley, at times between drifts ten feet deep. At Carson City we swing sharp left into the main range, hoping that the snow won't be so deep around Tahoe that we can't camp.

But the shores of Tahoe, what is left of them between the cottages, are either buried in snow or soggy with mud and water. We try the public camp at Meyers and find it flooded. It is practically dark; we are all chilled and starving, but we decide to pull over Echo Pass and camp on the west slope, where it will be drier.

On the first steep pitch of the pass the fuel pump gasps twice, coughs, and goes out. By frantic choking I keep the engine alive long enough to turn around, and we coast back into Meyers. Dave is unhappy that we haven't made it all the way home on his cobbled pump, and the rest of us are tired and sore. Only Page profits from this difficulty: he finds a snowbank and gets his hands blue for the first time in two years.

The new pump takes us a half hour. It is almost nine when we top the pass and start down past the ski lodges, through the snow-choked forest. Eventually we find a section of the old highway, marooned when the road was straightened. The wind off the snowbanks chatters our teeth, but wood is plentiful, and on this southern slope above the road it is dry. We fortify ourselves with giant-killer and the quickest food we can think of: soup and chili and bread, and for dessert the napoleons we bought at a French bakery in Bishop, away back in the Owens Valley.

Tonight we all hit the bottom of our sleeping bags, and even the sagebrushing Bonners go to bed in all their clothes. I pull my head in and do not come out until morning, either for air or for a look at the moon. By this time the moon is a pretty moth-eaten piece of merchandise anyway.

* * *

SUNDAY: SO BACK HOME now, the loop almost closed. Down the south fork of the American, past lumber mills and flumes and yards stacked with enough lumber to ease a small housing shortage, past new buildings enough to care for every veteran in the Western states. It seems that every vacant spot of ground in this quarter of the Sierra is being built on. The number of Bide-a-Wees and Shangri Las is due to be doubled shortly. We wonder why the taste of summer cottages in the West is so infallibly bad. It cannot be simply that many people build their own, because some of these we pass are manifestly neither amateur jobs nor inexpensive ones. And many of the people who commit atrocities in these mountains have chaste and impeccable homes in town. There is some madness in brown shingle, some itch for bright color, some suppressed impulse toward cuteness that borders every road through the Sierra with blue-shuttered horrors. Across the canyon we see a Civil War cannon that someone has towed up the pass, derricked across the river, and mounted on the cliff-like hill under a pergola. Why?

We are dangerously close to sounding like Henry Miller, and spitting the taste of this Camp Cozy nightmare from our puckered mouths. But it is healthy to remember John Muir, who practically invented the Sierra and who should certainly have been one to mourn the pollution of the clean wilderness. He wasn't. Instead of thinking what men did to the mountains, he kept his mind on what the mountains did to men, and he might not have considered even the wretched and pretentious ugliness along the shores of Tahoe and through the passes and on every Sierra lake too heavy a price for the health, the happiness, and eventually the cleansing of taste, that hundreds of thousands derive from the Snowy Range.

Out of the mountains now, through a half-and-half region of orchards and pines, and out onto the long green spurs that stretch down this side of the range. At Placerville we make our last gesture toward the back roads, turning off on a sub-major highway through the Mother-lode country. Here gulches and bars are upended and turned over by a succession of panners, hillsides are crazy with abandoned sluices, riverbeds are full of dredges feeding messily like hippopotamuses on the gravels that even after a hundred years give up gold. Sutter Creek, Mokelumne Hill—the names echo, but what charms us now is not these placer towns with their storefronts reminiscent of '49 and their graveyards full of history, but the dreamy, highspring, New England loveliness of this countryside. Like Tamsen Donner, Mary must botanize. She finds eighteen varieties of wild flowers in a space a yard square, and all around us there are blue hills, yellow swales, lavender and white and pink meadows, and everywhere the ecstatic green of California's brief and furious spring.

With home in sight, Page, who has been caged among grown-ups for ten days, shushed, pushed aside, and ignored, begins to generate unbearable pressures. His vocabulary is that of his third-grade kind—about five cant phrases, generally meaningless, interspersed with sound effects. I give him the long strong doubletalk of a father pretending to be good and annoyed, but I am really remembering a quarter of a century ago, when I sat in the back of a loaded car as this one sits now, surrounded by a Stoll auto tent, folding camp beds, tarpaulins, blankets, suitcases, and all the assorted paraphernalia we thought necessary for touring. We had a food box built onto the right front fender, a luggage carrier on the running board, and a trunk rack on the rear, with a dusty canvas lashed to it. I remember that old car and every item of that equipment and every volt and ampere that went through my squirming young body. I remember places we camped, roads we went over in Montana and Wyoming and Idaho and Utah. There were no back roads then, because everything was a back road. I remember the gumbo near Thermopolis, Wyoming, that stripped the rubber off both our rear tires and plugged it up under the fenders until we stalled. I remember the tire we hung on a tree in West Yellowstone, with its incredible mileage painted on it in white, "6,000 miles and still going!" In those days we counted twenty miles an hour a remarkable average for a hard day's drive. I remember the broken springs and the boiling radiators, the red dust of roads under construction, the waving of hands from every car, back in the days when touring was still only a step from the goggles-and-ulster stage and the roads were the lineal descendants of the Oregon Trail.

When I turn to look at the noisemaking buffoon who is my later duplicate, his eyes are bright as a squirrel's, and through his milk-bottle horn he lets me have it. His ricochet effect bounces off my skull, and I fall back to driving. But I am plenty content, because we shall hardly be well recovered from this desert trip before we shall be off again, across the continent. We shall not be following our pre-war custom of hitting the Lincoln Highway at sixty-five, driving seven hundred miles a day, and sleeping in motels. We'll be lugging our sleeping bags and jungling up in inner-spring washes. We shall see the Wah-Wah Mountains and the San Rafael Swell, the Goosenecks of the San Juan and Monument Valley, the Four Corners and the sandrock country and the western slope of the Colorado Rockies, and we shall probably stop somewhere on the banks of the Platte and eat lunch among primroses. And we shall meet most of America on the road.

Why I Like the West

from Marking the Sparrow's Fall

It has always been my belief and contention that if the *Mayflower* had happened to land somewhere on Puget Sound or in San Francisco Bay instead of at Plymouth Rock, men in coonskin hats would now be cautiously exploring the Berkshires and shooting carrier pigeons for their suppers, and the burghers of Brooklyn would still be speaking Dutch. I would go further: like those Francophile scholars who date English literature from the Norman Conquest and shove all the crude Anglo-Saxon beginnings back into a predawn twilight, I would be content to date American literature by its Americanism (that is, by its westernism), and start it not with John Smith or the Plymouth Compact but with Augustus Longstreet or Sut Lovingood or the Big Bear of the Arkansaw.

It is all very well to have Melvilles and Hawthornes, and even Emersons and Thoreaus, and certainly it is more than salutary to have Mark Twains, but to have to go for our first colonial cheepings to the sickly legend of Pocahontas or the dismal Providences of Increase Mather, this is a hard fate. By changing our dating procedure we might at a stroke eliminate the necessity of sending our young back to personages like John Cotton, who liked to "sweeten his mouth with a bit of Calvin" before closing out his eighteen hours of daily study and prayer. We might instead indoctrinate young Americans by contact with such true forefathers as John Phoenix, who once dashed out of a San Francisco saloon to accost the Eagle Baker's wagon and demand a baked eagle.

Cotton Mather would not have done that, nor Jonathan Edwards, nor even the Simple Cobbler of Agawam. They became what they became, and remained what they remained, by the accident of a New England landing, and not ten generations of western rebellion has succeeded in eradicating the provincial and hard-mouthed habits that might have melted away in a year in some climate farther from endurance and closer to indulgence. If this be ingratitude to our Mother East, then it is ingratitude, and that same John Phoenix has written the text: "How sharper than a serpent's thanks it is to have a toothless child."

A wild man from the West, I have always done my honest best to live up to what tradition says I should be. I have always tried to look like Gary Cooper and talk like the Virginian. I have endeavored to be morally upright, courteous to women; with an innate sense of right and wrong but without the polish that Yale College or European travel might have put upon me. I have consented to be forgiven my frontier gaucheries, and I did not hold it against the waiter in the Parker House bar when he removed my feet from the upholstery.

I have been breezy, frank, healthy, relaxed, with a drawling soul and an open heart and a friendly smile. I have obediently liked my beef well done and my r's hard and have let it be known that I eat fried potatoes with my scrambled eggs for breakfast. Without actually wilting when the population was more than ten to the square mile, I have expressed a sense of crowding; and I have publicly honored a friend of mine who moved on from his ranch when it got so crowded he had to put a door on his privy. I have done all this in obedience to the myth of the West; and while doing it I have served as a self-appointed evangelist to rescue unfortunate eastern heathens from the climate, topography, theology, prejudices, literature, railroads, traditions, narrowness, and geographical ignorance that are their heritage. I have not always been thanked, but I have been earnest.

Any conversation which has permitted me to discuss redwood trees, Sierra forests, western rivers, canyons, or plateaus, Pacific surf, Utah trout fishing, or long-distance views has been a honeyhead in which I could happily drown. I have been full of comparative statistics on areas, altitudes, distances; the fact that my favorite county in Utah is somewhat larger than the state of Massachusetts is something I cannot keep to myself. Under the hesitant, skeptical, and envious questioning of easterners I confess to the same sense of well-being that I once felt in Devon while trying to convince a mule-headed young Britisher that in the United States bread came ready-sliced. The paltry eastern landscape I have given my patronizing scorn; have never been able to refrain from telling easterners that Mount Washington, their pride, could be set down in the Grand Canyon— in a *ditch*—and never show above the rim. They try to greet these revelations with well-bred astonishment, or to laugh them off, but I have seen their souls warp under the strain. Anything they can cite, I can cite bigger.

But it is time to admit that during a long career of western chauvinism I have been trading on the general ignorance of my hearers. Friend or adversary, they have proposed a myth of the West that I have subscribed to, and I have even imposed it upon them sometimes. I have carefully concealed from them what I thought they should have known in the first place—that there is no such thing as the West. There are only Wests, as different from one another as New Hampshire from South Carolina or Brooklyn from Brookline. A few things they have in common, and some of them are important not only to boosters and evangelists but to historians and scholars, but in other ways they resemble each other about as much as Senator Glen Taylor resembles Will Rogers. The West, be it known to all those I have misled, is neither a region nor a way of life nor a state of mind. It is many regions, many states of mind, many ways of life.

* * *

WHEN I WENT "BACK EAST" to school in Iowa I took with me the belligerent thesis that all virtue, all good country, all pleasant people, and all pretty girls lay back of me, west of the Missouri if not west of the Rockies. But later, when I found myself an odd sparrow among the polite rustling of the Ivy League, I cheerfully acceded to local custom and included in the West the Iowa and Wisconsin and Illinois I had once fiercely attacked as effete, colorless, and insipid. One glance at the New Yorker's or the Bostonian's map of the United States will make it clear how I could get away with this, and also how great an advantage any Westerner has in a regional argument. Whatever he may *not* know, a Westerner is bound to know geography, and among the heathen he can claim anything for his province and get away with it. If he wants to, he can start the West at the Alleghenies, or the eastern edge of Indiana, and if he is challenged he can conduct a defense in depth. Ohio, Illinois, Iowa, Nebraska, eastern Colorado—he can retreat all the way to the Rockies, and by that time he will have his opponent extended and can whip around and cut his supply lines. And if he is still pressed there are Montana and Wyoming and Idaho and Utah and Nevada and California, New Mexico and Arizona and Texas, to wage a war of movement in. The Easterner who once lets it get established that there is such a thing as the West hasn't got a chance in a quarrel of regional patriotism. He is Napoleon in Russia.

If we admitted its existence, the West would have to be almost as big as Russia. By the test of dialect, which is a reasonable and fair test as far as it goes, there is veritably a West, and it extends from the Alleghenies to the Pacific, from Ohio and Missouri to the Canadian line, with only unimportant islands to interrupt its triumphant oneness. By comparison the dialects of the eastern seaboard are confined and provincial, and even the several variations on southern speech, widespread as they are, reveal themselves as a regional aberration. The speech of the various Wests is the authentic speech of America, purified of the *r* which soundeth not and the *r* which belongeth not and the squat *a* and the other blemishes.

But the Mid-West, which shares this normalized speech with the other Wests, doesn't share all the essentials. From the Alleghenies to the 98th meridian of longitude—roughly to the line of the Red and the Missouri Rivers—and from the Canadian line south to Missouri and Ohio, is one great region, a noble part of America, and worthy of honor. I was born in it and have gone to school in it and worked in it and traveled across it endlessly, and I respect it highly and speak its native tongue, but it is not part of the West, or one of the Wests, unless one is speaking with Bostonians or New Yorkers. It is Mid-West; it stops at the 98th meridian because at about that line the rainfall ceases to be adequate for unassisted agriculture and an entirely new set of conditions is imposed upon the inhabitants.

By this test of aridity, there are few sections west of the 98th meridian which do not qualify as part of the West. Only certain high mountain regions, the coastal parts of Washington, Oregon, and northern California, and the gulf of Texas can properly be exempted. And the aridity test is more meaningful than it might seem, much more meaningful than the test of language, for upon the lack of sufficient rain depend practically all the things that make the Wests western.

Aridity, for one thing, means an unmisted atmosphere, a low relative humidity; and low humidity means bluer skies, longer views, subtler effects of distance, better photography. Aridity means dust, and upon dust are built the much-advertised western sunsets. Aridity means a new set of animals—coyotes, antelope, jackrabbits, flickertails, lizards, roadrunners, desert tortoises—and a new set of plants, from sagebrush and shadscale to datura and tumbleweed. It means a changed landscape and bizarre topography, since erosion works very much differently in the absence of a protective mat of ground cover and persistent rains. In a dry land the brinks of hills will be clifflike, not rounded; valleys will often be canyons; hills are likely to be buttes and mesas and barerock movements; the coloration will be not the toned greens of wetter regions but the red and ochre and tan and gray and black of raw rock, the gray of sagebrush, the yellow of dry grass. The whole effect is harsher, bonier, farther, bigger, the difference between a weather-beaten face and one that is well padded and protected.

Aridity changes the agriculture of the West, turns a farmer's values upside down. In watered country, land is valuable, and water running through it is owned, according to the English precedents of riparian law, by the man who owns the land along the banks. But dry land is worthless without water, and riparian law has given way before changed conditions. In the Wests, most of them, water is life. No ownership of a strip of shore entitles any farmer to empty the stream upon his fields and deprive the man below. Through a water company, private or public, he shares ownership and responsibility, and takes his share at specified periods for specified lengths of time. Out of the conditions arising from dryness have come all the irrigation laws of the American books, all the cooperative systems of water use, and a whole battery of government agencies, especially the Reclamation Service, concerned with the public responsibility to impound and distribute the water that is too expensive and difficult for one man or a group of men to handle alone. That governmental responsibility has dotted the West with reclamation and power dams, public works on an enormous scale, which not only give the western landscape some of its quality, but provide the footings for an entirely new sort of civilization. Charge all this "socialism" to lack of rain.

That same blessed drought prevents, except in sections where water from mountain sources is available, the rabbit-hutch crowding, the intense and greedy occupation and transformation of the earth by numberless hives of people. The population center of the United States is still away back in Sullivan County, Indiana, less than a quarter of the way across the continent, where it can abide for all of me. And though by the 1940 census more people in the western states lived in cities than in the country, only California, Texas, Washington, Utah, and Colorado made that proportion possible. The rest of the West is rural; there is still a lot of space open, and there will continue to be for lack of water. Even the range will not be very heavily populated, because it takes many acres to support one whiteface or Shropshire. Arid and semiarid plains, inaccessible mountains and plateaus, uninhabitable desert comprise the great bulk of the western landscape. The arable land in Utah, for an example, does not exceed 3 percent of the total acreage of the state.

Wyoming Plateau, sagebrush and jackrabbits and gray plain, where it is sixty miles between towns. Nevada desert, miles of empty alluvial slope and alkali bottom swung between the ranges, and beyond the next range another valley, and the horizons scrawling with mountain crests and heat. The big open spaces of the Utah plateaus, the Idaho lava beds, the "scablands" below Spokane, the Mojave and Colorado deserts, the all but roadless Navajo reservation, bigger than some of the states—the spaces are still open, and the cities are a long way apart.

It is open country and great distances that compel the western railroads to pamper their long-haul passengers with better roadbeds, faster schedules, more and fancier gadgets such as the Vistadome. In an open country everyone is a traveler; most Westerners develop that habit of covering ground in gargantuan chunks. I suspect that the man who contemplates empty landscape while he drives his own car has something of a spiritual advantage on the one who, boxed in a subway or bus, contemplates tomorrow's news in the five o'clock final of some tabloid. I have no statistics on ulcers, but I have convictions and some evidence. I also have duodenal scars, but those are another matter, and from another source.

Beyond dialect and aridity, the Wests have not too much in common. Local developments, local economics, have produced even in the arid regions very different societies. The plains are one kind, cow country is another, mining country is another, Indian country, Mormon country, the Northwest lumber empire, the industrialized agriculture of California's Central Valley and the lower Rio Grande and parts of Arizona, are all economically distinct. The sub-Wests differ in climate, topography, racial composition, history, orientation. That is why, when an old Harvard friend wrote from Santa Fe that he knew now what I had used to blow off about, I held my peace and withheld judgment. Because Santa Fe is only one of many Wests; my friend may have seen them all, but I suspect he had hold of the elephant's tail and was yelling for dear life that the elephant was very like a rope.

It may be like a rope in New Mexico—or rather in the upper Rio Grande valley—where the combination of ancient Spanish villages and even more ancient Pueblo towns has withstood much of the transforming push of the Anglo-American frontier. New Mexico is bilingual, for one thing, and bi- or tri-cultural; nowhere else in America, perhaps, can you see such contrasts. Sleep out on a piney promontory above the seventeenth-century village of Peñasco, where in the afternoon you have seen peasants threshing oats by trampling the sheaves with horses and winnowing the grain by hand, and after dark look across the great valley and see the multiplex lights, the high, hanging glow like a city among the stars, far over westward on the Jemez Mountains. There is no better view of Los Alamos.

In New Mexico, the elephant is like a rope. In the high border country of Montana and Wyoming, cow country and dude country, the old hunting ground of Crow and Blackfoot, it may be like a wall. Out in Nebraska and Kansas and the Dakotas, out in the great staring exposed plains on the wheel of earth under the belljar of sky, blown on by every wind and torn at by dramatic and tormented weather, it is maybe like a tree. In the sleepy little Mormon towns under the Lombardy poplars, in the red-dirt streets snowed with cottonwood fluff, before the local ward house after Sunday meeting or Mutual, it is something else, perhaps a spear.

* * *

IN TEXAS, A WORLD IN ITSELF, the most provincial and fiercely local of all the Wests, it is again something different. On the Columbia and the Willamette it is new, in the California coast towns from Santa Barbara south it is like nothing else. And all of these sections and subsections bleed imperceptibly into one another: cow country stretches from Texas to Saskatchewan, from Nebraska and Colorado to William Randolph Hearst's duchy of San Simeon. Copper and gold and silver and lead, molybdenum and antimony, must be mined where they are found; so must the extrusions of soft yellow vanadium and uranium ore that crop out of canyon walls in western Colorado and southern Utah. Every section is a combination of ways of life and states of mind as it is likely to be a combination of topographies.

Just for a sample, try Arizona. It's West, it's arid, it talks American, it can show cowboys and Indians. More specifically, it is part of what, with Texas and New Mexico, is called the Great Southwest. But look at it: The Indians who give Arizona its characteristic color are not the town Indians, though the Hopi reservation lies within the borders of the Painted Desert. The characteristic Indians of Arizona are the nomadic Navajo, and they make an entirely different world from the settled world of Pueblo and Spaniard on the upper Rio Grande. But a good part of Arizona is Mormon, and another kind of life and people revolve around the Temple in Mesa. And in Arizona has grown up a segment of that industrial-agriculture economy dependent on conservation dams, floods of cheap migrant labor, and expensive Washington lobbies, and that is still a third world. Outside all these are the worlds of the tourists and the lungers. Admittedly these elements fuse somewhat, admittedly they are all recognizably western and recognizably American. One may go into the Hopi country and see a bunch of longhairs hanging around the post at Oraibi listening to a World Series broadcast, and in Monument Valley a traveler will encounter Navajo girls wearing saddle shoes and dark glasses, and chewing bubble gum. But the amalgamation is very imperfect, and in some areas the differences increase rather than decrease with time. Change is one constant condition of the West, as of any new country. One of the portentous changes comes with the spread of that industrial agriculture which the West invented. It is not an aspect of the West, of any of the Wests, that I brag of, but no one who has gone among pickers' camps in California, or watched Navajos loading at little remote Arizona posts to be hauled up into Idaho to pick potatoes, will underestimate it as a fact.

The elephant is a complex beast, and the Wests are everything one is looking for. Historically raw-material states, a colonial empire exploited from the first by eastern capital at high interest rates, victimized by short-haul rail tariffs and absentee ownership, they inherit now a new industrialism, and with it every backbreaking problem known to industry anywhere. Neither one people, one topography, one economic structure, nor one climate, the Wests are like a litter of pups, with nothing grown up about them but their feet, who have discovered some time since how to make a big noise with their mouths. This is what I have been helping in, and it is always a satisfaction. But now comes the growing up, and growing up is no particular fun; the "big power" feeling that California has shown with the counting of the 1950 census that will put her next to New York in Congressional representation is a most un-western feeling, up to now. It will become increasingly familiar.

The last time I looked, Colorado, Utah, Wyoming, Arizona, and New Mexico contained exactly half of our national parks and monuments, and the states around them contained twenty-two more.

Like aridity, and to a degree *because* of aridity, scenery is a bond among all the Wests, and "development," in most areas, has meant most of all hard roads and accommodations for tourists. Because scenery is one finished product that all the Wests can market, development will continue to mean roads, at least until men succeed in pumping passing clouds for extra rain, and transform the landscape. That tapping of clouds, by dry ice or otherwise, is not so fantastic as it sounds; there has already been a serio-comic exchange between Utah and Nevada over who owns water rights in those potential waters driving eastward across the mountains. If and when those clouds are tapped, I want to be in on the court sessions; the rhubarb that will ensue between California and all states eastward to the Rockies will make the controversies over the Colorado River's water seem pallid by comparison.

Meantime, I want to go on living in some one or another of the Wests, perhaps because they *are* new, perhaps because they are still in the stage of development, not of repair, possibly because of the excitement that accompanies the coming of age of an active and promising adolescent. The Wests are waxing rather than waning countries. I do not think they contain more hospitality than other regions, or more liberalism, or more good sense. Politically they are fairly often conservative and sometimes they are reactionary, and they are as capable of being run by political gangs as other places. But believing to some extent in the effect of place upon people, I think I can see somewhat more openness and frankness, somewhat less repression and inhibition, than is apparent in some other places where I have lived, and maybe I can see also more buoyancy and hopefulness.

Sitting here a few miles from the last sunsets on the continent I find myself as contented as I am likely to be anywhere in 1950, and the meadowlarks in the pasture next door remind me that for better or worse I am not far from my spiritual headquarters. For the meadowlark is another thing that all the Wests have in common. In California he sings more tunes, and sings them a little differently, than he sings in Montana or Saskatchewan, but California or Montana, it is the purest and sweetest birdsong I know, purer and sweeter even than the tune of Vermont's white-throated sparrow, which is saying much. Anywhere where meadowlarks sing any of their many tunes, that will be a satisfactory place for this evangelist. And that will be somewhere west of the Missouri.

The West Coast: Region with a View

from *One Way to Spell Man*

During the last two days of October, there gathered at the Highlands Inn, in Carmel, California, one of those conferences that are periodic within the learned professions. The subject, "Has the West Coast an Identifiable Culture?" was calculated to permit the discussion of everything from piety and local prejudice to statistical social analysis. The conferees included four historians, three professors of English, two anthropologists, a philosopher, a college president, a college chaplain, a professor of music, a sociologist, the director of an art museum, the director of the California Department of Beaches and Parks, the director of a university press, the editor of the West's most successful magazine, a music and art critic, an architectural writer, the San Francisco *Time* man, a distinguished architect, two novelists, and the vice-president of the American Council of Learned Societies, which was picking up the check.

Into this pleasant two-day conversation the term "regionalism" was introduced early. The terms of the conference seemed to force us toward the sin of cultural narcissism. What we decided (and it could be nothing very precise, because it was immediately clear to all of us that the region had had no such adequate studies as make generalization possible in some other regions, and was in such a state of flux that it was not likely to have any for a considerable time) is not my subject here. I was more interested in something else revealed by the talks: that among those twenty-five people there was not a single serious defender of the kind of regionalism that used to be argued, and sometimes chanted, during the years when I was growing up in the Rocky Mountains, an immature region, and the Midwest, a somewhat more developed one.

The self-conscious zeal and the mystique were missing at Carmel. Nobody much cared whether the West Coast was called one region or three: clearly it was either or both. Nobody much cared whether the architecture, music, painting, and literature of the Coast were mystically indigenous or not; nobody felt that it was vital for him to concern himself intensively with local themes, settings, characters, and "spirit." More important than those questions of idiosyncrasy in the local arts were the questions "How lively is any of these arts, as measured by both its local and its national or international acceptance?" and "How good is it?" And that is a big change from the organic theory of inevitable cultural maturation that most Americans have accepted, passively or aggressively, for more than a hundred years. By the organic theory, localism and virtue are all but synonymous.

I was not surprised to see regionalism in decline—it has been in decline in every region except in the rear-guard South for years. But I was surprised to see it in nearly total eclipse, especially on the West Coast, where the boom has forced an extreme self-awareness, and most especially in a conference which invited all the traditional responses.

We have always, as a civilization, been compelled to periodic examinations and self-appraisals. Trying to establish who we were—or that we really were somebody—we have smarted under the criticism of British travelers, and have pondered Tocqueville and Lord Bryce, and studied how imported institutions, habits, arts, and ways of thinking adapt themselves on a new continent or in new regions of the continent, and how (this is often pure hope) they become something new and (this is piety) better. Self-discovery has been our need and our theme. Patriotism and the organic theory were twin-born yokels. The critic who remarked back in Jefferson's time that "the chorus of every play is in the hearts of the audience" was implying an intimate bond between small-c culture and large-C Culture, between the society and the arts which expressed it. He did not say, though he might have, Mature the society and the arts will follow as the day the night, and they will echo in the hearts of the audience, because it is of and by and from the people that the matured cultural voice speaks.

Emerson and Whitman would say that for him later on. The Emerson who got tired of the courtly muses of Europe and celebrated the native and the low was at once acknowledging a historical trend and asserting a new value. The Whitman who visioned democratic archetypes and foreheard voices that spoke for a whole people was formulating doctrine that seventy or eighty years later consoled Iowa poets yearning for the slow Midland earth to get on with its essential production of a small-c culture so that they could speak with its voice. Ellis Parker Butler's motto for Iowa, "Ten million yearly for manure but not one cent for literature," would not indefinitely apply. Wait, only wait, and mature your powers. Like Marxism, a local literature was organic and inevitable. Like the classless society, it would come.

The organic theory was essential to the self-respect of us colonials and provincials. It gave us a critical touchstone and the beginnings of a literary history; our jobs were to evaluate local writings in terms of the organic expectations and to hang those which passed the test, like Christmas-tree balls, on the skimpy tree of the local tradition. The organic theory could be used as well in promoting Chicago against Boston, or Nashville or Iowa City against New York, as in asserting America against courtly Europe. When the national literature broke into sections after the Civil War, the organic theory broke with it. Eventually it took over, informed, and enlarged the local-color movement, purged its excesses, gave it a common doctrine, and set about replacing the tourist writers of local color with the Whitmanesque voices of local culture. The Great American Novel was now to come not single and whole from the nation but piecemeal from the regions.

William Dean Howells, in wanting American writers to be as American as they unconsciously could, admitted the self-consciousness of the movement he had steered for many years. He meant that the best writers grow as naturally as apples on a tree, the way he had grown in Ohio and Mark Twain in Missouri. When it happened according to the organic inevitabilities, nationalism or regionalism provided the highest kind of art, and locals were its best judges, as boys and blackbirds were the best judges of berry patches.

That was the doctrine I grew up on, and to a point I will still defend it. It has demonstrably worked, in region after region. Given the proper conditions, it will always work. But the proper conditions involve a relative homogeneity of life in relative isolation over a relatively long period, and that combination is increasingly hard to find. The national character as demonstrated by a Lincoln or analyzed by a Howells or Twain or James was being lost in the rush even while we thought we recognized his face. Industrialism was drumming him under, immigrations of a hundred nationalities and religions and cultural traditions were sweeping him away. Except in rural areas, especially the South, where isolation has not been broken down and the local patterns have remained nearly intact, regionalism has pretty well gone, and the organic theory, if not discredited, is indefinitely suspended in the face of incessant larger syntheses. So what we used to believe expressed a region has turned out, often, to express no more than a period. In the longer view, it looks not like a consummation but like a phase.

Obviously neither the West Coast nor any of its three subregions has a regional culture or regional arts in the traditional terms. For one thing, no part of it has really matured in isolation. Even the Northwest, relatively homogeneous and relatively the most isolated, has been a door to Alaska and a window on Asia, and it is primarily in its woods and its cow country, its James Stephenses and H. L. Davises, that it has developed a regional strain of literature. And what of those novels of rural California that Hamlin Garland foresaw, what of those sunny lads and lasses—or maidens—working and loving under the palms? Well, California agriculture began with cattle, shifted to wheat, developed water and shifted again to truck crops, rice, cotton, fruit. But it never had as its basis that 160-acre yeoman that the American gospels, and Garland with them, assumed. It has always been factories in the field. Jump from *Ramona* to *The Octopus* to *The Grapes of Wrath* and discover how discontinuous and broken is the California agricultural environment and how persistent is the "largeness" of the operations. Cattle persist, and cowboys, but go up into the foothills and meet them. They are largely second- and third-generation Italians. Not even in the rural areas is there a continuity even of ethnic stocks.

The West Coast, California especially, is actually profoundly nonrural. California's 80 percent urbanization matches that of the Middle Atlantic States. It is not inhabited by quaint provincials, and never was. San Francisco in particular has always been a city of an unsurpassed worldliness, a city of sin and excitement and gold. Not only was California a more persuasive image of the earthly paradise than Kansas or Dakota prairie land, but it demanded initiative and some capital to get there, and something like selective immigration took place. Though it drew people of every kind and class, it drew a relatively higher proportion of the educated and cultivated than did other parts of the West; and it drew them, in one of the most remarkable movements of population in recent times, from all over the world.

The advantages that San Francisco enjoyed were enjoyed in somewhat less lavishness by both the Northwest and the Los Angeles area. The setting of both is spectacular, the climate of both is mild. Los Angeles began its boom with a railroad price war and one-dollar tickets to the Pacific, and has mushroomed ever since on sunshine, oranges, oil, Hollywood, and airplanes. But it, too, has drawn heavily from the ranks of writers and artists and musicians, and it, too, if only because of its styles and its movie and television industries, is a variety of world city. So is Seattle. So is Portland. No isolation in any of them, and no homogeneity, and no holding still. To make social studies of any of those cities would be like trying to hold a stethoscope to the chest of an angry cat. And hence no traditional regionalism; perhaps no identifiable West Coast culture.

Quite obviously the twenty-five men sitting around a table in Carmel had much in common. They all lived in places strongly on the boom, places that multitudes of people move into but that few people ever move out of. They all shared a peculiarly West Coast view of the Pacific and of Asia, a degree of familiarity and awareness created entirely by propinquity. They shared big agriculture and except for the coastal strip from about Eureka, California, northward they shared a water shortage. Very largely, the West Coast, like all the rest of the Far West, is an oasis civilization. They shared a style of domestic architecture that more than any other single cultural manifestation deserves to be called regional in the old sense and that is probably imported more enthusiastically into other regions than any other West Coast product. They shared colossal headaches incident upon explosive growth, lack of planning, commercialism, and public apathy: overcrowded highways, double-session schools, housing developments that at their cheapest and worst are about as aesthetic and as socially healthful as ringworm. They acknowledged for their own subregions a bad case of togetherness and conformity, possibly brought on by the need of new immigrants to root themselves, conform, belong. They shared an anxiety probably more acute than that of the country at large, if religious cultism, a marked growth in the more conservative denominations, very high suicide and alcoholism rates, and a vast yeasty ferment of amateur creativeness may all be lumped together as indications of social unease.

Eagerness to conform and belong may in themselves be causes of anxiety when it is not clear what one can or should conform to. By the evidence of both the editor of *Sunset* and the director of the California Beaches and Parks, one common way is to seize upon the natural environment, make greedy use of the parks, forests, beaches, campsites, make a fetish of the barbecue and barbecue weather. Precisely because there are so many new migrants, most of them eagle-eyed for the patterns to which they ought to conform, the West Coast as a region shows a blurred image. No group, even an intimate group in one of the subregions, could sit down and find in common such things as the *Fugitive* group in Nashville found: a common agrarian tradition with a philosophy to match, a common Protestantism lit by revivalism, a common racial and cultural background, a common lost cause, a common hatred, a common guilt.

On the West Coast, no such unanimity of tradition and belief. No voices, no archetypes, no Great Pacific Slope Novel. And yet, from Seattle to San Diego a tremendous stir, a great swell of energy and optimism and creativity, and this may be the truest, though not necessarily the most traditional, expression of a really regional spirit. For the ferment is not simply economic, not just a building boom and the skyrocketing of the electronics and aircraft and missile industries. This society—urban, opulent, anxious, energetic, highly unionized, with a per-capita income exceeded by that of only four or five states, growing at a furious rate, situated in a region whose climate is on the whole more beatific and whose natural setting is more spectacular than those of any other section—this society is not sitting on its hands or relapsing into Spanish-Californian somnolence. In spite of the sports cars and the Rolls-Royces (thirteen of the forty U.S. Rolls-Royce agencies are in California), and in spite of the swimming pools and the homes that cost two, three, four hundred thousand dollars, this society strains for something more. Perhaps it is uneasily asking itself Max Lerner's question "After prosperity, what?" Perhaps it is conforming, or trying to conform, to some regional image of creativity, as my Norwegian grandparents consciously tried to conform to the outlines of midwestern character.

In any case there is a curious ambivalence detectable—or at least I seemed to detect it in the findings of the Carmel conference. For along with the uneasiness, the anxiety, the uncertainty and fumbling for identification, there is in the whole West Coast, and there was among the twenty-five conferees at Carmel, a confidence so sublime that it is hardly even conscious of itself. By the end of the meeting, we were assuring ourselves that it would be totally false to try to justify or even identify West Coast culture in organic or regional terms. Never having felt isolated or provincial or inferior, the Coast doesn't have to wedge itself forward.

Two days at Carmel convinced most of us that we felt pretty much like the rest of the United States, only more so. Our language is a representative amalgam almost undistinguished by local dialectal peculiarities; ethnically we are more mixed even than the eastern seaboard cities; in a prosperous country, we are more prosperous than most; in an urban country, more urban than most; in a gadget-happy country, more addicted to gadgets; in a mobile country, more mobile; in a tasteless country, more tasteless; in a creative country, more energetically creative; in an optimistic society, more optimistic; in an anxious society, more anxious.

Contribute regionally to the national culture? We *are* the national culture, at its most energetic end.

It is exhilarating when twenty-five intelligent and articulate people discover at the same time that they share so egregious and brash a confidence. Newcomer or native son, we all had it. We asked ourselves what was most characteristic about the architecture which was the Coast's most distinctive regional contribution, and we found that it was open, outward-turning, the reverse of the inward-turning and cavelike and protective. We looked out the windows down at the headland of Point Lobos, where land and water and sun met magnificently, and we knew one of the reasons people came—we among them—and seldom left. We began to add up the signs of cultural life, all the way from the San Francisco opera season and the somewhat magniloquent Hollywood Bowl to the unsponsored and spontaneous creative cutting edges: the jazz renaissance in San Francisco, the weekly theater on the campus of the University of Washington, the centers of poetry and fiction, the new patterns of neighborhood theater and neighborhood music in the sprawling noncity of Los Angeles, the art museums, the galleries, the painters of the so-called San Francisco School, who would actually be quite as much at home almost anywhere since most of them are abstract expressionists. We counted Nobel Prize winners in West Coast universities and the people we knew who had recently been filched by West Coast schools from the Ivy League, and artists, writers, musicians, painters, who had chosen to be born here or to come here. For a little while we were like a delighted bunch of regional patriots counting our successes—except that there was practically nothing of traditional regionalism in us. Half of the people we cited as signs of great creative growth were in-migrants, as were half of ourselves. That was no problem. That was precisely how the rest of the country and the rest of the world *did* contribute to us; that was simply greater evidence of centrality.

Robert Frost, whom if I were a regionalist I would instantly identify as having been born in San Francisco, had a test by which he judged a man: How well can he swing what he knows? The West Coast beyond question can afford to know more, but what it knows it can swing. It thinks it can swing the whole country. If I ever saw a region that feels its oats, this is it.

From its great eyes on Mount Palomar, Mount Wilson, Mount Hamilton, the West Coast looks farther into space than anyone anywhere. That is something to fasten upon. But take another symbol. On the grand prow of land above the Golden Gate, looking north across the soar and lift of the bridge to the Marin hills, and eastward across San Francisco's roofs and streets, and westward toward the last promontory below which the Pacific spreads vast and blue, sits one of San Francisco's three art museums, the Palace of the Legion of Honor. It is formally French, a replica. The late William Wurster, the dean of Bay Area architects as well as of the University of California School of Architecture, called it "the most inward-turning building upon the most outward-turning site in the world."

That building represents an old way of thinking; it demonstrates in a way the earliest, imitative, transplanted stage of the organic process. It is not likely that it or the spirit that produced it will have much influence on the future. For nothing else in this West Coast amalgam is inward-turning. America at its farthest West and its highest voltage, it is a region, if it can be called a region at all, with a view. Like lemmings, the nation has beaten its way to the western edge and the last sunsets on the continent, but only a few jump off the Golden Gate in frustration at having nowhere else to go. The rest of them are busy preparing the coast as a launching platform for the future.

I believe this truly is not a region but the mainstream, America only more so. Both the good and the bad are more so. Sight of what some builders have been permitted to do along the Skyline road south of San Francisco would bring tears to the eyes of a hangman. The North Beach bohemia that for some reason seemed to represent San Francisco to the world for a season was a dreary borrowing, an inward-turning if there ever was one, a death wish in a crying towel. Much of this, and much of every hideousness of our automotive civilization. And yet what a surge, how much life, how much exuberant and not always controlled power—above all, what confidence! The West Coast has the calm confidence of a Christian with four aces, and Mark Twain, who knew it in its earlier exuberance, would be the first to say so. If Lerner's "After prosperity, what?" is an answerable question, the West Coast is going to have a good deal to do about framing the answer.

Comments for Committee for Green Foothills' 25th Anniversary

May 9, 1987

Wendell Berry, commenting on the displaced quality of much American life, calls himself a "placed" person, and suggests that if you don't know where you are, you don't know who you are. Identity depends not on some intransigent independence and separateness, but upon membership in something—a community, region, tradition, place.

Most of us never become placed at all, and especially in the West we are a tribe of migrants. To the truly placed individual, most of us look footloose, unattached, irresponsible, asocial or antisocial. We have a current like the Platte, a mile wide and an inch deep. The dust never settles around us. As a species, though we consume territory and often deal in it, we are non-territorial. We lack a stamping ground, and we often escape responsibility by running from it. Rooted in no community, we are accountable to none. Culturally we are more often transplanters and discarders than conservers or builders.

The fact is, both we and the society or semi-society we have created show the symptoms of deficiency. We suffer from some obscure scurvy or pellagra of the soul. We have lost touch with the gods that elsewhere make places holy, and in our dealing with the earth we have become conscienceless and rootless. Our folk heroes are wanderers and orphans—Leatherstocking, Huckleberry Finn, the Ishmael of *Moby Dick*. What is the Lone Ranger's home town?

Much of our literature, from *Roughing It* to *On the Road*, from *The Log of a Cowboy* to *Lonesome Dove*, from *The Big Rock Candy Mountain* to *The Big Sky*, is a literature not of place but of motion. Here in the West our principal cultural invention is the motel and our characteristic towns are mere overnight stops on the Interstate. Nobody ever lives where he was born, or dies where he has lived.

I know about this. I was born on wheels. I know the excitement of newness and the relief when responsibility has been left behind. But I also know the dissatisfaction and hunger that result from placelessness. All through my childhood and youth, I no sooner began to know a place, and feel comfortable in it, than I was yanked out of it and set down among strangers in another strange town. The towns where I lived never became quite real to me; they were only the raw material of places, as I was the raw material of a person, and we needed a lot more mutual contact and shared memory before either of us could be complete. I spent my youth envying people who still lived in the house they were born in, in neighborhoods that they knew yard by yard, among people who had been familiars since earliest memory. I wanted an attic, to prove to myself that I had lived.

That is probably why, when we came to Stanford at the end of World War II, we were ripe to settle down. To those who had grown up in it, the Peninsula was a place, surely; but it was a place in jeopardy from sudden and violent change. It was beautiful, climatically invigorating, intellectually stimulating, with a great university at its heart and marvelous green and gold foothills for a backdrop. What happened to it was something that we participated in: there were a lot of people like the Stegners flocking to this part of the world then. We watched the orchards that had been a froth of blossoms every spring wither as if in the breath of a blowtorch. We watched houses being built, first a few, then many, in the foothills. We heard and read of plans for the kind of uninhibited development that scared us to death for the future of what we loved about the place. Very early, it became clear that if we didn't want our new place to be degraded and uglified and over-developed even while we were trying to live our way into it, we would have to be very careful how we ourselves treated it, and we would have to fight what threatened it.

We have now been here for forty-two years, light-years longer than we ever lived in any other place. More than half of our lives have been lived in one house, and we've got God's plenty of evidence, in sheds and storerooms if not in an attic, that we have lived there. We eagerly await the semi-annual trash pickups that will let us throw things away. That is a new experience, and a satisfying one.

Some things that we see as we look out our windows sicken us. But also, in those forty-two years we have participated in a few exhilarating victories of the long-range public good over short-range private greed. The Peninsula our children and grandchildren will inherit is not as healthy and beautiful as it might be, but it is not totally spoiled, either—and it could have been.

In this green and friendly garden of R.E.'s, among people, all of whom we know and respect, and many of whom we love, we can at last begin to feel placed. Since the night twenty-five years ago when we gathered in Ruth Spangenberg's living room to organize the Committee for Green Foothills, we have been through a lot of shared living. What was at first a mere contact, a temporary coagulation of near-strangers with like interests, has become a continuity and a tradition. I wish I could just call the roll, for I see some of those original members here this afternoon. But I won't. You know who you are because you know *where* you are; and you know what you have done, you and the hundreds who have joined Green Foothills since.

You should take great pride in what you have done; and you should brace yourselves to do more. The opportunity will not vanish, or the threats disappear. A place is not a place until people have lived their way deeply into it and it exists in their minds and memories and emotions as surely as it does on the map. And one of the best ways to get that feeling for a place is to fight for it.

The Committee for Green Foothills has helped to educate the citizens and officials of the area in responsible stewardship. It has saved, for the indifferent and the hostile as well as for its own members, some of the beauty and health of the Mid-Peninsula. And for me, at least, one of the best things it has done is to foster the spirit of community and the spirit of place—to create something valid and fine to which such random particles as the Stegners can adhere. Belonging is the heart of it; membership is the absolutely essential corrective to too much disaffiliated liberty.

On publicized reason for this afternoon's party is that you choose to honor me. I thank you for that, though I think you overestimate my importance. Many of you have been more dedicated and more effective than I have been. But I can tell you I am proud to be, and grateful to be, among such friends, and that our purpose is as strong as it ever was. This, finally, is my place.

The very first memories I have, from about the age of three, are of an orphanage in Seattle. I would be content if my last ones could be of a gathering like this, among these people, here.

STRIKING THE ROCK

from *The American West as Living Space*

The summer of 1948 my family and I spent on Struthers Burt's ranch in Jackson Hole. I was just beginning a biography of John Wesley Powell, and learning some things about the West that I had not understood before. During that busy and instructive interval my wife and I were also acting as western editors and scouts for a publishing house, and now and then someone came by with a manuscript or the idea for a book. The most memorable of these was a famous architect contemplating his autobiography. One night he showed us slides of some of his houses, including a million-dollar palace in the California desert of which he was very proud. He said it demonstrated that with imagination, technical know-how, modern materials, and enough money, an architect could build anywhere without constraints, imposing his designed vision on any site, in any climate.

In that waterless pale desert spotted with shadscale and creosote bush and backed by barren, lion-colored mountains, another sort of architect, say Frank Lloyd Wright, might have designed something contextual, something low, broad-eaved, thick-walled, something that would mitigate the hot light, something half underground so that people could retire like the lizards and rattlesnakes from the intolerable daytime temperatures, something made of native stone or adobe or tamped earth in the colors and shapes of the country, something no more visually obtrusive than an outcrop.

Not this architect. He had built of cinderblock, in the form of Bauhaus cubes, the only right angles in that desert. He had painted them a dazzling white. Instead of softening the lines between building and site, he had accentuated them, surrounding his sugary cubes with acres of lawn and a tropical oasis of oleanders, hibiscus, and palms—not the native Washingtonia palms either, which are a little scraggly, but sugar and royal palms, with a classier, more Santa Barbara look. Water for this *estancia*, enough water to have sustained a whole tribe of desert Indians, he had brought by private pipeline from the mountains literally miles away.

The patio around the pool—who would live in the desert without a pool?—would have fried the feet of swimmers, three hundred days out of the year, and so he had designed canopies that could be extended and retracted by push-button, and under the patio's concrete he had laid pipes through which cool water circulated by day. By night, after the desert chill came on, the circulating water was heated. He had created an artificial climate, inside and out.

Studying that luxurious, ingenious, beautiful, sterile incongruity, I told its creator, sincerely, that I thought he could build a comfortable house in hell. That pleased him; he thought so too. What I didn't tell him, what he would not have understood, was that we thought his desert house immoral. It exceeded limits, it offended our sense not of the possible but of the desirable. There was no economic or social reason for anyone's living on a barren flat, however beautiful, where every form of life sought shelter during the unbearable daylight hours. The only reasons for building there were to let mad dogs and rich men go out in the midday sun, and to let them own and dominate a view they admired. The house didn't fit the country, it challenged it. It asserted America's never-say-never spirit. It seemed to us an act of arrogance on the part of both owner and architect.

I felt like asking him, What if a super-rich Eskimo wanted a luxury house on Point Hope? Would you build it for him? Would you dam the Kobuk and bring megawatts of power across hundreds of miles of tundra, and set up batteries of blower-heaters to melt the snow and thaw the permafrost, and would you erect an international style house with picture windows through which the Eskimo family could look out across the lawn and strawberry bed and watch polar bears on the pack ice?

He might have taken on such a job, and he was good enough to make it work, too—until the power line blew down or shorted out. Then the Eskimos he had encouraged to forget igloo-building and seal-oil lamps would freeze into ice sculptures, monuments to human pride. But of course that is all fantasy. Eskimos, a highly adapted and adaptable people, would have more sense than to challenge their arctic habitat that way. Even if they had unlimited money. Which they don't.

That desert house seemed to me, and still seems to me, a paradigm—hardly a paradigm, more a caricature—of what we have been doing to the West in my lifetime. Instead of adapting, as we began to do, we have tried to make country and climate over to fit our existing habits and desires. Instead of listening to the silence, we have shouted into the void. We have tried to make the arid West into what it was never meant to be and cannot remain, the Garden of the World and the home of multiple millions.

* * *

THAT DOES NOT MEAN either that the West should never have been settled or that water should never be managed. The West—the habitable parts of it—is a splendid habitat for a limited population living within the country's rules of sparseness and mobility. If the unrestrained engineering of western water was original sin, as I believe, it was essentially a sin of scale. Anyone who wants to live in the West has to manage water to some degree.

Ranchers learned early to turn creeks onto their hay land. Homesteaders not on a creek learned to dam a run-off coulee to create a "rezavoy" as we did in Saskatchewan in 1915. Kansas and Oklahoma farmers set windmills to pumping up the underground water. Towns brought their water, by ditch or siphon, from streams up on the watershed. Irrigation, developed first by the Southwestern Indians and the New Mexico Spanish, and reinvented by the Mormons—it was a necessity that came with the territory—was expanded in the 1870s and 1880s by such cooperative communities as Greeley, Colorado, and by small-to-medium corporate ventures such as the one I wrote about in *Angle of Repose*—the project on the Boise River that after its failure was taken over by the Bureau of Reclamation and called the Arrowrock Dam.

Early water engineers and irrigators bit off what they and the local community could chew. They harnessed the streams that they could manage. Some dreamers did take on larger rivers, as Arthur Foote took on the Boise, and went broke at it. By and large, by 1890 individual, corporate, and cooperative irrigators had gone about as far as they could go with water engineering; their modest works were for local use and under local control. It might have been better if the West had stopped there. Instead, all through the 1890s the unsatisfied boosters called for federal aid to let the West realize its destiny, and in 1902 they got the Newlands Act. This *permitted* the feds to undertake water projects—remember that water was state-owned, or at least state-regulated—and created the Bureau of Reclamation.

Reclamation projects were to be paid for by fees charged irrigation districts, the period for paying off the interest-free indebtedness being first set at ten years. Later that was upped to twenty, later still to forty. Eventually much of the burden of repayment was shifted from the sale of water to the sale of hydro-power, and a lot of the burden eliminated entirely by the practice of river-basin accounting, with write-offs for flood control, job creation, and other public goods. Once it was lured in, the federal government—which meant taxpayers throughout the country, including taxpayers in states that resented western reclamation because they saw themselves asked to pay for something that would compete unfairly with their own farmers—absorbed or wrote off more and more of the costs, accepting the fact that reclamation was a continuing subsidy to western agriculture. Even today, when municipal and industrial demands for water have greatly increased, 80 to 90 percent of the water used in the West is used, often wastefully, on fields, to produce crops generally in surplus elsewhere. After all the billions spent by the Bureau of Reclamation, the total area irrigated by its projects is about the size of Ohio, and the water impounded and distributed by the Bureau is about 15 percent of all the water utilized in the

West. What has been won is only a beachhead, and a beachhead that is bound to shrink.

* * *

ONE OF THE THINGS Westerners should ponder, but generally do not, is their relation to and attitude toward the federal presence. The bureaus administering all the empty space that gives Westerners much of their outdoor pleasure and many of their special privileges and a lot of their pride and self-image are frequently resented, resisted, or manipulated by those who benefit economically from them but would like to benefit more, and are generally taken for granted by the general public.

The federal presence should be recognized as what it is: a reaction against our former profligacy and wastefulness, an effort at adaptation and stewardship in the interest of the environment and the future. In contrast to the principal water agency, the Bureau of Reclamation, which was a creation of the boosters and remains their creature, and whose prime purpose is technological conversion of the arid lands, the land-managing bureaus all have as at least part of their purpose the preservation of the West in a relatively natural, healthy, and sustainable condition.

Yellowstone became the first national park in 1872 because a party of Montana tourists around a campfire voted down a proposal to exploit it for profit, and pledged themselves to try to get it protected as a permanent pleasuring-ground for the whole country. The national forests began because the bad example of Michigan scared Congress about the future of the country's forests, and induced it in 1891 to authorize the reservation of public forest lands by presidential proclamation. Benjamin Harrison took large advantage of the opportunity. Later, Grover Cleveland did the same, and so did Theodore Roosevelt. The West, predictably, cried aloud at having that much plunder removed from circulation, and in 1907 western Congressmen put a rider on an agricultural appropriations bill that forbade any more presidential reservations without the prior consent of Congress. Roosevelt could have pocket-vetoed it. Instead, he and his Chief Forester, Gifford Pinchot, sat up all night over the maps and surveys of potential reserves, and by morning Roosevelt had signed into existence twenty-one new national forests, sixteen million acres of them. Then he signed the bill that would have stopped him.

It was Theodore Roosevelt, too, who created the first wildlife refuge in 1903, thus beginning a service whose territories, since the Alaska National Interest Lands Conservation Act of 1980, now exceed those of the National Park Service by ten million acres.

As for the biggest land manager of all, the Bureau of Land Management, it is the inheritor of the old General Land Office, whose job was to dispose of the Public Domain to homesteaders, and its lands are the leftovers once (erroneously) thought to be worthless. Worthless or not, they could not be indefinitely neglected and abused. The health of lands around them depended on their health.

They were assumed as a permanent federal responsibility by the Taylor Grazing Act of 1934, but the Grazing Service then created was a helpless and toothless bureau dominated by local councils packed by local stockmen—foxes set by other foxes to watch the henhouse, in a travesty of democratic local control. The Grazing Service was succeeded by the Bureau of Land Management, which was finally given some teeth by the Federal Land Policy and Management Act (FLPMA) of 1976. No sooner did it get the teeth that would have let it do its job than the Sagebrush Rebels offered to knock them out. The Rebels didn't have to. Instead, President Reagan gave them James Watt as Secretary of the Interior, and James Watt gave them Robert Burford as head of the BLM. The rebels simmered down, their battle won for them by administrative appointment, and BLM remains a toothless bureau.

All of the bureaus walk a line somewhere between preservation and exploitation. The enabling act of the National Park Service in 1916 charged it to provide for the *use without impairment* of the parks. It is an impossible assignment, especially now that more than three hundred million people visit the national parks annually, but the Park Service tries.

The National Forest Service, born out of Pinchot's philosophy of "wise use," began with the primary purpose of halting unwise use, and as late as the 1940s so informed a critic as Bernard DeVoto thought it the very best of the federal bureaus. But it changed its spots during the first Eisenhower administration, under the Mormon patriarch Ezra Taft Benson as Secretary of Agriculture, and began aggressively to harvest board feet. Other legitimate uses—recreation, watershed and wildlife protection, the gene-banking of wild plant and animal species, and especially wilderness preservation—it either neglected or resisted whenever they conflicted with logging.

By now, unhappily, environmental groups tend to see the Forest Service not as the protector of an invaluable public resource and the true champion of multiple use, but as one of the enemy, allied with the timber interests. The Forest Service, under attack, has reacted with a hostility bred of its conviction that it is unjustly criticized. As a consequence of that continuing confrontation, nearly every master plan prepared in obedience to the National Forest Management Act of 1976 has been challenged and will be fought, in the courts if necessary, by the Wilderness Society, the Sierra Club, the Natural Resources Defense Council, and other organizations. The usual charge: too many timber sales, too often at a loss in money as well as in other legitimate values, and far too much roading—roading being a preliminary to logging and a way of forestalling wilderness designation by spoiling the wilderness in advance.

What is taking place is that Congress has been responding to public pressures to use the national forests for newly-perceived social goods; and the National Forest Service, for many years an almost autonomous bureau with a high morale and, from a forester's point of view, high principles, is resisting that imposition of control.

Not even the Fish and Wildlife Service, dedicated to the preservation of wild species and their habitats, escapes criticism, for under pressure from stockmen it has historically waged war on predators, especially coyotes, and the 1080 poison baits that it distributed destroyed not only coyotes but hawks, eagles, and other wildlife that the agency was created to protect. One result has been a good deal of public suspicion. Even the current device of 1080 collars for sheep and lambs, designed to affect only an attacking predator, is banned in thirty states.

The protection provided by these various agencies is of course imperfect. Every reserve is an island, and its boundaries are leaky. Nevertheless this is the best protection we have, and not to be disparaged. All Americans, but especially Westerners whose backyard is at stake, need to ask themselves whose bureaus these should be. Half of the West is in their hands. Do they exist to provide bargain-basement grass to favored stockmen whose grazing privileges have become all but hereditary, assumed and bought and sold along with the title to the home spread? Are they hired exterminators of wildlife? Is it their function to negotiate loss-leader coal leases with energy conglomerates, and to sell timber below cost to Louisiana Pacific? Or should they be serving the much larger public whose outdoor recreations of backpacking, camping, fishing, hunting, river-running, mountain climbing, hang-gliding, and, God help us, dirt-biking are incompatible with clear-cut forests and overgrazed, poison-baited, and stripmined grasslands? Or is there a still higher duty—to maintain the health and beauty of the lands they manage, protecting from everybody, including such destructive segments of the public as dirt-bikers and pot-hunters, the watersheds and spawning streams, forests and grasslands, geological and scenic splendors, historical and archaeological remains, air and water and serene space, that once led me, in a reckless moment, to call the western public lands part of the geography of hope?

As I have known them, most of the field representatives of all the bureaus, including the BLM, do have a sense of responsibility about the resources they oversee, and a frequent frustration that they are not permitted to oversee them better. But that sense of duty is not visible in some, and at the moment is least visible in the political appointees who make or enunciate policy. Even when policy is intelligently made and well understood, it sometimes cannot be enforced because of local opposition. More than one forest ranger or BLM man who tried to enforce the rules has had to be transferred out of a district to save him from violence.

There are many books on the Public Domain. One of the newest and best is *These American Lands,* by Dyan Zaslowsky and the Wilderness Society, published by Henry Holt and Company.

I recommend it, not only for its factual accuracy and clarity, but for its isolation of problems and its suggestions of solutions. Here all I can do is repeat that the land bureaus have a strong, often disregarded influence on how life is lived in the West. They provide and protect the visible, available, unfenced space that surrounds almost all western cities and towns—surrounds them as water surrounds fish, and is their living element.

The bureaus need, and some would welcome, the kind of public attention that would force them to behave in the long-range public interest. Though I have been involved in controversies with some of them, the last thing I would want to see is their dissolution and a return to the policy of disposal, for that would be the end of the West as I have known and loved it. Neither state ownership nor private ownership—which state ownership would soon become—could offer anywhere near the disinterested stewardship that these imperfect and embattled federal bureaus do, while at the same time making western space available to millions. They have been the strongest impediment to the careless ruin of what remains of the Public Domain, and they will be necessary as far ahead as I, at least, can see.

The Bureau of Reclamation is something else. From the beginning, its aim has been not the preservation but the remaking—in effect the mining—of the West.

* * *

A PRINCIPAL JUSTIFICATION for the Newlands Act was that fabled Jeffersonian yeoman, that small freehold farmer, who was supposed to benefit from the Homestead Act, the Desert Land Act, the Timber and Stone Act, and other land-disposal legislation, and rarely did so west of the 98th meridian. The publicized purpose of federal reclamation was the creation of family farms that would eventually feed the world and build prosperous rural commonwealths in deserts formerly fit for nothing but horned toads and rattlesnakes. To insure that these small farmers would not be done out of their rights by large landowners and water users, Congress wrote into the act a clause limiting the use of water under Reclamation Bureau dams to the amount that would serve a family farm of 160 acres.

Behind the pragmatic, manifest-destinarian purpose of pushing western settlement was another motive: the hard determination to dominate Nature which historian Lynn White, in a well-known essay, identified as part of our Judeo-Christian heritage. Nobody implemented that impulse more uncomplicatedly than the Mormons, a chosen people who believed the Lord when He told them to make the desert blossom as the rose. Nobody expressed it more bluntly than a Mormon hierarch, John Widtsoe, in the middle of the irrigation campaigns: "The destiny of man is to possess the whole earth; the destiny of the earth is to be subject to man. There can be no full conquest of the earth, and no real satisfaction to humanity, if large portions of the earth remain beyond his highest control."

That doctrine offends me to the bottom of my not-very-Christian soul. It is related to the spirit that builds castles of incongruous luxury in the desert. It is the same spirit that between 1930 and the present has so dammed, diverted, used and reused the Colorado River that its saline waters now never reach the Gulf of California, but die in the sand miles from the sea; that has set the Columbia, a far mightier river, to tamely turning turbines; that has reduced the Missouri, the greatest river on the continent, to a string of ponds; that has recklessly pumped down the underground water table of every western valley and threatens to dry up even so prolific a source as the Ogalalla Aquifer; that has made the Salt River Valley of Arizona and the Imperial, Coachella, and great Central Valleys of California into gardens of fabulous but deceptive richness; that has promoted a new rush to the West fated, like the beaver and grass and gold rushes, to recede after doing great environmental damage.

The Garden of the World has been a glittering dream, and many find its fulfillment exhilarating. I do not. I have already said that I think of the main-stem dams that made it possible as original sin, but there is neither a serpent nor a guilty first couple in the story. In Adam's fall we sinned all. Our very virtues as a pioneering people, the very genius of our industrial civilization, drove us to act as we did. God and Manifest Destiny spoke with one voice urging us to "conquer" or "win" the West; and there was no voice of comparable authority to remind us of Mary Austin's quiet but profound truth, that the manner of the country makes the usage of life there, and that the land will not be lived in except in its own fashion.

Obviously, reclamation is not the panacea it once seemed. Plenty of people in 1987 are opposed to more dams, and there is plenty of evidence against the long-range viability and the social and environmental desirability of large-scale irrigation agriculture. Nevertheless, millions of Americans continue to think of the water-engineering in the West as one of our proudest achievements, a technology that we should export to backward Third World nations to help them become as we are. We go on praising apples as if eating them were an injunction of the Ten Commandments.

* * *

FOR ITS FIRST THIRTY YEARS, the Bureau of Reclamation struggled, plagued by money problems and unable to perform as its boosters had promised. It got a black eye for being involved, in shady ways, with William Mulholland's steal of the Owens Valley's water for the benefit of Los Angeles. The early dams it completed sometimes served not an acre of public land. It did increase homestead filings substantially, but not all those homesteads ended up in the hands of Jeffersonian yeomen: according to a 1922 survey, it had created few family farms; the 160-acre limitation was never enforced; three-quarters of the farmers in some reclamation districts were tenants.

Drouth, Depression, and the New Deal's effort to make public works jobs gave the Bureau new life. It got quick appropriations for the building of the Boulder (Hoover) Dam, already authorized, and it took over from the State of California construction of the enormous complex of dams and ditches called the Central Valley Project, designed to harness all the rivers flowing westward out of the Sierra. It grew like a mushroom, like an exhalation. By the 1940s the bureau that only a few years before had been hanging on by a shoestring was constructing, simultaneously, the four greatest dams ever built on earth up to that time—Hoover, Shasta, Bonneville, and Grand Coulee—and was already the greatest force in the West. It had discovered where power was, and allied itself with it: with the growers and landowners, private and corporate, whose interests it served, and with the political delegations, often elected out of this same group, who carried the effort in Washington for more and more pork-barrel projects. In matters of western water there are no political parties. You cannot tell Barry Goldwater from Mo Udall; or Orrin Hatch from Richard Lamm.

Nevertheless there was growing opposition to dams from nature lovers, from economists and cost-counters, and from political representatives of areas that resented paying these costs to subsidize their competition. Uniting behind the clause in the National Park Act that enjoined "use without impairment," environmental groups in 1955 blocked two dams in Dinosaur National Monument and stopped the whole Upper Colorado River Storage Project in its tracks. Later, in the 1960s, they also blocked a dam in Marble Canyon, on the Colorado, and another in Grand Canyon National Monument, at the foot of the Grand Canyon.

In the process they accumulated substantial evidence—economic, political, and environmental—against dams, the bureau that built them, and the principles that guided that bureau. President Jimmy Carter had a lot of public sympathy when he tried to stop nine water-project boondoggles, most of them in the West, in 1977. Though the hornet's nest he stirred up taught him something about western water politics, observers noted that no new water projects were authorized by Congress until the very last days of the 99th Congress, in October 1986.

The great days of dam-building are clearly over, for the best damsites are used up, most of the rivers are "tamed," costs have risen exponentially, and public support of reclamation has given way to widespread and searching criticism. It is not a bad time to assess what the big era of water engineering has done to the West.

The voices of reappraisal are already a chorus. Four books in particular, all published within the past five years, have examined western water developments and practices in detail. They are Philip Fradkin's *A River No More,* about the killing of the Colorado; William A. Kahrl's *Water and Power,* on the rape of the Owens Valley by Los Angeles; Donald Worster's *Rivers of Empire,* a dismaying survey of our irrigation society in the light of Karl Wittvogel's studies of the ancient hydraulic civilizations of Mesopotamia and China; and Marc Reisner's *Cadillac Desert,* a history that pays particular and unfriendly attention to the Bureau of Reclamation and its most empire-building director, Floyd Dominy.

None of those books is calculated to please agribusiness or the politicians and bureaucrats who have served it. Their consensus is that reclamation dams and their little brother the centrifugal pump have made an impressive omelet but have broken many eggs, some of them golden, and are in the process of killing the goose that laid them.

* * *

BEGIN WITH SOME ENVIRONMENTAL consequences of "taming" rivers, if only because the first substantial opposition to dams was environmental.

First, dams do literally kill rivers, which means they kill not only living water and natural scenery but a whole congeries of values associated with them. The scenery they kill is often of the grandest, for most main-stem dams are in splendid canyons, which they drown. San Francisco drowned the Hetch Hetchy Valley, which many thought as beautiful as Yosemite itself, to insure its future water supply. Los Angeles turned the Owens Valley into a desert by draining off its natural streams. The Bureau of Reclamation drowned Glen Canyon, the most serene and lovely rock funhouse in the West, to provide peaking power for Los Angeles and the Las Vegas Strip.

The lakes formed behind the dams are sometimes cited as great additions to public recreation, and Floyd Dominy even published a book to prove that the Glen Canyon Dam had beautified Glen Canyon by drowning it. But draw-down reservoirs rarely live up to their billing. Nothing grows in the zone between low-water-mark and high-water-mark, and except when brimming full, any draw-down reservoir, even Glen Canyon which escapes the worst effects because its walls are vertical, is not unlike a dirty bathtub with a ring of mud and mineral stain around it.

A dammed river is not only stoppered like a bathtub, but it is turned on and off like a tap, creating a fluctuation of flow that destroys the riverine and riparian wildlife and creates problems for recreational boatmen who have to adjust to times when the river is mainly boulders and times when it rises thirty feet and washes their tied boats off the beaches. And since dams prohibit the really high flows of the spring runoff, boulders, gravel and detritus pile up into the channel at the mouths of side gulches, and never get washed away.

Fishing too suffers, and not merely today's fishing but the future of fishing. Despite their fish ladders, the dams on the Columbia seriously reduced the spawning runs of salmon and steelhead, and they also trapped and killed so many smolts on their way downriver that eventually the federal government had to regulate the river's flow. The reduction of fishing is felt not only by the off-shore fishing fleets and by Indian tribes with traditional or treaty fishing rights, but by sports fishermen all the way upstream to the Salmon River Mountains in Idaho.

If impaired rafting and fishing and sightseeing seem a trivial price to pay for all the economic benefits supposedly brought by dams, reflect that rafting and fishing and sightseeing are not trivial economic activities. Tourism is the biggest industry in every western state. The national parks, which are mainly in the public lands states, saw over three hundred million visitors in 1984. The national forests saw even more. A generation ago, only 5,000 people in all the United States had ever rafted a river; by 1985, 35 million had. Every western river from the Rogue and the Owyhee to the Yampa, Green, San Juan, and Colorado is booked solid through the running season. As the rest of the country grows more stressful as a dwelling place, the quiet, remoteness, and solitude of a week on a wild river become more and more precious to more and more people. It is a good question whether we may not need that silence, space, and solitude for the healing of our raw spirits more than we need surplus cotton and alfalfa, produced for private profit at great public expense.

The objections to reclamation go beyond the obvious fact that reservoirs in desert country lose a substantial amount of their impounded water through surface evaporation; and the equally obvious fact that all such reservoirs eventually silt up and become mud flats ending in concrete waterfalls; and the further fact that an occasional dam, because of faulty siting or construction, will go out, as the Teton Dam went out in 1976, bringing disaster to people, towns, and fields below. They go beyond the fact that underground water, recklessly pumped, is quickly depleted, and that some of it will only be renewed in geological time, and that the management of underground water and that of surface water are necessarily linked. The ultimate objection is that irrigation agriculture itself, in deserts where surface evaporation is extreme, has a limited though unpredictable life. Marc Reisner predicts that in the next half century as much irrigated land will go out of production as the Bureau of Reclamation has "reclaimed" in its whole history.

Over time, salts brought to the surface by constant flooding and evaporation poison the soil: the ultimate, natural end of an irrigated field in arid country is an alkali flat. That was the end of fields in every historic irrigation civilization except Egypt, where, until the Aswan Dam, the annual Nile flood leached away salts and renewed the soil with fresh silt.

Leaching can sometimes be managed if you have enough sweet water and a place to put the run-off. But there is rarely water enough—the water is already 125 percent allocated and 100 percent used—and what water is available is often itself saline from having run through other fields upstream and having brought their salts back to the river. Colorado River water near the headwaters at Grand Lake is 200 parts per million salt. Below the Wellton-Mohawk District on the Gila it is 6300 ppms salt. The 1 ½ million acre-feet that we are pledged to deliver to Mexico is so saline that we are having to build a desalinization plant to sweeten it before we send it across the border.

Furthermore, even if you have enough water for occasional leaching, you have to have somewhere to drain off the waste water, which is likely not only to be saline, but to be contaminated with fertilizers, pesticides, and poisonous trace minerals such as selenium. Kesterson Reservoir, in the Central Valley near Los Banos, is a recent notorious instance, whose two-headed, three-legged, or merely dead waterfowl publicized the dangers of draining waste water off into a slough. If it is drained off into a river, or out to sea, the results are not usually so dramatic. But the inedible fish of the New River draining into the Salton Sea, and the periodically-polluted beaches of Monterey Bay near the mouth of the Salinas River, demonstrate that agricultural runoff is poison anywhere.

The West's irrigated bounty is not forever, not on the scale or at the rate we have been gathering it in. The part of it that is dependent on wells is even more precarious than that dependent on dams. In California's San Joaquin Valley, streams and dams supply only 60 percent of the demand for water; the rest is pumped from wells—hundreds and thousands of wells. Pumping exceeds replenishment by a half trillion gallons a year. In places the water table has been pumped down 300 feet; in places the ground itself has sunk thirty feet or more. But with those facts known, and an end clearly in sight, nobody is willing to stop, and there is as yet no state regulation of groundwater pumping.

In Arizona the situation is if anything worse. Ninety percent of Arizona's irrigation depends on pumping. And in Nebraska and Kansas and Oklahoma, old Dust Bowl country, they prepare for the next dust bowl, which is as inevitable as sunrise though a little harder to time, by pumping away the groundwater through center-pivot sprinklers.

Add to the facts about irrigation the fact of the over-subscribing of rivers. The optimists say that when more water is needed, the engineers will find a way—"augmentation" from the Columbia or elsewhere for the Colorado's overdrawn reservoirs, or the implementation of cosmic schemes such as NAWAPA (North American Water and Power Alliance), which would dam all the Canadian rivers up against the east face of the Rockies, and from that Mediterranean-sized reservoir supply water to every needy district from Minneapolis to Yuma. I think that there are geological as well as political difficulties in the way of water-redistribution on that scale. The solution of western problems does not lie in more grandiose engineering.

Throw into the fact-barrel, finally, a 1983 report from the Council of Environmental Quality which concludes that desertification—the process of converting a viable arid-lands ecology into a lifeless waste—proceeds faster in the western United States than in Africa. Some of that desertification is the result of overgrazing, but the salinization of fields does its bit. When the hydraulic society falls back from its outermost frontiers, it will have done its part in the creation of new deserts.

* * *

THE HYDRAULIC SOCIETY. I borrow the term from Donald Worster, who borrowed it from Karl Wittvogel. Wittvogel's studies convinced him that every hydraulic society is by necessity an autocracy. Power, he thought, inevitably comes to reside in the elite that understands and exercises the control of water. He quotes C. S. Lewis: "What we call man's power over nature turns out to be a power exercised by some men over other men with nature as its instrument"; and Andre Gorz: "The total domination of nature inevitably entails a domination of people by the techniques of domination." Those quotations suggest a very different approach from the human domination advocated by such as John Widtsoe.

The hydraulic society involves the maximum domination of nature. And the American West, Worster insists, is the greatest hydraulic society the world ever saw, far surpassing in its techniques of domination the societies on the Indus, the Tigris-Euphrates, or the Yellow River. The West, which Walter Webb and Bernard DeVoto both feared might remain a colonial dependency of the East, has instead become an empire and got the East to pay most of the bills.

The case as Worster puts it is probably overstated. There are, one hopes, more democratic islands than he allows for; more areas outside the domination of the water managers and users. Few parts of the West are totally controlled by what Worster sees as a hydraulic elite. Nevertheless, no one is likely to call the agribusiness West—with most of its power concentrated in the Iron Triangle of growers, politicians, and bureaucratic experts and its work done by a permanent underclass of dispossessed, mainly alien migrants—the agrarian democracy that the Newlands Act was supposed to create.

John Wesley Powell had understood that a degree of land monopoly could easily come about in the West through control of water. A thorough Populist, he advocated cooperative rather than federal waterworks, and he probably never conceived of anything on the imperial scale later realized by the Bureau of Reclamation. But if he were alive today he would have to agree at least partway with Worster: water experts ambitious to build and expand their bureau and perhaps honestly convinced of the worth of what they were doing have allied themselves with landowners and politicians, and by making land monopoly through water control immensely profitable for their backers, they have made it inevitable.

How profitable? Worster cites figures from one of the most recent of the mammoth projects, the Westlands, that brought water to the western side of the San Joaquin Valley. Including interest over forty years, the cost to the taxpayers was $3 billion. Water is delivered to the beneficiaries, mostly large landholders, at $7.50 an acre foot—far below actual cost, barely enough to pay operation and maintenance costs. According to a study conducted by economists Philip LaVeen and George Goldman, the subsidy amounted to $2,200 an acre, $352,000 per quarter section—and very few quarter-section family farmers were among the beneficiaries. Large landholders obliged by the 160-acre limitation to dispose of their excess lands disposed of them to cronies, paper farmers, according to a pattern by now well established among water users.

So much for the Jeffersonian yeoman and the agrarian democracy. As for another problem that Powell foresaw, the difficulty that a family would have in handling even 160 acres of intensively-farmed irrigated land, both the corporate and the family farmers solve it the same way: with migrant labor, much of it illegally recruited below the Rio Grande. It is anybody's guess what will happen now that Congress has passed the Immigration Bill, but up to now the border has been a sieve, carefully kept open from this side. On a recent rafting trip through the Big Bend canyons of the Rio Grande, my son twice surprised sheepdog functionaries herding wetbacks to safety in America.

Those wetbacks are visible not merely in California and Texas, but pretty much throughout the West. Visiting Rigby, Idaho, up in the farming country below the washed-out Teton Dam, I found a shanty-town whose universal language was Spanish. Wherever there are jobs to do, especially laborious or dirty jobs—picking crops, killing turkeys—there have been wetbacks brought in to do them. Like drug-running, the importation of illegals has resulted from a strong, continuing American demand, most of it from the factories in the field of the hydraulic society. One has to wonder if penalties for such importations will inhibit growers any more than the 160-acre limitation historically did.

* * *

MARC REISNER, IN *Cadillac Desert,* is less concerned with the social consequences than with the costs and environmental losses and the plain absurdities of our long battle with aridity. "Only a government that disposes of a billion dollars every few hours would still be selling water in deserts for less than a penny a ton. And only an agency as antediluvian as the Bureau of Reclamation, hiding in a government as elephantine as ours, could successfully camouflage the enormous losses the taxpayer has to bear for its generosity."

Charles P. Berkey of Columbia University, a hydrologist, wrote in 1946, "The United States has virtually set up an empire on impounded and redistributed water. The nation is encouraging development, on a scale never before attempted, of lands that are almost worthless except for the water that can be delivered to them by the works of man. There is building up, through settlement and new population, a line of industries foreign to the normal resources of the region....One can claim (and it is true) that much has been added to the world; but the longer-range view in this field, as in many others, is threatened by apparently incurable ailments and this one of slowly choking to death with silt is the most stubborn of all. There are no permanent cures."

Raphael Kazmann, in *Modern Hydrology,* agrees: "The reservoir construction program, objectively considered, is really a program for the continued and endless expenditure of ever-increasing sums of public money to combat the effects of geologic forces, as these forces strive to reach positions of relative equilibrium in the region of rivers and the flow of water. It may be that future research in the field of modern hydrology will be primarily to find a method of extricating ourselves from this unequal struggle with minimum loss to the nation."

And Donald Worster pronounces the benediction: "The next stage after empire is decline." The West, aware of its own history, might phrase it differently: The next stage after boom is bust. Again.

* * *

WHAT SHOULD ONE MAKE of facts as depressing as these? What do such facts do to the self-gratifying image of the West as the home of freedom, independence, largeness, spaciousness, and of the Westerner as total self-reliance on a white stallion? I confess they make this Westerner yearn for the old days on the Milk and the Missouri when those rivers ran free, and we were trying to learn how to live with the country, and the country seemed both hard and simple, and the world and I were young, when irrigation had not yet grown beyond its legitimate bounds and the West provided for its thin population a hard living but a wonderful life.

Sad to say, they make me admit, when I face them, that the West is no more the Eden that I once thought it than the Garden of the World that the boosters and engineers tried to make it; and that neither nostalgia nor boosterism can any longer make a case for it as the geography of hope.

FROM *BEYOND THE HUNDREDTH MERIDIAN*

Editor's note: During the summer of 1869 Major John Wesley Powell and nine companions made the first known descent of the Colorado River, traveling from Green River, Wyoming, to its confluence with the Virgin River near present-day Las Vegas. The following passage, based heavily on the diaries of Powell and George Bradley, describes the final three weeks of that exhausting trip—the run through the Grand Canyon from the Little Colorado to the Grand Wash Cliffs, 217 miles of some of the most awesome and unforgiving white water to be found anywhere in the world.

There is a rough physical law to the effect that the carrying power of water increases as the sixth power of its velocity, which is to say that a stream moving two miles an hour will carry particles sixty-four times as large as the same stream moving one mile an hour, and that one moving ten miles an hour will carry particles a million times as great.[1] A stream that in low water will deposit even its fine silt and sand, in high water will roll enormous boulders along its bed, and sometimes one can stand near the bank and see a rock that looks as big as a small house yield and sway with the force of the current.

Where the Colorado River entered the granite a few miles below the Little Colorado the channel was narrow, the river engorged, very deep, and very swift. It took hold of a boat irresistibly: the characteristic reaction of our diarists was awe. More times than once Bradley was led to report rapids as the worst of the trip so far, and all of them felt the gloom of that black inner gorge and the poverty of the narrow sky.[2] To add to undernourishment and exhaustion and strain they had nights of rain that caught them miserable and unprotected on bouldery shores, days of alternating sun and rain that first drenched them and then boiled them in temperatures of 115°. Rarely was there a decent camping place; they stopped where daylight or endurance ran out on them. With very little shore, the river did not even provide adequate firewood. Curling up on the edges of cliffs, among boulders, on wet spits of sand, they made out as they could. And along with their discomforts there was an increasing but unspoken fear.

Partly the lack of shores did it, the way the river sometimes took up all the space and left them no place for lining, no trail for a portage. Rapids that they feared to run they ran because they could do nothing else, and as they came plunging through the waves, tossed from one side to the other by the cushion of the water piling against great rocks, they often had no chance to inspect the river ahead, to search out channels, to guard against falls. They went with the recklessness of Sam Adams, not for lack of better sense but in sheer helplessness.

The pretense that it was a scientific expedition had worn thin. Every barometer they had was out of commission, so that they had lost track of their altitude and had no way of telling how much fall there was before the Virgin. Even an accurate view of where they had been was denied them, after Howland lost in a swamping his map of the river from the Little Colorado down, and all his notes with it. Anxiety closed around them like the dark rock, and looking up lateral gorges to the outer walls so high and far above, to the buttes and towers and enormous pediments and alcoves of the cliff-edged plateaus that now rose above them more than a vertical mile, they could add claustrophobia to their burdens, and the haunting speculation of what it would mean if they had to try to climb out.

Unrelieved labor, incessant strain and anxiety, continuing rain, a river that seemed every day to grow worse, and for food the same moldy bread, spoiled bacon, stewed apples, and for commander a man who they felt would risk all their lives for an extra hour of geologizing, an extra night of squinting at a star.

When they ran into the granite on the second day below the Little Colorado—one of the days that Bradley recorded as the wildest thus far—the *Emma Dean* was smashed under by a wave and ran swamped for half a mile before its crew got it into an eddy. Bradley and Walter Powell brought their boat through with the loss of an oar, the third escaped with a shaking up and a ducking. That night as they slept among boulders and on ledges so narrow that only Sumner and Major Powell found space wide enough to make a double bed, Bradley huddled off by himself and wrote up his secret diary in the rain. They had better lie quiet, he said, or one of them would be in the river before morning.

Some of them were in the river every day now. Hawkins capsized and lost his oars the next morning, and after only two and a half days in the Grand Canyon their supplies were again wet and spoiling. At the mouth of a beautiful clear creek coming in from the north they camped to saw out more oars and dry the food. That was Silver Creek, which Powell later, on a lecture tour, rechristened Bright Angel Creek to make a singularly happy contrast with the Dirty Devil above. The cutwater of the *Emma Dean* was broken and all of them were exhausted. Even Bradley was willing to lay over a day for a rest. Immediately Powell, seizing the opportunity, took off up the canyon to geologize.

As if to emphasize the need for haste, the Bright Angel layover was hard on the rations. There they finally threw away what remained of the bacon, so many times spoiled and dried and boiled and redried that they gagged at it. And Billy Hawkins, making biscuits on a rock, had the misfortune to let the saleratus get sawed off into the river by the line of one of the boats. From that time on they ate unleavened bread.

Below Bright Angel they got through one laborious day without accident. On the afternoon of the next a furious thunder shower drove them to what shelter they could find among the rocks, where they sat dripping and heard the thunder bounce from cliff to cliff and saw hundreds of flash-flood rivulets burst over the walls above them. The more their need for haste, the less haste they seemed able to make. "Hard work and little distance seems to be the characteristic of this canyon," Bradley wrote. Then on the 19th the *Emma Dean* swamped again, and Bradley's boat, sweeping to the rescue, struck on her cutwater with a jolt that started her nails. Two more oars went in that rapid, and all the boats now were so battered that they had to be calked every day. For the sixth day out of the last seven they lay down in soaking blankets. But that night when it cleared off, a great drying fire restored them. So bedraggled were they that they did not start until noon the next day. They were all looking ahead, watching for that break in the walls that might be the Grand Wash Cliffs.

It seemed as if they might have reached it, or neared it, for the walls did fall back a little and the rapids were further apart. In a half day's run, including a portage and two linings, they ran ten miles. The next day was again for Bradley "first for dashing wildness of any day we have seen or *will* see." Swept broadside down upon a rapid, Powell's boat rebounded from the cliff and was carried into a narrow slot with no shores to land on. Ahead a bend cut off the view. From around it came the "mad roar" that had taught them caution many times already. Here they could not be cautious if they would. Powell stood up, hanging to a strap that ran from gunwale to gunwale, trying to spot a channel through the long, winding chute of white water. Their luck held. All they got out of that one was a tremendously exhilarating ride for ten precious miles before the roar of another heavy fall below made them pull ashore to reconnoiter. By the time they had portaged that, they were out of the granite.

Their cheers had in them something of the hysteria of strain, and they did not stay cheerful long. Barely had they adjusted themselves to milder water when the river turned sharply from its north-by-west course and bored back almost straight east into the granite again. Overhead the clouds gathered blackly, and it rained.

* * *

THEIR HYPNOTIZED SPIRITS now rose and fell with the river, and changed with its course. When, away back at the Little Colorado, they had discovered their latitude to be as low as that of Callville, they had been cheered, but the river taught them to wait and see, for it persisted in running back toward the north with them. Now it rubbed in the lesson of skepticism by taking them back into the hard rock they feared. "If it keeps on this way," Bradley wrote, "we shall be back where we started from, which would make us feel very much as I imagine the old hog felt when he moved the hollow log so that both ends came on the outside of the fence."[3]

Still, there was nothing they could do except to keep rooting at the log. They fought their way down to spend another night on the rocks, with a bad rapid facing them as soon as they should wake up, and its roar an uneasy sound in their dreams. But next day the unpredictable river switched again. After two hard miles the hated granite sank under toward its home at the earth's core. The rapids, though tremendous, seemed by Grand Canyon standards lighter.[4] On the afternoon when they ran out of the granite they made ten miles.

The following day they made twenty-two with great cheerfulness, and their cheer was doubled by the great marble cave in which the Major chose to camp—dry and spacious and out of the interminable rain. Around their fire they sat speculating on how far Grand Wash might be, for the Mormons whose notes on the river from Grand Wash to Callville were in the Major's pocket put the Wash no more than seventy or eighty miles below the mouth of the Little Colorado. On the dogleg river they had already gone more than one hundred twenty. They must be very close, perhaps within a day's running. Ahead, they convinced themselves, the river seemed to widen and the current to slack off. They examined their flour—one sack plus enough for a meal or two—and gauged the skimpy supply against the possible miles ahead. They were half naked, bearded, skinny, and their dreams were haunted by visions of gargantuan meals, but they knew they would make it now.

The river relented. On August 25 they made thirty-five marvelous miles, in spite of a hard portage around what they called Lava Falls, where a basalt flow had first dammed the canyon and then been cut clean through, and in spite of a near accident when the iron strap in the bow of one boat pulled loose and almost let the boat get away in a rapid. All the boats, clearly, were about as used up as the men. They drove themselves.

The opening of their last sack of flour was a solemn moment, and a warning. Down a violent stretch of river where lava made continuous but not major rapids they ran the battered boats recklessly, lining only once in thirty-five miles when they landed on the wrong side of a rapid and couldn't get across to run it safely. Another good omen: the dry abandoned dwellings and granaries of ancient Indians that they had been seeing among the cliffs ever since Glen Canyon gave way to signs of life. In an Indian garden they found squash big enough to eat, and stole a dozen to make green squash sauce, their first fresh vegetable food since the disastrous potato-top greens in Uinta Valley fifty days before. Though the nearly vertical walls of the inner gorge grew higher and higher, their two-day run of seventy miles put them close to two hundred miles below the Little Colorado. "A few days like this," Powell said, "and we are out of prison."

It was a prison even to him now, not a happy hunting ground of science. And the river knew better than they did. On the morning of August 27 it swung south, and since the dip of the beds was to the north, they rapidly ran into lower and lower formations. If it kept up this way they would be back in the granite. By nine o'clock they saw the dreaded rock, brown here instead of black, but unmistakable, rising up from the shoreline. They had to portage at the very entrance to the granite gorge. By eleven they came to a place that forced them ashore with sinking hearts.

Later river runners, with some justification, have disputed Powell's description of that rapid, both as to its violence and to its shape.[5] There can be no doubting the fact that it looked to them, in their demoralized and discouraged state, like the worst thing on the river. Sumner's journal calls it "a hell of foam"; Powell and Bradley agree in calling it the worst they had met. "The billows are huge," said Bradley, "and I fear our boats could not ride them if we could keep them off the rocks. The spectacle is appalling to us."[6]

It should have been. They had five days' rations remaining. Above the narrow inner gorge the outer walls stepped back in lofty and perhaps unclimbable cliffs. The nearest Mormon settlement was miles away to the north across unknown plateaus and deserts. To run the rapid was, as far as Powell could see, pure self-destruction. Above the pounding water rose abrupt granite cliffs. Trying the right bank, they could find no way either to portage or to line. Crossing over above the rapid, they tried the left, working along the craggy granite to try to get a view of the river below the first fall. The cliff shut off the water.

Telling about that day in his published *Report,* Powell records an adventure that neither his own daily notes nor the journals of Bradley and Sumner mention. He says that, intent upon seeing and appraising the rapid, he worked out upon the pinnacles and crags of the cliff and once more, as in Desolation Canyon, got himself "rimmed." He was four hundred feet above the boulder-strewn water, clinging to the rock with his one hand, when he called for help. He says that the men climbed close above him and dropped him a rope, but that he dared not let go to grab for it. Hanging grimly, unable even to advise them because he could not see his own position, he clung while two men hurried down the cliff and came back with a pair of the largest oars. Themselves working on a perilous edge, they reached out an oar and finally jammed it in a crevice beyond Powell so that they could pinch him in against the cliff and hold him there. Then they jammed the second oar below him, and carefully he turned himself until he could step on this oar and inch back to safety.

How they may have looked at one another, whether or not they may have cursed him to themselves for being maimed and a burden, how fully they may have laid their situation at his door, no one will ever know. Since the journals do not mention the episode at all, it may not even be true. It may be a piece of fiction suggested by his previous rimming and inserted into the narrative as peculiarly effective here.[7] Perhaps it is part of that impulse to self-dramatization that had led Powell to make speeches on top of Long's Peak, and sit on a spectacular crag above Flaming Gorge producing rhetoric for the Chicago *Tribune.* But even if the story is not true, it ought to be. There could have been no more striking symbolic summary of the fix the whole expedition was in than the spectacle of the maimed leader hanging perilously between advance and retreat, unable to move either way, on a crag of the hated granite.

Without getting a really good view, they spent another hour trying to see from the left-hand cliff, and in the afternoon crossed again to try the right, but without success.

After almost a full day of studying the situation, Powell could see no way except to let down over the first fall, run the rapid to the head of the second, and then pull like fury to the left to avoid a great rock against which the river poured a curving, boiling wall of water. It was not a plan that appealed to him; it appealed even less to some of the men. Bradley, who had reported rebelliousness before, reported it again: "There is discontent in camp tonight and I fear some of the party will take to the mountains but hope not."[8]

Crossing the river again and camping in the mouth of a lateral gorge, they had both certainties and uncertainties to contemplate as they chewed on their leathery unleavened bread. There were the alternative uncertainties of a fearful nest of rapids with an unknown river below, and a perhaps equally dangerous climb out some side gorge onto the plateau and across it to the Mormon settlements northward. And there were the desperate certainties of failing supplies, failing boats, failing strength, failing nerve. Sitting apart from the others and writing up his notes, Bradley called it "decidedly the darkest day of the trip."[9]

Of all the men who had accompanied Major Powell through a summer of natural history in the Colorado parks, a winter of studying Indians and topography from the base camp on White River, and more than three tense months in the canyons, O. G. Howland was best fitted by education and interests to be a companion for the commander. He was the oldest in the party, though at thirty-six, less than a year older than Powell, he was hardly decrepit to match his beard. Like Sumner, Hawkins, and his brother Seneca, he was technically entered on the expedition's roll as a hunter, but he was no buckskin savage. Since arriving in Denver in 1860 on the tide of the Colorado gold rush he had been a printer and editor of Byer's *Rocky Mountain News,* business agent for a Methodist Episcopal magazine known as the *Sunday School Casket,* member and later vice-president of the Denver Typographical Union Local No. 49, and secretary and member of the board of the Nonpareil Prospecting and Mining Company. Judged by his letters to the *News,* he was the most literate and articulate of the group. By Powell's own testimony, he was of a "faithful, genial nature." When Powell took a companion with him on his exploratory climbs around the canyon rims and up side gulches he almost always took his brother, Bradley, or the elder Howland. Bradley was the only member of the party over thirty, outside of Howland and Powell, and he had been an army non-com long enough to learn discipline.

But the same qualities that made Howland a companion and friend for Powell half unfitted him for the grueling adventure of the river. He had a certain scientific and literary curiosity, and part of his job was to map the river and make notes as they went, but his appetite for knowledge was nothing like Powell's omnivorous passion, and though he was an outdoor man and a sportsman he had not quite the hardihood or the youth of the hunters and Andy Hall. Also, he had been the unlucky one. His momentary error of sight or judgment had led to the wreck of the No-Name, the loss of a third of their provisions, and their present starving and desperate condition. The comparative meagerness of their scientific results could be traced to his misfortune in twice losing his maps and notes in swampings. Possibly the sense of personal failure troubled him. Just possibly Powell or his brother, under the increasing strain, may in some moment of irritation have thrown it up to him. Conceivably too, as Sumner and Hawkins many years after the fact asserted, the Major and Bill Dunn may have rubbed each other the wrong way, or trouble may have brewed between the moody Walter Powell and Dunn. Bradley's journal mentions no such cause of discontent, however, and he was not one to spare the Major when he thought Powell needed criticism. Sumner's journal is equally bare.

Put it down to strain, to the steady corrosion of strength and nerve. Lay it to the dark oppressive granite, to the repeated hope that they had run out of it for good and the each-time-greater anger and disappointment when the river switched them back into it. Put it down to the rapid they now faced without a clear chance to run, line, or portage. Put it down to a growing lack of confidence in Powell's judgment or the reliability of his scientific observations, to the gnawing need for a square meal or to the arrival at an ultimate ceiling of endurance. Whatever it is put down to, it was clear to Powell on the night of August 27 that the whole expedition was close to where he himself had been that afternoon on the cliff, unable to go forward or back.

That was even clearer when Howland came to him after supper and asked him to walk up the side canyon for a little talk. Howland had been talking things over with his brother and Bill Dunn. It was madness and suicide to try to go on. He proposed that the whole expedition abandon the river and make its way out to the Mormon settlements on the Virgin. If Powell would not take the whole party out, the Howlands and Dunn would go by themselves. They had had enough.

Powell had strong arguments. He knew that they could not be more than a few days' run from Grand Wash, he knew that the river had been falling so fast that it could not possibly have much further to fall to the level of Callville. But Howland had a stronger one. He had only to point to the furious string of rapids that blocked their way downriver. Even if past them there were calm water all the rest of the way to the Virgin, those were enough.

In the end they agreed not to say anything to the other men until Powell had had time to plot their position by dead reckoning to find out exactly where they were. It was a clear night; he got a meridian observation with the sextant and found that it agreed pretty closely with the plot. By airline, they could not be more than forty-five miles from the mouth of the Virgin, twenty miles from which there were Mormon towns. Moreover, for a good many miles above the Virgin the Mormon party under Jacob Hamblin had found low walls and no bad rapids on the Colorado. The eighty or ninety meandering miles of river still ahead might contain no more than a day or two of bad water.

He was several hours establishing to his own satisfaction that there was no possibility of serious error in his calculations. Then he woke Howland and spread the plot on the sand and showed him. This is how he told it later:

> We have another short talk about the morrow, and he lies down again;
> but for me there is no sleep. All night long, I pace up and down a
> little path, on a few yards of sand beach, along by the river. Is it wise
> to go on? I go to the boats again, to look at our rations. I feel satisfied

that we can get over the danger immediately before us; what there may be below I know not. From our outlook yesterday, on the cliffs, the cañon seemed to make another great bend to the south, and this, from our experience heretofore, means more and higher granite walls. I am not sure that we can climb out of the cañon here, and, when at the top of the wall, I know enough of the country to be certain that it is a desert of rock and sand, between this and the nearest Mormon town, which, on the most direct line, must be seventy-five miles away. True, the late rains have been favorable to us, should we go out, for the probabilities are that we shall find water still standing in holes, and, at one time, I almost conclude to leave the river. But for years I have been contemplating this trip. To leave the exploration unfinished, to say that there is a part of the cañon which I cannot explore, having already almost accomplished it, is more than I am willing to acknowledge, and I determine to go on.[10]

He woke Walter Powell and told him of the decision that must be made. Walter promised to stay with him. He woke Billy Hawkins, the irrepressible, and Andy Hall, the lighthearted, and Sumner, the hardy, and Bradley, the saturnine, and they promised the same. Though reduced, it would still be an expedition.

Breakfast on August 28 was "solemn as a funeral." In silence except for the pounding roar of the rapid, deep in the gloomy rock where the early sun could not reach, they ate Hawkins' flat biscuits and drank their coffee and avoided each others' eyes. They had finished eating when Powell asked his question. With five men behind him he could ask it bluntly. Did the three want to come along, or climb out?

Seneca Howland, left to himself, would have stuck, but neither he nor the other six could persuade his brother and Bill Dunn. They had all climbed enough on the walls to know the possibility of unbroken, unscalable cliffs stretching for miles. But they thought they could make their way out one of the side canyons, and they were sure they could kill game on the plateau. They were mountain men, the wilderness was their natural home. Listening to the arguments of the others, they shook their heads; in the end Seneca Howland decided to stay with his brother.

They were given two rifles and a shotgun and invited to take their share of the miserable rations. It was to their credit, and evidence of friendliness between the two groups, that they refused. The three crossed the river with the others, helped them unload the leaky *Emma Dean,* which was to be abandoned, and assisted in portaging the two large boats over a thirty-foot rock and lining them down the first fall. Hawkins left a pan of biscuits on the rock for them. Sumner gave Howland his watch to deliver to his sister, Mrs. William Byers, in Denver. Powell wrote a letter to his wife. The records of the expedition were, as Powell thought, divided, each party taking one complete copy. At the head of a two-hundred-yard rapid between the two falls each entreated the other to change its mind. They shook hands; there were tears. "They left us with good feelings," Bradley wrote, "though we deeply regret their loss for they are as fine fellows as I ever had the good fortune to meet."[11] Bradley was a grumbler, but he rose nobly to occasions.

So the parting at Separation Rapid was not quite Sam Adams' experience of collecting a purse and sending someone home as a "common nuisance," nor was it marked by the quarreling and accusation and blame that attended the breakup of Adams' volunteers. Neither was it what some unaccountably virulent enemies of Powell asserted later: a harsh discharge of three men at a place and in circumstances that might mean their death. Neither was it what some of Powell's defenders have tried to make it, a craven desertion by three cowards. It was a sad parting at the brink of two dangers, by men who respected one another.[12]

The original ten were now six, the four boats two. What had been rations for ten months was now rations for five days. What had been thrilling was grim. From up on the cliff the Howlands and Dunn watched as Powell stepped into the *Maid of the Canyon* and the men shoved off into the waves along the right-hand wall. The river seized them. They shot down a hollow, up a wave, past a rock half buried in the foaming water. The oarsmen pulled madly at the clumsy oars—a job of enormous difficulty in a boat leaping through waves at a speed of twenty miles an hour, tossed now up, now down, the water falling away suddenly so that the oarblade bites air, then surging up to bury the oar to the handle. To hit a hidden rock with an oar was to risk shattering it or having it driven into the oarsman's body; to catch a crab was to lose all chance of control. They rowed as the river had taught them to row, pulling hard for the tongue of the second fall. There the boat was all but snatched from under them. They shot down the fall and burst into the great back-cresting waves at its foot. Instantly they were full of water, but half swamped they still rowed like madmen, pulling across the current. The wild pile-up of water against the righthand rock caught them only partially. They raced up the sloping wall of water, fell away to the left, down into a hole, and were through into the diminishing tailwaves. The whole rapid had taken perhaps a minute. While they pulled for shore to bail out, the *Kitty Clyde's Sister* plunged through the tailwaves and was with them, safe. Powell afterward thought the rapid, in spite of its fearful look, no worse than others they had run. Bradley continued to think it the worst to date, until they met another one that afternoon.

Below the rapid, according to Powell's *Report,* they landed and fired off their guns in the hope that the three hunters would climb down and rejoin them. But they did not come, and the boats went on.[13] They had dangers enough of their own to occupy them. Powell's journal entry for the day of parting is indication of how even so serious an event had to take its place in the day's routine. His journal reads simply, "Boys left us. Ran rapid. Bradley boat. Make camp on left bank. Camp 44."[14]

In that one brief entry are contained not merely the schism that all but destroyed the expedition, but the incident that of all their summer's adventures was perhaps most hair-raising. "Bradley boat," the Major says. What he thus reminded himself of was a climactic little episode. As the wreck of the *No-Name* in Lodore initiated them to disaster and taught them caution, so Bradley's adventure below Separation Rapid ended their river dangers in desperation and cool skill. They had come a long way from the initial amateurishness and inattention to Bradley's complete adequacy to his job, from Powell's first caution to his final recklessness.

Like many another rapid, the big one (Lava Cliff) six and a half miles below Separation struck Bradley as the worst they had met on the river. The stage of water has such an unpredictable, even unbelievable effect upon specific rapids that there would be little chance of checking his judgment, even if that rapid were not now silted up at the head of Lake Mead.[15] But it was bad enough. Sumner referred to it as "another hell." Powell landed to look it over, and found that along one side a line could be taken up on the basalt cliff and the boats lined from above. But when he arrived back on the riverbank he found that the men had already started one boat, Bradley's, down toward the head of the fall. She was in fast water, too much in the sweep of the current for them to pull her back, and their line was not long enough to be taken up over the cliff. They took a bight around a rock and hung on while one went for more rope.

Meantime Bradley, in the very sag of the fall, found himself swinging at the end of a mighty pendulum. The current set in close and fierce against the basalt wall, and suspended as he was from above, he yawed in a wide arc out into the rapids and then was slammed back in against the cliff. Standing in the boat, he fended himself off with an oar, but the moment he stopped the inward swing the waves snatched him outward again. Powell saw him take quick looks down river, saw him look at the straining, worn line, saw him reach in his pocket for his knife.

Before he could cut the line the whole sternpost was jerked out of the boat, rope and cutwater flew thirty feet into the air, and the *Sister* was off like a horse from the starting line. Bradley dropped his knife and leaped to the steering oar, fighting to get her bow pointed downstream, for to go over broadside-on would be certain wreck. One stroke, two, three, and just as he hit the fall he turned her. She went clear under in a welter of white, came up on a huge crest, went down again and out of sight beyond some rocks. In half a breath she shot into the open, Bradley still standing, and swung into an eddy. Bradley waved his hat in triumph, but from where Powell stood it was impossible to see how badly the boat was damaged, and he feared both it and Bradley might go down into the whirlpool.

Powell shouted at his brother and Sumner to run along the cliff to help below. Then with Hawkins and Hall he leaped into the second boat, pushed off, and went over the falls any way the water took them, endways and sideways, blind with water, beaten almost out of the boat by waves. It was an act totally uncharacteristic, reckless beyond anything he had permitted himself or his men all the way down the river. It is as good documentation as any for the desperation of their case.

Bradley had to rescue them, capsized and strangling, and help them pull their boat to safety against the cliff. There was handshaking around to match that when the Howlands and Goodman were rescued from their island at Disaster Falls. Powell said nothing ever thrilled him so much as to see Bradley swing his hat from the spinning boat after running her through. It is clear from his various accounts of the trip that Bradley, more than any other member of the party, had his complete respect as a man of skill and courage. As for Bradley, his diary was getting used to superlatives. This ride, he said, "stands A No. 1 of the trip."

That was the last big roar from the river dragon. Two or three miles below that great rapid the river swung northwest. By nightfall they were out of the granite. By noon of the next day, after a swift uneventful run, they passed through the sudden portal in the Grand Wash Cliffs and saw rolling country, low walls, distant mountains.

Where they camped that night is not certain. To be appropriate, it should have been in the little loop that now, as part of Lake Mead, on the Nevada-Arizona boundary, is known as God's Pocket. They were in God's pocket sure enough. Their joy, Powell says, was almost ecstasy, though even in that relaxed and triumphant camp, in the clear night, with an unreal wide sky over them, they speculated a long time on how the Howlands and Dunn were faring, how they had managed on the cliffs, whether they might now be in the high plateau forest filling themselves with venison or wild mutton or whether they might be stuck in some gulch groping for a way up and out. They could say I-told-you-so; they could also, more generously, hope the others' luck had been equal to their own.

For there was no doubt that they were now "out of prison." On August 30 they scared away one band of naked Paiutes and talked to another family that Powell coaxed near by speaking Ute to them. From the Indians, however, they learned little and got no food, and so they pushed on. Just after the noon stop they saw four men pulling a seine in the river. They were a Mormon named Asa and his two sons and an Indian, and they were there on instructions from Church headquarters in Salt Lake City to watch the river for wreckage or bodies from the Powell Expedition, reported lost weeks ago in the depths of the Colorado canyons.

That was the first official notice Brigham Young ever paid to Major Powell. He would pay him more later; the two would become something like friends, and Brigham would draw on Powell for scientific information useful to his empire. His interest now was something more than mortuary, something more than merely humanitarian. For Powell's river party was in a way doing Brigham's business for him, exploring the heart of the country on whose fringes Brigham's colonists had scratched out precarious toeholds of settlement. If Asa and his sons and their Indian companion waiting in the glare of the red mudflats at the mouth of the Virgin saw no bodies floating by, they might at least intercept something else— records or wreckage—from which to piece together information about the canyons. They intercepted more than they expected, and yet their humanitarian and mortuary gesture was not to be entirely wasted either.

Nine men had plunged into the unknown from the last outpost of civilization in the Uinta Valley on the sixth of July, 1869. On August 30 six came out.

Notes

1. In practice, the moving power of a stream is conditioned by numerous unpredictable factors such as the smoothness of the bed, the straightness of the course, and so on. An early and extremely lucid discussion of the corrasive and moving power of streams is in G. K. Gilbert, *Report on the Geology of the Henry Mountains*, in which Gilbert develops many observations first made by Powell himself.

2. Evidence of the morbid effect of being confined in the dark and narrow inner canyon is contained in most of the river journals. The *imaginary* effects upon people who have not been there or who let their imaginations run free are much more extreme, as in many of the early canyon illustrations, where towering height, acute narrowness, and cavernous darkness are wildly exaggerated. In this key, simply as random examples, see the picture of James White losing his companion, George Strole, in Bell, *New Tracks in North America*; or the illustrations made by F. W. von Egloffstein for the Ives report—the first pictures made of the Grand Canyon...; or Frederick Dellenbaugh's

painting, "Running the Sockdologer," reproduced in his *Romance of the Colorado River*, p. 329; or many of the Thomas Moran woodcuts illustrating Powell's *Exploration of the Colorado River of the West.*

3. Bradley, Journal, August 22, 1869. Bradley several times remarks how much farther it is from the Little Colorado to Grand Wash than they expected it to be from Mormon estimates. The reason is simply that through the plateaus into which it has cut the Grand Canyon the Colorado runs a very tortuous course. At its junction with the Little Colorado it is flowing almost due south; it shortly swings west, then northwest, then almost south again, then north, then again west, then southwest, then south, and then, with many minor twists, northwest to its break out of the Grand Wash Cliffs.

4. They seem to have had no special trouble with Dubendorff Rapid, a mile below the end of the Middle Granite Gorge, though it is held by modern boatmen to be one of the twenty stiffest on the river.

5. Stanton thought this rapid the worst on the entire Colorado, but Julius Stone, on his excursion in 1909 (Julius F. Stone, *Canyon Country* [New York, 1932]), found it neither so rough as Powell' report had led him to expect, nor obscured by any turns. Except for a brief time when a flood scoured it out in 1952, the rapid has long been buried under Lake Mead silt, but photographs taken before the lake filled in show it as a straight reach with a creek coming in on each side to form an almost perfect cross. It was up the northern cross canyon that the Howlands and Dunn made their way out onto the Shivwits Plateau. Powell's statement that after running the rapid they were out of sight of the three men is certainly an error—an error which is perhaps less damning if we remember that Powell's notes by this time were almost in code, and that he never saw this rapid again, since the second Powell expedition left the river at Kanab Wash. Stone, a contentious and literal-minded man, was undoubtedly right in rejecting some of Powell's detailed statements of fact; he was undoubtedly wrong in others, for he was himself deceived by the profound changes that a difference in water level can make in the canyons. Otis Marston's investigations of river history have indicated that Separation, while it existed, capsized more boats than any other on the river. (Letter of February 6, 1953.)

6. Bradley, Journal, August 27, 1869.

7. The only corroboration for this dramatic story of Powell's is in Hawkins' reminiscences, notoriously unreliable and written down years later, after he could have read the Powell report and could easily have confused details in it with things actually remembered. Nevertheless, Hawkins does report that Powell got stuck on a cliff and had to be rescued by oars pressed into crevices so as to afford him a foothold. The difficulty is that Hawkins places the incident far back in the Canyon of Lodore, on the day when Powell was on the cliff and the camp was swept by a flash fire, the day when Hawkins lost most of the messkit in the Green. It is conceivable

that Hawkins was right, and that Powell deliberately moved the story for dramatic effect to a more climactic place in his narrative. But Hawkins within two lines of telling this story has jumped from Lodore to the junction of Grand and Green, and is so obviously scrambling his memories that his account is worth very little.

8. Bradley, Journal, August 27, 1869.

9. Ibid.

10. Powell, *Exploration*, pp. 98–9.

11. Bradley, Journal, August 28, 1869.

12. There is little point in dragging a reader through the dreary controversy over the precise status in history of the three who left the party. Powell himself never called them deserters, and in his report spoke of them as "faithful men." Much of the debate was stirred up by the omission of the names of the three from the Powell monument on the south rim of the Grand Canyon—an omission which, however unfortunate, can hardly be blamed upon Powell, since he had been a dozen years dead when the monument was unveiled.

13. Powell's detractors, concentrating on the details, in which he was sometimes umistakably inaccurate, have questioned his statement that the party waited and shot off guns to see if the three would not rejoin them. Both Powell's account in Bell's *New Tracks in North America* and his *Exploration* say that they waited two hours. Sumner's journal mentions no wait. Bradley's, probably the most reliable, says, "The three boys stood on the cliff looking at us [while the party was bailing out after running Separation Rapid] and having waved them adieu we dashed through the next rapid and then into an eddy where we stopped to catch our breath and bail out the water from our now nearly sunken boats." It was perhaps to this second wait, still within range of the three if they wanted to rejoin the boat party, that Powell referred, though from Bradley's record it would not seem to have lasted anything like two hours.

14. Powell, Journal, August 28, 1869.

15. This was Lava Cliff, which according to Otis Marston was briefly uncovered in 1952 by the same flood that scoured out Separation Rapid. It seems to have been more scary than dangerous. (Letter of February 6, 1953.)

FICTION

How Do I Know What I Think Till I See What I Say?

from *All the Little Live Things*

A half hour after I came down here, the rains began. They came without fuss, the thin edge of a circular Pacific storm that is probably dumping buckets on Oregon. One minute I was looking out my study window into the greeny-gold twilight under the live oak, watching a towhee kick up the leaves, and the next I saw that the air beyond the tree was scratched with fine rain. Now the flagstones are shining, the tops of the horizontal oak limbs are dark-wet, there is a growing drip from the dome of the tree above, the towhee's olive back has melted into umber dusk and gone. I sit here watching evening and the winter rains come on together, and I feel as slack and dull as the day or the season. Or not slack so much as bruised. I am like a man so stiff from a beating that every move reminds him and fills him with outrage.

In the face of what has happened, Ruth is more resilient than I, she has taken up little life-saving jobs. It would not surprise me to see a FOR SALE sign on the cottage that for me still trembles a little, like settling dust in evening sunlight, with the ghost of Marian's presence. But Ruth, making the cookies and casseroles and whole-wheat bread that she used to take there as offerings, puts the future under the pressure of sympathetic magic. She wills continuity, she chooses to believe that before too long we will hear the slam of the old station wagon's door down below, or have brought to us on the wind the voices of father and daughter talking to the piebald horse.

I? I came down here vaguely mumbling about finally starting on the memoirs. But the last thing I want to think about is what a retired literary agent used to do before he retired, and the people he used to do it among. I am concerned with gloomier matters: the condition of being flesh, susceptible to pain, infected with consciousness and the consciousness of consciousness, doomed to death and the awareness of death. My life stains the air around me. I am a tea bag left too long in the cup, and my steepings grow darker and bitterer.

Coming home this noon, Ruth and I said hardly ten words to each other. Our minds were back there on the lawn among the blunt stones. But when we eased over the stained and sagging bridge and saw the brush broken and trampled at its side, and a minute later when we rolled past the cottage with its weed-grown yard that I suppose expresses Marian without in the least resembling her, and a minute after that when the turning lane brought into view the gable of Peck's treehouse, something jumped the gap between us each time, a succession of those moments that you come to depend on during a long life together. But neither of us dared look fully at the reminding things we drove by. Ruth sat studying her hands, rubbing one white-gloved thumb over the other. In silence we drove through the open gates, between the big eucalyptus trees, and on up the steep shelf of road under the oaks.

October is the worst month for us. Nothing I saw pleased me. The oaks were dusty, with many brown terminal twigs killed by borers. The buckeyes were bare. Only a few dull-red leaves dangled from the poison-oak bushes. Brittle weeds grew into the edges of the road, and as we swung around the buttonhook and onto the hilltop I saw in the adobe ground cracks wide enough to break an ankle in.

And there on the right as we coasted toward the carport was the cherry tree, its leaves drooping and its foolish touching untimely blossoms wilted. Ruth drew an audible breath. Cherry blossoms in October were exactly the sort of thing from which Marian would have derived one of her passionate lessons about life.

Ruth got out of the car. "I'm going to lie down for a while. Shouldn't you?"

"Maybe I'll work around the yard."

The white hand was laid like a policeman's on my arm. "Joe," she said, "don't take it out in highballs, now."

"What do you think I am?" I said, but her clairvoyance had put a barrier between me and a place I had half-consciously planned to visit. When I get sad or upset I can be a pantry drinker, and she knows it.

She pecked me with a kiss. "Poor lamb"—and then as our eyes met, "Poor Marian. Poor all of us."

I followed her inside and changed the dark suit for old garden clothes and poked morosely out into the yard again. I found that I had maligned the day. Until the rain moved in just now it was one of those Indian-summer days, warm and windless, brown-colored, even the air faintly and purely brown like the water of some Vermont streams. It smelled leathery and cured—the oak leaves, maybe. On the bank the pyracantha was ripening heavy clusters, and the toyon along the hill was top-heavy with berries. I stood by the carport looking down across the gone-by vegetable garden and the baby orchard, and of course what stood up in my view as if it were a hundred feet high was that cherry tree.

My hands began to shake and my eyes got moist—outrage, outrage. To take all that trouble of digging, fertilizing, planting, spraying, pruning, coddling, only to have a blind vermin come burrowing brainlessly underground to destroy everything! My head was full of some poet's bitter question: Was it for this the clay grew tall?

I walked down to look. The basin was disturbed by no more humps of loose dirt, but something drastic had happened underground. The leaves that a few days before had been green now drooped like heat-withered cellophane. Along the branches, here and there, were the browning wisps of blossoms that the tree had frantically put out when the gopher began working on its roots. Before I even saw that it had begun, it was finished. Trying to produce flower and fruit and complete its cycle within a few days and way out of season, the tree was dead without knowing it. The sore sense of guilt that I felt told me I should have done something. But what?

I took hold of the sapling trunk and wiggled it, and with a slight threadlike tearing the whole tree came up in my hand. Except for the tiny root I had just broken away, there was nothing. The thing was as bare as a fishpole, gnawed off and practically polished about six inches below the surface.

Off in the brownish air a great flock of Brewer's blackbirds flashed into sudden dense visibility, roughened the sky a moment the way a school of fish can roughen the sea, and flashed off again, disappearing, as they all sheared edgewise at once. It was like something seen through a polarizer. The big red-tailed hawk that lives in Shields's pasture was perched, I saw, high in a eucalyptus. Probably he was watching me with his X-ray eyes and wondering what I was doing, standing in my October orchard and brandishing the gnawed stub of what was once a promising Lambert cherry tree.

It was a fair question, and I could have answered it. I was pondering the vanity of human wishes and the desperation of human hope, the tooth of time, the vulnerability of good and the unseen omnipresence of evil, and the frailty and passion of life. That is all I was pondering, and I was overwhelmingly aware as I poked around that it was Marian who had exposed me to feeling as I had hoped not to be exposed again. I almost blamed her. Until she appeared, I had succeeded in being a retired putterer remarkable for nothing much except a capacity to fiddle while Rome burned and crack jokes while Troy fell. Now I feel the cold. I felt it up there in the orchard and I feel it now, I feel it as icily as I felt it after Curtis died. But where the death of my son drove me to find a hole and crawl in it, the death of this girl I knew for barely half a year keeps driving me into the open, and I hate it.

I threw the cherry tree onto the pile of cuttings that I would burn as soon as the fire hazard was over. The withered blossoms of that sapling, with their suggestion of unfulfilled April, put an ache and an anger in me where resignation might have been. Marian's philosophy of acceptance was never mine—I remain a Manichee in spite of her. The forces of blind life that work across this hilltop are as irresistible as she said they were, they work by a principle more potent than fission. But I can't look upon them as just life, impartial and eternal and in flux, an unceasing interchange of protein. And I can't find proofs of the crawl toward perfection that she believed in.

Maybe what we call evil is only, as she told me the first day we met, what conflicts with our interests; but maybe there are such realities as ignorance, selfishness, jealousy, malice, criminal carelessness, and maybe these things are evil no matter whose interests they serve or conflict with. Maybe there is good life and bad life, good choice and bad choice, and unending war between them as in the Sunday-school hymns I sang as a boy. And maybe the triumph of the good is less sure than my Sunday-school teachers believed.

Nevertheless, Marian has invaded me, and though my mind may not have changed I will not be the same. There is a sense in which we are all each other's consequences, but I am more her consequence than she knew. She turned over my rock.

Looking at my ruined cherry tree, I could do nothing to repair what had happened. I could only act out a pantomime of impotence. Like a dwarf in a tantrum, some Grumpy out of a witch-haunted comedy, I dug in the basin of the tree until I found the run by which evil had entered and by which it had gone away. I set a trap facing each direction, knowing that even if I caught this gopher I would gain nothing but an empty revenge. If I ringed the hill with traps, others would still get through. If I put poisoned carrots in every burrow in Shields's pasture, some fertile pair would still survive.

I can see Marian smiling.

Riddled with ambiguous evil, that is how I think of it. All of us tainted and responsible—Weld, Peck, the LoPrestis and their sullen daughter, myself, John, even Marian. And yet until a few months ago this place was Prospero's island. It never occurred to us to doubt its goodness; we wouldn't have dreamed of trading it for our old groove in Manhattan's overburdened bedrock, or for one of those Sunshine Cities where tranquilized senior citizens (people our age) move to Muzak up and down an eternal shuffleboard court. Coming here, we kept at least the illusion of making our own choices, and we found that this sanctuary kept us physically alive, more alive than I at least have felt since those springs a millennium ago in Maquoketa, Iowa, when I used to go skinny-dipping in the creek with other boys and crawl out into an icy wind, shaking and blue, to pull on the bliss of a cotton union suit over my goose pimples.

For more than two years, physical well-being has been enough to make a life of. The expanding economy has had no boost from us. We have gone on no credit-card vacations to Oahu or Palm Springs, we never set off for the mountains towing a trailer or a boat, we belong to no country club, seldom dine out, possess no blue blue pool with lily-pad cocktail tables and expensive guests afloat in it. It will hardly do to confess aloud, in this century, how little it took to content us. We walked, gardened, read; Ruth cooked, I built things. We simplified feeling, as we had already anesthetized memory. The days dripped away like honey off a spoon. Once in a while we went for drinks or dinner to the house of someone like the LoPrestis, with whom our relationship was easy and friendly because it was shallow. Once in a while we were tempted out to San Francisco for a concert or show. That was all. Enough.

Yet, if I had really been so fierce for withdrawal, wouldn't I have fenced Tom Weld away when I had the chance? Wouldn't we have kept Fran LoPresti at wary arm's length? Wouldn't I have sprayed for Jim Peck and his crowd before they got like weevils into everything?

I am as responsible as anyone. When we first met Peck in the bottoms I should have come away cackling and clutching my brows, crying, "A fool! A fool! I met a fool i' the forest, a motley fool!" Instead I came away implicated, entangled, and oppressed, and I knew exactly why. He was like a visitation—beard, motorcycle, and all, and his head rattled with all the familiar loose marbles. He angered me in a remembered way, he made me doubt myself all afresh. And there was a threat in him, a demand that he and his bughouse faiths be somehow dealt with or they would undermine peace forever.

But the Welds and the LoPrestis, who merely involved us in neighborhood complications, and even Jim Peck, who challenged every faith I hold, threatened our serenity far less than did Marian Catlin, who only offered us love.

These ironies are circular, without resolution. I drift from grief to anger, and from anger to a sense of personal failure that blackens whole days and nights; and from that all too familiar agenbit of inwyt

I circle back to the bitter aftertaste of loss. All anew, I am assailed by ultimate questions.

The other night, standing in the patio watching the stars and the lights lost among the hills, I had a flash as if my veins had been shot full of menthol, a cold convulsion of panicked awareness that I was I, that for sixty-four years I have inhabited this skull which from the inside seems comfortably habitual, but which I might not even recognize if I could stand six feet away and see its hairless shine in the starlight. That old baldpate I? Good God. Is that what Ruth sees? What Marian regarded with affection and amusement? What Curtis rejected and was rejected by? And if I am so strange from the outside, am I so sure I know myself any better from within?

How do I know what I think till I see what I say, somebody asks, kidding the Philistines. But I can't think the question so stupid. How *do* I know what I think unless I have seen what I say? For two years I cultivated the condition that Marian called twilight sleep. Now my eyelids flutter open, and I am still on the table, the gown is pulled away to reveal the incision, the clamps, the sponges, and the blood, the masks are still bent over me with an attention at once impersonal and profound.

Escape was a dream I dreamed, and waking I am confused and a little sick. Sitting here sorting out the feelings and beliefs of Joseph Allston, while the rain sweeps in on gusts of soft Pacific air, I am sure of hardly anything, least of all of the code I thought I lived by. Some of it, yes; maybe more of it than I now think, for certainly I don't believe in conversions and character changes any more than I believe you can transform a radio into a radar by rewiring one or two of its circuits. But I do believe you can replace a blown tube or solder a broken wire. I have always said that the way to deal with the pain of others is by sympathy, which in first-year Greek they taught me meant "suffering with," and that the way to deal with one's own pain is to put one foot after the other. Yet I was never willing to suffer with others, and when my own pain hit me I crawled into a hole.

Sympathy I have failed in, stoicism I have barely passed. But I have made straight A in irony—that curse, that evasion, that armor, that way of staying safe while seeming wise. One thing I have learned hard, if indeed I have learned it now: it is a reduction of our humanity to hide from pain, our own or others'. To hide from anything. That was Marian's text. Be open, be available, be exposed, be skinless. Skinless? Dance around in your bones.

So I will have to see what I say about this sanctuary, these entanglements, these unsought amputations and wounds, this loss. In the saying, I suppose there will be danger of both self-pity and masochism. That Roman who drove a dagger into his thigh and broke it off at the hilt for a reminder, who would dare say he didn't enjoy the stoical spectacle he made? But I will have Marian at my elbow to mend me with laughter.

* * *

THE RAIN HAS COME ON harder. I should go up to the house and bring in wood and light a grate fire and prepare such comforts as the first night of winter prescribes. Ruth has been by herself long enough. But I know I must come back down here to my study shack, regularly and often, until I have either turned light into these corners or satisfied myself that there is no light to be switched on. If every particle in the universe has both consciousness and choice, as Marian believed, then it also has responsibility, including the responsibility to try to understand. I am not exempt, no matter how I may yearn for the old undemanding darkness under the stone.

FROM *ANGLE OF REPOSE*

Now I believe they will leave me alone. Obviously Rodman came up hoping to find evidence of my incompetence—though how an incompetent could have got this place renovated, moved his library up, and got himself transported to it without arousing the suspicion of his watchful children, ought to be a hard one for Rodman to answer. I take some pride in the way I managed all that. And he went away this afternoon without a scrap of what he would call data.

So tonight I can sit here with the tape recorder whirring no more noisily than electrified time, and say into the microphone the place and date of a sort of beginning and a sort of return: Zodiac Cottage, Grass Valley, California, April 12, 1970.

Right there, I might say to Rodman, who doesn't believe in time, notice something: I started to establish the present and the present moved on. What I established is already buried under layers of tape. Before I can say I *am*, I was. Heraclitus and I, prophets of flux, know that the flux is composed of parts that imitate and repeat each other. Am or was, I am cumulative, too. I am everything I ever was, whatever you and Leah may think. I am much of what my parents and especially my grandparents were—inherited stature, coloring, brains, bones (that part unfortunate), plus transmitted prejudices, culture, scruples, likings, moralities, and moral errors that I defend as if they were personal and not familial.

Even places, especially this house whose air is thick with the past. My antecedents support me here as the old wistaria at the corner supports the house. Looking at its cables wrapped two or three times around the cottage, you would swear, and you could be right, that if they were cut the place would fall down.

Rodman, like most sociologists and most of his generation, was born without the sense of history. To him it is only an aborted social science. The world has changed, Pop, he tells me. The past isn't going to teach us anything about what we've got ahead of us. Maybe it did once, or seemed to. It doesn't any more.

Probably he thinks the blood vessels of my brain are as hardened as my cervical spine. They probably discuss me in bed. *Out of his mind, going up there by himself...How can we, unless...helpless...roll his wheelchair off the porch who'd rescue him? Set himself afire lighting a cigar, who'd put him out?...Damned old independent mule-headed...worse than a baby. Never consider the trouble he makes for the people who have to look after him...House I grew up in, he says. Papers, he says, thing I've always wanted to do...All of Grandmother's papers, books, reminiscences, pictures, those hundreds of letters that came back from Augusta Hudson's daughter after Augusta died...A lot of Grandfather's relics, some of Father's, some of my own...Hundred year chronicle of the family. All right, fine. Why not give that stuff to the Historical Society and get a fat tax deduction? He could still work on it. Why box it all up, and himself too, in that old crooked house in the middle of twelve acres of land we could all make a good thing out of if he'd consent to sell? Why go off and play cobwebs like a character in a Southern novel, out where nobody can keep an eye on him?*

They keep thinking of my good, in their terms. I don't blame them, I only resist them. Rodman will have to report to Leah that I have rigged the place to fit my needs and am getting along well. I have had Ed shut off the whole upstairs except for my bedroom and bath and this study. Downstairs we use only the kitchen and library and the veranda. Everything tidy and shipshape and orderly. No data.

So I may anticipate regular visits of inspection and solicitude while they wait for me to get a belly full of independence. They will look sharp for signs of senility and increasing pain—will they perhaps even hope for them? Meantime they will walk softly, speak quietly, rattle the oatbag gently, murmuring and moving closer until the arm can slide the rope over the stiff old neck and I can be led away to the old folks' pasture down in Menlo Park where the care is so good and there is so much to keep the inmates busy and happy.

If I remain stubborn, the decision may eventually have to be made for me, perhaps by computer. Who could argue with a computer? Rodman will punch all his data onto cards and feed them into his machine and it will tell us all it is time.

I would have them understand that I am not just killing time during my slow petrifaction. I am neither dead nor inert. My head still works. Many things are unclear to me, including myself, and I want to sit and think. Who ever had a better opportunity? What if I *can't* turn my head? I can look in any direction by turning my wheelchair, and I choose to look back. Rodman to the contrary notwithstanding, that is the only direction we can learn from.

Increasingly, after my amputation and during the long time when I lay around feeling sorry for myself, I came to feel like the contour bird. I wanted to fly around the Sierra foothills backward, just looking. If there was no longer any sense in pretending to be interested in where I was going, I could consult where I've been. And I don't mean the Ellen business. I honestly believe this isn't that personal. The Lyman Ward who married Ellen Hammond and begot Rodman Ward and taught history and wrote certain books and monographs about the Western frontier, and suffered certain personal catastrophes and perhaps deserved them and survives them after a fashion and now sits talking to himself into a microphone—he doesn't matter that much any more. I would like to put him in a frame of reference and comparison. Fooling around in the papers my grandparents, especially my grandmother, left behind, I get glimpses of lives close to mine, related to mine in ways I recognize but don't completely comprehend. I'd like to live in their clothes awhile, if only so I don't have to live in my own. Actually, as I look down my nose to where my left leg bends and my right leg stops, I realize that it isn't backward I want to go, but downward. I want to touch once more the ground I have been maimed away from.

In my mind I write letters to the newspapers, saying Dear Editor, As a modern man and a one-legged man, I can tell you that the conditions are similar. We have been cut off, the past has been ended and the family has broken up and the present is adrift in its wheelchair. I had a wife who after twenty-five years of marriage took on the coloration of the 1960s. I have a son who, though we are affectionate with each other, is no more my true son than if he breathed through gills. That is no gap between the generations, that is a gulf. The elements have changed, there are whole new orders of magnitude and kind. This present of 1970 is no more an extension of my grandparents' world, this West is no more a development of the West they helped build, than the sea over Santorin is an extension of that once-island of rock and olives. My wife turns out after a quarter of a century to be someone I never knew, my son starts all fresh from his own premises.

My grandparents had to live their way out of one world and into another, or into several others, making new out of old the way corals live their reef upward. I am on my grandparents' side. I believe in Time, as they did, and in the life chronological rather than in the life existential. We live in time and through it, we build our huts in its ruins, or used to, and we cannot afford all these abandonings.

And so on. The letters fade like conversation. If I spoke to Rodman in those terms, saying that my grandparents' lives seem to me organic and ours what? hydroponic? he would ask in derision what I meant. Define my terms. How do you measure the organic residue of a man or a generation? This is all metaphor. If you can't measure it, it doesn't exist.

Rodman is a great measurer. He is interested in change, all right, but only as a process; and he is interested in values, but only as data. X people believe one way, Y people another, whereas ten years ago Y people believed the first way and X the second. The rate of change is therefore. He never goes back more than ten years.

Like other Berkeley radicals, he is convinced that the post-industrial post-Christian world is worn out, corrupt in its inheritance, helpless to create by evolution the social and political institutions, the forms of personal relations, the conventions, moralities, and systems of ethics (insofar as these are indeed necessary) appropriate to the future. Society being thus paralyzed, it must be pried loose. He, Rodman Ward, culture hero born fully armed from this history-haunted skull, will be happy to provide blueprints, or perhaps ultimatums and manifestoes, that will save us and bring on a life of true freedom. The family too. Marriage and the family as we have known them are becoming extinct. He is by Paul Goodman out of Margaret Mead. He sits in with the sitter-inners, he will reform us *malgré* our teeth, he will make his omelet and be damned to the broken eggs. Like the Vietnam commander, he will regretfully destroy our village to save it.

The truth about my son is that despite his good nature, his intelligence, his extensive education, and his bulldozer energy, he is as blunt as a kick in the shins. He is peremptory even with a doorbell button. His thumb never inquires whether one is within, and then waits to see. It pushes, and ten seconds later pushes again, and one second after that goes down on the button and stays there. That's the way he summoned me this noon.

* * *

I RESPONDED SLOWLY, for I guessed who it was: his thumb gave him away. I had been expecting his visit, and fearing it. Also I had been working peacefully and disliked being disturbed.

I love this old studio of Grandmother's. It is full of sun in the mornings, and the casual apparatus and decorations of living, which age so swiftly in America, have here kept a worn, changeless comfortableness not too much violated by the tape recorder and the tubular desk light and other things I have had to add. When I have wheeled my chair into the cut-out bay in the long desk I can sit surrounded on three sides by books and papers. A stack of yellow pads, a mug of pens and pencils, the recorder's microphone are at my elbow, and on the wall before my face is something my grandmother used to have hanging there all through my childhood: a broad leather belt, a wooden-handled cavalry revolver of the Civil War period, a bowie knife, and a pair of Mexican spurs with 4-inch rowels. The minute I found them in a box I put them right back where they used to be.

The Lord knows why she hung them where she would see them every time she looked up. Certainly they were not her style. Much more in her style are the trembling shadows of wistaria clusters that the morning sun throws on that wall. Did she hang them here to remind herself of her first experience in the West, the little house among the liveoaks at New Almaden where she came as a bride in 1876? From her letters I know that Grandfather had them hanging there in the arch between dining room and parlor when she arrived, and that she left them up because she felt they meant something to him. The revolver his brother had taken from a captured rebel, the bowie he himself had worn all through his early years in California, the spurs had been given to him by a Mexican packer on the Comstock. But why did she restore his primitive and masculine trophies here in Grass Valley, half a lifetime after New Almaden? Did she hang those Western objects in her sight as a reminder, as an acknowledgment of something that had happened to her? I think perhaps she did.

In any case, I was sitting here just before noon, contented in mind and as comfortable in body as I am ever likely to be. The slight activity of rising and breakfasting, which I do without Ada, and the influence of coffee and the day's first aspirin, and the warmth of the sun against my neck and left side, these are morning beneficences.

Then that thumb on the bell.

I pushed back from among the sun-dazzled papers and rotated my chair. Two years' practice has not fully accustomed me to the double sensation that accompanies wheelchair locomotion. Above, I am as rigid as a monument; below, smooth fluidity. I move like a piano on a dolly. Since I am battery-powered, there is no physical effort, and since I cannot move my head up, down, or to either side, objects appear to rotate around me, to slide across my vision from peripheral to full to opposite peripheral, rather than I to move among them. The walls revolve, bringing into view the casement windows, the window seat, the dusters of wisteria outside; then the next wall with photographs of Grandmother and Grandfather, their three children, a wash drawing of the youngest, Agnes, at the age of three, a child who looks all eyes; and still rotating, the framed letters from Whittier, Longfellow, Mark Twain, Kipling, Howells, President Grover Cleveland (I framed them, not she); and then the spin slows and I am pointed toward the door with the sunlight stretching along the worn brown boards. By the time I have rolled into the upper hall, my visitor is holding down the bell with one hand and knocking with the other.

Though I have got handier in the ten days I have been here, it took me a minute to get into position over the brace that locks my chair onto the lift, and I felt like yelling down at him to for God's sake let up, I was coming. He made me nervous. I was afraid of doing something wrong and ending up at the bottom in a mess of twisted metal and broken bones.

When I was locked in, I flipped the wall switch, and the lift's queer, weightless motion took hold of me, moved me smoothly, tipped me with the inevitable solar plexus panic over the edge. I went down like a diver submerging, the floor flowed over my head. Without haste the downstairs wall toward which my rigid head was set unrolled from top to bottom, revealing midway the print of that Pre-Raphaelite seadog and his enchanted boy listeners—a picture my grandmother might have painted herself, it is so much in her key of aspiration arising out of homely realism. Then I was level with the picture, which meant that my chair had come into view from the front door, and the ringing and pounding stopped.

The chair grounded in light as murky and green as the light of ten fathoms: the ambition of that old wistaria has been to choke off all the lower windows. I tipped up the brace with one crutch, and groped the crutch back to its cradle on the side of the chair—and carefully, too, because I knew he was watching me and I wanted to impress him with how accidentproof my habits were. A touch on the motor switch, a hand on the wheel, and I was swinging again. The wall spun until Rodman's face came into focus, framed in the door's small pane like the face of a fish staring in the visor of a diver's helmet—a bearded fish that smiled, distorted by the beveled glass, and flapped a vigorous fin.

* * *

THESE ARE THE RESULTS, mainly negative from his point of view, of Rodman's visit:

(1) He did not persuade me—nor to do him justice did he try very hard—to come back and live with them or start arrangements for the retirement home in Menlo Park.

(2) He did not persuade me to stop running around alone in my

wheelchair. Sure I bumped my stump, showing off how mobile I am and how cunningly I have converted all stairs to ramps. Could he tell by my face how much I hurt, sitting there smiling and smiling, and wanting to take that poor sawed-off twitching lump of bones and flesh in my two hands and rock back and forth and grit my teeth and howl? What if he could? When I am not showing off to prove my competence to people who doubt it, I can go in this chair almost anywhere he can go on his legs, and just as safely.

(3) I am not going to install a walkie-talkie on the chair so if I get in trouble I can call the Highway Patrol. He had that all worked out, and pushed it. But the only emergency I ever have is that sometimes when I am far from the bathroom and too achy to get out of my chair to perform, my urine bottle overflows. It is called the Policeman's Friend, and the cops and I might have a pleasant time exchanging yarns about awkward times when we have been caught with it full, but I doubt that any cop would take it seriously as an emergency.

(4) I am not made anxious about "getting like my father." Clearly they are afraid these things run in the family, which is the sort of acknowledgment that under other circumstances I would like Rodman to make to history. Sure my father had a queer unhappy life, and sure he stayed on and on here after the mine closed down, and finally got so addled that Ada and Ed Hawkes had to look after him as they would have looked after a willful and irresponsible child. Rodman all but asks, What if he came up here some day and found me talking to myself like Grandpa? But I could tell him I talk to myself all the time, into this microphone, and sort of like the company. He knows as well as I do that when I quit making even approximate sense he can get the support of the law to take me away, as I had to take Father.

(5) I am not going to ask Ed and Ada to move in downstairs. They have lived all their life in the cottage down the hill, and they are as close as I need them.

(6) I am not going to give up this business of Grandmother's papers and write a book on "somebody interesting." Rodman pretends to be afraid that out of sentiment I will waste what he flatteringly calls major talents (he disparages history but was touchingly proud when

I won the Bancroft Prize) on a nobody. His notion of somebody interesting is numbingly vulgar. Having no historical sense, he can only think that history's interest must be "color." How about some Technicolor personality of the Northern Mines, about which I already know so much? Lola Montez, say, that wild girl from an Irish peat bog who became the mistress of half the celebrities of Europe, including Franz Liszt and Dumas, *père* or *fils* or both, before taking up with King Ludwig I of Bavaria, who made her Countess of Landsfeld. And from there, in 1856, to San Francisco, where she danced the spider dance for miners and fortune hunters (*No, Lola, no!*) and from there to Grass Valley to live for two years with a tame bear who couldn't have been much of an improvement on Ludwig.

That's Rodman's idea of history. Every fourth-rate antiquarian in the West has panned Lola's poor little gravel. My grandparents are a deep vein that has never been dug. They were *people*.

I am sure Rodman knows nothing whatever about Grandfather, nothing about his inventiveness or his genius for having big ideas twenty years ahead of their time or his struggle to do something grand and humanly productive and be one of the builders of the West. I know that his taking the job as superintendent of the Zodiac was a kind of surrender, though I don't yet know the details. Rodman probably feels that that was the sort of job Grandfather bucked for all his life and finally made. He probably thinks of him as a lesser George Hearst, neither quite crooked enough nor quite successful enough to be interesting.

But it is interesting that, apparently in an attempt to comprehend my present aberration, Rodman should have taken the trouble to read some of Grandmother's stories and look at some magazines containing her drawings. Characteristically he saw nothing in them. All full of pious renunciations, he says, everything covered up with Victorian antimacassars. He cited me her own remark that she wrote from the protected point of view, the woman's point of view, as evidence that she went through her life from inexperience to inexperience.

Her pictures the same. If, as I assured him with quotations from the histories of American art, she was the best-known woman illustrator of her time, and the only woman who ever did anything significant about drawing the early West, how come nobody collects her? And *woman* illustrator, he repeats with good-humored condescension. Yet his name is always in the papers as a defender of disadvantaged minorities, and only last week he had his picture in the *Chronicle* in a Woman's Liberation Front picket line.

Well, Grandmother, let me back out of this desk and turn around and look at you over there in your walnut frame next to the letters of people who wrote to you as a respected contemporary. Should I take an interest in you even if you were historical, white, a woman, and my grandmother? Did all your talents, and Grandfather's, and all the efforts of a long strenuous life go for no more than to produce Rodman and me, a sociologist and a cripple? Nothing in your life or art to teach a modern or one-legged man something?

A Quaker lady of high principles, the wife of a not-very-successful engineer whom you supported through years of delayed hope, you lived in exile, wrote it, drew it—New Almaden, Santa Cruz, Leadville, Michoacán, the Snake River Valley, the deep quartz mines right under this house—and you stayed a cultural snob through it all. Even when you lived in a field camp in a canyon, your children had a governess, no less, unquestionably the only one in Idaho. The dream you had for your children was a dream of Eastern cultivation.

Yet do you remember the letters you used to get from isolated miners and geologists and surveyors who had come across a copy of *Century* or *Atlantic* and seen their lives there, and wrote to ask how a lady of obvious refinement knew so much about drifts, stopes, tipples, pumps, ores, assays, mining law, claim jumpers, underground surveying, and other matters? Remember the one who wanted to know where you learned to handle so casually a technical term like "angle of repose"?

I suppose you replied, "By living with an engineer." But you were too alert to the figurative possibilities of words not to see the phrase as descriptive of human as well as detrital rest. As you said, it was too good for mere dirt; you tried to apply it to your own wandering and uneasy life. It is the angle I am aiming for myself, and I don't mean the rigid angle at which I rest in this chair. I wonder if you ever reached it. There was a time up there in Idaho when everything was wrong; your husband's career, your marriage, your sense of yourself, your confidence, all came unglued together. Did you come down out of that into some restful 30° angle and live happily ever after? When you died at ninety-one, the New York *Times* obituary spoke of you as a Western woman, a Western writer and artist. Would you have accepted the label? Or did you cling forever to the sentiment you wrote to Augusta Hudson from the bottom of failure in Boise Canyon—that not even Henry James's expatriates were so exiled as you? We shared this house all the years of my childhood, and a good many summers afterward. Was the quiet I always felt in you really repose? I wish I thought so. It is one of the questions I want the papers to answer.

If Henry Adams, whom you knew slightly, could make a theory of history by applying the second law of thermodynamics to human affairs, I ought to be entitled to base one on the angle of repose, and may yet. There is another physical law that teases me, too: the Doppler Effect. The sound of anything coming at you—a train, say, or the future—has a higher pitch than the sound of the same thing going away. If you have perfect pitch and a head for mathematics you can compute the speed of the object by the interval between its arriving and departing sounds. I have neither perfect pitch nor a head for mathematics, and anyway who wants to compute the speed of history? Like all falling bodies, it constantly accelerates. But I would like to hear your life as *you* heard it, coming at you, instead of hearing it as I do, a sober sound of expectations reduced, desires blunted, hopes deferred or abandoned, chances lost, defeats accepted, griefs borne. I don't find your life uninteresting, as Rodman does. I would like to hear it as it sounded while it was passing. Having no future of my own, why shouldn't I look forward to yours?

You yearned backward a good part of your life, and that produced another sort of Doppler Effect. Even while you paid attention to what you must do today and tomorrow, you heard the receding sound of what you had relinquished. It came to you secondhand in the letters of Augusta Hudson. You lived vicariously in her, dined with the literary great, visited La Farge at Newport, lunched at the White

House, toured Italy and the Holy Land. The daily gorgeousness of Augusta's social obligations lighted your strenuous poverty in the way you liked to illuminate your drawings, with a wash of light from above and to one side. Witness this letter I was just reading, written when Augusta was moving into her Stanford White Mansion on Staten Island: "Before you put a fire in your new fireplace, gather up your children and have them stand in it, looking up, and then, with the light falling on them so, paint them and send them to me."

Where was Grandmother living when she had that sentimental whim? In a dugout in Boise Canyon.

Except for her marriage she would have been a respected part of what, marrying whom she did, she had to leave behind. I think her love for my grandfather, however real, was always somewhat unwilling. She must unconsciously have agreed with his judgment that she was higher and finer than he. I wonder if there was some moment when she fully comprehended and appreciated him? I wonder if there was a time when the East and all that Edith Wharton gentility had been lived out of her as surely as the cells of her girlhood had been replaced in her body?

Not that she made a fetish of her gifts, or held herself above anyone. She plunged into things with energy, she was never afraid of work. John Greenleaf Whittier said she was the only girl he knew who could conduct a serious discussion of the latest *North American Review* while scrubbing her mother's floor. She endured, and even enjoyed, considerable physical hardship on occasion. In Leadville she kept house in a one-room cabin, and in that one room presided over talk that she insisted (and she would have known) was as good as the best in America. All her life she loved conversation, discussion, company. When I was a child we were always being visited by people like the president of Yale College and the American Ambassador to Japan. They sat on the piazza and talked with Grandmother while Grandfather listened, working quietly among his roses.

But that was after she had reached, or appeared to have reached, the angle of repose. I can remember her as Susan Burling Ward, an old lady. It is harder to imagine her as Susan Burling, a girl, before the West and all the West implied had happened to her.

Ever since Ada left me eating supper, and went home to get supper for Ed, I have been bolting through the papers covering her early years. Among them is an article that Augusta wrote, sometime after 1900, for a magazine called *The Booklover*. It is as good a thing to start with as any.

> Botanists tell us that the blossom is an evolution of the leaf—but they cannot say just why that particular bud should take from the same air and sunshine a fairer substance, a deeper color, a more permanent existence, and become something at which each passerby pauses, and goes on his way happier for the sight. Why on the sturdy stem of farmers and merchants should one girl blossom into a storyteller in pencil and in words?
>
> Susan Burling comes from a line of farmers, on the father's side, who have lived at Milton on the Hudson for many generations; on the mother's side from the Mannings, merchants; but on both sides members of the Society of Friends.
>
> Growing up the youngest and darling of the family, always surrounded by the atmosphere of love and duty where harsh words and looks were unknown, she gained a certain discipline of independence by being sent to New York to study art. She was still a very young girl, having only gone through a high school in Poughkeepsie where she had distinguished herself in mathematics. She had from babyhood tried to draw, and the little compositions of her twelfth year have quite an idea of "placing" and story.
>
> The School of Design for Women at the Cooper Institute was the only place, at that time, where anything approaching an art education could be had for a girl. The Academy of Design schools were hedged about by all sorts of restraints, and the Art Students' League was not yet in existence. It was here that I first saw her—very youthful in figure, delicate yet full of vigor. She rode well; an accomplishment that stood her in good stead in Mexico and the West, where indeed no one is really respected who cannot manage a horse. She skated on her little feet like a swallow flying, and danced with the same grace and lightness. She could outskate and outdance us all.

And that's enough. Skating, dancing. It tires me to think of all that young vitality, and makes me unaccountably sad to look at her there on the wall, an old woman who has given up vivacity for resignation.

But still presenting the clean profile, the small neat cameo head, that her earliest pictures show, and lighted—I am sure she imposed this on the painter—by a dusky radiance from above and to one side. Despite the downcast eyes, there is something intractable about you, Grandmother, but I am too tired and sore to deal with it. I have been at this desk too long, and Rodman's visit was no help. Ada, come on, hurry up. I ache all over—neck, shoulders, back, wrists, stump. I want your key in the door, I will you to clatter my supper dishes into the sink and start laboring up the stairs.

This house creaks and shifts in the dark. It is even older than I am, and nearly as warped, and it may ache as much. Come on, Ada, before I begin to think Rodman and Leah are right. Too long a day. I must never go this long again. Tomorrow, with the sun in the room, it will be better. Mornings, and maybe an hour or two in the evening, that's enough. Ada, come on, come on. Appear in that doorway. Let me hear your gravelly Cousin Jack voice. "Eh, Mister Ward, ain't you about ready for bed?"

Mister Ward, she will say, not Lyman. Fifty years ago we used to play together, never quite with Grandmother's approval. What would she have said if she'd seen us with our pants down in the dusty loft of Attles' barn? But Ada never presumes on childhood acquaintance. None of the legendary Western democracy operated in our relations, only the democracy of childhood. Her grandfather worked for mine, and her father for my father, in this same old Zodiac whose mole holes riddle the hill under us (that's why the house has settled so crookedly). Three generations of Trevithicks and Hawkeses working for three generations of Wards. The West is not so new as some think.

Bless God, she is six feet tall and strong as a man. She is cheerful, dependable, common. She deals with my person and my problems as matter-of-factly as she would change a baby's diaper. I suppose I *am* her baby, as my father was in his last years. Does she wish all the Wards would die off and give her a rest, or would she be empty without one of us to look after? Does the sight of my nakedness trouble her when she undresses and bathes me? Is she given cold shivers by my stump? Turned to stone by my rigid Gorgon head? Does she think of me as an old friend, as poor Lyman, as that unlucky Mister Ward, as a grotesque, or simply as an object to be dealt with, like a caked saucepan?

Whatever you think, come on, Ada. I need that bath and that bed and that bedtime bourbon. Whatever you think, I have learned to think nothing. I run by routine, I accept from hired women services that I would never have accepted from my wife before I became a grotesque. When you block the doorway with your bulk, and shuffle in on your bunioned arthritic feet making comfortable noises, my soul rushes out of me with gratitude.

Already we have a comfortable rut, we go through habitual motions whose every stage is reassuring. While she starts the bath water I wheel my chair into the bedroom, just beside the bathroom door. We don't bother with the crutches. She helps her grotesque doll to stand up, and it clings to her while her gnarled hands, the end joints twisted almost at right angles, fumble with zippers and buttons. She has never complained of her arthritis to me—thinks it amounts to nothing beside mine. Grunting with effort she lifts me—she would say "hefts" me—off the chair's step, and I cling there, in pain as always, naked, helpless, while she flops a testing hand in the water. Then she returns and hefts her maimed doll bodily into the air until the last clothing falls from its foot, and lowers it with grunts and sighs into the tub.

The water is so hot that it makes the cicatriced stump prickle and smart, but it must be that hot if it is to ease the aches away enough to permit sleep. Painfully she wallows down on her knees and without diffidence soaps and rinses me all over. Her crooked fingers drag across the skin stiff as twigs. Her doll sits stiffly, pointed straight ahead at the fixtures that emerge from the wall. When she is finished she bends far over and guides its arms around her neck. Then she rears upward, and up it comes, naked and pink, her hairy baby, its stump bright red. Its dripping wets the front of her dress, its rigid head glares over her shoulder.

Holding it, clucking and murmuring as she works, she towels it down as far as the knees, and then she takes it around the waist and tilts it upon her great bosom and rotates until its leg, bent to miss the tub's rim, can straighten down on the mat. Pressing it against her as intimate as husband, she towels the rest of it and eases it into the chair and wheels it to the bed. Another lift—the buttocks sink in softness. It sits there shivering in its damp towel until she comes with urine bottle and tube. When I have attached them she checks the hookup with a casual tug.

Now the pajamas, delicious to the chilling skin, and the ease backward until the body that has been upright too long is received by mattress and pillows. She sets the telephone close, she tucks up the covers. Finally she waddles over to the cabinet by the desk and gets the bottle and two glasses, and we have a comfortable nightcap together like cronies.

Oh, hurry, Ada Hawkes. I don't want to telephone. That would demonstrate something that I don't want demonstrated.

My grandfather, long before your grandfather Trevithick knew him, before he put on weight and fell in love with flowers and learned to take his consolation from a lonely bottle, was an indefatigable worker. He often rode a horse a hundred miles a day, four hunched miles in a week, accepting the testing that such journeys implied. Despite bad eyes and migraines, he used sometimes to work all night on maps and reports. When he was making an underground survey of the New Almaden mine he stayed underground for twenty hours at a stretch. He would not understand, any more than my grandmother would, this weakness that yearns for a motherly bosom and a pair of warped gentle hands.

"Best egg in the basket," he used to say of me when I was a small boy and wanted to help him plant and prune and prop and espalier his Burbank fruit freaks. I would like to be that kind of egg. I refer my actions to his standards even yet. If I were talking to anyone but myself I would have shut up long ago. Probably it's a mistake to complain even to myself. I won't do it.

But oh, Ada, Ada, get over here, it's already past nine.

And there, like a bell tardily ringing the hour, is her key in the lock downstairs.

FROM *The Big Rock Candy Mountain*

I.

In the summer it was the homestead, the little round-roofed shack that looked like a broad freight car with one side extended into a sleeping porch where the two beds were, the single room with the kerosene stove against one wall and the cupboards built up beside it, the table and the benches and the couch where the cat slept all day long, curled up dozing, but sleeping so lightly that a finger placed on one hair of him, anywhere, would bring him instantly awake with a *pr-r-r-rt!*

The homestead was the open, flat plain, unbroken clear to the horizon on every side except the south, where the Bearpaw Mountains, way down across the line in Montana, showed in a thin white line that later in summer turned to brown. In August, when the heat was intense, the mountains faded out of sight in the haze and heat waves, but almost any day in June and early July they could be seen, and they were an important part of the farm.

There were other important things about the farm, the intimate parts like the pasture, a half mile long and two hundred yards wide, fenced with three tight strands of barbed wire on peeled cedar posts, the whole thing a pride to Bruce because there was no fence anywhere near as tight and neat on the other farms nearby. His father was a thorough man on a job; when he put in a fence he put in a fence that he need not be ashamed of, he set the posts deep in the ground and tamped them in tight, he bought a wire-stretcher and strung the strands like guitar strings.

The pasture was cut diagonally by the coulee, and just below the house was the reservoir, and across the reservoir and through the fence was the long sixty-acre wheat field, and the smaller field of flax, and the end of those fields was both the south line of their property and the international boundary. The farm was that feeling, too, the sense of straddling two nations, so that even though you were American, living in Canada, you lost nothing by it, but really gained, because the Fourth of July was celebrated in Canada and Canadian holidays like Victoria Day and the King's birthday were celebrated in Montana, and you got in on both. And you lived in Saskatchewan, in one nation, but got your mail in Montana, in another.

The farm was every summer between June and September. It was the long trip, in the first year by wagon but later by car, from Whitemud out; it was the landmarks on that trail, the Frenchman's house with a dozen barefooted children streaking for the barn, the gates that had to be opened, the great horse ranch where they travelled hours without seeing a living thing except herds of horses as wild as coyotes. It was Robsart, a little clot of dwellings with a boarding house that they generally tried to make for the noon meal, and then scattered farms again along the grass-grown wagon-track, and a couple of little streams to ford, and Gadke's where they always stopped while Pa talked things over with Mr. Gadke because Mr. Gadke was a smart dry-farmer, until finally the last gate and the last ford just past the twin tarpapered shacks that all the homesteaders called Pete and Emil, and then their own house, and the familiar-unfamiliar look of the fence and fireguard and pasture the first time in the spring.

Farm was the shut-up, mousy smell of the house, the musty smell of packed quilts, the mattresses out in the sun on the first morning. It was the oil that had to be wiped off his gopher traps, and the first walk out along the pasture fence to the edge of the field with the traps over his shoulder. It was trouble with water, sometimes, when the well-hole beside the reservoir had caved in and they had to haul drinking water in barrels for two miles, and stories like the one his father told about the Picketts, down in Montana. The Picketts had no well, only a little creekbed that often dried up on them, and then they hoarded water, according to Pa, like nothing you ever saw. A pan of water would be used to boil eggs in the morning. Then the dishes would be washed in it. Then all the family would wash, one after the other. Then the water would be strained to get the grease and dirt out, and saved to put in the radiator of the Picketts' old car. Pa swore you could tell whether the Picketts had had cabbage or beans or sweetcorn for dinner just by smelling the boiling radiator of that old McLaughlin.

Farm ordinarily was the things he and Chet did together, the guns they whittled out of sticks, the long campaigns in the coulee and the patch of sweetcorn when it got high enough to make good cover. It was the Russian thistle they hoed out of garden and fireguard, and the swearing his father did when the thistle got a good start in the wheat field. It was long days of blazing sun, and violent rains, and once it was a cyclone that passed a mile south of them. That was when they were still living in the tent, before Pa got the house built, and Pa roped them all down in the section hole until he was sure the twister wasn't going to hit them.

In this summer of 1918, because Chet was staying in town to be delivery boy for Mr. Babcock in the confectionery store, the homestead was isolation and loneliness, though he never felt it or knew it for what it was. Only when his mother looked at his father and said they should never have let Chet take that job, it left Brucie too much alone. Then he felt vaguely disturbed and faintly abused, but he never did really believe he was lonely, because he loved the homestead, and the Sunday school hymns he sang to himself down in the flowered coulee meant to him very definite and secret and precious things, meant primroses and space and the wet slap of a rare east wind, and those tunes would mean those things to him all his life.

Still he was almost always alone, and that summer he somehow lost his identity as a name. There was no other boy to confuse him with; he wasn't Bruce, but "the boy," and because he was the only thing of his kind in all that summer world he needed no name, but only his own sense of triumphant identity. He knew the homestead in intimate and secret detail because there was so little variety in it that the small things took the senses. He knew the way the grass grew curling over the lip of a burnout, and how the prairie owls nested under those grassy lips. He knew how the robins tucked their nests back under the fringes of the prairie wool, and their skyblue eggs were always a wonder. He could tell, by the way the horses clustered in a corner of the pasture, when something was wrong, as when Dick got wound up in the lower strand of the fence and almost cut his leg off trying to break loose. He could tell instantly when a weasel was after the hens by the kind of clamor they made. Nothing else, for some reason, ever caused that fighting squawk from the mother hens. He could tell a badger's permanent burrow from the one he made in digging out a gopher. The yapping of coyotes on a moonlit night was lonely and beautiful to him, and the yard and chicken house and fireguard and coulee were as much a part of him as his own skin.

He lived in his own world in summer, and only when hail or wind or gophers or Russian thistle threatened the wheat on which he knew his father yearly gambled everything, was there much communication with the adult world whose interests were tied down to the bonanza farming and the crop. Wheat, he knew, was very high. The war did that. And he knew too that they were not well off, that every spring his father scraped together everything he had for seed and supplies and hoped for a good year so that he could clean up. He knew that they had less than most of the homesteaders around: they didn't have a barn, a cow (they had two in town, but it was a hard trip to bring them out), a seeder, a binder, a disc, a harrow. They didn't have much of anything, actually, except a team, a plow, and a stoneboat. Anything he didn't have tools for his father either borrowed tools to do, or hired done. But that frantic period of plowing and seeding came early, before his senses had adjusted themselves completely to the homestead, and later, in the period when they did practically nothing but sit and wait and hope that the weather would give them a crop, he moved in a tranced air of summer and loneliness and delight.

At the end of the first week in this summer he caught a weasel in one of his gopher traps, and brought it, still twisting and fighting in the trap, to the house. His father and mother came to the door; his mother made a face and shivered.

"Ugh!" she said. "Ugly, snaky thing!"

But his father showed more interest. "Got something special, uh?" he said. He came down and took the ringed chain from the boy's hand, held the weasel up. The weasel hissed in his face, trying to jump at him, and he straightened his arm to hold the swinging trap away.

"You've got to hand it to them," he said. "There isn't anything alive with more fight in it."

"Take it and kill it," Elsa said. "Don't just keep it in the trap torturing it."

Bruce was looking at his father. He ignored his mother's words because this was men's business. She didn't understand about weasels. "Maybe I could keep him till he turns into an ermine," he said.

"Why not?" his father said. "You could get three bucks for his pelt, these days. We ought to be able to make a cage that'd hold him."

"Oh, Bo," Elsa said. "Keep a weasel?"

"Give Boopus here something to do," Bo said. "You've been telling me we ought to get him a pet."

Bruce looked from one to the other, wondering when they had talked over getting him a pet. "We've got old Tom now," he said.

"Old Tom," his father said, "is so full of mice his mind is all furry."

"We ought to get a dog," Elsa said. "Not a vicious thing like a weasel."

"Well, we've got the weasel, and we don't know any place to get a dog." Bo looked down at the boy and grinned. He swung the weasel gently back and forth, and it arched its long yellow body against the trap and lunged. "Let's go make a cage for this tough guy," Bo said.

"Can I have a dog too?"

"Maybe. If I can find one."

"Holy catartin," Bruce said. "A cat, a dog, and a weasel. Maybe I can catch some more and start a weasel farm."

"I'd move out," his mother said. She waved them away. "Hurry up, if you're going to keep that bloodthirsty thing. Don't leave it in the trap with its broken leg."

They made a cage out of a beer-case, screened under the hinged top and with a board removed at the bottom, leaving an opening over which they tacked a strip of screen. They had trouble getting the weasel out of the trap, and finally Bo had to smother him in a piece of horse blanket and spring the jaws loose and throw blanket and all in the cage. For three days the weasel sulked in the corner and would eat nothing, but when the boy said he didn't think it was going to live his father laughed at him. "You can't kill a weasel just by breaking his leg. Put a mouse in there and see what happens."

Next day the boy rescued a half-dead mouse that Tom was satedly toying with under the bed, and dropped it in the cage. Nothing happened, but when he came back later the mouse was dead, with a hole back of his ear and his body limp and apparently boneless. The boy fished the carcass out with a bent wire, and from then on there was no question of the weasel's dying. The problem was to find enough mice, but after a few days he tried a gopher, and then it was all right.

* * *

THERE HAD BEEN A WIND during the night, and all the loneliness of the world had swept up out of the southwest. The boy had heard it wailing through the screens of the sleeping porch where he lay, and he had heard the wash tub bang loose from the outside wall and roll on down the coulee, and the slam of the screen door, and his mother's padding feet as she rose to fasten things down. Through one half-open eye he had peered up from his pillow to see the moon skimming windily in a luminous sky. In his mind's eye he had seen the prairie outside with its woolly grass and cactus white under the moon, and the wind, whining across that endless oceanic land, sang in the screens, and sang him back to sleep.

Now, after breakfast, when he set out through the pasture on the round of his traps, there was no more wind, but the air smelled somehow recently swept and dusted, as the house in town smelled after his mother's cleaning. The sun was gently warm on the bony shoulder blades of the boy, and he whistled, and whistling turned to see if the Bearpaws were in sight to the south. There they were, a tenuous outline of white just breaking over the bulge of the world; the Mountains of the Moon, the place of running streams and timber and cool heights that he had never seen—only dreamed of on days when the baked gumbo of the yard cracked in the heat and the sun brought cedar smells from fenceposts long since split and dry and odorless, when he lay dreaming on the bed with a Sears Roebuck or a T. Eaton catalogue before him, picking out the presents he would buy for his mother and his father and Chet and his friends next Christmas, or the Christmas after that. On those days he looked often and long at the snowy mountains to the south, while dreams rose in him like heat waves, blurring the reality of the unfinished shack and the bald prairie of his home.

The Bearpaws were there now, and he watched them a moment, walking, his feet automatically dodging cactus clumps, before he turned his attention to the scattered stakes that marked his traps. He ran the line at a half-trot, whistling.

At the first stake the chain was stretched tightly down the hole. The pull on its lower end had dug a little channel in the soft earth of the mound. Gently, so as not to break the gopher's leg off, the boy eased the trap out of the burrow, held the chain in his left hand, and loosened the stake with his right. The gopher tugged against the trap, but it made no noise. There were only two places where they made a noise: at a distance, when they whistled a warning, and in the weasel's cage. Otherwise they kept still.

For a moment he debated whether to keep this one alive for the weasel or to wait so he wouldn't have to carry a live one all the way around. Deciding to wait, he held the chain out, measured the rodent, and swung. The knobbed end of the stake crushed the skull, and the eyes popped out of the head, round and blue. A trickle of blood started from nose and ears. The feet kicked.

Releasing the gopher, the boy lifted it by the tail and snapped its tail fur off with a smart flip. Then he stowed the trophy carefully in the breast pocket of his overalls. For the last two years he had won the grand prize offered by the province to the school child who destroyed the most gophers. On the mantel in town were two silver loving cups, and in the cigar box under his bed in the farmhouse were already seven hundred forty tails, the catch of three weeks. In one way, he resented his father's distributing poison along the wheat field, because poisoned gophers generally got down their holes to die, and he didn't get the tails. So he spent most of his time trapping and snaring in the pasture, where poison could not be spread because of the horses.

Picking up trap and stake, Bruce kicked the dead gopher down its burrow and scooped dirt over it with his toe. They stunk up the pasture if they weren't buried, and the bugs got into them. Frequently he had stood to windward of a dead and swollen gopher, watching the body shift and move with the movements of the beetles and crawling things in it. If such an infested corpse were turned over, the carrion beetles would roar out, great, hard-shelled, orange-colored, scavenging things that made his blood curdle at the thought of their touching him, and after they were gone and he looked again he would see the little black ones, undisturbed, seething through the rotten flesh. So he always buried his dead, now.

Through the gardens of red and yellow cactus blooms he went whistling, half-trotting, setting his traps afresh whenever a gopher shot upright, whistled, and ducked down its hole. All but two of the first seventeen traps held gophers, and he came to the eighteenth confidently, expecting to take this one alive. But this gopher had gone in head first, and the boy put back in his pocket the salt sack he had brought along for a game bag. He would have to trap or snare one down by the dam.

On the way back he stopped with bent head while he counted the morning's catch of tails, mentally adding this lot to the seven hundred forty he already had, trying to remember how many he and Chet had had this time last year. As he finished his mathematics his whistle broke out again, and he galloped down through the pasture, running for very abundance of life, until he came to the chicken house just within the fireguard.

Under the eaves of the chicken house, so close that the hens were constantly pecking up to its door and then almost losing their wits with fright, was the weasel's cage. The boy lifted the hinged top and looked down through the screen.

"Hello," he said. "Hungry?"

The weasel crouched, its snaky body humped, its head thrust forward and its malevolent eyes steady and glittering.

"Tough, ain't you?" the boy said. "Just you wait, you bloodsucking old stinker, you. Won't I skin you quick, hah?"

There was no dislike or emotion in his tone. He took the weasel's malignant ferocity with the same indifference he displayed in his gopher killing. Weasels, if you kept them long enough, were valuable. He would catch some more and have an ermine farm. He was the best gopher trapper in Saskatchewan. Why not weasels? Once he and Chet had even caught a badger, though they hadn't been able to take him alive because he was caught by only three hind toes, and lunged so savagely that they had to stand off and stone him to death in the trap. But weasels you could catch alive, and Pa said you couldn't hurt a weasel short of killing him outright. This one, though virtually three-legged, was as lively and vicious as ever.

Every morning now he had a live gopher for breakfast, in spite of Elsa's protests that it was cruel. She had argued and protested, but he had talked her down. When she said that the gopher didn't have a chance in the weasel's cage, he retorted that it didn't have a chance when the weasel came down the hole after it, either. When she said that the real job he should devote himself to was destroying all the weasels, he replied that then the gophers would get so thick they would eat the wheat down to stubble. Finally she had given up, and the weasel continued to have his warm meals.

For some time the boy stood watching his captive. Then he turned and went into the house, where he opened the oatbox in the kitchen and took out a chunk of dried beef. From this he cut a thick slice with the butcher knife, and went munching into the sleeping porch where his mother was making the beds.

"Where's that little double-naught?" he said.

"That what?"

"That little wee trap I use for catching live ones for Lucifer."

"Hanging out by the laundry bench, I think. Are you going trapping again now?"

"Lucifer hasn't been fed yet."

"How about your reading?"

"I'ne take the book along and read while I wait. I'm just going down by the dam."

"I can, not I'ne, son."

"I can," the boy said. "I am most delighted to comply with your request of the twenty-third inst." He grinned at his mother. He could always floor her with a quotation out of a letter or the Sears Roebuck catalogue.

With the trap swinging in his hand, and under his arm the book— *Narrative and Lyric Poems*, edited by Somebody-or-Other—which his mother kept him reading all summer so that "next year he could be at the head of his class again," the boy walked out into the growing heat.

From the northwest the coulee angled down through the pasture, a shallow swale dammed just above the house to catch the spring run-off of snow water. Below the dam, watered by the slow seepage from above, the coulee bottom was a parterre of flowers, buttercups in broad sheets, wild sweet pea, and stinkweed. On the slopes were evening primroses pale pink and white and delicately fragrant, and on the flats above the yellow and red burgeoning of the cactus.

Just under the slope of the coulee a female gopher and three half-grown pups basked on their warm mound. The boy chased them squeaking down the hole and set the trap carefully, embedding it partially in the earth. Then he retired back up on the level, where he lay full length on his stomach, opened the book, shifted so that the glare of the sun across the pages was blocked by the shadow of his head and shoulders, and began to read.

From time to time he looked up from the book to roll on his side and stare out across the coulee, across the barren plains pimpled with gopher mounds and bitten with fire and haired with dusty, woolly grass. Apparently as flat as a table, the land sloped imperceptibly to the south, so that nothing interfered with his view of the ghostly mountains, looking higher now as the heat increased. Between his eyes and that smoky outline sixty miles away the heat waves rose writhing like fine wavy hair. He knew that in an hour Pankhurst's farm would lift above the swelling knoll to the west. Many times he had seen that phenomenon, had seen Jason Pankhurst watering the horses or working in the yard when he knew that the whole farm was out of sight. It was heat waves that did it, his father said.

The gophers below had been thoroughly scared, and for a long time nothing happened. Idly the boy read through his poetry lesson, dreamfully conscious of the hard ground under him, feeling the gouge of a rock under his stomach without making any effort to remove it. The sun was a hot caress between his shoulder blades, and on the bare flesh where his overalls pulled above his sneakers it bit like a burning glass. Still he was comfortable, supremely relaxed and peaceful, lulled into a half trance by the heat and the steamy flower smells and the mist of yellow from the buttercup coulee below him.

And beyond the coulee was the dim profile of the Bearpaws, the Mountains of the Moon.

The boy's eyes, pulled out of focus by his tranced state, fixed on the page before him. Here was a poem he knew...but it wasn't a poem, it was a song. His mother sang it often, working at the sewing machine in winter.

It struck him as odd that a poem should also be a song, and because he found it hard to read without bringing in the tune, he lay quietly in the full glare of the sun, singing the page softly to himself. As he sang the trance grew on him again, he lost himself entirely. The bright hard dividing lines between senses blurred, and buttercups, smell of primrose, feel of hard gravel under body and elbows, sight of the ghosts of mountains haunting the southern horizon, were one intensely-felt experience focussed by the song the book had evoked.

And the song was the loveliest thing he had ever heard. He felt the words, tasted them, breathed upon them with all the ardor of his captivated senses.

The splendor falls on castle walls
And snowy summits old in story...

The current of his imagination flowed southward over the shoulder of the world to the ghostly outline of the Mountains of the Moon, haunting the heat-distorted horizon.

Oh hark, oh hear, how thin and clear,
And thinner, clearer, farther going,
Oh sweet and far, from cliff and scar...

In the enchanted forests of his mind the horns of elfland blew, and his breath was held in the cadence of their dying. The weight of the sun had been lifted from his back. The empty prairie of his home was castled and pillared with the magnificence of his imagining, and the sound of horns died thinly in the direction of the Mountains of the Moon.

From the coulee below came the sudden metallic clash of the trap, and an explosion of frantic squeals smothered almost instantly in the burrow. The boy leaped up, thrusting the book into the wide pocket of his overalls, and ran to the mound. The chain, stretched down the hole, jerked convulsively, and when he took hold of it he felt the life on the other end trying to escape. Tugging gently, he forced loose the digging claws and hauled the squirming gopher from the hole.

On the way up to the chicken house the dangling gopher with a tremendous muscular effort convulsed itself upward from the broken and imprisoned leg, and bit with a rasp of teeth on the iron. Its eyes, the boy noticed impersonally, were shiny black, like the head of a hatpin. He thought it odd that when they popped out of the head after a blow they were blue.

At the cage he lifted the cover and peered down through the screen. The weasel, scenting blood, backed against the far wall of the box, yellow body tense as a spring, teeth showing in a tiny soundless snarl.

Undoing the wire door with his left hand, the boy held the trap over the hole. Then he bore down with all his strength on the spring, releasing the gopher, which dropped on the straw and scurried into the corner opposite its enemy.

The weasel's three good feet gathered under it and it circled, very slowly, along the wall, its lips still lifted to expose the soundless snarl. The abject gopher crowded against the boards, turned once and tried to scramble up the side, fell back on its broken leg, and whirled like lightning to face its executioner again. The weasel moved carefully, circling, its cold eyes hypnotically steady.

Then the gopher screamed, a wild, agonized, despairing squeal that made the boy swallow and wet his lips. Another scream, wilder than the first, and before the sound had ended the weasel struck.

There was a fierce flurry in the straw before the killer got its hold just back of the gopher's right ear, and then there was only the weasel looking at him over the dead and quivering body. In a few minutes, the boy knew, the gopher's carcass would be as limp as an empty skin, with all its blood sucked out and a hole as big as the ends of his two thumbs where the weasel had dined.

Still he remained staring through the screen top of the cage, face rapt and body completely lost. After a few minutes he went into the sleeping porch, stretched out on the bed, opened the Sears Roebuck catalogue, and dived so deeply into its fascinating pictures and legends that his mother had to shake him to make him hear her call to lunch.

2.

Things greened beautifully that June. Rains came up out of the southeast, piling up solidly, moving toward them as slowly and surely as the sun moved, and it was fun to watch them come, the three of them standing in the doorway. When they saw the land east of them darken under the rain Bo would say, "Well, doesn't look as if it's going to miss us," and they would jump to shut windows and bring things in from yard or clothesline. Then they could stand quietly in the door and watch the good rain come, the front of it like a wall and the wind ahead of it stirring up dust, until it reached them and drenched the bare packed earth of the yard, and the ground smoked under its feet, and darkened, and ran with little streams, and they heard the swish of the rain on roof and ground and in the air.

They always watched it a good while, because rain was life in that country. When it didn't stop after twenty minutes or a half hour Bo would say with satisfaction, "She's a good soaker. That'll get down to the roots. Not so heavy it'll all run off, either." Then they would drift away from the door, because it was sure to be a good rain and there was another kind of satisfaction to be gained from little putter jobs while the rain outside made a crop for you. Elsa would carry her plants outside, the wandering Jew and the foliage plants and the geraniums stalky like miniature trees, and set them in the rain.

During that whole month there was much rain, and the boy's father whistled and hummed and sang. The boy lay in bed many mornings and heard him singing while he fried the bacon for breakfast. He always fried the bacon; he swore no woman knew how to do anything but burn it. And these days he always sang, fool songs he had learned somewhere back in the remote and unvisualizable past when he had worked on the railroad or played ball or cut timber in Wisconsin.

Oh I was a bouncing baby boy,
The neighbors did allow;
The girls they hugged and kissed me then,
Why don't they do it now?

He had a deep, big-chested voice, and he sang softly at first, rattling the pans, or whistled between his teeth with concentrated pauses between sounds, so that from the bed you knew he was slicing bacon off the slab. Then a match would scrape on the tin front of the stove, and he would be singing again,

Monkey married the baboon's sister,
Smacked his lips and then he kissed her.
Kissed so hard he raised a blister...

You lay in bed and waited, feeling fine because it had rained yesterday but today was fair, a good growing day, and you could almost feel how the wheat would be pushing up through the warm and steaming earth. And in the other room your father sang in great good humor,

She's thin as a broomstick, she carried no meat.
She never was known to put soap on her cheek.
Her hair is like rope and the color of brass—
But Oh, how I love her, this dear little lass!
Dear Evelina, Sweet Evelina...

After a minute or two he would poke his head into the porch and frown blackly, turn his head and frown even more blackly at the other bed where your mother lay stretching and smiling. "I plow deep while sluggards sleep!" he would say sepulchrally, and vanish. Then the final act, the great beating on the dishpan with a pewter spoon, and his singsong, hog-calling voice, "Come and get it, you potlickers, or I'll throw it away!"

It was fun to be alive and awake, and wait for your father to go through his whole elaborate ritual. It was fun to get up and souse in the washbasin outside the door, and throw the soapy water on the packed earth, and come in and eat, while Pa joked at you, saying he thought sure you were dead, he had been in there five times, pinching and slapping like a Pullman porter, but no sign of life. "You sure do sleep heavy," he would say. "It's a wonder you don't break down the bed. I better put some extra slats in there."

You joked back at him, and after breakfast you had a sparring match that left your ears all red and tingling, and then Pa went out to harrow to keep the earth broken up and the moisture in, and you went around your traps.

All through June there were good mornings, but the best of them all was the day Bo went down to Cree for the mail, and when he came back there was a dog sitting in the car seat beside him, a big-footed, lappy-tongued, frolicsome pup with one brown and one white eye and a heavy golden coat. The boy played with him for an hour, rolling him over and pulling his clumsy feet out from under him. Finally he lay down on the ground and the pup attacked his ears, sticking a red tongue into them, diving for openings, snuffling and snorting and romping. When the boy sat up, his mother and father were standing with their arms around one another, watching him. He went up very seriously and hugged them both in thanks for the pup.

"You'll have to teach him tricks," his father said. "A dog's no good unless you educate him. He gets the habit of minding you that way."

"How'll I do it?"

"Show you tonight." His father reached out and cuffed him on the ear and grinned. "Anything you can think of you'd like to do next week?"

The boy stared, wondering. "What?"

"What? What?" his father said, mimicking him. "Can't you think of anything you'd like to do?"

"I'd like to drive the stoneboat next time you use it."

"I don't think you know what fun is," his father said. "Don't you know what date it is?"

"Sure. It's June 27. No, June 28."

"Sure. And what comes after the week of June 28?"

The boy wondered, looking at first one, then another. They were both laughing at him. Then it hit him. "Fourth of July!" he said.

"Okay," his father said. He cuffed at him again, but missed. "Maybe we'll go into Chinook for the Fourth. Fireworks, ballgame, parade, pink lemonade sold in the shade by an old maid."

"Whee!" the boy said. He stooped and wrestled the pup, and afterward, when he lay panting on the ground, resting, and the pup gave up lapping his ears and lay down too, he thought that he had the swellest Ma and Pa there was.

That night his father showed him how to get the pup in a corner and make him sit up, bracing his back against the wall. For long, patient hours in the next few days he braced the pup there and repeated, "Sit up! Sit up! Sit up!" while he shoved back the slipping hind feet, straightened the limp spine, lifted the dropping front paws. You had to say the command a lot, his father said, and you had to reward him when he did it right. And you had to do only one trick at a time. After he learned to sit up you could teach him to jump over a stick, roll over, speak, shake hands, and play dead. The word for playing dead was "charge!" He would teach him, Bruce thought, to do that next, so they could play war. It would be better than having Chet there, because Chet never would play dead. He always argued and said he shot you first.

When he wasn't training the pup he was dreaming of Chinook and the ballgame and parade and fireworks, sky rockets, Roman candles, pinwheels. He was curious about pinwheels, because he remembered a passage in *Peck's Bad Boy and His Pa* where a pinwheel took after Pa and cornered him up on the sofa. But he was curious about all fireworks; he had never seen any except firecrackers. And the finest thing of all to imagine was the mountains, because Pa and Ma decided that since they were that close, they might as well drive up to the mountains too, and take the whole day.

His father teased him. Probably, he said, it would rain pitchforks on the Fourth. But his mother said Oh Pa, don't talk like that.

Then on the afternoon of the third they all stood in the yard and watched the southeast. Thunderheads were piling up there, livid white in front and black and ominous behind. Thunder rumbled like a wagon over a bridge.

"It'll pass over," Elsa said, and patted Bruce on the back. "It just wouldn't be fair if it rained now and spoiled our holiday."

The boy looked up and saw his father's dubious expression. "Do you think it'll blow over, Pa? Hardly any have blown over yet."

"Bound to blow over," his father said. "Law of averages. They can't all make a rain."

But the boy remembered three rains from that same quarter that same month that had gone on for twenty-four hours. He stayed in the yard watching, hoping against hope until the wall of dark was almost to the fireguard and the advance wind was stirring dust in the yard, stayed until the first large drops fell and puffed heavily in the dust, stayed until his mother pulled him inside with dark speckles all over his shirt. "Don't you worry," she said. "It'll be clear tomorrow. It has to be."

That night he stayed up until nine, waiting to see if the steady downpour would stop, hating the whisper of the rain outside and the gravelly patter on the roof. The tomcat awoke and stretched on the couch, jumped off with a sudden soft thud and went prowling into the sleeping porch, but the boy sat up. His parents were reading, not saying much. Once or twice he caught them looking at him, and always the house whispered with the steady, windy sound of the rain. This was no thunder shower. This was a drencher, and it could go on for two days, this time of year. His father had said so, with satisfaction, of other rains just like it.

When his mother finally sent him off to bed he went unwillingly, undressed slowly to see if the rain wouldn't stop before he got his shoes off, his stockings off, his overalls off. But when he was in his nightshirt it still rained steadily and insistently, and he turned into his pillow wanting to cry. A big tear came out and he felt it hanging on the side of his nose. He lay very still for fear it would fall off. He strangled the sob that jumped in his throat because that would make the drop fall, and while he was balancing the drop he fell asleep.

* * *

After the night's rain the yard was spongy and soft under the boy's bare feet. He stood at the edge of the packed dooryard in the flat thrust of sunrise looking at the ground washed clean and smooth and trackless, feeling the cool mud under his toes. Experimentally he lifted his right foot and put it down in a new place, pressed, picked it up again to look at the neat imprint of straight edge and curving instep and the five round dots of toes. The air was so fresh that he sniffed as he would have sniffed the smell of cinnamon.

Lifting his head, he saw how the prairie beyond the fireguard looked darker than in dry times, healthier with green-brown tints, smaller and more intimate somehow than it did when the heat waves crawled over scorched grass and carried the horizons backward into dim and unseeable distances. And standing in the yard above his one clean footprint, feeling his own verticality in all that spread of horizontal land, he sensed that as the prairie shrank he grew. He was immense. A little jump would crack his head on the sky; a stride would take him to any horizon.

His eyes turned into the low south sky, cloudless, almost colorless in the strong light. Just above the brown line of the horizon, faint as a watermark on pale blue paper, was the tracery of the mountains, tenuous and far-off, but today accessible for the first time. His mind had played among those ghostly summits for uncountable lost hours: today, in a few strides, they were his. And more. Under the shadow of those peaks, those Bearpaws that he and his mother always called the Mountains of the Moon, was Chinook, the band, the lemonade stands, the parade, the ballgame, the fireworks.

The pup lay watching, belly down on the damp ground. In a gleeful spasm the boy stooped to flap the dog's ears, then bent and spun in a wild wardance while the pup barked. And when his father came to the door in his undershirt, yawning, running a hand up the back of his head and through his hair, peering out from gummed eyes to see how the weather looked, the boy's voice was one deep breathing relief from yesterday's rainy fear.

"It's clear as a bell," he said.

His father yawned again, clopped his jaws, rubbed his eyes, mumbled something from a mouth furry with sleep. He stood on the step scratching himself comfortably, looking down at boy and dog.

"Going to be hot," he said slyly. "Might be too hot to drive."

"Aw, Pa!"

"Going to be a scorcher. Melt you right down to axle grease riding in that car."

The boy regarded him doubtfully, saw the lurking sly droop of his mouth. "Aw, we are too going!"

At his father's laugh he burst from his immobility like a sprinter starting, raced one complete circle around the house with the dog after him. When he flew around past his father again his voice trailed out behind him at the corner. "Gonna feed the hens," he said. His father looked after him, scratched his knee, laughed suddenly, and went back indoors.

Through chores and breakfast the boy moved with the dream of a day's rapture in his eyes, but that did not keep him from swift and agile helpfulness. He didn't even wait for commands. He scrubbed himself twice, slicked down his hair, hunted up clean clothes, wiped the mud from his shoes and put them on. While his mother packed the shoebox of lunch he stood at her elbow proffering aid. He flew to stow things in the topless old Ford. He got a rag and polished the brass radiator. Once or twice, jumping around to help, he looked up to see his parents looking at each other with the knowing, smiling expression in the eyes that said they were calling each other's attention to him.

"Just like a racehorse," his father said, and the boy felt foolish, swaggered, twisted his mouth down, said "Aw!" But in a moment he was hustling them again. They ought to get going, with fifty miles to drive. Long before they were ready he was standing beside the Ford, licked and immaculate and so excited that his feet jumped him up and down without his own volition or knowledge.

It was eight o'clock before his father came out, lifted off the front seat, poked the flat stick down into the gas tank, and pulled it out dripping. "Pretty near full," he said. "If we're going to the mountains too we better take a can along, though. Fill that two-gallon one with the spout."

The boy ran, dug the can out of the shed, filled it at the spigot of the drum that stood on a plank support to the north of the house. When he came back, his left arm stuck straight out and the can knocking against his leg, his mother was settling herself into the back seat among parcels and waterbags.

"Goodness," she said. "This is the first time I've been the first ready since I don't know when. I should think you'd have done all this last night."

"Plenty time." The father stood looking down at the boy. "All right, racehorse. You want to go to this shindig you better hop in."

The boy was up in the front seat like a squirrel. His father walked around to the front of the car. "Okay," he said. "Look sharp, now. When she kicks over, switch her to magneto and pull the spark down."

The boy said nothing. He looked upon the car with respect and a little awe. They didn't use it much, and starting it was a ritual like a firedrill. The father unscrewed the four-eared brass plug, looked down into the radiator, screwed the cap back on, and bent to take hold of the crank. "Watch it, now," he said.

The boy felt the gentle heave of the springs, up and down, as his father wound the crank. He heard the gentle hiss in the bowels of the engine as the choke wire was pulled out, and his nose filled with the strong, volatile odor of gasoline. Over the slope of the radiator his father's brown strained face looked up. "Is she turned on all right?"

"Yup. She's on battery."

"Must have flooded her. Have to let her rest a minute."

They waited, and then after a few minutes the wavelike heaving of the springs again, the rise and fall of the blue shirt and bent head over the radiator, the sighing swish of the choke, a stronger smell of gasoline. The motor had not even coughed.

The two voices came simultaneously from the car. "What's the matter with it?"

His brow puckered in an intent scowl, Bo stood back blowing mighty breaths. "Son of a gun," he said. Coming round, he pulled at the switch, adjusted the spark and gas levers. A fine mist of sweat made his face shine like dark oiled leather.

"There isn't anything really wrong, is there?" Elsa said, and her voice wavered uncertainly on the edge of fear.

"I don't see how there could be," Bo said. "She's always started right off, and she was running all right when I drove her in here."

The boy looked at his mother sitting erect and stiff among the things on the seat. She was all dressed up, a flowered dress, a hat with hard green varnished grapes on it pinned to her red hair. For a moment she sat, stiff and nervous. "What will you have to do?" she said.

"I don't know. Look at the motor."

"Well, I guess I'll get out of the sun while you do it," she said, and fumbled her way out of the clutter.

The boy felt her exodus like a surrender, a betrayal. If they didn't hurry up they'd miss the parade. In one motion he bounced out of the car. "Gee whiz!" he said. "Let's do something. We got to get started."

"Keep your shirt on," his father grunted. Lifting the hood, he bent his head inside. His hand went out to test wires, wiggle spark-plug connections, make tentative pulls at the choke. The weakly-hinged hood slipped and came down across his wrist, and he swore. "Get me the pliers," he said.

For ten minutes he probed and monkeyed. "Might be the plugs," he said at last. "She doesn't seem to be getting any fire through her."

Elsa, sitting on a box in the shade, smoothed her flowered dress nervously. "Will it take long?"

"Half hour."

"Any day but this!" she said. "I don't see why you didn't make sure last night."

Bo breathed through his nose and bent into the engine again. "It was raining last night," he said.

One by one the plugs came out, were squinted at, scraped, the gap tested with a thin dime. The boy stood on one foot, then the other, time pouring like a flood of uncatchable silver dollars through his hands. He kept looking at the sun, estimating how much time there was left. If they got started right away they might still make it for the parade, but it would be close. Maybe they'd drive right up the street while the parade was on, and be part of it...

"Is she ready?" he said.

"Pretty quick."

He wandered over by his mother, and she reached out to put an arm around him. "Well, anyway we can get there for the band and the ballgame and the fireworks," he said. "If she doesn't start till noon we can make it for those."

She said, "Pa'll get it going in a minute. We won't miss anything, hardly."

"You ever seen skyrockets, Ma?"

"Once."

"Are they fun?"

"Wonderful," she said. "Just like a million stars all colors all exploding at once."

His feet took him back to his father, who straightened up with a belligerent grunt. "Now!" he said. "If the sucker doesn't start now..."

And once more the heaving of the springs, the groaning of the turning engine, the hiss of the choke. He tried short, sharp half-turns, as if to catch the motor off guard. Then he went back to the stubborn, laboring spin. The back of his shirt was stained darkly, the curving dikes of muscles along the spine's hollow showing cleanly where the cloth stuck. Over and over, heaving, stubborn at first, then furious, till he staggered back panting.

"God damn!" he said. "What you suppose is the matter with the thing?"

"She didn't even cough once," the boy said, and staring up at his father's face full of angry bafflement he felt the cold fear touch him. What if it wouldn't start at all? What if, all ready to go, they had to unload the Ford and not even get out of the yard? His mother came over and they stood close together looking at the car and avoiding each other's eyes.

"Maybe something got wet last night," she said.

"Well, it's had plenty of time to dry out," Bo said.

"Isn't there something else you can try?"

"We can jack up the hind wheel, I guess. But there's no damn reason we should have to."

"Well, if you have to, you'll have to," she said briskly. "After planning it for a week we can't just get stuck like this. Can we, son?"

Bruce's answer was mechanical, his eyes steady on his father. "Sure not," he said.

His father opened his mouth to say something, looked hard at the boy, and shut his lips again. Without a word he pulled out the seat and got the jack.

The sun climbed steadily while they jacked up one hind wheel and blocked the car carefully so it wouldn't run over anybody if it started. The boy let off the brake and put it in high, and when they were ready he sat in the seat so full of hope and fear that his whole body was one tight concentration. His father stooped, his cheek pressed against the radiator as a milker's cheek touches the flank of a cow. His shoulder dropped, jerked up. Nothing. Another jerk. Nothing. Then he was rolling in a furious spasm of energy, the wet dark back of his shirt rising and falling. Inside the motor there was only the futile swish of the choke and the half-sound, half-feel of cavernous motion as the crankshaft turned over. The Ford bounced on its spring as if its front wheels were coming off the ground on every upstroke. Then it stopped, and the father was hanging on the radiator, breathless, dripping wet, swearing: "Son of a dirty, lousy, stinking, corrupted...!"

The boy stared from his father's angry wet face to his mother's, pinched with worry. The pup lay down in the shade and put its head on its paws. "Gee whiz!" the boy said. "Gee whiz!" He looked at the sun, and the morning was half gone.

Jerking with anger, his father threw the crank halfway across the yard and took a step or two toward the house. "The hell with the damn thing!" he said.

"Bo, you can't!"

He stopped, glared at her, took an oblique look at Bruce, bared his teeth in an irresolute, silent swearword. "But God, if it won't go!"

"Maybe if you hitched the horses to it," she said.

His laugh was short and choppy. "That'd be fine!" he said. "Why don't we just hitch the team to this damned old boat and pull it into Chinook?"

"But we've got to get it started. Why wouldn't it be all right to let the team pull it around? You push it on a hill sometimes and it starts."

He looked at the boy again, jerked his eyes away exasperatedly, as though he held his son somehow accountable. The boy stared, mournful, defeated, ready to cry, and his father's head swung back unwillingly. Then abruptly he winked, mopped his head and neck, and grinned. "Think you want to go, uh?"

The boy nodded. "All right," his father said crisply. "Fly up in the pasture and get the team. Hustle!"

On the high lope the boy was off up the coulee bank. Under the lip of the swale, a quarter of a mile west, the bay backs of the horses and the black dot of the cold showed. Usually he ran circumspectly across that pasture, because of the cactus, but now he flew. With shoes it was all right, and even without shoes he would have run. Across burnouts, over stretches so undermined with gopher holes that sometimes he broke through to the ankle, skimming over patches of cactus, soaring over a badger hole, plunging into the coulee and up the other side, he ran as if bears were after him. The black colt, spotting him, lifted his tail and took off in a spectacular stiff-legged sprint, but the bays merely lifted their heads and watched. He slowed, came up walking, laid a hand on the mare's neck and untied the looped halter rope. She stood for him while he scrambled and kicked himself up, and then they were off, the mare in an easy lope, the gelding trotting after, the colt stopping his wild showoff career and wobbling hastily and ignominiously after his departing mother.

They pulled up before the Ford, and the boy slid off to throw the halter rope to his father. "Shall I get the harness?" he said, and before anyone could answer he was off running, to come back dragging one heavy harness with the tugs trailing. He dropped it, turned to run again, his breath laboring in his lungs. "I'll get the other'n," he said.

With a short, almost incredulous laugh Bo looked once at Elsa and threw the harness over the mare. When the second one came he laid it on the gelding, pushed against the heavy shoulder to get the horse into place. The gelding resisted, pranced a little, got a curse and a crack across the nose, jerked back and trembled and lifted his feet nervously, and set one shod hoof on his owner's instep. Bo, unstrung by the heat and the hurry and the labor and the exasperation of a morning when nothing went right, kicked the gelding in the belly.

"Get in there, you damned big blundering ox! Back, back up. Whoa now, whoa!"

With a heavy rope for a towline and the disengaged trees of the wagon for a rig he hitched the now-skittish team to the car. Without a word he stooped and lifted the boy to the mare's back. "All right," he said, and his face relaxed in a quick grin. "This is where we start her. Ride them around in a circle, not too fast."

Then he climbed into the Ford, turned the switch to magneto, fussed with the levers. "Let 'er go!" he said.

The boy kicked the mare ahead, twisting as he rode to watch the Ford heave forward off the jack as a tired, heavy man heaves to his feet, and begin rolling after him over the uneven ground, jerking and kicking and growling when his father put it in gear. The horses settled as the added weight came on the line, flattened into their collars, swung in a circle, bumped each other, skittered. The mare reared, and the boy shut his eyes and clung. When he came down, her leg was entangled in the tug and his father was climbing cursing out of the car to straighten her out. His father was mad again and yelled at him. "Keep 'em apart! There isn't any tongue. You got to keep Dick over on his own side."

Now again the start, the flattening into the collars, the snapping tight of the tugs. This time it went smoothly, the Ford galloped after the team in lumbering, plunging jerks. The mare's eyes rolled white, and she broke into a trot, pulling the gelding after her. Desperately the boy clung to the knotted and shortened reins, his ears alert for the grumble of the Ford starting behind him. The pup ran beside the team yapping, crazy with excitement.

They made three complete circles of the back yard between house and chicken coop before the boy looked back again. "Won't she start?" he yelled. He saw his father rigid behind the wheel, heard his ripping burst of swearwords, saw him bend and glare down into the mysterious inwards of the engine through the pulled-up floorboards. Guiding the car with one hand, he fumbled down below, one glaring eye just visible over the cowl.

"Shall I stop?" the boy shouted. Excitement and near-despair made his voice a tearful scream. But his father's wild arm waved him on. "Go on, go on! Gallop 'em! Pull the guts out of this thing!"

And the galloping—the furious, mud-flinging, rolling-eyed galloping around the circle already rutted like a road, the Ford, now in savagely-held low, growling and surging and plowing behind; the mad yapping of the dog, the erratic scared bursts of runaway from the colt, the boy's mother in sight briefly for a quarter of each circle, her hands to her mouth and her eyes sick, and behind him in the Ford his father in a strangling rage, yelling him on, his lips back over his teeth and his face purple.

Until finally they stopped, the horses blowing, the boy white and tearful and still, the father dangerous with unexpended wrath. The boy slipped off, his lip bitten between his teeth, not crying now but ready to at any moment, the corners of his eyes prickling with it, and his teeth locked on his misery. His father climbed over the side of the Ford and stood looking as if he wanted to tear it apart with his bare hands.

Shoulders sagging, tears trembling to fall, jaw aching with the need to cry, the boy started toward his mother. As he came near his father he looked up, their eyes met, and he saw his father's blank with impotent rage. Dull hopelessness swallowed him. Not any of it, his mind said. Not even any of it. No parade, no ballgame, no band, no fireworks. No lemonade or ice cream or paper horns or firecrackers. No close sight of the mountains that throughout four summers had called like a legend from his horizons. No trip, no adventure, none of it, nothing.

Everything he felt was in that one still look. In spite of him his lip trembled, and he choked on a sob, his eyes on his father's face, on the brows pulling down and the eyes narrowing.

"Well, don't blubber!" his father shouted at him. "Don't stand there looking at me as if I was to blame for your missed picnic!"

"I can't—help it," the boy said, and with terror he felt the grief swelling up, overwhelming him, driving his voice out of him in a wail. Through the blur of his crying he saw the convulsive tightening of his father's face, and then all the fury of a maddening morning concentrated itself in a swift backhand blow that knocked the boy staggering.

He bawled aloud, from pain, from surprise, from outrage, from pure desolation, and ran to bury his face in his mother's lap. From that muffled sanctuary he heard her angry voice. "No," she said. "Go on away somewhere till he gets over it."

She rocked him against her, but the voice she had for his father was bitter. "As if he wasn't hurt enough already!" she said.

He heard the heavy quick footsteps going away, and for a long time he lay crying into the voile flowers. When he had cried himself out, and had listened apathetically to his mother's soothing promises that they would go in the first chance they got, go to the mountains, have a picnic under some waterfall, maybe be able to find a ballgame going on in town, some Saturday—when he had listened and become quiet, wanting to believe it but not believing it at all, he went inside to take his good clothes and his shoes off and put on his old overalls again.

It was almost noon when he came out to stand in the front yard looking southward toward the impossible land where the Mountains of the Moon lifted above the plains, and where, in the town below the peaks, crowds would now be eating picnic lunches, drinking pop, getting ready to go out to the ball ground and watch heroes in real uniforms play ball. The band would be braying now from a bunting-wrapped stand, kids would be playing in a cool grove, tossing firecrackers...

In the still heat his eyes searched the horizon for the telltale watermark. There was nothing but waves of heat crawling and lifting like invisible flames; the horizon was a blurred and writhing flatness where earth and sky met in an indistinct band of haze. This morning a stride would have taken him there; now it was gone.

Looking down, he saw at his feet the clean footprint he had made in the early morning. Aimlessly he put his right foot down and pressed. The mud was drying, but in a low place he found a spot that would still take an imprint. Very carefully, as if he performed some ritual for his life, he went around, stepping and leaning, stepping and leaning, until he had a circle six feet in diameter of delicately exact footprints, straight edge and curving instep and the five round dots of toes.

The Women on the Wall

The corner window of the study overlooked a lawn, and beyond that a sunken lane between high pines, and beyond the lane a point of land with the old beach club buildings at one end and a stone wall around its tip. Beyond the point, through the cypresses and eucalyptuses, Mr. Palmer could see the Pacific, misty blue, belted between shore and horizon with a band of brown kelp.

Writing every morning in his study, making over his old notebooks into a coherent account of his years on the Galápagos, Mr. Palmer could glance up from his careful longhand and catch occasional glimpses, as a traveler might glance out of the window of a moving train. And in spite of the rather special atmosphere of the point, caused by the fact that until the past year it had been a club, there was something homey and neighborly and pleasant about the place that Mr. Palmer liked. There were children, for one thing, and dogs drifting up and down, and the occasional skirr of an automobile starting in the quiet, the diminishing sound of tires on asphalt, the distant racket of a boy being a machine-gun with his mouth.

Mr. Palmer had been away from the States a long time; he found the noises on the point familiar and nostalgic and reassuring in this time of war, and felt as if he had come home. Though California differed considerably from his old home in Ohio, he fell naturally and gratefully into its procession of morning and afternoon, its neighborhood routines, the pleasant breathing of its tides. When anything outside broke in upon his writing, it was generally a commonplace and familiar thing; Mr. Palmer looked up and took pleasure in the interruption.

One thing he could be sure of seeing, every morning but Sunday. The section was outside the city limits, and mail was delivered to a battery of mailboxes where the sunken lane joined the street. The mail arrived at about eleven; about ten-thirty the women from the beach club apartments began to gather on the stone wall. Below the wall was the beach, where the tides leaned in all the way from Iwo and Okinawa. Above it was the row of boxes where as regularly as the tide the mail carrier came in a gray car and deposited postmarked flotsam from half a world away.

Sometimes Mr. Palmer used to pause in his writing and speculate on what these women thought of when they looked out across the gumdrop-blue water and the brown kelp and remembered that across this uninterrupted ocean their husbands fought and perhaps bled and possibly died, that in those far islands it was already tomorrow, that the green water breaking against the white foot of the beach might hold in suspension minute quantities of the blood shed into it thousands of miles away, that the Japan Current, swinging in a great circle up under the Aleutians and back down the American coast, might as easily bear the mingled blood or the floating relics of a loved one lost as it could bear the glass balls of Japanese net-floats that it sometimes washed ashore.

Watching the women, with their dogs and children, waiting patiently on the stone wall for that most urgent of all the gods, that Mercury in the gray uniform, Mr. Palmer thought a good deal about Penelope on the rocky isle of Ithaca above the wine-dark sea. He got a little sentimental about these women. Sometimes he was almost frightened by the air of patient, withdrawn seriousness they wore as they waited, and the unsmiling alacrity with which they rose and crowded around the mailman when he came. And when the mail was late, and one or two of them sat out on the wall until eleven-thirty, twelve, sometimes twelve-thirty, Mr. Palmer could hardly bear it at all.

Waiting, Mr. Palmer reflected, must cause a person to remove to a separate and private world. Like sleep or insanity, waiting must have the faculty of making the real unreal and remote. It seemed to Mr. Palmer pathetic and somehow thrilling that these women should have followed their men to the very brink of the West, and should remain here now with their eyes still westward, patiently and faithfully suspending their own normal lives until the return of their husbands. Without knowing any of the women, Mr. Palmer respected and admired them. They did not invite his pity. Penelope was as competent for her waiting as Ulysses was for his wars and wiles.

* * *

MR. PALMER HAD BEEN WORKING in his new house hardly a week before he found himself putting on his jacket about eleven and going out to join the women.

He knew them all by sight just from looking out the window. The red-haired woman with the little boy was sitting on the wall nearest him. Next was the thin girl who always wore a bathing suit and went barefooted. Next was the dark-haired one, five or six months pregnant. And next to her was the florid, quick, wrenlike woman with the little girl of about five. Their faces all turned as Mr. Palmer came up.

"Good morning," he said.

The red-haired woman's plain, serious, freckled face acknowledged him, and she murmured good morning. The girl in the bathing suit had turned to look off over the ocean, and Mr. Palmer felt that she had not made any reply. The pregnant girl and the woman with the little girl both nodded.

The old man put his hands on his knees, rounded his mouth and eyes, and bent to look at the little boy hanging to the red-haired woman's hand. "Well!" he said. "Hi, young fella!"

The child stared at him, crowding against his mother's legs. The mother said nothing, and rather than push first acquaintance too far, Mr. Palmer walked on along the wall. As he glanced at the thin girl, he met her eyes, so full of cold hostility that for a moment he was shocked. He had intended to sit down in the middle of the wall, but her look sent him on further, to sit between the pregnant girl and the wrenlike woman.

"These beautiful mornings!" Mr. Palmer said, sitting down with a sigh.

The wrenlike woman nodded; the pregnant one regarded him with quiet ox-eyes.

"This is quite a ritual, waiting for the mail," Mr. Palmer said. He pointed to the gable of his house across the lane. "I see you from my window over there, congregating on the wall here every morning."

The wrenlike woman looked at him rather oddly, then leaped to prevent her daughter from putting out the eyes of the long-suffering setter she was mauling. The pregnant girl smiled a slow, soft smile. Over her shoulder Mr. Palmer saw the thin girl hitch herself up and sit on her hands. The expression on her face said that she knew very well why Mr. Palmer had come down and butted in, and why he watched from his window.

"The sun's so warm out here," the pregnant girl said. "It's a way of killing part of the morning, sitting out here."

"A very good way," Mr. Palmer said. He smoothed the creases in his trousers, finding speech a little difficult. From the shelter of his mother's legs the two-year-old boy down the wall stared at him solemnly. Then the wrenlike woman hopped off the wall and dusted her skirt.

"Here he is!" she said.

They all started across the mouth of the lane, and for some reason, as they waited for the mailman to sort and deliver, Mr. Palmer felt that his first introduction hadn't taken him very far. In a way, as he thought it over, he respected the women for that, too. They were living without their husbands, and had to be careful. After all, Penelope had many suitors. But he could not quite get over wanting to spank the thin girl on her almost-exposed backside, and he couldn't quite shake the sensation of having wandered by mistake into the ladies' rest room.

After that, without feeling that he knew them at all, he respected them and respected their right to privacy. Waiting, after all, put you in an exclusive club. No outsider had any more right on that wall than he had in the company of a bomber crew. But Mr. Palmer felt that he could at least watch from his window, and at the mailboxes he could, almost by osmosis, pick up a little more information.

The red-haired woman's name was Kendall. Her husband was an Army captain, a doctor. The thin girl, Mrs. Fisher, got regular letters bearing a Marine Corps return. The husband of Mrs. Corson, the wrenlike woman, commanded a flotilla of minesweepers in the western Pacific. Of the pregnant girl, Mrs. Vaughn, Mr. Palmer learned little. She got few letters and none with any postmarks that told anything.

From his study window Mr. Palmer went on observing them benignly and making additions to his notes on the profession of waiting. Though the women differed sharply one from another, they seemed to Mr. Palmer to have one thing in common: they were all quiet, peaceful, faithful to the times and seasons of their vigil, almost like convalescents in a hospital. They made no protests or outcries; they merely lived at a reduced tempo, as if pulse rate and respiration rate and metabolic rate and blood pressure were all turned down. Mr. Palmer had a notion how it might be. Sometimes when he awoke very quietly in the night he could feel how quietly and slowly and regularly his heart was pumping, how slow and regular his breathing was, how he lay there mute and cool and inert with everything turned down to idling speed, his old body taking care of itself. And when he woke that way he had a curious feeling that he was waiting for something.

* * *

EVERY MORNING AT TEN-THIRTY, as regular as sun and tide, Mrs. Kendall came out of the beach club apartments and walked across the point, leading her little boy by the hand. She had the child turned down, too, apparently. He never, to Mr. Palmer's knowledge, ran or yelled or cried or made a fuss, but walked quietly beside his mother, and sat with her on the big stump until five minutes to eleven, and then walked with her across to the end of the stone wall. About that time the other women began to gather, until all four of them were there in a quiet, uncommunicative row.

Through the whole spring the tides leaned inward with the same slow inevitability, the gray car came around and stopped by the battery of mailboxes, the women gathered on the wall as crows gather to a rookery at dusk.

Only once in all that drowsy spring was there any breaking of the pattern. That was one Monday after Mr. Palmer had been away for the weekend. When he strolled out at mailtime he found the women not sitting on the wall, but standing in a nervous conversational group. They opened to let him in, for once accepting him silently among them, and he found that the thin girl had moved out suddenly the day before: the Saturday mail had brought word that her husband had gone down in flames over the Marianas.

The news depressed Mr. Palmer in curious ways. It depressed him to see the women shaken from their phlegmatic routine, because the moment they were so shaken they revealed the raw fear under their quiet. And it depressed him that the thin girl's husband had been killed. That tragedy should come to a woman he personally felt to be a snob, a fool, a vain and inconsequent chit, seemed to him sad and incongruous and even exasperating. As long as she was one of the company of Penelopes, Mr. Palmer had refused to dislike her. The moment she made demands upon his pity he disliked her very much.

After that sudden blow, as if a hawk had struck among the quiet birds on the wall, Mr. Palmer found it less pleasant to watch the slow, heavy-bodied walking of Mrs. Kendall, her child always tight by the hand, from apartment to stump to wall. Unless spoken to, she never spoke. She wore gingham dresses that were utterly out of place in the white sun above the white beach. She was plain, unattractive, patient, the most remote, the most tuned-down, the quietest and saddest and most patient and most exasperating of the Penelopes. She too began to make wry demands on Mr. Palmer's pity, and he found himself almost disliking her. He was guilty of a little prayer that Mrs. Kendall's husband would be spared, so that his pity would not have to go any farther than it did.

* * *

THEN ONE MORNING Mr. Palmer became aware of another kind of interruption on the point. Somebody there had apparently bought a new dog. Whoever had acquired it must have fed it, though Mr. Palmer never saw anyone do so, and must have exercised it, though he never saw that either. All he saw was that the dog, a half-grown cocker, was tied to the end of a rose trellis in the clubhouse yard. And all he heard, for two solid days, was the uproar the dog made.

It did not like being tied up. It barked, and after a while its voice would break into a kind of hysterical howling mixed with shuddering diminuendo groans. Nobody ever came and told it to be still, or took care of it, or let it loose. It stayed there and yanked on its rope and chewed at the trellis post and barked and howled and groaned until Mr. Palmer's teeth were on edge and he was tempted to call the Humane Society.

Actually he didn't, because on the third morning the noise had stopped, and as he came into his study to begin working he saw that the dog was gone. Mrs. Corson was sitting in a lawn chair under one of the cypresses, and her daughter was digging in the sandpile. There was no sign either of Mrs. Kendall or Mrs. Vaughn. The owner of the house was raking leaves on the lawn above the seawall.

Mr. Palmer looked at his watch. It was nine-thirty. On an impulse he slipped on a jacket and went down and out across the lawn and down across the lane and up the other side past the trellis. Where the dog had lain the ground was strewn with chewed green splinters.

Mrs. Corson looked up from her chair. Her cheeks were painted with a hatchwork of tiny ruddy veins, and her eyes looked as if she hadn't slept. They had a stary blankness like blind eyes, and Mr. Palmer noticed that the pupils were dilated, even in the bright light. She took a towel and a pack of cigarettes and a bar of coco-butter off the chair next to her.

"Good morning," she said in her husky voice. "Sit down."

"Thank you," Mr. Palmer said. He let himself down into the steeply slanting wooden chair and adjusted the knees of his slacks. "It is a good morning," he said slyly. "So quiet."

Mrs. Corson's thin neck jerked upward and backward in a curious gesture. Her throaty laughter was loud and unrestrained, and the eyes she turned on Mr. Palmer were red with mirth.

"That damned dog," she said. "Wasn't that something?"

"I thought I'd go crazy," Mr. Palmer said. "Whose dog was it, anyway?"

Mrs. Corson's rather withered, red-nailed hand, with a big diamond and a wedding ring on the fourth finger, reached down and picked up the cigarettes. The hand trembled as it held the pack out.

"No, thank you," he said.

Mrs. Corson took one. "It was Mrs. Kendall's dog," she said. "She took it back."

"Thank God!" said Mr. Palmer.

Her hands nervous with the matchbox in her lap, Mrs. Corson sat and smoked. Mr. Palmer saw that her lips, under the lipstick, were chapped, and that there was a dried, almost leathery look to her tanned and freckled skin.

He slid deeper into the chair and looked out over the water, calm as a lake, the long light swells breaking below him with a quiet, lulling swish. Up the coast heavier surf was breaking farther out. Its noise came like a pulsating tremble on the air, hardly a sound at all. Everything tuned down, Mr. Palmer was thinking. Even the lowest frequency of waves on the beach. Even the ocean waited.

"I should think you'd bless your stars, having a place like this to wait in," he said.

One of Mrs. Corson's eyebrows bent. She shot him a sideward look.

"Think of the women who are waiting in boardinghouse rooms," Mr. Palmer said, a little irritated at her manner. "Think of the ones who are working and leaving their children in nurseries."

"Oh, sure," Mrs. Corson said. "It's fine for Anne, with the beach and yard."

Mr. Palmer leaned on the arm of the chair and looked at her quizzically. He wished any of these women would ever put away their reticence and talk about their waiting, because that was where their life lay, that was where they had authority. "How long has your husband been gone?" he asked.

"Little over two years."

"That's a long time," Mr. Palmer said, thinking of Penelope and her wait. Ten years while the war went on at Troy, ten more years while Ulysses wandered through every peril in the Mediterranean, past Scylla and Charybdis and Circe and the Cyclops and the iron terrors of Hades and the soft temptations of Nausicaa. But that was poetry. Twenty years was too much. Two, in all conscience, was enough.

"I shouldn't kick," the woman said. "Mrs. Kendall's husband has been gone for over three."

"I've noticed her," Mr. Palmer said. "She seems rather sad and repressed."

For a moment Mrs. Corson's eyes, slightly bloodshot, the pupils dilated darkly, were fixed questioningly on Mr. Palmer's. Then the woman shook herself almost as a dog does. "I guess," she said. She rose with a nervous snap and glanced at her watch. From the sandpile the little girl called, "Is it time, Mommy?"

"I guess so," Mrs. Corson said. She laid the back of her hand across her eyes and made a face.

"I'll be getting along," Mr. Palmer said.

"I was just taking Anne down for her pony ride. Why don't you ride down with us?"

"Well..."

"Come on," Mrs. Corson said. "We'll be back in less than an hour."

The child ran ahead of them and opened the car doors, down in the widened part of the lane. As Mr. Palmer helped Mrs. Corson in she turned her face a little, and he smelled the stale alcohol on her breath. Obviously Mrs. Corson had been drinking the night before, and obviously she was a little hung over.

But my Lord, why not? he said to himself. Two years of waiting, nothing to do but sit and watch and do nothing and be patient. He didn't like Mrs. Corson any less for occasional drinking. She was higher-strung than either Mrs. Vaughn or Mrs. Kendall. You could almost lift up the cover board and pluck her nerves like the strings of a piano. Even so, she played the game well. He liked her.

At the pony track Anne raced down the fenced runway at a pink fluttering gallop, and Mr. Palmer and Mrs. Corson, following more slowly, found her debating between a black and a pinto pony.

"Okay," the man in charge said. "Which'll it be today, young lady?"

"I don't know," the girl said. Her forehead wrinkled. "Mommy, which do you think?"

"I don't care, hon," her mother said. "Either one is nice."

Pretty, her blonde braids hanging in front and framing her odd pre-Raphaelite face, Anne stood indecisive. She turned her eyes up to Mr. Palmer speculatively. "The black one's nice," she said, "but so's the..."

"Oh, Anne," her mother said. "For heaven's sake make up your mind."

"Well...the black one, then," Anne said. She reached out a hand and touched the pony's nose, pulling her fingers back sharply and looking up at her mother with a smile that Mr. Palmer found himself almost yearning over.

"You're a nitwit," her mother said. "Hop on, so we can get back for the mailman."

The attendant swung her up, but with one leg over the saddle Anne kicked and screamed to get down. "I've changed my mind," she said. "Not this one, the pinto one."

The attendant put her up on the pinto and Mrs. Corson, her chapped lips trembling, said, "Another outburst like that and you won't get on any, you little...!"

The pony started, led by the attendant who rocked on one thick-soled shoe. For a moment Mrs. Corson and Mr. Palmer stood in the sun under the sign that said "Pony Rides, 10 Cents, 12 for $1.00." They were, Mr. Palmer noticed, in the Mexican part of town. Small houses, some of them almost shacks, with geraniums climbing all over them, strung out along the street. Down on the corner beyond the car was a tavern with a dusty tin sign. Mrs. Corson unsnapped her purse and fished out a wadded bill and held it vaguely in her hand, looking off up the street past the track and the pinto pony and the pink little huddle on its back and the attendant rocking along ahead on his one thick shoe.

"I wonder," she said. "Would you do me a favor?"

"Anything."

"Would you stay here five minutes while I go to the store? Just keep an eye on her?"

"Of course," he said. "I'd be glad to go to the store for you, if you'd like."

"No," she said. "No, I'd better get it." She put the crumpled bill into his hand. "Let her have all the rides she wants. I'll be back in a few minutes."

Mr. Palmer settled himself on a chair against the stable wall and waited. When Anne and the attendant got back he waved the bill at them. "Want another ride?"

"Yes!" Anne said. Her hands were clenched tightly in the pony's mane, and her eyes danced and her mouth was a little open. The attendant turned and started down the track again. "Run!" Anne cried to him. "Make him run!"

The crippled hostler broke into a clumsy hop-skip-and-jump for a few yards, pulling the pony into a trot. The girl screamed with delight. Mr. Palmer yawned, tapped his mouth, smiled a little as he smelled the powder-and-perfume smell on the dollar bill, yawned again. Say what you would, it was decent of the woman to come out with a hangover and take her child to the pony track. She must feel pretty rocky, if her eyes were any criterion.

He waited for some time. Anne finished a second ride, took a third, finished that, and had a fourth. The attendant was sweating a little. From the fence along the sidewalk two Negro children and a handful of little Mexicans watched. "How about it?" Mr. Palmer said. "Want another?"

She nodded, shaken with giggles and sudden shyness when she looked around and found her mother gone.

"Sure you're not getting sore?" Mr. Palmer patted his haunch suggestively.

She shook her head.

"Okay," the hostler said. "Here we go again, then."

At the end of the fifth ride Anne let herself be lifted off. The hostler went inside and sat down, the pony joined its companion at the rail, cocked its hip and tipped its right hoof and closed its eyes. Anne climbed up into Mr. Palmer's lap.

"Where's Mommy?"

"She went to buy something."

"Darn her," Anne said. "She does that all the time. She better hurry up, it's getting mailtime."

"Don't you like to miss the mail?"

"Sometimes there's packages and things from Daddy," Anne said. "I got a grass skirt once."

Mr. Palmer rounded his mouth and eyes. "You must like your daddy."

"I do. Mommy doesn't, though."

"What?"

"Mommy gets mad," Anne said. "She thinks Daddy could have had shore duty a long time ago, he's had so much combat, but she says he likes the Navy better than home. He's a commander."

"Yes, I know," Mr. Palmer said. He looked up the street, beginning to be fretful. The fact that the woman spent her whole life waiting shouldn't make her quite so callous to how long she kept other people waiting. "We *are* going to miss the mailman if your mommy doesn't hurry," he said.

Anne jumped off his lap and puckered her lips like her mother. "And today's a package!"

Mr. Palmer raised his eyebrows. "How do you know?"

"The fortune teller told Mommy."

"I see," the old man said. "Does your mother go to fortune tellers often?"

"Every Saturday," Anne said. "I went with her once. You know what she said? And it came true, too."

Mr. Palmer saw the girl's mother coming down the sidewalk, and stood up. "Here comes Mommy," he said. "We'd better meet her at the car."

"She said we'd get good news, and right away Daddy was promoted," Anne said. "And she said we'd get a package, and that week we got *three*!"

Mrs. Corson was out of breath. In the bright sun her eyes burned with a curious sightless brilliance. The smell of alcohol on her was fresher and stronger.

"I'm sorry," she said as she got in. "I met a friend, and it was so hot we stopped for a beer."

On the open highway, going back home, she stepped down hard on the throttle, and her fingers kept clasping and unclasping the wheel. Her body seemed possessed of electric energy. She radiated something, she gave off sparks. Her eyes, with the immense dark pupils and suffused whites, were almost scary.

When they pulled up and parked in front of Mr. Palmer's gate, opposite the mailboxes, the little red flags on some of the boxes were still up. On the stone wall sat Mrs. Kendall, her son, Tommy, and the pregnant girl, Mrs. Vaughn. "Late again," Mrs. Corson said. "Damn that man."

"Can I play, Mommy?" Anne said.

"Okay." As the child climbed out, the mother said, "Don't get into any fixes with Tommy. Remember what I told you."

"I will," Anne said. Her setter came up and she stooped to pull its ears.

Her mother's face went pinched and mean. "And stop abusing that dog!" she said.

Mr. Palmer hesitated. He was beginning to feel uncomfortable, and he thought of the pages he might have filled that morning, and the hour that still remained before noon. But Mrs. Corson was leaning back with the back of her hand across her eyes. Through the windshield Mr. Palmer could see the two women and the child on the wall, like a multiple Patience on a monument. When he looked back at Mrs. Corson he saw that she too was watching them between her fingers. Quite suddenly she began to laugh.

She laughed for a good minute, not loudly but with curious violence, her whole body shaking. She dabbed her eyes and caught her breath and shook her head and tried to speak. Mr. Palmer attended uneasily, wanting to be gone.

"Lord," Mrs. Corson said finally. "Look at 'em. Vultures on a limb. Me too. Three mama vultures and one baby vulture."

"You're a little hard on yourself," Mr. Palmer said, smiling. "And Anne, I'd hardly call her a vulture."

"I didn't include her," Mrs. Corson said. She turned her hot red eyes on him. "She's got sense enough to run and play, and I hope I've got sense enough to let her."

"Well, but little Tommy..."

"Hasn't had his hand out of mamma's since they came here," Mrs. Corson said. "Did you ever see him play with anybody?"

Mr. Palmer confessed that he hadn't, now that he thought of it.

"Because if you ever do," Mrs. Corson said, "call out all the preachers. It'll be Christ come the second time. Honest to God, sometimes that woman..."

Bending forward, Mr. Palmer could see Mrs. Kendall smoothing the blue sweater around her son's waist. "I've wondered about her," he said, and stopped. Mrs. Corson had started to laugh again.

When she had finished her spasm of tight, violent mirth, she said, "It isn't her child, you know."

"No?" he said, surprised. "She takes such care of it."

"You're not kidding," Mrs. Corson said. "She won't let him play with Anne. Anne's too dirty. She digs in the ground and stuff. Seven months we've lived in the same house, and those kids haven't played together once. Can you imagine that?"

"No," Mr. Palmer confessed. "I can't."

"She adopted it when it was six months old," Mrs. Corson said. "She tells us all it's a love-child." Her laugh began again, a continuous, hiccoughy chuckle. "Never lets go its hand," she said. "Won't let him play with anybody. Wipes him off like an heirloom. And brags around he's a love-child. My God!"

With her thin, freckled arm along the door and her lips puckered, she fell silent. "Love-child!" she said at last. "Did you ever look at her flat face? It's the last place love would ever settle on."

"Perhaps that explains," Mr. Palmer said uncomfortably. "She's childless, she's unattractive. She pours all that frustrated affection out on this child."

Mrs. Corson twisted to look almost incredulously into his face. "Of course," she said. Her alcoholic breath puffed at him. "Of course. But why toot it up as a love-child?" she said harshly. "What does she think my child is, for God's sake? How does she think babies are made?"

"Well, but there's that old superstition," Mr. Palmer said. He moved his hand sideward. "Children born of passion, you know— they're supposed to be more beautiful..."

"And doesn't that tell you anything about her?" Mrs. Corson said. "Doesn't that show you that she never thought of passion in the same world with her husband? She has to go outside herself for any passion, there's none in her."

"Yes," Mr. Palmer said. "Well, of course one can speculate, but one hardly knows..."

"And that damned dog," Mrs. Corson said. "Tommy can't play with other kids. They're too dirty. So she gets a dog. Dogs are cleaner than Anne, see? So she buys her child this nice germless dog, and then ties him up and won't let him loose. So the dog howls his head off, and we all go nuts. Finally we told her we couldn't stand it, why didn't she let it loose and let it run. But she said it might run away, and Tommy loved it so she didn't want to take a chance on losing the pup. So I finally called the Society for the Prevention of Cruelty to Animals, and they told her either to give it regular running and exercise or take it back. She took it back last night, and now she hates me."

As she talked, saliva had gathered in the corner of her mouth. She sucked it in and turned her head away, looking out on the street. "Lord God," she said. "So it goes, so it goes."

Through the windshield Mr. Palmer watched the quiet women on the wall, the quiet, well-behaved child. Anne was romping with the setter around the big stump, twenty feet beyond, and the little boy was watching her. It was a peaceful, windless morning steeped in sun. The mingled smell of pines and low tide drifted across the street, and was replaced by the pervading faint fragrance of ceanothus, blooming in shades of blue and white along Mr. Palmer's walk.

"I'm amazed," he said. "She seems so quiet and relaxed and plain."

"That's another thing," Mrs. Corson said. "She's a cover-yourself-up girl, too. Remember Margy Fisher, whose husband was killed a few weeks ago? You know why she never wore anything but a bathing suit? Because this old biddy was always after her about showing herself."

"Well, it's certainly a revelation," Mr. Palmer said. "I see you all from my window, you know, and it seems like a kind of symphony of waiting, all quiet and harmonious. The pregnant girl, too—going on with the slow inevitable business of life while her husband's gone, the rhythm of the generations unchanged. I've enjoyed the whole thing, like a pageant, you know."

"Your window isn't a very good peek-hole," Mrs. Corson said drily.

"Mm?"

"Hope's husband was killed at Dieppe," said Mrs. Corson.

For a moment Mr. Palmer did not catch on. At first he felt only a flash of pity as he remembered the girl's big steady brown eyes, her still, rather sad face, her air of pliant gentleness. Then the words Mrs. Corson had spoken began to take effect. Dieppe—almost three years ago. And the girl six months pregnant.

He wished Mrs. Corson would quit drumming her red nails on the car door. She was really in a state this morning, nervous as a cat. But that poor girl, sitting over there with all that bottled up inside of her, the fear and uncertainty growing as fast as the child in her womb grew...

"Some naval lieutenant," Mrs. Corson said. "He's right in the middle of the fighting, gunnery officer on a destroyer. You ought to hear Hope when she gets scared he'll never come back and make a decent woman of her."

"I'd not like to," Mr. Palmer said, and shook his head. Across the lane the placid scene had not changed, except that Mrs. Kendall had let Tommy toddle fifteen feet out from the wall, where he was picking up clusters of dry pine needles and throwing them into the air.

The figures were very clean, sharp-edged in the clear air against the blue backdrop of sea. An Attic grace informed all of them: the girl stooping above the long-eared red setter, the child with his hands in the air, tossing brown needles in a shower, the curving seated forms of the women on the wall. To Mr. Palmer's momentarily tranced eyes they seemed to freeze in attitudes of flowing motion like figures on a vase, cameo-clear in the clear air under the noble trees, with the quiet ocean of their watchfulness stretching blue to the misty edge. Like figures on a Grecian urn they curved in high relief above the white molding of the wall, and a drift of indescribable melancholy washed across the point and pricked goose-pimples on Mr. Palmer's arms. "It's sad," he said, opening the door and stepping down. "The whole thing is very sad."

With the intention of leaving he put his hand on the door and pushed it shut, thinking that he did not want to stay longer and hear Mrs. Corson's bitter tongue and watch the women on the wall. Their waiting now, with the momentary trance broken and the momentary lovely group dispersed in motion, seemed to him a monstrous aberration, their patience a deathly apathy, their hope an obscene self-delusion.

He was filled with a sense of the loveliness of the white paper and the cleanly sharpened pencils, the notebooks and the quiet and the sense of purpose that waited in his study. Most of all the sense of purpose, the thing to be done that would have an ending and a result.

"It's been very pleasant," he said automatically. At that moment there came a yowl from the point.

He turned. Apparently Anne, romping with the dog, had bumped Tommy and knocked him down. He sat among the pine needles in his blue play-suit and squalled, and Mrs. Kendall came swiftly out from the wall and took Anne by the arm, shaking her.

"You careless child!" she said. "Watch what you're doing!"

Instantly Mrs. Corson was out of the car. Mr. Palmer saw her start for the point, her lips puckered, and was reminded of some mechanical toy tightly wound and tearing erratically around a room giving off sparks of ratchety noise. When she was twenty feet from Mrs. Kendall she shouted hoarsely, "Let go of that child!"

Mrs. Kendall's heavy gingham body turned. Her plain face, the mouth stiff with anger, confronted Mrs. Corson. Her hand still held Anne's arm. "It's possible to train children..." she said.

"Yes, and it's possible to mistreat them," Mrs. Corson said. "Let go of her."

For a moment neither moved. Then Mrs. Corson's hands darted down, caught Mrs. Kendall's wrist, and tore her hold from Anne's arm. Even across the lane, fifty feet away, Mr. Palmer could see the white fury in their faces as they confronted each other.

"If I had the bringing up of that child...!" Mrs. Kendall said. "I'd..."

"You'd tie her to your apron strings like you've tied your own," Mrs. Corson said. "Like you tie up a dog and expect it to get used to three feet of space. My God, a child's a little animal. He's got to run!"

"And knock other children down, I suppose."

"Oh, my God!" Mrs. Corson said, and turned her thin face skyward as if to ask God to witness. She was shaking all over; Mr. Palmer could see the trembling of her dress. "Listen!" she said, "I don't know what's the matter with you, and why you can't stand nakedness, and why you think a bastard child is something holier than a legitimate one, and why you hang on to that child as if he was worth his weight in diamonds. But you keep your claws off mine, and if your little bastard can't get out of the way, you can just..."

Mrs. Kendall's face was convulsed. She raised both hands above her head, stuttering for words. From the side the pregnant girl slipped in quietly, and Mr. Palmer, rooted uneasily across the lane, heard her quiet voice. "You're beginning to draw a crowd," she said. "For the love of Mike, turn it down."

Mrs. Corson swung on her. Her trembling had become an ecstasy. When she spoke she chewed loudly on her words, mangling them almost beyond recognition. "You keep out of this, you pregnant bitch," she said. "Any time I want advice on how to raise love-children, I'll come to you too, but right now I haven't got any love-children, and I'm raising what I've got my own way."

A window had gone up in the house next to Mr. Palmer's, and three boys were drifting curiously down the street, their pants sagging with the weight of armament they carried. Without hesitating more than a moment, Mr. Palmer crossed the street and cut them off. "I think you'd better beat it," he said, and pushed his hands in the air as if shooing chickens. The boys stopped and eyed him suspiciously, then began edging around the side. It was clear that in any contest of speed, agility, endurance, or anything else Mr. Palmer was no match for them. He put his hand in his pocket and pulled out some change. The boys stopped. Behind him Mr. Palmer heard the saw-edged voice of Mrs. Corson. "I'm not the kind of person that'll stand it, by God! If you want to..."

"Here," Mr. Palmer said. "Here's a quarter apiece if you light out and forget anything you saw."

"Okay!" they said, and stepped up one by one and got their quarters and retreated, their heads together and their armed hips clanking together and their faces turning once, together, to stare back at the arguing women on the point. Up the street Mr. Palmer saw a woman and three small children standing in the road craning. Mrs. Corson's voice carried for half a mile.

In the hope that his own presence would bring her to reason, Mr. Palmer walked across the lane. Mrs. Corson's puckered, furious face was thrust into Mrs. Kendall's, and she was saying, "Just tell me to my face I don't raise my child right! Go on, tell me so. Tell me what you told Margy, that Anne's too dirty for your bastard to play with. Tell me, I dare you, and I'll tear your tongue out!"

Mr. Palmer found himself standing next to Mrs. Vaughn. He glanced at her once and shook his head and cleared his throat. Mrs. Corson continued to glare into the pale flat face before her. When Mrs. Kendall turned heavily and walked toward the wall, the wrenlike woman skipped nimbly around her and confronted her from the other side. "You've got a lot of things to criticize in me!" she said. Her voice, suddenly, was so hoarse it was hardly more than a whisper. "Let's hear you say them to my face. I've heard them behind my back too long. Let's hear you say them!"

"Couldn't we get her into the house?" Mr. Palmer said to the pregnant girl. "She'll raise the whole neighborhood."

"Let her disgrace herself," Mrs. Vaughn said, and shrugged.

"But you don't understand," Mr. Palmer said. "She had a beer or so downtown, and I think that, that and the heat..."

The girl looked at him with wide brown eyes in which doubt and contempt and something like mirth moved like shadows on water. "I guess *you* don't understand," she said. "She isn't drunk. She's hopped."

"Hopped?"

"I thought you went downtown with her."

"I did."

"Did she leave you at the pony track?"

"Yes, for a few minutes."

"She goes to a joint down there," Mrs. Vaughn said. "Fortune telling in the front, goofballs and reefers in the rear. She's a sucker for all three."

"Goofballs?" Mr. Palmer said. "Reefers?"

"Phenobarb," Mrs. Vaughn said. "Marijuana. Anything. She doesn't care, long as she gets high. She's high as a kite now. Didn't you notice her eyes?"

Mrs. Kendall had got her boy by the hand. She was heavily ignoring Mrs. Corson. Now she lifted the child in her arms and turned sideways, like a cow ducking to the side to slip around a herder, and headed for the stone wall. Mrs. Corson whipped around her flanks, first on one side, then on the other, her hoarse whisper a continuing horror in Mr. Palmer's ears.

"What I ought to do," Mrs. Corson said, "is forbid Anne to even speak to that bastard of yours."

Mrs. Kendall bent and put the child on the ground and stood up. "Don't you call him that!" she shouted. "Oh, you vulgar, vicious, drunken, depraved woman! Leave me alone! Leave me alone, can't you?"

She burst into passionate tears. For a moment Mr. Palmer was terrified that they would come to blows and have to be pulled apart. He started forward, intending to take Mrs. Corson by the arm and lead her, forcefully if necessary, to the house. This disgraceful exhibition had gone on long enough. But the pregnant girl was ahead of him.

She walked past the glaring women and said over her shoulder, carelessly, "Mail's here."

Mr. Palmer caught his cue. He put out his hand to Anne, and walked her down across the mouth of the lane. He did not look back, but his ears were sharp for a renewal of the cat-fight. None came. By the time the man in gray had distributed the papers and magazines to all the battery of boxes, and was unstrapping the pack of letters, Mr. Palmer was aware without turning that both Mrs. Corson and Mrs. Kendall were in the background by the gray car, waiting quietly.

The Double Corner

The summer sun was fierce and white on the pavement, the station, the tracks, the stucco walls of buildings, but the pepper tree made a domed and curtained cave of shade where they waited—the twins languidly playing catch with a tennis ball, Tom and Janet on the iron bench. Sitting with her head back, looking up into the green dome, Janet saw the swarming flies up among the branches, hanging like smoke against the ceiling of a room. They made a sleepy sound like humming wires.

"I wish I thought you knew what you're doing," Tom said.

She looked at him. He was leaning forward, his hat pushed back, and with his toe he was keeping a frantic ant from going where it wanted to with a crumb. He had worked on cattle ranches as a young man, and she had always said he had cowpuncher's eyes, squinty and faded, the color of much-washed jeans.

"She's your mother," she reminded him.

"I know."

"If I'm glad to have her, I should think you'd be."

The boys were throwing the tennis ball up into the branches, bringing down showers of leaves and twigs. "Hey, kids, cut it out," Tom said. To Janet he said, "We've been all through it. Let it ride."

"But you had some reason," she persisted.

"Reason?" he said, and picked his calloused palm. "She'd be better off in an institution."

That made Janet sit up stiffly and try to hold his eyes. "That's what I can't understand, why you'd be willing to send your mother to an asylum." He was squinting, moving his head slowly back and forth, but he would not look up.

"I wish I could understand you," Janet said, watching the dark cheek, the long jaw, the leathery sunburned neck, the tipped-back rancher's hat that showed the graying temple. "Suppose you died, and I got old and needed care. Would you expect the boys to send me off to an asylum, or would you expect they'd have enough love and gratitude to give me a room in their house?"

"You're not out of your mind," Tom said.

"I would be, if they treated me the way she's been treated. Four or five months with Albert, and then he palmed her off on Margaret; and Margaret kept her a little while and sent her to George; and George keeps her two months and wants to ship her to an institution—would have if we hadn't telephoned."

Tom removed a leaf from a twig. "It isn't that she's not wanted. She just hasn't got all her buttons any more. She can't be fitted into a family."

"Well, I tell you one thing," Janet said. "In our family she's going to feel wanted! She's like a child, Tom. She's got to feel that she has a place."

"Okay," he said. He leaned forward and spit on the ant he had been herding. The boys had given up their ball and were sitting on the edge of the rocked-in well from which the pepper's trunk rose.

Janet watched her husband a minute. She did not like him when his face went wooden and impenetrable. "Tom," she said, "will having her around bother you? Will it make you feel bad?"

His faded blue eyes turned on her, almost amused. "Relax," he said.

The train whistled for the crossing at Santa Clara, and Janet swung around to the boys. "Remember?" she said. "We're all going to be extra nice to Grandma. We're not going to laugh, or pester, or tease. We're going to be as polite and kind as we know how to be. Oliver, can you remember that? Jack, can you?"

The twins stared back at her, identical in T-shirts and jeans, with identical straight brown hair and identical expressions of hypocritical piety. Unsure of what their expressions meant, she waved them out through the curtain of branches, and they stood on the blazing platform in the ovenlike heat until the train rolled in and the Pullmans came abreast of them and the train stopped.

Janet felt above her the cool air-conditioned stares of passengers; she saw porters swing out, down the long train. A redcap pushed a truckload of baggage against the steps of a car. Then, down toward the rear of the train, a man in a blue slack suit stepped down and waited with his hand stretched upward. In a moment he climbed up again and came down leading an old lady by the arm. Janet hurried down the platform.

The man in blue, a fattish man with bare hairy arms, clung to Grandma's elbow and smiled a sickly smile as Janet came up. He had sweated through the armpits of his shirt. Grandma Waldron leaned away from him, her little brown eyes darting constantly, her lips trembling on a soundless stream of talk. She looked agitated, and her arms were folded hard across the breast of her heavy coat as if she were protecting something precious. She wore black shoes and a black hat, and she looked intolerably hot. In her unsuitable clothes amid the white heat and the pastel stucco of a California town, she tugged at Janet's sympathy like a lost and unhappy child.

"Hello, Mom," Tom said, and came forward to kiss her, but she twisted away with her arms still clenched across her breast. She appeared to wrestle with something; her face was strained, and drops of perspiration beaded her upper lip. Then the head of a cat thrust violently up above the lapels of the coat, a panting cat, ears back, pink mouth snarling. Under Grandma's clutching arms its body struggled, but it could not work free. It yowled, strangling.

Grandma ducked around Tom and the man in blue and came up to Janet. Her soundless talking became audible as a stream of words so unaccented that Janet wondered if she heard them herself, if she knew when she was speaking aloud and when only thinking with her lips. Paying no attention to the cat writhing weakly under the old lady's coat, she put out her hands and made her voice warm. "Grandma, it's awfully nice to have you here!"

Grandma's voice rode over the greetings, and she did not relax her clutch around the cat to touch the welcoming hands. "...never get rid of that man," she said. "Came up before I even got settled in my seat and stuck like a burr all the way I know what he wanted, he wanted into my bag so he could steal my picture of Tom's family, said he wanted to see what they looked like if there'd been a policeman there I'd have had him arrested trying to get into my suitcase I've had to watch every minute."

Her brown, prying eyes lighted on Janet, then on the staring twins; darted up the platform, swung suspiciously to the man in blue, who was talking quietly to Tom. Janet saw Tom's face, expressionless, and all in an instant she wanted to shout at him, "Don't you think that! She's strange and scared, that's all. This is what shunting her all around has done to her. George should have known better than to send her all the way from Los Angeles with a stranger."

But she could not say this. She barely had time to think it before the long warning cry went up along the train, the porters swung aboard, the train jerked and began to roll. The cat was struggling again in Grandma's arms. The man in blue jumped clumsily and got aboard, waving to them from the steps. Above them the bands of windows with the air-conditioned faces and the stares of strangers moved smoothly past, and then emptiness and a hot wind closed around the last Pullman.

"Well, here we are," Janet said gently. "You remember the twins. Jack and Oliver."

Grandma's eyes darted over the boys. Her talk had gone underground, but her lips still moved. After almost a minute of absolutely soundless vehement talking, the words came to the surface again. "...torturing the cat, chasing it through the house. Broke the wandering Jew right off."

One of her hands let go long enough to cram the cat's head down again. "Kept wanting my cat," she said. "That man did. Kept all the time wanting my cat away from me like those other things he took, all my money and my picture and my best mittens. That man took them."

Tom came up and stood smiling into his mother's face. "Don't you know me, Ma?"

Her head shaking slightly, Grandma looked at him. "Always was wild. Running away to the North Pole. I told my husband all about him, you bet. My husband's the constable." She looked around sharply. "Is that man gone? If we had any proper laws he'd been in jail long ago he got my mittens and my money and he tried to get my cat."

"Come on," Janet said, and took Grandma's elbow with the gentlest of fingers. "Let's get home out of this sun."

After a moment of resistance, Grandma came along. At the car, while Tom was running down the windows to let out the accumulated heat, he caught Janet's eye. The corners of his mouth went down soberly, and she felt that she had been challenged. "Grandma," she said, "don't you think you should let the poor cat out so it can breathe? That man's gone now."

The old lady jerked her shoulders and looked around her hard, but did not relax her arms. Janet helped her into the back seat, climbed in after her, sat down scrupulously on her own side. "Please," she said, and smiled into Grandma's strained face. "It can't get away in the car."

For just a moment, holding the brown intent eyes, she felt that she was being probed and tested. Then Grandma's clenched arms loosened slightly, and the cat shot up under her chin in a convulsive squirming effort, twisted and clawed its way loose, and sprang to the floor, where it crouched with tail flicking. Grandma started half to her feet as if to grab it up again, shot a sidelong look at Janet, and settled back. Outside the car the boys were watching. Jack shoved Oliver, and Oliver returned the shove. "Meowwrrrr!" Jack said. Their eyes glistened, and they giggled.

"Get in," Janet said harshly. The two climbed in beside Tom, and in a bleak admonitory silence they turned into the street. When they had gone a few blocks Jack leaned over the seat to look at the crouching cat.

"Boy, that sure is a beat-up old cat," he said. Oliver turned to look too, and then they huddled down in the front seat. Janet heard their smothered mirth, and catching Tom's eye in the rear-view mirror, she thought she saw laughter there too.

For a moment she relaxed, almost ready to laugh herself. But when she turned to Grandma, sitting stiffly with her watchful eyes on the cat, she saw Grandma's open coat. Under it the black dress was plucked and snagged and the white neck was bloody with scratches.

But what a commentary! Janet thought. What a revelation of the old lady's fear and suspicion, when she would think it necessary to cram her cat into her bosom and cling to it in protection though it clawed her heart out.

She reached out and patted Grandma's arm. The old lady looked at her, and it seemed to Janet that there was no longer suspicion in her eyes, but only inquiry. "It's nice to have you with us," Janet said.

Words flowed over the old lady's lips, but none of them made any sound.

They topped the hill and came into their own valley, the slope falling away below them in orchard and hay meadow, rising again on the far side to the dark chaparral of the coast hills. Little ranches, squares of apricot and almond and pear trees, angular lines of pasture and corral, patterned the valley and the sides of the hills, and the sight of that sheltered country beauty made Janet turn to Grandma to see if she felt it too. But Grandma was soundlessly telling herself something. Of course she couldn't see it. Not yet. Grandma's mind was a terrified little animal trembling in a dark hole while danger walked outside.

"There's our place," Janet said. "The one with the white water tower."

Grandma's eyes darted, but Janet could not be sure whether they really looked or whether they only cunningly pretended to. Then the car turned into the driveway and stopped under the holly oak with the yellow climbing roses incredibly hanging forty feet up among its branches. The fuchsias drooped ripe purple on both sides of the front door; the hill went up behind in a regimented jungle of orchards. The air was hot, heady, full of brandied fruit smell and the intoxication of tarweed. Down at the stable, under the old pear tree by the fence, the two horses stood with their heads companionably over each other's backs, making a two-tailed machine against the flies.

"Isn't it lovely!" Janet said. "Isn't it perfectly lovely!" Very carefully and tenderly she picked up the cat, stroked its fur smooth; and watching Grandma, half expecting the old lady to snatch the cat away, she took it as a small triumph that nothing of the sort happened.

Grandma got out, and Janet got out after her. "You'll love it here," she said, and smiled.

Through the whole ritual of arrival she kept that tone. Every gesture was a calculated reassurance; every word soothed. When she led Grandma down into the bedroom wing she threw open the door confidently, feeling that this room, like the valley and the fruit-scented ranch, ought to strike even a sick mind as sheltered and secure. The bed had a blue and white ship quilt for a spread; the cotton rugs were fresh from the laundry; the roses she had put on the bed table that morning breathed sweetly in the room; the curtains moved coolly, secretly at the north windows.

She still had the cat in her arms. It had relaxed there, its eyes half closed. "This is your room," she said to Grandma, and smiled again into the strained brown eyes. She opened the bathroom door and showed the white tile, the towels neat on the racks, the new oval of green soap. Her own quick glance pleased her: it was a room and bath she would have liked to be brought into herself.

"Boys," she said, "I think the kitty would like some milk. Maybe you could bring a dish in here."

They brought it in a minute, their manners still quelled, their eyes speculative. Jack set the dish by the bed and Oliver poured it full. Janet, stooping to set the cat on the floor, glanced up to catch on Grandma's face a look not of suspicion and unfriendliness, but a softened expression that almost erased the hard crease between her eyes. She looked for a moment like anybody's grandmother, soft-faced and gentle.

The cat's feet found the floor, and it crouched, looking up at the people above it. With his toe Oliver moved the dish of milk closer, and the cat fled under the bed. Grandma started forward, the wrinkle hard between her eyes again, her mouth beginning to go, and Janet stopped her with a hand on her arm.

"It's still scared," she said softly to the boys. "It'll be all right after it's got used to us. We'll leave it with Grandma now so they can both take a rest."

As she was herding the twins up the hall Oliver said, "Boy, that cat needs a rest."

"So does Grandma," Tom said from the dining room. "You guys can rest by getting some hay up into the mow."

"Can we ride Peppermint after?"

"She's got a saddlesore."

"We'll ride her bareback."

"All right."

They went out, and Tom looked at Janet with a peculiar sidelong expression. "The eminent psychiatrist," he said.

"It's working, isn't it?" Janet said. "She let me take her cat, and she's already starting to relax a little."

"I hope it's working," he said.

"Tom, don't you want her to be better?"

"Of course. I'd give an arm."

"She's just like her poor cat," Janet said. "She's been so pushed down and crammed under that she—"

They both began to laugh.

"Probably we shouldn't," Janet said. But she added, "At least it's human to laugh! At least she's part of the family. Isn't that better than some old inhuman institution where she'd just be a number and a case history? They wouldn't laugh at her in a place like that. They wouldn't have the humanity to."

* * *

NEXT MORNING GRANDMA came with them to the orchard. She was quite calm, and for five minutes at a time her lips, instead of trembling on a stream of soundless words, were quiet, a little puckered; her eyes followed the preparation for picking with what seemed to Janet interest. Tom set up the ladders and laid out a string of lugs in the shade, and Grandma watched the four of them climb into the foliage among the bright globes of fruit.

Oliver picked a ripe apricot and stood on the ladder ready to toss it. "Here, Grandma," he said, "have an apricot."

He held it out, but the old lady made no move to come near and get it. "Just help yourself off the trees anywhere, Grandma," Janet said, and gave Oliver a sign to go on picking. When they were all up on ladders and busy, Grandma stooped quickly and snatched up a windfall apricot from the ground.

"No, Grandma," Janet said. "From the trees. Pick all you want. Those on the ground may be spoiled."

Grandma dropped the windfall and wiped her fingers on her dress. After a moment she started at her hurrying, shoulder-forward walk down the orchard toward the lower fence.

"Do you want her taking off across country?" Tom said.

"Who do you think you are, a jailer?" Janet said. "Let her feel free for once."

"I haven't got time to go out every half hour and round her up."

"You won't have to. She'll come back."

"Sure?"

"Absolutely sure," Janet said. "Wait and see."

Thrust up among leaves and branches, they looked down to where Grandma's figure had stopped at the fence. The old lady looked around furtively, then stooped, picked up something from the ground and popped it into her mouth.

"You've got a ways to go," Tom said, and his voice from the other tree was so impersonal and dry that she was angry with him.

"Give her a little time!" she said. "Give her a chance!"

She was confident, yet when Grandma had not returned at eleven her faith began to waver. She did not want Tom to catch her anxiously looking down the orchard, but every time she dumped a pail in the lug she snatched quick looks all around, and she was almost at the point of sending the boys out searching when she saw the gingham figure marching homeward along the upper fence.

She threw an apricot into the tree where Tom was picking. "See?" she said. "What did I tell you?"

Every morning thereafter, Grandma took a walk through the orchards and along the lanes. Every afternoon she settled down in the wicker rocker on the porch, and rocked and talked and told herself things. Janet, working around the house, heard the steady voice going, and sometimes she heard what it said. It said that Simms, the drayman, had his eye on Grandma's house and was trying to get her moved out so that he could move his daughter and her husband in. It said that the minister was angry at her, ever since she sided with the evangelicals, and wanted the Ladies' Aid to leave her out of things. It said that George's wife was trying everything to get George to send Grandma away. Just the other day Grandma had overheard George's wife talking to the cleaning woman, plotting to leave Grandma's room dirty and then blame her in front of George. These were things Grandma knew, and she proved them with great vehemence and circumstantiality.

Sometimes Janet came and sat beside Grandma. When she did, the talk went underground; the lips moved, sometimes fervidly, and the little brown eyes snapped, but there was no conversation between them. Janet might comment on how the air cooled down when fog rolled over the crest of the coast hills, or might point out a hummingbird working the flower beds, but she did not expect replies. She took it as a hopeful sign that her presence did not drive Grandma away or stop her enthusiastic rocking, and sometimes it seemed to her that the rhythmic motion erased the strain from the old lady's face and smoothed the wrinkle between her eyes.

Then one afternoon Janet came quietly on the porch and found Grandma rocking like a child in the big chair, pushing with her toes lifting off the floor, rocking back down to push with her toes again. She was not talking at all, but was humming a tuneless little song to herself.

It was early August, and dense heat lay over the valley. The apricots were long gone; in the upper orchard the prunes were purple among the leaves, the limbs of the trees propped against the weight of fruit. The unirrigated pasture was split by cracks three inches wide, and even in the shade one felt the dry panting of the earth for the rain that would not come for another three months. Looking out over the heat-hazed valley, Grandma pushed with her toes, rocking and humming. Her face was mild and soft, and Janet slipped into the next chair, almost holding her breath for fear of breaking the moment. It was so easy to make a mistake. Weeks of improvement could be canceled by one false move that the sick mind could seize on as it had seized on a harmless conversation between George's wife and her cleaning woman.

It was Grandma herself who spoke first. She looked over at Janet brightly and said, "Tom's a handsome man."

"Yes," Janet said.

"He's filled out," Grandma said. "He was a skinny boy."

She went back to her humming. For ten more minutes Janet sat still, wishing that Tom were there to see his mother as she had once been, speculating on how the moment might be stretched, wondering if possibly this was a turning point, if Grandma had come out of the twilight where she lived and would from now on shake off the suspicions and the fears. The vines over the porch moved sluggishly and were still again.

Janet stood up. "It's hot," she said. "Shall we get ourselves a lemonade, Grandma?"

She appraised the quick look, the interrupted humming, the break in the even rocking, and knew that everything was all right, she hadn't broken any spell. Grandma started to rise but Janet said, "Don't get up. I'll bring it out."

"I'll come along," the old lady said. In the kitchen she stood behind Janet and watched the lemons squeezed, the sugar added, the ice cubes pushed from the rubber tray.

"I like it better with fizz water, don't you?" Janet said. Grandma appeared not to understand, but she watched carefully as Janet filled the glasses. "Now a cherry," Janet said. "We might as well be festive." She looked at Grandma and laughed, surprising a tremble of a smile. Out on the porch she heard steps, and in the hope that Tom might have come in, and that she could demonstrate this miracle to him, she hugged the old lady around the shoulders and walked her through the French doors.

The steps had not been Tom's. Oliver was sprawled in the wicker rocker, his legs clear across the porch, his face sweaty. He looked up limply, brightened at sight of the glasses of lemonade.

"Hey! Can I have one?"

"If you want to fix it yourself. Grandma and I are having a party."

"Aw corn," Oliver said. "I haven't got the strength." He lay out even flatter in the chair, egg-eyed, his tongue hanging out. "This is the way they look when Popeye hits them," he said.

"Weak as you are, you'll have to move," Janet said. "You're in Grandma's chair."

He opened one eye. "Grandma's chair? How come?"

"Oliver!" his mother said. "Haven't you mislaid your manners?"

He rose promptly enough, a little surprised, and Janet ruffled his hair as he went by. But she couldn't miss the way Grandma's mouth had tightened and trembled, and how when she sat down again she sat on the front of the chair, unrelaxed, the mild look that had been briefly on her face replaced by a look of petulance and injury.

* * *

THREE DAYS LATER, when they were just beginning to pick the prune crop, Grandma moved.

Janet was preparing lunch when Tom and the boys came in from the orchard and started for the bathroom to clean up. Within a minute Oliver was back. "She's in our room! Mom, she's moved into our room with all her stuff!"

In Oliver's footsteps Janet went down the hall. Grandma sat stiffly on the boy's bed. The end of her suitcase showed under the bed, and the dresser was heaped with her clothing. From across the hall Tom appeared, scrubbing with a towel. Janet, stepping softly, went into the room and said, "Why, Grandma, don't you like your own room?"

The old lady's finger leaped out to point at Jack, who ducked as if the finger were a gun. The finger shifted smartly over to Oliver. "He told me to move. That boy of yours. He didn't want me to have the nice room with the bath when he only had this little one. He told me to get out."

Oliver's brow wrinkled, and his mouth opened. Tom took a step forward, but Janet stopped him with a look and squeezed hard on Oliver's shoulder. "There's just been a mistake," she said. "If either of the boys said that, he didn't mean it. The nice room with the bath is yours."

"He told me."

"If he did he didn't mean it. Did you, Oliver?"

"I never said anything of the kind. I was out in the orchard all morning."

"If you said it you didn't mean it, did you?"

"I never...No, I didn't mean it."

"Now let's get Grandma moved back before lunch," Janet said brightly, and motioned Jack to take some clothes from the dresser. When he moved to lift them off, Grandma took them from him with a hard look; he stood back and let her carry her own things to her room.

Back in the kitchen, Oliver said, "Boy, she's crazy as a bedbug. I never said a word to her. Where does she get it I made her move? She's nutty."

"Say she gets notions," Janet said. "I shouldn't have to tell you again. She's had a hard life. If we humor her and treat her nicely maybe she'll get well."

Oliver thoughtfully ate a prune off the work table. "How'd she get that way, fall downstairs or something?"

"I don't know," Janet said. "It just grew on her, I guess."

That was on Friday. On Sunday afternoon, when the prune orchard was dotted with people from the city who had come down to pick their own fruit, and Tom and the boys were out distributing ladders and pails and weighing up baskets and keeping the unpracticed pickers from breaking down limbs, Janet took a cool limeade in to Grandma and found her gone. Her closet was empty; her bureau drawers cleaned out.

Janet went out through the porch, across a road's-width of passionate sun, and under the shade of the oaks, where Tom had his scales. She waited while he weighed two baskets of prunes and carried them to a car. "Grandma's gone," she said when he came back.

She saw his patience bend and crack, and she stood guiltily, granting him the right to blame her but at the same time not admitting that she was in any way wrong. After a moment Tom said, "How long?"

"I don't know. I just took a drink in, and she was gone, with all her stuff. Sometime since dinner. Maybe an hour."

"We'd have seen her if she'd come out through here," he said. He looked across into the orchard, where three different parties were picking. "I just about have to stay here till these folks clear out. Can you and the kids look?"

She called the boys and they came at once, intent, sun-blackened, interested like setters being called up for a walk, and she thought as they came under the bronze shade: My nice boys! She thought it with a rush of affection, irrelevantly, grateful to them for their clear eyes and their health.

Trying to forestall in them the impatience that had jumped into Tom's face, she put on a crooked and rueful smile. "Grandma's abandoned us," she said, making it a joke between them.

They groaned, but more to acknowledge the joke than for any other reason, and wobbled their knees and crossed their eyes in dismay. Jack ran up the ladder of the tree house built in the oak and stood like a sailor on the crosstrees, peering into the empty shanty with a hand cupped over his eyes. Oliver sniffed the foot of the tree, followed an imaginary trail into the garage, through the car, around the woodshed, and back to the driveway. "Hey!" they said. "No Grandma. Man overboard. Fireman, save my child."

The three of them went across the brittle oat stubble, stopped to search the pump house, glanced into the chicken house and disturbed some matronly hens. They went through the stable and tackroom, and Janet stayed below while the boys climbed up into the mow. A drift of straw and dust fell from the trapdoor and filled the slant sunbeams with constellations.

The boys came down again. "No Grandma," they said. "Call the St. Bernards; she must be lost in the snow."

They went to the stable door and looked down across the lower orchard and the dry creek bed toward Hillstrom's. There was a breeze coming around the corner, a cool, horsy breath. They stood in it, searching the neighboring orchard and pastures, looking along the quarter-mile of white road that showed on the ridge above Kuhn's.

"She couldn't have gone far, with the suitcase," Janet said. "Did you look carefully in the garage, Oliver?"

"She wasn't there. I looked all over."

At a slight sound behind her, Janet turned. Grandma's cat came out of one of the horse stalls, balancing his tail, blinking slit-eyed in the bright doorway, rubbing against her legs.

"Now where'd you come from, kitty?" Janet said. "Where's your mistress?"

"He comes down here to catch mice," Jack said. "I saw him with one the other day."

"But where's your boss?" Janet said, and stooped to let the lifting furry back pass under her hand.

There were footsteps in the tackroom, and Tom came in. "Find her?"

"Not a sign."

Tom stood with his hands in his back pockets, chewing his upper lip. "Oh, damn!" he said, without real anger.

Jack picked up the cat and stood petting it, watching his parents, and the noise of the cat's purring was loud in the stable until the noise of a car ground over it and drowned it out, and a green sedan came around the corner and stopped in the barnyard. "Is this where you can pick your own prunes?" the driver said. A woman and three children were crowding to look through the rear window.

"Up above," Tom said. "If you'll drive back up to the house I'll be with you in a minute." He looked at Janet. "You want me to go hunting, or handle the pickers, or what?"

"The boys and I can cruise around."

Then their voices filled the stable. "Mom! Here she is. Here she is, Mom!"

The sedan started to turn around. Back in against the manger of the second stall there was a threshing and rustling, and as Janet squinted into the shadows she saw Grandma sitting up in the manger. She reared up and scolded the boys, "...never get a minute's peace somebody always prying around spying on a person go away you boys or I'll tell your father he sent me down here now you leave me be go 'way."

"For the love of God, Ma, come out of there," Tom said. He went in and half lifted her over the front of the manger. Rigid with anger, muttering, she jerked away and came at a half run out into the doorway. The sedan was just leaving; Janet saw the faces staring, and then she grabbed Grandma and held her until Tom pulled her back inside. Grandma's clothes were slivered with hay, gray with dust. There were oat hulls caught on her lip.

"Oliver," Janet said. "Jump on that man's running board and show him where to go."

"Aw, Ma!"

"Please!" she said. "Get those people out of here!"

Tom hung on to Grandma's arm till the sound of the car had died. "I don't suppose it will do any good to ask you what you thought you were doing down here," he said.

Grandma sniffed. "I know I don't count for anything here," she said. "When I had my own home it was different, before Henry died, but around here I only do as I'm told. If you tell me to live in the stable and eat with the horses that's all right with me. I know I'm on charity, I don't complain."

Abruptly Tom let go of her arm. "You handle this," he said to Janet, and went out into the hot light that lay like a sea around the warm dark island of the stable.

"You must trust us, Grandma," Janet said softly. Without really watching him, she was aware how Jack stared with the cat purring in his arms, and she reached out to pull him against her, knowing how Grandma's queerness must trouble his understanding. "You must let us love you and take care of you," she said. "Don't feel that any of us are against you. We all love you. You don't have to move out of your room, or eat out of the horse's box..."

Before she could move Grandma had lunged forward and snatched the sleepy tomcat out of Jack's arms. She clenched it against her fiercely, fighting its clawing desperate feet, and turned half around to shield it from their sight. The cat yowled, a frantic squashed sound, as Grandma retreated into the stall from which she had just come.

Janet shook her head at Jack and whispered, "You'd better run up and help Dad and Oliver." She steered him to the edge of the hard sunlight, whispering, "We'll just let her alone a few minutes. She's so excited she shouldn't be pushed around. I'll bring her up in a little while."

"What if she—"

"Run along. She'll be all right."

Her own nerves were on edge; she was trembling. Back in the shadow the cat squalled again, and then the sounds were muffled, as if Grandma had got the animal under her sweater. After a minute or two they stopped entirely. Either the old lady had got over her fright and stopped squeezing the cat, or it had escaped.

Janet waited another five minutes. It was perfectly quiet; she heard the slightest tick of falling straw. She did not like to think of Grandma back there in the shadow, her mouth going on some vehement silent tirade, her mind full of suspicion and crazy notions.

She went to the front of the stall and said casually, "Shall we go back to the house, Grandma?"

Grandma jerked around. She had been bending over the manger, and now she pulled out the brown suitcase, the arm or leg of a suit of winter underwear trailing out of its corner. Janet smiled. "Did the cat get away? Never mind, he likes it here. He'll be back."

"That boy tried to steal it," Grandma said.

She came out quietly enough, but when Janet offered to carry the suitcase she swung it far over on one side, guarding it jealously, and Janet sighed. It was so easy to make a mistake. The slightest gesture of kindness was likely to rouse suspicion. You had to be as soft and smooth and easy as cottonwool, or you did harm instead of good. She watched Grandma marching ahead of her; as the old lady turned the sun was golden on the oat husks caught on her lip. Janet smiled, following her up to the house and into the cool porch, and, still smiling, followed her down the hall to her room.

It was not until two hours later, after she had calmed the old lady and talked her into taking a tepid bath, and had then started to unpack and put away Grandma's clothes, that she discovered about the cat. It was jammed into the suitcase, tangled among long drawers and petticoats and damask napkins. And it was desperately and resistantly dead. Its eyes were half open, its mouth wide so that the needle teeth showed in a grin. Its front legs were stiffened straight out, as if it had died pushing against the smothering lid.

That evening after dinner Janet sat on the porch looking across the little valley and feeling how the heat left the earth as the night came on. The boys were playing checkers in the living room behind her; she felt their presence in the lamplight that yellowed the windows. Tom was hammering at something down in the pump house. Grandma was in her room.

Over the ridge of the stable the pasture knoll beyond the Wilson place shone a lovely fawn color in the last flat sun. But all around, in the valley itself, the earth was already going gray and shadowy. In a little while the light would lift off the last knoll; the clouds would change and darken back of the coast hills; the ranches would begin to melt back into the trees; lights would wink on; the clean sky would be pricked with stars.

It was a most peaceful place and a peaceful life. Half irritably, she thought that Grandma should find healing in every hour of it. But she knew she would have to talk to Tom about Grandma later; for now she put the whole problem away, sitting with her hands turned palm upward in her lap and listening to the lulling rise of the night noises, crickets and tree frogs and the far musical cry of a train down toward San Jose. When it was all but dark she leaned near one of the open lighted windows and said, "Time for bed, boys."

"Just till we finish this game," Oliver said, and looking in, she saw them hunched head to head over the card table. There was a rhythm in that too, the same rhythm through which she herself swung, moving evenly through the warm, temperate, repetitive events of a life that was not going anywhere because it was already there; it lived at the center.

She heard Tom coming through the dusk, his steps soft in the disked ground as he crossed a strip of orchard, then grating in the gravel drive, and he came up on the porch and sat down heavily in the wicker chair beside her.

"Boy, I've got you cornered now!" Oliver said from inside. "You give up?"

"Like heck," Jack said. "Not as long as I'm in a double corner."

"Time they were in bed?" Tom said.

"They're just finishing a game."

They sat on without speaking in the dark. Out over the main valley, moving smoothly among the orderly stars, the running lights on the wing tips of an air liner winked on and off. Sometimes, when clouds bridged the main valley trough, the motors of a plane like that could fill their little hollow with sound, but now in the clear night the noise was only a remote and diminishing hum. The lights winked unfailingly far down toward the south until the hills rose and cut them off.

Inside, the boys broke up their game and snapped off the light. For a minute or two they stood together at the French doors looking out on the porch. "Well, I guess we'll go to bed now," one of them said, and Janet was amused that in the dark she really couldn't tell which one had spoken.

"I'll look in on you later," she said. "It's so nice out I think I'll sit awhile."

When they had gone, she and Tom sat on. The wicker chair squeaked; she knew he had turned his head.

"Well?" he said.

"Well?" She did not want to make it hard for him to begin; she even wanted with an odd sense of urgency to try again to tell him how she felt, how she knew that even a thing badly done, if it was done with love, was better than a thing done efficiently but without love. But she was in a defensive position, like Jack in his double corner. Tom had to move first...."You realize she has to be sent away," Tom said.

"Why?" She would not move until he absolutely forced her.

"My God!" he said. "Why?"

She heard his chair squeak again. Another plane was coming up the valley, its motors a distant even drone. "I'll tell you why," he said. "Just because she breaks everything up. She can't live with sane people. She'll bust the whole pattern of our lives."

"By pattern you mean comfort," Janet said, and heard her own voice, stiff and resistant, and the irritation that jumped in Tom's voice when he answered.

"No, I don't mean comfort! I mean the way we live, the way the kids grow up. Do you think it does them any good, seeing her batting at empty air?"

Janet had thought of the boys herself, plenty of times. But they were steady and well-balanced. It might even teach them forbearance and kindliness to have the old lady around. It wasn't fair of Tom to bring them into it now.

"I wonder how the boys would like to be responsible for condemning Grandma to prison for life, just to protect their own routine?" she said.

"That's better than letting her break up other people's lives."

"Oh, break up our lives!" Janet said. "The little trouble we've had..." She leaned forward, trying to reach the vague shadow of her husband with her eyes and voice. "Don't you realize what it would mean if we sent her away? We'd be treating her exactly as strangers might treat her, as if we had no feeling for her at all. We'd be washing our hands of her, just so we could be more comfortable." She sat back, suddenly so angry and hurt that her hands shook. "I'm surprised you don't..."

"Don't what?" Tom's voice said.

"Nothing."

"Nazi methods?" Tom said. "That's what you were going to say, isn't it? You're surprised I don't want to cyanide her."

"You know I didn't—"

"Sometimes you have to do a thing you don't want to do," Tom said. "You can do it kindly, even when it's something hard."

"But that's just what I wish you could see!" Janet cried. "There's no chance of any kindness in an institution, and it's kindness she needs."

There was a pause. "So you don't want to send her away," Tom said. "Not even after that cat business."

"I couldn't forgive myself if we did," she said. "It would be throwing her out when she was crying for help and not knowing how to say the words. That cat was the one thing she had left to love. Remember how afraid she was that the man on the train was going to steal it? That cat was half her life."

"And she killed it."

"Out of fear! We haven't got her over her fear, that's all. She was getting along fine, till this last spell. I've got enough confidence in the way we live to think we can change her pattern instead of her changing ours."

"Then you're crazier than she is."

Janet stood up. Her knees were trembling a little, and the thought crossed her mind that now, without the cat, Grandma was going to be harder than ever to win over. Maybe she would even get the notion that someone in the family had killed it. But that was not the question. The question was whether they could feel right about giving her over to some cold-blooded aseptic hospital that would surely drive her deeper into her persecuted dream.

"I don't see how we could respect ourselves," she said. "It's at least worth a better try than we've given it."

For a time the little night noises were still. Then a cricket started up again, a tinny fiddling under the porch. Tom's face was lost in the dark, but finally he spoke. "Okay. You're the doctor."

"Just the thought of giving up after less than two months."

"Okay, okay."

"I wish you could see it, Tom."

"I see it," he said. "I just don't believe it."

She hesitated. Then she went past him, walking quietly as if he were sleeping and she did not want to disturb him, and opened the screen and let it close softly behind her. The house was still. The padded living-room rug muffled her steps, and she had a feeling that it was very late at night, though she knew it couldn't be past ten. There was a light burning in the hall, and by the diffused glow she made her way to the hall leading down the bedroom wing.

As if a hand had closed around her heart she stopped dead still at the entrance. Halfway down the hall Grandma was standing, looking into the open door of the boys' room. Her head was sunk between her shoulders with the intensity of her stare, and her mouth moved on some secret malevolence. She made no move to enter, but only stood there staring, stooping forward a little. Then she heard Janet and whirled, and all the light that filtered into the hall flashed in her eyeballs, and she scuttled down the hall and into her own room.

Janet fought her breath free, but the cold paralysis of fear was still in her legs. She took four quick steps to the children's door, listened. Their breathing came quiet and steady in the dark, and she sagged against the door in relief. From down the hall there was a muffled click, and she saw the shadowy crack along Grandma's door widen. When she stepped full into the hall again the crack softly closed.

Janet put her hand down, felt the skeleton key in the lock of the boys' door. That key would work in any of the bedroom doors. She slipped it out and started down the hall, and the stealthy crack which had opened along Grandma's door closed again as she came. Janet stood a moment at the door, listening. There was not a sound. With a quick movement she inserted the skeleton key into the lock and turned it. She leaned against the door with the key in her hand and said, "Oh, Grandma, I'm sorry, I'm so terribly sorry!"

All through the darkened house there was not a sound. Up the hall her boys slept undisturbed, and out on the porch her husband sat in the dark, looking down over the even pattern of his orchards. She thought of the windows that Grandma could climb out of, the screens that should be nailed tight shut, and though the key in her hand was still a rigid reproach, she hurried. She hurried with fear driving her, and she was crying, not entirely from fear, when she called to Tom through the open French doors.

Pop Goes the Alley Cat

Getting up to answer the door, Prescott looked into the face of a Negro boy of about eighteen. Rain pebbled his greased, straightened hair; the leather yoke of his blazer and the knees of his green gabardine pants were soaked. The big smile of greeting that had begun on his face passed over as a meaningless movement of the lips. "I was lookin'," he said, and then with finality, "I thought maybe Miss Vaughn."

"She's just on her way out."

The boy did not move. "I like to see her," he said, and gave Prescott a pair of small, opaque, expressionless eyes to look into. Eventually Prescott motioned him in. He made a show of getting the water off himself, squee-geeing his hair with a flat palm, shaking his limber hands, lifting the wet knees of his pants with thumb and finger as he sat down. He was not a prepossessing specimen: on the scrawny side, the clothes too flashy but not too clean, the mouth loose and always moving, the eyes the kind that shifted everywhere when you tried to hold them but were on you intently the moment you looked away.

But he made himself at home. And why not, Prescott asked himself, in this apartment banked and stacked and overflowing with reports on delinquency, disease, crime, discrimination; littered with sociological studies and affidavits on police brutality and the mimeographed communications of a dozen betterment organizations? The whole place was a temple to the juvenile delinquent, and here was the god himself in the flesh, Los Angeles Bronzeville model.

Well, he said, I am not hired to comment, but only to make pictures.

Carol came into the hall from her bedroom, and Prescott saw with surprise that she was glad to see this boy. "Johnny!" she said. "Where did you drop from?"

Over the boy had come an elaborate self-conscious casualness. He walked his daddylonglegs fingers along the couch back and lounged to his feet, rolling the collar of the blazer smooth across the back of his neck. Prescott was reminded of the slickers of his high school days, with their pinch-waisted bell-bottomed suits and their habit of walking a little hollow-chested to make their shoulders look wider. The boy weaved and leaned, pitching his voice high for kidding, moving his shoulders, his mouth, his pink-palmed hands. "Start to *rain* on me," he said in the high complaining humorous voice. "*Water* start comin' down on me I think I have to drop *in*."

"How come you're not working?"

"That job!" the boy said, and batted it away with both hands. "That wasn't much of a job, no kiddin'."

"Wasn't?"

"*You* know. Them old flour bags *heavy*, you get tired. Minute you stop to rest, here come that old foreman with the *gooseroo*. Hurry up there, boy! Get along there, boy! They don't ride white boys like that."

Carol gave Prescott the merest drawing down of the lips. "That's the third job in a month," she said, and added, "Johnny's one of my boys. Johnny Bane. This is Charlie Prescott, Johnny."

"Pleased to meet you," Johnny said without looking. Prescott nodded and withdrew himself, staring out into the dripping garden court.

"You know a fact?" Johnny said. "That old strawboss keep eyeballin' me and givin' me that old hurry-up, hurry-up, that gets *old*. I get to carryin' my knife up the sleeve of my sweatshirt, and he comes after me once *more*, I'm goin' *cut* him. So I quit before I get in bad trouble out there."

Carol laughed, shaking her head. "At least that's ingenious. What'll you do now?"

"Well, I don't *know*." He wagged his busy hands. "No future pushin' a truck around or cuttin' *lemons* off a tree. I like me a job with some *class*, you know, something where I could *learn* something."

"I can imagine how ambition eats away at you."

"No kiddin'!" the burbling voice said. "I get real industrious if I had me the right *kind* of a job. Over on Second Street there's this Chinaman, he's on call out at Paramount. Everytime they need a Chinaman for a mob scene, out he goes and runs around for a couple of hours and they hand him all this *lettuce*, man. You know anybody out at MGM, Paramount, anywhere?"

"No," she said. "Do you, Charlie?"

"Nobody that needs any Chinamen." Prescott showed her the face of his watch. Johnny Bane was taking in, apparently for the first time, the camera bag, the tripod, the canvas sack of flash bulbs beside Prescott's chair.

"Hey, man, you a photographer?"

"Charlie and I are doing a picture study of your part of town for the Russell Foundation," Carol said.

"Take a long time to be a photographer?" Johnny's mouth still worked over his words, but now that his attention was fixed his eyes were as unblinking as an alligator's.

"Three or four years."

"Man, that's a rough *sentence*! Take a long time, uh? Down by the station there's this place, mug you for a quarter. Sailors and their chicks always goin' in. One chick I was watchin' other night, she had her picture five times. Lots of cats and chicks, every night. *Money* in that, man."

She shook her head, saying, "Johnny, when are you going to learn to hold a job? You make it tough for me, after I talk you into a place."

"I get me in trouble, I stay over there," he said. "I know you don't want me gettin' into trouble." Lounging, crossing his feet, he said, "I like to learn me some trade. Like this photography. I bet I surprise you. That ain't like pushin' a truck with some *foreman* givin' you the eyeballs all the time."

Prescott lifted the camera bag to the chair. "If we're going to get anything today we'll have to be moving."

"Just a minute," Carol said. To Johnny she said, "Do you know many people over on your hill?"

"Sure, man. *Multitudes.*"

"Mexicans too?"

"They're mostly Mexicans over there. My chick's Mexican." He staggered with his eyes dreamily shut. "Solid, solid!" he said.

"He might help us get in some places," Carol said. "What do you think, Charlie?"

Prescott shrugged.

"He could hold reflectors and learn a little about photography."

Prescott shrugged again.

"Do you mind, Charlie?"

"You're the doctor." He handed the sack of flash bulbs and the tripod to Johnny and picked up the camera bag. "Lesson number one," he said. "A photographer is half packhorse."

* * *

THE *BARRIO* WAS A DOUBLE ROW of shacks tipping from a hilltop down a steep road clayily shining and deserted in the rain, every shack half buried under climbing roses, geraniums, big drooping seedheads of sunflowers, pepper and banana trees, and palms: a rural slum of the better kind, the poverty overlaid deceptively with flowers. Across the staggering row of mailboxes Prescott could see far away, over two misty hilltops and an obscured sweep of city, the Los Angeles Civic Center shining a moment in a watery gleam of sun.

Johnny hustled around, pulling things from the car. As Prescott took the camera bag, the black face mugged and contorted itself with laughter. "You want me and my chick? How about me and my chick cuttin' a little *jive*, real mean? Colored and Mexican hobnobbin'. That okay?"

"First some less sizzling shots," Carol said dryly. "Privies in the rain, ten kids in a dirt-floored shack. How about Dago Aguirre's? That's pretty bad, isn't it?"

"Dago's? Man, that's a real *dump*. You want dumps, uh? Okay, we try Dago's."

He went ahead of them, looking back at the bag Prescott carried.

"Must cost a lot of lettuce, man, all those *cameras*."

Prescott shook the bag at him. "That's a thousand dollars in my hand," he said. "That's why I carry it myself."

Rain had melted the adobe into an impossible stickiness; after ten steps their feet were balls of mud. Johnny took them along the flat hilltop to a gateless fence under a sugar palm, and as they scraped the mud from their shoes against a broken piece of concrete a Mexican boy in Air Force dungarees opened the door of the shack and leaned there.

"*Ese, Dago*," Johnny said.

"*Hórale, cholo.*" Dago looked down without expression as Johnny shifted the tripod and made a mock-threatening motion with his fist.

"We came to see if we could take some pictures," Carol said. "Is your mother home, Dago?"

Dago oozed aside and made room for a peering woman with a child against her shoulder. She came forward uncertainly, a sweet-faced woman made stiff by mistrust. Carol talked to her in Spanish for five minutes before she would open her house to them.

Keeping his mouth shut and working fast as he had learned to on this job, Prescott got the baby crawling on the dirt floor between pans set to catch the drip from the roof. He got the woman and Dago and the baby and two smaller children eating around the table whose one leg was a propped box. By backing into the lean-to, between two old iron bedsteads, and having Carol, Johnny, and Dago hold flashes in separate corners, he got the whole place, an orthodox FSA shot, Standard Poverty. That was what the Foundation expected. As always, the children cried when the flashes went off; as always, he mollified them with the blown bulbs, little Easter eggs of shellacked glass. It was a dump, but nothing out of the ordinary, and he got no picture that excited him until he caught the woman nursing her baby on a box in the corner. The whole story was there in the protective stoop of her figure and the drained resignation of her face. She looked anciently tired; the baby's chubby hand was clenched in the flesh of her breast.

Johnny Bane, eager beaver, brisk student, had been officious about keeping extension cords untangled and posing with the reflector. By the time Prescott had the camera and tripod packed Johnny had everything else dismantled. "How you get all them *lights* to go off at *once?*" he said.

Prescott dropped a reflector and they both stooped for it, bumping heads. The boy's skull felt as hard as cement; for a moment Prescott was unreasonably angry. But he caught Carol's eye across the room, and straightening up without a word, he showed Johnny and Dago how the flashes were synchronized, he let them look into the screen of the Rolleiflex, he explained shutter and lens, he gave them a two-minute lecture on optics. "Okay?" he said to Carol in half-humorous challenge.

She smiled. "Okay."

The Aguirre family watched them to the door and out into the drizzle. Johnny Bane, full of importance, a hep cat, a photographer's assistant, punched the shoulder of the lounging Dago. "*Ay te wacho,*" he said. Dago lifted a languid hand.

"Now what?" Prescott asked.

"More of the same," Carol said. "Unfortunately, there's plenty."

"Overcrowding, malnutrition, lack of sanitation," he said. "Four days of gloom. Can't we shoot something pretty?"

"There's always Johnny's chick."

"Maybe she comes under the head of lack of sanitation."

They were all huddled under the sugar palm. "What about my chick?" Johnny demanded. "You want my chick now?"

Carol stood tying a scarf over her fair hair. In raincoat and saddle shoes, she looked like a college sophomore. "Does your chick's family approve of you?" she said. "Most Mexican families aren't too happy to see boy friends hanging around."

Tickled almost to idiocy, he cackled and flapped his hands. "Man, they think I'm *rat* poison, no kiddin'. They think *any* cat's rat poison. They got this old Mexican jive about keepin' chicks at *home.* But I come there with *you,* they got to let me *in,* don't they?"

"So who's helping whom?" Prescott said.

That made him giggle and mug all the way down the slippery hill. "Hey, man," he said once, "you know these Mexicans believe in this

Evil Eye, this *ojo*. When I hold up that old reflector I'm sayin' the Lord's *Prayer* backwards and puttin' the eyeballs on him, and when here comes that big flash, man, her old man really think he got the *curse* on him. I tell him I don't take it off till he let Lupe go out any time she want. Down to that *beach*, man. She look real mean down there on that sand gettin' the eyeballs from all the cats. *Reety!*"

"Spare us the details," Carol said, and turned her face from the rain, hanging to a broken fence and slipping, laughing, coming up hard against a light pole. Prescott slithered after her until before a shack more pretentious than most, almost a cottage, Johnny kicked the mud from his shoes and silently mugged at them, with a glassy, scared look in his odd little eyes, before he knocked on the home-made door.

It was like coming into a quiet opening in the woods and startling all the little animals. They were watched by a dozen pairs of eyes. Prescott looked past the undershirted Mexican who had opened the door and saw three men with cards and glasses and a jug before them on a round table. A very pregnant woman stood startled in the middle of the floor. On a bed against the far wall a boy had lowered his comic book to stare. There was a flash of children disappearing into corners and behind the stove. The undershirted man welcomed them with an enveloping winy breath, but his smile was only for Carol and Prescott; his recognition of Johnny was a brief, sidelong lapse from politeness. Somewhere behind the door a phonograph was playing "*Linda Mujer*"; now it stopped with a squawk.

Once, during the rapid Spanish that went on between Carol and the Mexican, Prescott glanced at Johnny, but the boy's face, with an unreal smile pasted on it, blinked and peered past the undershirted man as if looking for someone. His forehead was puckered in tense knots. Then the undershirted man said something over his shoulder, the men at the table laughed, and one lifted the jug in invitation. The host brought it and offered it to Carol, who grinned and tipped and drank while they applauded. Then Prescott, mentally tasting the garlic and chile from the lips that had drunk before him, coldly contemplating typhoid, diphtheria, polio, drank politely and put the jug back in the man's hands with thanks and watched him return it to the table without offering it to Johnny Bane. They were pulled into the room, the door closed, and he saw that the old hand-cranked Victrola had been played by a Mexican youth in drape pants and a pretty girl, short-skirted and pompadoured. The girl should be Lupe, Johnny's chick. He looked for the glance of understanding between them and saw only the look on Johnny's face as if he had an unbearable belly-ache.

This was a merry shackful. The men were all a little drunk, and posed magnificently and badly, their eyes magnetized by the camera. The boy was lured from his comic book. Lupe and the youth, who turned out to be her cousin Chuey, leaned back and watched and whispered with a flash of white teeth. As for Johnny, he held reflectors where Prescott told him to, but he was no longer an eager beaver. His mouth hung sullenly, his eyes kept straying to the two on the couch.

Dutifully Prescott went on with his job, documenting poverty for humanitarianism's sake and humanizing it as he could for the sake of art. He got a fair shot of the boy reading his comic book under a hanging image of the Virgin, another of two little girls peeking into a steaming kettle of frijoles while the mother modestly hid her pregnancy behind the stove. He shot the card players from a low angle, with low sidelighting, and when an old grandmother came in the back door with a pail of water he got her there, stooping to the weight in the open door, against the background of the rain.

Finally he said into Carol's ear, with deliberate malice, "Now do we get that red-hot shot of Johnny jiving with his chick?"

"You're a mean man, Charlie," she said, but she smiled, and looking across to where Johnny stood sullen and alone, she said, "Johnny, you want to come over here?"

He came stiff as a stick, ugly with venom and vanity. When Carol seated him close to Lupe the girl rolled her eyes and bit her lip, ready to laugh. The noise in the room had quieted; it was as if a dipperful of cold water had been thrown into a boiling kettle. Carol moved Chuey in close and laid some records in Lupe's lap. Prescott could see the caption coming up: *Even in shacktown, young people need amusement. Lack of adequate entertainment facilities one of greatest needs. Older generation generally disapproves of jive, jive talk, jive clothes.*

The girl was pretty, even with her ridiculous pompadour. Her eyes were soft, liquid, very dark, her cheekbones high, and her cheeks planed. With a *rebozo* over her head she might have posed for Murillo's Madonna. She did not stare into the camera as her elders did, but at Prescott's word became absorbed in studying the record labels. Chuey laid his head close to hers, and on urging, Johnny sullenly did the same. The moment the flash went off Johnny stood up.

Prescott shifted the Victrola so the crank handle showed more, placed Chuey beside it with a record in his hands. "All right, Lupe, you and Johnny show us a little rug-cutting."

He watched the girl glance from the corners of her eyes at her parents, then come into Johnny's arm. He held her as if she smelled bad, his head back and away, but she turned her face dreamily upward and sighed like an actress in a love drama and laid her face against his rain-wet chest. "*Qúe chicloso!*" she said, and could not hold back her laughter.

"*Surote!*" Johnny pushed her away so hard she almost fell. His face was contorted, his eyes glared. Spittle sprayed from his heavy lips. "*Bofa!*" he said to Lupe, and suddenly Prescott found himself protecting the camera in the middle of what threatened to become a brawl. Chuey surged forward, the undershirted father crowded in from the other side, the girl was spitting like a cat. With a wrench Johnny broke away and got his back to the wall, and there he stood with his hand plunged into the pocket of his blazer and his loose mouth working.

"Please!" Carol was shouting, "Chuey! Lupe! Please!" She held back the angry father and got a reluctant, broken quiet. Over her shoulder she said, "Johnny, go wait for us in the car."

For a moment he hung, then reached a long thin hand for the latch and slid out. The room was instantly full of noise again, indignation, threats. Prescott got his things safely outside the door away from their feet, and by that time politeness and diplomacy had triumphed. Carol said something to Lupe, who showed her teeth in a little white smile; to Chuey, who shrugged; to the father, who bowed over her hand and talked close to her face. There was handshaking around, Carol promised them prints of the pictures,

Prescott gave the children each a quarter. Eventually they were out in the blessed rain.

"What in hell did he call her?" Prescott said as they clawed their way up the hill.

"Pachuco talk. Approximately a chippy."

"Count on him for the right touch."

"Don't say anything, Charlie," she said. "Let me handle him."

"He's probably gone off somewhere to nurse his wounded ego."

But as he helped her over the clay brink on to the cinder road he looked towards the car and saw the round dark head in the back seat. "I must say you pick some dillies," he said.

Walking with her face sideward away from the rain, she said seriously, "I don't pick them, Charlie. They come because they don't have anybody else."

"It's no wonder this one hasn't got anybody else," he said, and then they were at the car and he was opening the door to put the equipment inside. Johnny Bane made no motion to get his muddy feet out of the way.

"Lunch?" Carol said as she climbed under the wheel. Prescott nodded, but Johnny said nothing. In the enclosed car Prescott could smell his hair oil. Carol twisted around to smile at him.

"Listen!" she said. "Why take it so hard? It's just that Chuey's her cousin, he's family, he can crash the gate."

"Agh!"

"Laugh it off."

He let his somber gaze fall on her. "That punk!" he said. "I get him good. Her too. I kill that mean little bitch. You wait. I kill her sometime."

For a moment she watched him steadily; then she sighed. "If it helps to take it out on me, go ahead," she said. "I'll worry about you, if that's what you want."

A few minutes later she stopped at a diner on Figueroa, but when she and Prescott climbed out, Johnny sat still. "Coming?" she said.

"I ain't hungry."

"Oh, Johnny, come off it! Don't sulk all day."

The long look he gave her was so deliberately insolent that Prescott wanted to reach through the window and slap his loose mouth. Then the boy looked away, picked a thread indifferently from his sleeve, stared moodily as if tasting some overripe self-pity or some rich revenge. Prescott took Carol's arm and pulled her into the diner.

"Quite a young man," he said.

Her look was sober. "Don't be too hard on him."

"Why not?"

"Because everybody always has been."

He passed her the menu. "Mother loved me, but she died."

"Stop it, Charlie!"

He was astonished. "All right," he said at last. "Forget it."

While they were eating dessert she ordered two hamburgers to go, and when she passed them through the car window Johnny Bane took them without a word. "What do you want to do?" she said. "Come along, or have us drop you somewhere?"

"Okay if I go along?"

"Sure."

"Okay."

In a street to which she drove, a peddler pushed a cart full of peppers and small Mexican bananas through the mud between dingy frame buildings. No one else was on the street, but two children were climbing through the windows of a half-burned house. The rain angled across, fine as mist.

"What's here?" Prescott said.

"This is a family I've known ever since I worked for Welfare," Carol said. "Grandmother with asthma, father with dropsy, half a dozen little rickety kids. This is to prove that bad luck has no sense of proportion."

Fishing for a cigarette, Prescott found the package empty. He tried the pockets of coat and raincoat without success. Carol opened her purse; she too was out. Johnny Bane had been smoking hers all morning.

"We can find a store," she said, and had turned the ignition key to start when Johnny said, "I can go get some for you."

"Oh, say, would you, Johnny? That would be wonderful."

Prescott felt dourly that he was getting an education in social workers. One rule was that the moment your delinquent showed the slightest sign of decency, passed you a cigarette or picked up something you had dropped, you fell on his neck as if he had rescued you from drowning. As a matter of fact, he had felt his own insides twitch with surprised pleasure at Johnny's offer. But then what? he asked himself. After you've convinced him that every little decency of his deserves a hundred times its weight in thanks, then what?

"No stores around here," Johnny said. "Probably the nearest over on Figueroa."

"Oh," she said, disappointed. "Then I guess we'd better drive down. That's too far to walk."

"You go ahead, do your business here," Johnny said. He leaned forward with his hands on the back of the front seat. "I take the car and go get some weeds, how's that?"

Prescott waited to hear what she would say, but he really knew. After a pause her quiet voice said, "Have you got a driver's license?"

"Sure, man, right here."

"All right," she said, and stepped out. "Don't be long. Charlie dies by inches without smokes."

While Prescott unloaded, Johnny slid under the wheel. He was as jumpy as a greyhound. His fingers wrapped around the wheel with love.

"Wait," Carol said. "I didn't give you any money."

With an exclamation Prescott fished a dollar bill from his pocket and threw it into the seat, and Johnny Bane let off the emergency and rolled away.

"What was that?" Prescott said. "Practical sociology?"

"Don't be so indignant," she said. "You trust people, and maybe that teaches them to trust you."

"Why should anybody but a hooligan have to be *taught* to trust you? Are you so unreliable?"

But she only shook her head at him, smiling and denying his premises, as they went up the rotted steps.

This house was more than the others. It was not merely poor, it was dirty, and it was not merely dirty, but sick. Prescott looked it over for picture possibilities while Carol talked with a thin Mexican woman, worn to the bleak collarbones with arms like sticks. In the kitchen the sink was stopped with a greasy rag, and dishes swam in water the color of burlap. On the table were three bowls with brown juice dried in them. There was a hole clear through the kitchen wall. In the front room, on an old taupe overstuffed sofa, the head of the house lay in a blanket bathrobe, his thickened legs exposed, his eyes mere slits in the swollen flesh of his face. By the window in the third room an old woman sat in an armchair, and everywhere, in every corner and behind every broken piece of furniture, were staring broad-faced children, incredibly dirty and as shy as mice. In a momentary pause in Carol's talk he heard the native sounds of this house: the shuffle of children's bare feet and the old woman's harsh breathing.

He felt awkward, and an intruder. Imprisoned by the rain, quelled by the presence of the Welfare lady and the strange man, the children crept soft as lizards around the walls. Wanting a cigarette worse than ever, Prescott glanced impatiently at his watch. Probably Johnny would stop for a malt or drive around showing off the car and come in after an hour expecting showers of thanks.

"What do you think, Charlie?" Carol's voice had dropped; the bare walls echoed to any noise, the creeping children and the silent invalids demanded hushed voices and soft feet. "Portrait shots?" she whispered. "All this hopeless sickness?"

"They'll be heartbreakers."

"That's what they ought to be."

Even when he moved her chair so that gray daylight fell across her face, the old woman paid no attention to him beyond a first piercing look. Her head was held stiffly, her face as still as wood, but at every breath the cords in her neck moved slightly with the effort. He got three time exposures of that half-raised weathered mask; flash would have destroyed what the gray light revealed.

Straightening up from the third one, he looked through the doorway into the inhuman swollen face of the son. It was impossible to tell whether the Chinese slits of eyes were looking at him or not. He was startled with the thought that they might be, and wished again, irritably, for a cigarette.

"Our friend is taking his time," he said to Carol, and held up his watch.

"Maybe he couldn't find a store."

Prescott grunted, staring at the dropsical man. If he shot across the swollen feet and legs, foreshortening them, and into the swollen face, he might get something monstrous and sickening, a picture to make people wince.

"Can he be propped up a little?" he asked.

Carol asked the thin, hovering wife, who said he could. The three of them lifted and slid the man up until his shoulders were against the wall. It troubled Prescott to see Carol's hands touch the repulsive flesh. The man's slits watched them; the lips moved, mumbling something.

"What's he say?"

"He says you must be a lover of beauty," Carol said.

For a moment her eyes held his, demanding of him something that he hated to give. Once, on his only trip to Mexico, he had gone hunting with his host in Michoacán, and he remembered how he had fired at a noise in a tree and brought something crashing down, and how they had run up to see a little monkey lying on the bloodied leaves. It was still alive; as they came up its eyes followed them, and at a certain moment it put up its arms over its head to ward off the expected death blow. To hear this monster make a joke was like seeing that monkey put up its arms in an utterly human gesture. It sickened him so that he took refuge behind the impersonality of the camera, and when he had taken his pictures he said something that he had not said to a subject all day. "Thanks," he said. "*Gracias, señor.*"

Somehow he had to counteract that horrible portrait with something sweet. He posed the thin mother and one of the children in a sentimental Madonna and Child pose, pure poster art suitable for a fund-raising campaign. While he was rechecking for the second exposure he heard the noise, like a branch being dragged across gravel. It came from the grandmother. She sat in the same position by the window of the other room, but she seemed straighter and more rigid, and he had an odd impression that she had grown in size.

The thin woman was glancing uneasily from Prescott to Carol.

The moment he stepped back she was out of her chair and into the other room.

The grandmother had definitely grown in size. Prescott watched her with a wild feeling that anyone in this house might suddenly blow up with the obscene swelling disease. Under the shawl the old woman's chest rose in jerky breaths, but it didn't go down between inhalations. Her gray face shone with sudden sweat; her mouth was open, her head held stiffly to one side.

"Hadn't I better try to get a doctor?" Prescott said.

Bending over the old woman, Carol turned only enough to nod.

Prescott went quickly to the door. The peddler had disappeared, the children who had been climbing in the burned house were gone, the street lay empty in the rain. Johnny Bane had been gone for over an hour; if this woman died he could take the credit. In a district like this there might not be a telephone for blocks. Prescott would have to run foolishly like someone shouting fire.

A girl of ten or so, sucking her thumb, slid along the wall, watching him. He trapped her. "Where's there a telephone?"

She stared, round-eyed and scared.

"*Teléfono? You sabe teléfono?*"

He saw comprehension grow in her face, slapped a half-dollar into her hand, motioned her to start leading him. She went down the steps and along the broken sidewalk at a trot.

It took four calls from the little neighborhood grocery before he located a doctor who could come. Then, the worst cause for haste removed, he paused to buy cigarettes for himself and a bag of suckers for the children. His guide put a sucker in her mouth and a hand in his, and they walked back that way through the drizzle.

The street before the house was still empty, and he cursed Johnny Bane. Inside, the grandmother was resting after her paroxysm, but her head was still stiffly tilted, and a minute after he entered she fell into a fit of coughing that pebbled her lips with mucus and brought her halfway to her feet, straining and struggling for air. Carol and the thin woman held her, eased her back.

"Did you get someone?" Carol said.

"He's on his way."

"Did he tell you anything to do?"

"There's nothing to do except inject atropine or something. We have to wait for him."

"Hasn't Johnny come back?"

"Did you really expect him to?"

Her eyes and mouth were strained. She no longer looked like a college sophomore; a film from the day's poverty and sickness had rubbed off on her. Without a word she turned away, went into the kitchen, and started clearing out the sink.

As Prescott started to pack up it occurred to him that a picture of an old woman choking to death would add to the sociological impact of Carol's series, but he was damned if he would take it. He'd had enough for one day. The dropsical man turned his appalling swollen mask, and on an impulse Prescott stood up and gestured with the packet of cigarettes. The monster nodded, so Prescott inserted a cigarette between the lips and lighted it. Sight of the man smoking fascinated him.

The Rolleiflex was just going into the bag when it struck him that he had not seen the Contax. He rummaged, turned things out on to the floor. The camera was gone. Squatting on his heels, he considered how he should approach the mother of the house, or Carol, to get it back from whichever child had taken it. And then he began to wonder if it had been there when he unpacked for this job. He had used it at the Aguirre house for one picture, but not since. The bag had been in the car all the time he and Carol had been eating lunch. So had Johnny Bane.

Carefully refusing to have any feeling at all about the matter, he took his equipment out on the porch. Four or five children, each with a sucker in its mouth, came out and shyly watched him as he smoked and waited for the doctor.

The doctor was a short man with an air of unhurried haste. He examined the grandmother for perhaps a minute and got out a needle. The woman's eyes followed his hands with terror as he swabbed with an alcohol-soaked pad, jabbed, pushed with his thumb, withdrew, dropped needle and syringe into his case. It was like an act of deadpan voodoo. Within minutes the old woman was breathing almost normally, as if the needle had punctured her swelling and let her subside. For a minute more the doctor talked with Carol; he scribbled on a pad. Then his eyes darted into the next room to where the swollen son lay watching from his slits.

"What's the matter in here?"

"Dropsy," Carol said. "He's been bedridden for months."

"Dropsy's a symptom, not a disease," the doctor said, and went over.

In ten more minutes they were all out on the porch again. "I'll expect you to call me then," the doctor said.

"I will," Carol said. "You bet I will."

"Are you on foot? Can I take you anywhere?"

"No thanks. We're just waiting for my car."

It was then four-thirty. Incredulously Prescott watched her sit down on the steps to wait some more. The late sun, scattering the mist, touched her fair hair and deepened the lines around her mouth. Behind her the children moved softly. Above her head the old porch pillar was carved with initials and monikers: GJG, Mingo, Lola, Chavo, Pina, Juanito. A generation of lost kids had defaced even the little they had, as they might deface and abuse anyone who tried to help them in ways too unselfish for them to understand.

"How long do you expect to sit here?" he said finally.

"Give him another half hour."

"He could have gone to Riverside for cigarettes and been back by now."

"I know."

"You know he isn't going to come back until he's brought."

"He was upset about his girl," she said. "He felt he'd been kicked in the face. Maybe he went up there."

"To do what? Cut her throat?"

"It isn't impossible," she said, and turned her eyes up to his with so much anxiety in them that he hesitated a moment before he told her the rest.

"Maybe it isn't," he said then, "but I imagine he went first of all to a pawnshop to get rid of the camera."

"Camera?"

"He swiped the Contax while we were having lunch."

"How do you know?"

"Either that or one of the kids here took it."

Her head remained bent down; she pulled a sliver from the step. "It couldn't have been here. I was here all the time. None of the children went near your stuff."

She knew so surely what Johnny Bane was capable of, and yet she let it trouble her so, that he was abruptly furious with her. Social betterment, sure, opportunities, yes, a helping hand, naturally. But to lie down and let a goon like that walk all over you, abuse your confidence, lie and cheat and steal and take advantage of every unselfish gesture!

"Listen," he said. "Let me give you a life history. We turn him in and he comes back in handcuffs. Okay. That's six months in forestry camp, unless he's been there before."

"Once," she said, still looking down. "He was with a bunch that swiped a truck."

"Preston then," Prescott said. "In half a year he comes back from Preston and imposes on you some more, and you waste yourself keeping him out of trouble until he gets involved in something in spite of you, something worse, and gets put away for a stretch in San Quentin. By the time they let him out of there he'll be ripe for really big-time stuff, and after he's sponged on you for a while longer he'll shoot somebody in a hold-up or knife somebody in a whorehouse brawl, and they'll lead him off to the gas chamber. And nothing you can do will keep one like him from going all the way."

"It doesn't have to happen that way. There's a chance it won't."

"It's a hell of a slim chance."

"I know it," she said, and looked up again, her face not tearful or sentimental as he had thought it would be, but simply thoughtful. "Slim or not, we have to give it to him."

"You've already given him ten chances."

"Even then," she said. "He's everything you say—he's mean, vicious, dishonest, boastful, vain, maybe dangerous. I don't like him any better than you do, any better than he likes himself. But he's told me things I don't think he ever told anyone else."

"He never had such a soft touch," he said.

"He grew up in a slum, Harlem. Routine case. His father disappeared before he was born, his mother worked, whatever she could find. He took care of himself."

"I understand that," Prescott said. "He's a victim. He isn't to blame for what his life made him. But he's still unfit to live with other people. He isn't safe. Nine out of ten, maybe, you can help, but not his kind. It's too bad, but he's past helping."

"He wasn't a gang kid," she said. "He's unattractive, don't you see, and mean. People don't like him, and never did. He tries to run with the neighborhood Mexican gang here, but you saw how Chuey and Dago and Lupe just tolerate him. He doesn't belong. He never did. So he prowled the alleys and dreamed up fancy revenges for people he hated, and played with stray cats."

Prescott moved impatiently, and the children slid promptly further along the wall. Carol was watching him as steadily as the children were.

"He told me how he ran errands to earn money for liver and fish to feed them. He wanted them to come to him and be *his* cats."

Prescott waited, knowing how the script ran but surprised that Carol, a hardened case worker, should have fallen for it.

"But they were all alley cats, as outcast as he was," she said. "He'd feed a cat for a week, but when he didn't have anything for it, it would shy away, or he'd grab it and get clawed. So he used to try to tie cats up when he caught them."

Prescott said nothing.

"But when a cat wouldn't let itself be petted, or when it fought the rope—and it always did—he'd swing it by the rope and break its neck," Carol said.

She stirred the litter in the step corner and a sow bug rolled into its ball and bounced down into the dirt. "'I give them every chance, Miss Vaughn,' that's what he told me. 'I give them every chance and if they won't come and be my friend I pop their neck.'"

Cautiously Prescott moved the camera bag backwards with his foot. He looked at the afternoon's grime in the creases of his hands. "That's a sad story," he said at last. "I mean it, it really is. But it only proves what I said, that he's too warped to run loose. He might try that neck-popping on some human being who wouldn't play his way—Lupe, for instance."

"Would you pop a cat's neck if it wouldn't come to you?" Carol said softly.

"Don't be silly."

"But you'd pop Johnny's."

They stared at each other in the rainy late afternoon.

Prescott told himself irrelevantly that he had not fallen in love with her on this job. Anyone who fell in love with her would have to share her with every stray in Greater Los Angeles. But he liked her and respected her and admired her; she was a fine human being. Only she carried it too far.

And yet he had no answer for her. "Good God," he said, "do you know what you're asking?"

"Yes," she said. "I know exactly. But I know you can't come with liver and fish heads six days a week and on the seventh come with a hangman's rope. You can't say, 'I gave him every chance,' unless you really did."

The brief sun had disappeared again in the mist and smog. The street was muddy and gray before them. Behind them the thin woman came to the door and opened it, shooing the children in with an unexpected harsh snarl in her voice. Prescott felt disturbed and alien, out of his proper setting and out of his depth. But he still could find no answer for her. You could not come with liver and fish heads six days a week and with a hangman's knot on the seventh. You could not put limits on love—if love was what you chose to live by.

"All right," he said. "We don't call the cops, is that it?"

She smiled a crooked smile. "Let's try to get along without the police as long as we can."

The thin woman stood in the doorway and said good-bye and watched them down the steps, and the children pressing around her flanks watched too. Prescott waved, and the woman smiled and nodded in reply. But none of the children, solemnly staring, raised a hand. After a moment he was angry with himself for having expected them to.

A Field Guide to the Western Birds

I must say that I never felt better. I don't feel sixty-six, I have no gerontological worries; if I am on the shelf, as we literally are in this place on the prow of a California hill, retirement is not the hangdog misery that I half expected it to be. When I stepped out of the office, we sold our place in Yorktown Heights because even Yorktown Heights might be too close to Madison Avenue for comfort. The New Haven would still run trains; a man might still see the old companions. I didn't want to have to avoid the Algonquin at noon or the Ritz bar after five. If there is anything limper than an ex-literary agent it is an ex-literary agent hanging around where his old business still goes on. We told people that we were leaving because I wanted to get clear away and get perspective for my memoirs. Ha! That was to scare some of them, a little. *What I Have Done for Ten Percent.* I know some literary figures who wish I had stayed in New York where they could watch me.

But here I sit on this terrace in a golden afternoon, finishing off an early, indolent highball, my shanks in saddle-stitched slacks and my feet in brown suede; a Pebble Beach pasha, a Los Gatos geikwar. What I have done for ten percent was never like this.

Down the terrace a brown bird alights—some kind of towhee, I think, but I can't find him in the bird book. Whatever he is, he is a champion for pugnacity. Maybe he is living up to some dim notion of how to be a proper husband and father, maybe he just hates himself, for about ten times a day I see him alight on the terrace and challenge his reflection in the plate glass. He springs at himself like a fighting cock, beats his wings, pecks, falls back, springs again, slides and thumps against the glass, falls down, flies up, falls down, until he wears himself out and squats on the bricks, panting and glaring at his hated image. For about ten days now he has been struggling with himself like Jacob with his angel, Hercules with his Hydra, Christian with his conscience, old retired Joe Allston with his memoirs.

I drop a hand and grope up the drained highball glass, tip the ice cubes into my palm, and scoot them down the terrace. "Beat it, you fool." The towhee, or whatever he is, springs into the air and flies away. End of problem.

Down the hill that plunges steeply from the terrace, somewhere down among the toyon and oak, a tom quail is hammering his ca-whack-a, ca-whack-a, ca-whack-a. From the horse pasture of our neighbor Shields, on the other side of the house, a meadowlark whistles sharp and pure. The meadowlarks are new to me. They do not grow in Yorktown Heights, and the quail there, I am told, say Bob White instead of ca-whack-a.

This terrace is a good place just to lie and listen. Lots of bird business, every minute of the day. All around the house I can hear the clatter of house finches that have nested in the vines, the drainspouts, the rafters of the carport. The liveoaks level with my eyes flick with little colored movements: I see a red-headed woodpecker working spirally around a trunk, a nuthatch walking upside down along a limb, a pair of warblers hanging like limes among the leaves.

It is a thing to be confessed that in spite of living in Yorktown Heights among the birdwatchers for twenty-four years I never got into my gaiters and slung on my binoculars and put a peanut butter sandwich and an apple in my pocket and set off lightheartedly through the woods. I have seen them come straggling by on a Sunday afternoon, looking like a cross between the end of a Y.W.C.A. picnic and Hare and Hounds at Rugby, but it was always a little too tweedy and muscular to stir me, and until we came here I couldn't have told a Wilson thrush from a turkey. The memoirs are what made a birdwatcher out of Joseph Allston; I have labored at identification as much as reminiscence through the mornings when Ruth has thought I've been gleaning the busy years.

When we built this house I very craftily built a separate study down the hill a hundred feet or so, the theory being that I did not want to be disturbed by telephone calls. Actually I did not want to be disturbed by Ruth, who sometimes begins to feel that she is the Whip of Conscience, and who worries that if I do not keep busy I will start to deteriorate. I had a little of that feeling myself: I was going to get all the benefits of privacy and quiet, and I even put a blank wall on the study on the view side. But I made the whole north wall of glass, for light, and that was where I got caught. The wall of glass looks into a deep green shade coiling with the python limbs of a liveoak, and the oak is always full of birds.

Worse than that for my concentration, there are two casement windows on the south that open on to a pasture and a stripe of sky. Even with my back to them, I can see them reflected dimly in the plate glass in front of me, and the pasture and the sky are also full of birds. I wrote a little thumbnail description of this effect, thinking it might go into the memoirs somewhere. It is something I learned how to do while managing the affairs of writers: "Faintly, hypnotically, like an hallucination, the reflected sky superimposed on the umbrageous cave of the tree is traced by the linear geometry of hawks, the vortical returnings of buzzards. On the three fenceposts that show between sky and pasture, bluejays plunge to a halt to challenge the world, and across the stripe of sky lines of Brewer's blackbirds are pinned to the loops of telephone wire like a ragged black wash." I have seen (and sold) a lot worse.

I am beginning to understand the temptation to be literary and indulge the senses. It is a full-time job just watching and listening here. I watch the light change across the ridges to the west, and the ridges are the fresh gold of wild oats just turned, the oaks are round and green with oval shadows, the hollows have a tinge of blue. The last crest of the Coast Range is furry with sunstruck spikes of fir and redwood. Off to the east I can hear the roar, hardly more than a hum from here, as San Francisco pours its commuter trains down the valley, jams El Camino from Potrero to San Jose with the honk and stink of cars, rushes its daytime prisoners in murderous columns down the Bayshore. Not for me, not any more. Hardly any of that afternoon row penetrates up here. This is for the retired, for the no-longer-commuting, for contemplative ex-literary agents, for the birds.

Ruth comes out of the French doors of the bedroom and hands me the pernicious silver necklace that my client Murthi once sent her in gratitude from Hyderabad. The bird who made it was the same kind of jeweler that Murthi is a writer; why in *hell* should anyone hand-make a little set screw for a fastener, and then thread the screw backward?

I comment aloud on the idiocy of the Hyderabad silversmith while I strain up on one elbow and try to fasten the thing around her neck, but Ruth does not pay attention. I believe she thinks complaints are a self-indulgence. Sometimes she irritates me close to uxoricide. I do not see how people can stay healthy unless they express their feelings. If I had that idiot Murthi here now I would tell him exactly what I think of his smug Oxonian paragraphs and his superior sniffing about American materialism. If I hadn't sold his foolish book for him he would never have sent this token of gratitude, and all the comfortable assumptions of my sixty-six years would be intact. I drop the screw on the bricks; *invariably* I try to screw it the wrong way. Cultural opposites; never the twain shall meet. Political understanding more impossible than Murthi thinks it is, because the Indians insist on making and doing and thinking everything backward.

"No fog," Ruth says, stooping. At Bryn Mawr they taught her that a lady modulates her speaking voice, and as a result she never says anything except conspiratorially. A writer who wrote with so little regard for his audience wouldn't sell a line. On occasion she has started talking to me while her head was deep inside some cupboard or closet so that nothing came out but this inaudible thrilling murmur, and I have been so exasperated that I have deliberately walked out of the room. Five minutes later I have come back and found her still talking, still with her head among the coats and suits and dresses. "*What?*" I am inclined to say then. The intent is to make her feel chagrined and ridiculous to have been murmuring away to herself. It never does. A Bryn Mawr lady is as unruffled as her voice.

"*What?*" I say now, though this time I have heard her well enough.

It just seems to me that out on the terrace, in the open air, she might speak above a whisper.

"No fog," she says in exactly the same tone. "Sue was afraid the fog would come in and chase everybody indoors."

I get the necklace screwed together at last and sink back exhausted. I am too used up even to protest when she rubs her hand around on my bald spot—a thing that usually drives me wild.

"Are you ready?" she says.

"That depends. Is this thing black tie or hula shirt?"

"Oh, informal."

"Slacks and jacket all right?"

"Sure."

"Then I'm ready."

For a minute she stands vaguely stirring her finger around in my fringe. It is very quiet; the peace seeps in upon the terrace from every side. "I suppose it isn't moral," I say.

"What isn't?"

"This."

"The house? What?"

"All of it."

I rear up on my elbow, not because I am sore about anything but because I really have an extraordinary sense of well-being, and when I feel anything that strongly I like a reaction, not a polite murmur. But then I see that she is staring at me and that her face, fixed for the party, is gently and softly astonished. It is as definite a reaction as they taught her, poor dear. I reach out and tweak her nose.

"I ought to invest in a hair shirt," I say. "What have I done to deserve so well-preserved and imperturbable a helpmeet?"

"Maybe it's something you did for ten percent," she whispers, and that tickles me. I was the poor one when we were married. Her father's money kept us going for the first five or six years.

She laughs and rubs her cheek against mine, and her cheek is soft and smells of powder. For the merest instant it feels *old*—too soft, limp and used and without tension and resilience, and I think what it means to be all through. But Ruth is looking across at the violet valleys and the sunstruck ridges, and she says in her whispery voice, "Isn't it beautiful? Isn't it really perfectly beautiful!"

So it is; that ought to be enough. If it weren't I would not be an incipient birdwatcher; I would be defensively killing myself writing those memoirs, trying to stay alive just by stirring around. But I don't need to stay alive by stirring around. I am a bee at the heart of a sleepy flower; the things I used to do for a living and the people I did them among are as remote as things and people I knew in prep school.

"I am oppressed with birdsong," I say. "I am confounded by peace. I don't want to move. Do we have to go over to Bill Casement's and drink highballs and listen to Sue's refugee genius punish the piano?"

"Of course. You were an agent. You know everybody in New York. You own or control Town Hall. You're supposed to help start this boy on his career."

I grunt, and she goes inside. The sun, very low, begins to reach in under the oak and blind me with bright flashes. Down at the foot of our hill two tall eucalyptuses rise high above the oak and toyon, and the limber oval leaves of their tips, not too far below me, flick and glitter like tinsel fish. From the undergrowth the quail cackles again. A swallow cuts across the terrace and swerves after an insect and is gone.

It is when I am trying to see where the swallow darted to that I notice the little hawk hovering above the tips of the eucalyptus trees. It holds itself in one spot like a helicopter pulling somebody out of the surf. The sparrow hawk or kestrel, according to the bird book, is the only small hawk, maybe the only one of any kind, that can do that.

From its hover, the kestrel stoops like a falling stone straight into the tip of the eucalyptus and then shoots up again from among the glitter of the leaves. It disappears into the sun, but just when I think it has gone it appears in another dive. Another miss: I can tell from its angry *kreeeeee!* as it swerves up. All the other birds are quiet; for a second the evening is like something under a belljar. I watch the kestrel stop and hover, and down it comes a third time, and up it goes screeching. As I stand up to see what it can be striking at, it apparently sees me; it is gone with a swift bowed wingbeat into the sun.

And now what? Out of the eucalyptus, seconds after the kestrel has gone, comes a little buzzing thing about the size of a bumblebee. A hummingbird, too far to see what kind. It sits in the air above the tree just as the kestrel did; it looks as if it couldn't hold all the indignation it feels; I think of a thimble-sized Colonel Blimp with a red face and asthmatic wheezings and exclamations. Then it too is gone as if shot out of a slingshot.

I am tickled by its tiny wrath and by the sense it has shown in staying down among the leaves where the hawk couldn't hit it. But I have hardly watched the little buzzing dot disappear before I am rubbing my eyes like a man seeing ghosts, for out of this same eucalyptus top, in a kind of Keystone Kop routine where fifty people pour out of one old Model T, lumbers up a great owl. He looks as clumsy as a buffalo after the speed and delicacy of the hawk and the hummingbird, and like a lumpish halfwit hurrying home before the neighborhood gang can catch and torment him, he flaps off heavily into the woods.

This is too much for Joseph Allston, oppressed with birdsong. I am cackling to myself like a maniac when Ruth comes out on to the terrace with her coat on. "Ruthie," I tell her, "you just missed seeing Oliver Owl black-balled from the Treetop Country Club."

"What?"

"Just as Big Round Red Mr. Sun was setting over the California hills."

"Have you gone balmy, poor lamb," Ruth whispers, "or have you been nibbling highballs?"

"Madame, I am passionately at peace."

"Well, contain your faunish humor tonight," Ruth says. "Sue really wants to do something for this boy. Don't you go spoiling anything with your capers."

Ruth believes that I go out of my way to stir up the animals. Once our terrier Grumpy—now dead, but more dog for his pounds than ever lived—started through the fence in Yorktown Heights with a stick in his mouth. He didn't allow for the stick and the pickets, and he was coming fast—he never came any other way. The stick caught solidly on both sides and pretty near took his head off. That, Ruth told me in her confidential whisper, was the way I had approached every situation in my whole life. In her inaudible way, she is capable of a good deal of hyperbole. I have no desire to foul up Sue's artistic philanthropies. I can't do her boy any good, but I'll sip a drink and listen, and that's more help than he will get from any of the twelve people who will be there when he finally plays in Town Hall.

II

IN CALIFORNIA, AS ELSEWHERE, alcohol dulls the auricular nerves and leads people to raise their voices. The noise of cocktail parties is the same whether you are honoring the Sitwells in a suite at the Savoy Plaza, or whether you are showing off a refugee pianist on a Los Gatos patio. It sounds very familiar as we park among the Cadillacs and Jaguars and one incredible sleek red Ferrari and the routine Plymouth suburbans and Hillman Minxes of the neighbors. The sound is the same, only the setting is different. But that difference is considerable.

Dazed visitors from the lower, envious fringes of exurbia—and those include the Allstons, or did at first—are likely to come into the Casement cabaña and walk through it as if they have had a solid thump on the head. This cabaña has a complete barbecue kitchen with electrically operated grills thirty feet long. It has a bar nearly that size, a big television screen and a hi-fi layout, a lounge that is sage and gray and tangerine or lobster, I am not decorator enough to tell. It is chaste and hypnotically comfortable and faintly oppressive with money, like an ad for one of the places where you will find *Newsweek* or see men of distinction.

The whole glass side of the cabaña slides back and the cabaña becomes continuous with a patio that spreads to the edge of the pool, which is the color of one of the glass jars that used to sit in the windows of drugstores in Marshalltown, Iowa, when I was a boy. Across the pool, strung for a long distance along the retaining wall that holds the artificial flat top on to this hill, are the playing fields of Eton. I think I have never toured them all, but I have seen a croquet ground; a putting green; a tennis court and a half-sized paddle-tennis court; a Ping-Pong table; a shuffle-board court of smooth concrete;

and out beyond, a football field, full-sized and fully grassed, that was built especially for young Jim Casement and his friends and so far as I have observed is never used. Beyond the retaining wall the hill falls away steeply, so that you look out across it and across the ventilators of the stables below the wall, and into the dusk where lights are beginning to bloom in beds and borders down the enormous garden of the Santa Clara Valley.

A neighborhood couple of modest means—and there are some—contemplate gratefully their admission to these splendors. A standing invitation amounts to a guest card at an exclusive club, and the Casements are generous with invitations. At some stage of their first tour through the layout any neighbor couple is sure to be found standing with their heads together, their eyes gauging and weighing and estimating, and you can hear the IBM machinery working in their heads. Hundred thousand? More than that, a lot more. Hundred and fifty? God knows what's in the house itself, in which the Casements do not entertain but only live. Couldn't touch the whole thing for under two hundred thousand, probably. A pool that size wouldn't have come at less than ten thousand; the cabaña alone would have cost more than our whole house....

I have been around this neighborhood for more than six months, and in six months the Casements can make you feel like a lifelong friend. And I have not been exactly unfamiliar in my lifetime with conspicuous consumption and the swindle sheet. But I still feel like whistling every time I push open the gate in the fence that is a design by Mondrian in egg crates and plastic screen, and look in upon the pool and the cabaña and the patio. The taste has been purchased, but it is taste. The Casement Club just misses being extravagantly beautiful; all it needs is something broken or incomplete, the way a Persian rug weaver will leave a flaw in his pattern to show that Allah alone is perfect and there is no God but God. This is all muted colors, plain lines, calculated simplicities. As I hold open the gate for Ruth, with the noise of the party already loud in the air, I feel as if I were going aboard a brand new and competitively designed cruise ship, or entering the latest Las Vegas motel.

We have not more than poked our heads in, and seen that the

crowd is pretty thick already, before Sue spots us and starts over. She has a high-colored face and a smile that asks to be smiled back at, a very warm good-natured face. You think, the minute you lay eyes on her, What a nice woman. And across clusters of guests I see Bill Casement, just as good-natured, waving an arm, and with the same motion savagely beckoning a white-coated Japanese to intercept us with a tray. It is one of Bill's beliefs that guests at a Casement party spring into the splendid patio with bent elbows and glasses in their hands. He does not like awkward preliminaries; he perpetuates a fiction that nobody is ahead of anybody else.

"Ah," Sue says, "it's wonderful of you to come!" The funny thing is, you can't look at that wide and delighted smile and think otherwise. You are doing her an enormous favor just to *be*; to be at her party is to put her forever in your debt.

I scuff my ankles. "It is nothing," I say. "Where are the people who wanted to meet me?"

Sue giggles, perfectly delighted. "Lined up all around the pool. Including the next-most-important guest. You haven't met Arnold, have you?"

"I don't think he has met me," I say with dignity.

She has us by the elbows, starting us in. I twist and catch up two glasses off the tray that has appeared beside me, and I exchange a face of fellowship with the Japanese. Then the stage set swallows us. Mr. and Mrs. Allston, Ruth and Joe, the Allstons, neighbors, we are repeated every minute or two to polite inattentive people, and we get people thrown at us in turn. Names mean less than nothing, they break like bubbles on the surface of the party's sound. We are two more walk-ons with glasses in our hands; our voices go up and are lost in the clatter that reminds my bird-conscious ears of a hundred blackbirds in a tree.

Groups open and let us in and hold us a minute and pass us on. My recording apparatus makes note of Mr. Thing, a white-haired and astonishingly benevolent-looking music critic from San Francisco; and of Mr. and Mrs. How-d'ye-do, whose family has supported music in the city since Adah Menken was singing "Sweet Betsy from Pike" to packed houses at the Mechanics' Hall. We shake the damp glass-chilled hand of Mr. Monsieur, whom we have seen on platforms as the accompanist of a celebrated Negro soprano, and Ruth has her hand kissed by a gentleman whom I distinguish as Mr. Budapest, a gentleman who makes harps, or harpsichords, and who wears a brown velvet jacket and sandals.

Glimpses of Distinguished Guests, *filets* of conversation *au vin, verschiedener kalter Aufschnitt* of the neighborhood:

Sam Shields, he of the robust cement mixer and the acres of home-made walks and patios and barbecue pits and incinerators, close neighbor to the Joseph Allstons; home-builder who erected by hand his own house, daring heaven and isostasy, on the lip of the San Andreas fault. With a Navy captain and a Pan Am pilot, both of the neighborhood (the pilot owns the Ferrari) he passes slowly, skinny-smiling, blue-bearded, with warts, ugly as Lincoln, saying: *I do not kid you. A zebra. I rise up from fixing that flat tire and I am face to face with a zebra. I am lucky it wasn't a leopard. Hearst stocked that whole damn duchy with African animals, including giraffes. It wouldn't surprise me if pygmies hunt warthogs through those hills with blowguns....*And as he passes, the raised glass, the *salud:* Ah there, Joe!

Four Unknowns, two male and two female, obviously not related by marriage because too animated, but all decorous, one lady with cashmere sweater draped shawl-like over her shoulders, the other winking of diamonds as she lifts her glass; the gentlemen deferential, gray, brushed, double-breasted, bent heads listening: *Bumper to bumper, all the way across, and some idiot out of gas on the bridge...*

Mrs. Williamson, beagle-breeder extraordinary, Knight of the AKC, leather-faced, hoarse-voiced (*Howdy, Neighbor!*) last seen on a Sunday morning across the canyon from the Allstons' house, striding corduroy-skirted under the oaks, blowing her thin whistle, crying in the bar-room voice to a pack of wag-tailed long-coupled hounds, *Pfweeeet! Here Esther! come Esther!* Here we go a-beagling. Wrists like a horsewoman, maybe from holding thirty couple of questing hounds on leash. Now, from quite a distance, rounding the words on the mouth, with a white smile, brown face, tweed shoulders, healthy-horsy-country woman, confidential across forty feet of lawn: *How are the memoirs?*

More Unknowns, not of the local race. City or Upper Peninsula, maybe Berkeley, two ladies and a gentleman, dazzled a little by the Casement Club, watchful. Relax and pass, friends. It is no movie set, it was made for hospitality. The animals who come to drink at this jungle ford are not what they seem. No leopards they, nor even zebras. Yon beagle-breeding Amazon is a wheelhorse of the League of Women Voters, those two by the dressing-room doors at the end of the pool spend much of their time and all of their surplus income promoting Civil Liberties and World Government. Half the people here do not work for a living, for one reason or other, but they cannot be called idlers. They all do something, sometimes even good. And you do not need, as on Martha's Vineyard, to distinguish between East Chop and West Chop. Here we live in a mulligan world, though it is made of prime sirloin....*Ah, how do you do? Yes, isn't it? Lovely...*

Bill Casement, with his golfer's hide, one eye on the gate for new arrivals—shake of the head, *Quite a struggle, boy,* stoops abstractedly to listen to a short woman with a floury face. Somebody comes in. *Excuse me, please.* Short woman looks around for another anchorage—turn away, quick.

And what of the arts? Ah there, again, in a group: Mr. Thing, Mr. Budapest, Mr. and Mrs. How-d'ye-do, surnamed Ackerman, a tight enclave of the cognoscenti, on their fringes an eager young woman, not pretty, perhaps a piano teacher somewhere; this her big moment, probably, thrilled to be asked here, voice shaking and a little too loud as she wedges something into the conversation, *But Honegger isn't really—do you think? He seems to me...*And to me, thou poor child. You have not gone to heaven, you do not have to prove angelhood, you are still in the presence of mortals. Listen and you shall hear.

And what of the Great Man? He is coming closer. There is a kind of progress here, though constantly interrupted, like walking the dog around Beekman Place and up to 51st and back down First Avenue. Magnetic fields, iron filings, kaleidoscopic bits of colored glass that snap into pattern and break again.

On around the diving board, on to the lawn, softer and quieter and with a nap like a marvelous thick rug. Something underfoot— whoop! what the hell? Croquet wicket. Half a good drink gone—on Ruth's dress? No. To the rescue another Japanese, out of the lawn like a mushroom. Thank you, thank you. Big tooth-gleaming grin, impossible to tell what they think. Contempt? Boozing Americans? But what then of all the good nature, the hospitality, the generosity? What of that, my toothy alert impeccable friend? Would you prefer us to be French aristocrats out of Henry James? Absurd. Probably has no such thoughts at all, good waiter, well trained.

"Ah," Sue says, "there he is!"

It is in her face like a sentence or a theorem: Here is this terrific musician, the best young pianist in the world. And here is this ex-literary agent, knows everybody in New York, owns Town Hall, lunches with S. Hurok twice a week. And here I have brought them together, carbide and water, and what will happen? Something will—there will be an explosion, litmus paper will change color, gases will boil and fume, fire will appear, a gleaming little nugget of gold or radium will form in the crucible.

Mr. Kaminski, Mr. and Mrs. Allston. Arnold, Joe and Ruth.

Now hold your breath.

III

MY FIRST IMPRESSION, in the flick of an eye, is *What in hell can Sue be thinking of?* My second, all but simultaneous with the first, is *Bill Casement had better look out.*

Taking inventory during the minute or two of introductions and Ruth's far inland murmur and Sue's explanations of who we all are, I can't pick out any obvious reason why Kaminski should instantly bring my hackles up. His appearance is plus-minus. His skin is bad, not pitted by smallpox or chickenpox but roughened and lumpy, the way a face may be left by a bad childhood staphylococcus infection. His head is big for his body, which is both short and slight, and his crew-cut hair, with that skin, makes him look like a second in a curtain-raiser at some third-rate boxing arena: his name somehow ought to be Moishe, pronounced Mushy. But he has an elegant air too, and he has dressed for the occasion in a white dinner jacket. His eyes are large and brown and slightly bulging; some women would probably call them "fine." They compensate for his mouth, a little purse-slit like the mouth of a Florida rock fish.

The proper caption for the picture in its entirety is "Glandular Genius." I suppose if you are sentimental about artistic sensibility, or fascinated by the neurotic personality, you might look at a face like Kaminski's with attention, respect, perhaps sympathy and a shared anguish. He has all the stigmata of the type, and it is a type some people respond to. But if you are old Joe Allston, who has had to deal in his time with a good many petulant G.G.'s, you look upon this face with suspicion if not distaste.

It makes, of course, no difference to me what he is. Nevertheless, Bill Casement had better look out. This pianist is pretty expressionless, but such expression as he permits himself is so far a little shadowy sneer, a kind of controlled disdain. Bill might note not only that expression, but the air of almost contemptuous ownership with which Kaminski wears Sue's hand on his white sleeve. And it does not seem to me that even Sue can look as delighted and proud as she looks now out of simple good nature. It is true that she is as grateful for a friendly telephone call as if it had cost you fifty dollars to make it, and true that if you notice her and speak to her and joke with her a little she is constitutionally unable to look upon you as less than wonderful. It is a kind of idiotic and appealing humility in her; she is as happy for a smile as Sweet Alice, Ben Bolt. But right now she looks at Kaminski in a way that can only be called radiant; no woman of fifty should look at any young man that way, even if he *can* play the piano. If she knew how she looks, she would disguise her expression. The whole tableau embarrasses me, because I like Sue and automatically dislike the cool smirk on Kaminski's face, and I am sorry for Sue's sake that no chemical wonder is going to take place at our meeting. As for Kaminski, he is not stupid. Within three seconds he is giving me back my dislike as fast as I send it.

Sue stands outside the closed circuit of our hostility like a careless person gossiping over an electric fence.

"People who have as much to give as you two ought to know each other. Though what the rest of us do to deserve you both is more than I know. It's so *good* of you to be here! And shall I tell you something, Joe? Do you mind being *used*? Isn't that an awful question! But you see, Arnold, Joe was a literary agent for years and years in New York—the best, weren't you, Joe? For who? Hemingway? John Marquand? Oh,

James Hilton and James M. Cain and all sorts of people. And we know he couldn't be what he was without having a lot of influence in the other arts too. So we're going to use you, unscrupulously. Or *I* am. Because it's so difficult to make a career as a concert pianist. It's as if there were a conspiracy...."

She is holding a glass, but does not seem to have drunk from it. Her hand is on Kaminski's arm, and her face shines with such goodness that I am ready to grind my teeth.

It is Ruth's belief that I take instant and senseless dislikes to people and that when I do I go out of my way to pick quarrels. Nothing, in fact, could be more unjust. Right now I am aching to harpoon this Kaminski and take the smirk off his face, or at least make him say something dishonestly modest, but what do I say? I say, "I'm afraid you're wrong about my having any influence where it would count. But we're looking forward to hearing you play." I could not have bespoke him more fair. He drops his arrogant head a little to acknowledge that I live.

"It's a wonder you haven't heard him clear over on your hill," Sue says. "All he does all day and night is sit down in the cottage and practice and practice and practice—terribly difficult things. He doesn't even remember meals half the time; I have to send them down on a tray." She gives his arm a slap—you naughty boy. "And he's got such power," she cries. "Look at his hands!"

She turns over his hand, which is the hand of a man half again as big as he is, a big thick meaty paw like a butcher's. The little contemptuous shadow of his expression turns towards her. "If I make too much noise?" he says. These are the first actual words we have heard him say.

I am not a Glandular Genius. I am not even an Artist, and hence I am not Sensitive. But I can recognize a challenge when I hear one, especially when there is an edge of insult in it. Poor Sue takes his remarks, apparently, as some sort of apology.

"Too much noise nothing! If the neighbors hear you, that's their good luck. And when you break down and play Chopin—which is never often enough—then they're double lucky. You know what we did the other night, Ruth—Joe? We heard Arnold playing Chopin down below, to relax after all the terribly difficult things, and we all just pulled up chairs on the patio and had a marvelous concert for over an hour. Even Jimmy, and if you can make *him* listen! Really, *nobody* plays Chopin the way Arnold does."

Arnold's expression says that he concurs in this opinion, though generally opinions from this source are uninformed.

He stands there aloofly, not contaminating his art by brushing too close to Conspicuous Consumption. I am reminded irritably of my ex-client Murthi, who would have been astonished by nothing in this whole evening; he would have recognized it as the American Way from old Bob Montgomery movies. He would have recognized Kaminski too: the Artist (imported, of course—the technological jungle could only borrow, not create) captive to the purse and whim of the Nizam-rich, the self-indulgent plutocracy. Murthi would have welcomed in Kaminski a fellow devotee of the Spirit.

Nothing gives me a quicker pain than that sort of arrogance, whether it is Asian, European, or homegrown. I suppose I am guilty of impatience. Our neighbor Mrs. Shields, who does a good deal of promoting of International Understanding among foreign and native students at Stanford, ropes us in now and then for receptions and such. Generally we stand around making polite international noises at one another, but sometimes we really get a good conversation going. It seems to me that invariably, when I get into the middle of a bunch of thoroughly sensible Indians and Siamese and West Germans and Italians and Japanese and Guamanians, and we begin to get very interested in what the other one thinks, there is sure to come up someone in the crowd with a seed in his teeth about American materialism. This sets my spirituality on edge, and we're off.

It will not do for me to be too close to Kaminski tonight. He has hardly said a word, but I can see the Spirit sticking out all over him.

The Japanese passes with a tray. "Arnold?" Sue says. He makes a gesture of rejection with his meaty hand. He is above a drink. But I am pleased to see that when Ruth engages him in one of her conspiratorial conversations he is as vulnerable as other mortals. He listens with his head bent and a pucker between his eyes, not hearing one damned word, but forced to listen.

Well out of it, I stand back and watch, and remember nights when my ten percent involvement in artists didn't permit me to stand back, such a night as the Book-of-the-Month party when the Time-Life boy got high and insulted his publisher's wife, and punches flew, and in the melee someone—I swear it was a *Herald Tribune* reviewer—bit a chunk out of the lady's arm. She got blood poisoning and nearly died. A critic's bite is as deadly as a camel's, apparently. None of that for me, ever again. Let Art pursue its unquiet way, be content to be a birdwatcher of Los Gatos.

I hear Sue say lightly, "You're so dressed *up*, Arnold. You're the dressiest person at your party."

And wouldn't that be true, too; wouldn't Caliban, in this crowd where nothing is conventional except the thinking, just have to be correct as a haberdasher's clerk? Oh, a beauty. I bury my nose in a third highball, feeling ready and alert and full of conversational sass, but not wanting to get involved with Kaminski, and having no one else handy. Sue and her pianist are listening intently to Ruth's whisper. Teetering on my toes, I catch fragments of talk from people passing by, and think of Sam Shields and his zebra, and of Murthi again, and of how zebras roaming the California hills would not surprise Murthi at all. He would have seen them in some movie. Spiritually empty Americans are always importing zebras or leopards or crocodiles for pets. Part of the acquisitive and sensational itch. Roman decadence.

The whole subject irritates me. How in hell do zebras get into an intelligent conversation?

Some god, somewhere, says Let there be light, and a radiance like moonlight dawns over the patio and the clusters of guests. A blue underwater beam awakes in the pool; the water smokes like a hot spring. Sue's eyes are on the velvet-coated man, who is describing something with gestures to the music-patronizing Ackermans. One of the neighbors, in a loud plaid tweed, stands aside watching the musicians as he would watch little animals digging a hole. I have a feeling that I have failed Sue; Kaminski and I have already practically dropped one another's acquaintance. Her eyes wander around to me. She looks slightly puzzled, a little tired. She rounds her eyes to indicate how pleasantly difficult all this is, and bursts into laughter.

"Everybody here?" I ask.

"Almost, I think. At least the ice seems to be getting broken. Honestly, I don't know half the people here myself. Isn't that a giveaway? This is the first stock I ever bought in musical society."

"Very pretty party," I say. It is. From across the pool it is strikingly staged: light and shade, composition of heads and shoulders, moving faces, glints of glass and bright cloth. For a moment it has the swirl and flash of a Degas ballet, and I say so to Sue. I hear Bill Casement's big laugh; white coats dart around; the Mondrian gate opens to spill four late arrivals into the patio.

"Excuse me," Sue says. "I must go greet somebody. But I particularly wanted Arnold to meet the Ackermans, so I'm going to steal him now. Arnold, will you come..."

He stands with his fish mouth flattened; he breathes through his nose; he does not trouble to keep his voice down. He says, "For God's sake, how long is this going to go on?"

Sue's eyes jump to his; her lips waver in an imbecilic smile. Her glance swerves secretly to me, then to Ruth, and back to Kaminski. "Well, you know how people are," she says. "They don't warm up without a..."

"Good God!" says Kaminski, in a sudden, improbable rage, gobbling as if his throat were full of phlegm. "I am supposed to play for pigs who swill drinks and drinks and drinks until they are falling-down drunk and then will stuff themselves and sleep in their chairs? These are not people to listen to music. I can't play for such people. They are the wrong people. It is the wrong kind of party, nothing but drinks."

Ruth is already trying to pull me away, and I am pretending to go with her while at the same time holding back for dear life; I wouldn't for a fat fee miss hearing what this monster will say next. Sue swings him lightly around, steers him away from us, and I hear her: "Oh, please, Arnold! There's no harm done. We talked about it, remember? We thought, break the ice a little first. Never mind. I'm sorry if it's wrong. We can serve any time now, they'll be ready to listen as soon as..."

I am dragged out of earshot, and wind up beside Ruth, over

against the dressing rooms under a cascade of clematis. Ruth looks like someone who has just put salt in her coffee by mistake. With her white hair and black eyebrows, she has a lot of lady-comedian expressions, but she doesn't seem to know which one to use this time. Our backs against the dressing-room wall, we sneak a cautious look back where we have just casually drifted from. Sue's Roman-striped cotton and Kaminski's white coat are still posed there at the far edge of the illumination. Then he jerks his arm free and walks off.

Ruth and I look at each other and make a glum mouth. There goes the attempt of a good-natured indiscreet well-meaning culture-craving woman to mother an artistic lush. Horrible social bust, tiptoes, hush-hush among her friends. Painful but inevitable. She looks forlorn at the edge of the artificial moonlight of her patio. A performance is going on, but not the one she planned. The audience is there, but it will have no recital to attend, and will not see the real show, which is already over.

Now don't be stupid and go after him, I say to Sue in my mind, but I have hardly had the thought before she does just that. What an utter fool.

That is the moment when the white coats line up in front of the cabaña, and one steps out ahead of the others. He raises his hands with the dramatics of an assistant tympani player whose moment comes only once, and knocks a golden note from a dinner gong.

An arm falls across my shoulders, another sweeps Ruth in. "Come on," says Bill Casement's gun-club golf-course dressing-room voice. "Haven't had a word with you all night. By God, it's a pleasure to see a familiar face. How's it going? O.K.? Good, let's get us some food."

IV

ASSEMBLY LINE ALONG A REACH of stainless steel; the noisy, dutiful, expectant shuffling of feet, the lift of faces sniffing, turning to comment or laugh, craning to look ahead. *Mnnnnnnnn!* Trenchers as big as cafeteria trays, each hand-turned from a different exotic wood. Behind the counter white coats, alert eyes, ready tongs, spoons, spatulas. A state fair exhibit of salads—red lettuce crinkly-edged, endive, romaine, tomatoes like flowers, hearts of artichokes *marinée,* little green scallions, *caveat emptor.* Aspic rings all in a row. A marvelous molded crab with pimento eyes afloat in a tidepool of mayonnaise. Some of that...that...that.

Refugees from Manhattan. Load these folks up, they haven't had a square meal since 1929.

A landslide, an avalanche: slabs of breast from barbecued turkeys, gobs of oyster dressing, candied yams dripping like honeycomb. A man with a knife as long as a sword and as limber as a razorblade whips off paper-thin slices from a ham, leafs them on to trenchers. Another releases by some sleight of hand one after another of a slowly revolving line of spits from a Rube Goldberg grill. Shishkebab. Tray already dangerous, but still pickles, olives, celery frizzled in crushed ice, a smörgasbord of smoked salmon, smoked eel, smoked herring, cheeses. Ovens in the opulent barbecue yield corn fingers, garlic bread.

No more, not another inch of room—but as we turn away we eye three dessert carts burdened with ice-cream confections shaped like apples, pears, pineapples, all fuming in dry ice. Also pastries, petits fours, napoleons, éclairs. Also batteries of coffee flasks streaming bright bubbles. Also two great bowls in which cherries and fat black berries and chunks of pineapple founder in wine-colored juice. Among the smokes of broiling, freshness of scallions, stink of camembert, roquefort, liederkranz, opulence of garlic butter, vinegar-bite of dressings, sniff that bouquet of cointreau and kirsch in which the fruits are soaked. Lucullus, Trimalchio, *adsum.*

But hardly Trimalchio. Instead, this Bill Casement, tall and brown, a maker and a spender loaded with money from lumber mills in the redwood country; no sybarite, but only a man with an urgent will to be hospitable and an indulgent attitude towards his wife's whims. He herds us to a table, looks around. "Where the hell's Sue?" A man behind the counter flashes him some signal. "Excuse me, back in a second. Any of these musical characters tries to sit down here, say it's saved, uh?" Down-mouthed, with his head ducked, he tiptoes away laughing to show that this party is none of his doing, he only works here.

The lawn where Sue and Kaminski have been standing until just a few minutes ago stretches empty and faultless in the dusk. No hostess, no guest of honor. "Quite an evening," I say.

Ruth smiles in a way she has. "Still oppressed with birdsong?"

"Why don't you save that tongue to slice ham with?" I reply crossly. "I'm oppressed all right. Aren't you?"

"If she weren't so nice it would be almost funny."

"But she *is* so nice."

"Yes," she says. "Poor Sue."

As I circle my nose above the heaped and delectable trencher, the thought of Kaminski's bald scorn of food and drink boils over in my insides. Is he opposed to nourishment? "A pituitary monster," I say, "straight out of Dostoevsky."

"Your distaste was a little obvious."

"I can't help it. He curdled my adrenal glands."

"You make everything so endocrine," she says. "He wasn't that bad. In fact, he had a point. It *is* a little alcoholic for a musicale."

"It's the only kind of party they know how to give."

"But it still isn't quite the best way to show off a pianist."

"All right," I say. "Suppose you're right. Is it his proper place to act as if he'd been captured and dragged here? He's the beneficiary, after all."

"I expect he has to humiliate her," Ruth says.

Sometimes she can surprise me. I remark that without an M.D. she is not entitled to practice psychiatry. So maybe he does have to humiliate her. That is exactly one of the seven thousand two hundred and fourteen things in him that irritate the hell out of me.

"But it'll be ghastly," says Ruth in her whisper, "if she can't manage to get him to play."

I address myself to the trencher. "This is getting cold. Do we have to wait for Bill?" When I fill my mouth with turkey and garlic bread, my dyspeptic stomach purrs and lies down. But Ruth's remark of a minute before continues to go around in me like an auger, and I burst out again: "Humiliate her, uh? How to achieve power. How to recover from a depressing sense of obligation. How to stand out in every gathering though a son of a bitch. Did it ever strike you how much attention a difficult cross-grained bastard gets, just by being difficult?"

"It strikes me all the time," Ruth murmurs. "Hasn't it ever struck you before?"

"You suppose she's infatuated with him?"

"No."

"Then why would she put up with being humiliated?"

Her face with its black brows and white hair is as clever as a raccoon's. But as I watch it for an answer I see it flatten out into the pleasant look of social intercourse, and here is Bill, his hand whacking me lightly on the back. "Haven't been waiting for me, have you? Fall to, fall to! We're supposed to be cleared away by nine-thirty. I got my orders."

* * *

OUR TALK IS OF BARBECUING. Do we know there are eighteen different electric motors in that grill? Cook anything on it. The boys got it down to a science now. Some mix-ups at first, though. Right after we got it, tried a suckling pig, really a shambles. Everybody standing around watching Jerry and me get this thing on the spit, and somebody bound to say how much he looks like a little pink scrubbed baby. Does, too. Round he goes, round and round over the coals with an apple in his mouth and his dimples showing, and as his skin begins to shrink and get crisp, damn if his eyes don't open. By God! First a little slit, then wide open. Every time he comes round he gives us a sad look with these baby blue eyes, and the grease fries out of him and sizzles in the fire like tears. If you'd squeezed him he'd've said mama. He really clears the premises, believe me. Two or three women are really *sick*....

Big Bill Casement, happy with food and bourbon, looks upon us in friendship and laughs his big laugh. "Pigs and all, barbecuing is more in my line than this music business. About the most musical I ever get is listening to Cottonseed Clark on the radio, and Sue rides me off the ranch every time she catches me." He rears back and looks around, his forehead wrinkles clear into his bristly widow's peak. "Where d'you suppose she went to, anyway?"

Ruth gives him one of her patent murmurs. It might as well be the Lord's Prayer for all he hears of it, but it comforts him anyway.

Sue and Kaminski are nowhere to be seen—having a long confab somewhere. Thinking of what is probably being said at that meeting, I blurt out, "What about the performer? Who is he? Where'd Sue find him?"

"Well," Bill says, "he's a Pole. Polish Jew," he adds apologetically, as if the word were forbidden. "Grew up in Egypt, went back to Poland before the war, just in time to get grabbed by the Polish army and then by the Nazis. His mother went into an incinerator, I guess. He never knew for sure. I get all this from Sue."

His animation is gone. I am damned if he doesn't peek sideways and bat his eyes in a sheepish way around the patio pretending to be very disinterested and casual. He seems set to start back to attention at any slightest word with "What? Who? Me?"

"Very bright guy," he says with about the heartiness of a postscript sending love to the family. "Speaks half a dozen languages—German, Polish, French, Italian, Arabic, God knows what. Sue found him down here in this artist's colony, What's-its-name. He was having a hell of a time. The rest of the artists were about ready to lynch him—they didn't get along with him at all for some reason. Sue's been on the board of this place, that's how she was down there. She can see he's this terrific prospect, and not much luck so far except a little concert here and there, schools and so on. So she offers him the use of the cottage, and he's been here three weeks."

I watch his hand rubbing on the creased brown skin of cheek and jaw. The hand is manicured. I can imagine him kidding the manicurist in his favorite barbershop. He is a man the barbers all know and snap out their cloths for. He brings a big grin to the shoeshine boy. The manicurist, working on his big clean paw, has wistful furtive dreams.

"You met him yet?" Bill asks.

"We talked for a little while."

"Very talented," Bill says. "I *guess*. Make a piano talk. You'd know better than I would—artists are more in your line. I'm just a big damn lumberjack out of the tall timber."

In that, at least, he speaks with authority and conviction. Right now he would be a lot more at home up to his neck in a leaky barrel in some duck marsh than where he is.

Now I see Sue coming down along the fence from the projecting wing of the main house. She is alone. She stops at a table, and in the artificial moonlight I can see her rosy hostess's smile. "Here comes your lady now," I say.

Bill looks. "About time. I was beginning to...Say, I wonder if that means I should be...Where's Kaminski? Seen *him?*"

"Over across the pool," Ruth whispers, and sure enough there he is, walking pensively among the croquet wickets with his hands behind his white back. The Artist gathering his powers. I cock my ear to the sounds of the party, but all is decorous. All's well, then.

"Maybe I better push the chow line along, I guess," Bill says. He raises an arm and a white coat springs from beside the cabaña wall. In a minute we are confronted by a pastry cart full of all those éclairs and petits fours and napoleons and creampuffs. An arm reaches down and whisks my plate away, slides another in. Right behind the pastry cart comes another with a bowl of kirsch-and-cointreau-flooded fruit and a tray of fruity ice-cream molds. Forty thousand calories stare me in the face; my esophagus produces a small protesting conscientious *pwwk!* From the pastry man with his poised tongs and poised smile Ruth cringes away as if he were Satan with a fountain pen.

"Pick something," I tell her. "Golden apples of the sun, silver apples of the moon. You have a duty."

"Ha, yeah, don't let that bother you," Bill says, like a man who gets a nudge without letting it distract him from what he is looking at. Sue has stopped at a nearby table to talk to the Ackermans and the white-haired critic and the harpsichord man. The little music teacher, typecast for the homely sister of a Jane Austen novel, has managed to squeeze into the musical company. It is all out of some bird book, how the species cling together, and the juncoes and the linnets and the seed-eaters hop around in one place, and the robins raid the toyon berries *en masse,* and the jaybirds yak away together in the almond trees. The party has split into its elements, neighbors and unknown visitors and the little cluster of musicians. And now Sue, bending across them, beckons Kaminski, and he comes around the diving board, the hatchings of some cuckoo egg whose natural and unchangeable use it is to thrust his bottomless gullet up from the nest and gobble everything a foolish foster mother brings.

The rather dour accompanist moves to make place for him. Sue will not sit down; she stands there animated, all smiles. And Kaminski has changed his front. His politeness is as noticeable as perfume. He talks. He shows his teeth in smiles. The little music teacher leans forward, intent to hear.

With a tremendous flourish the waiter serves Ruth a bowl of fruit. "You do that like Alfredo serving noodles," I say, but Ruth, who knows what I mean, does not say anything, and the waiter, who may or may not, smiles politely, and Bill, who hasn't the slightest idea, comes back beaming into the conversation as if glad of any innocent conversational remark. With a bite of éclair in my mouth I wag my head at him, how delicious. I force down a few spoonfuls of ambrosial fruit. I succeed in forestalling ice-cream. The carts go away. Jerry comes around with a coffee flask. I dig out a couple of cigars.

I am facing the musical table, but I have lost my interest in how they all act. Full of highballs, food, smoke, coffee, my insides coil around heavily like an overfed boa constrictor. The only reason I don't slide down in my chair and get really comfortable is that Kaminski is sitting where he can see *me,* and I will not give him the satisfaction of seeing me contented and well nourished. For his performance I shall make it a point to be as wide-awake as a lie detector, and though I shall listen with an open mind, I shall not be his most forgiving critic.

But there is a clash between comfort and will, and a little balloony pressure in my midsection. Damn Kaminski. Damn his Asiatic spirituality and his coddled Art and his ghetto defensiveness and his refugee arrogance. My esophagus comes again with a richly flavored *brwwp!* Just an echo, hoo hoo.

"Say," says Bill, "how would a brandy go? Or calvados? I got some damn good calvados. You never had any till you taste this."

The impetuous arm goes up, but Sue, who must have had her eye sharp on him, is there before the waiter. "Bill, do me a favor?"

"Surest thing you know. What?"

"Have Jerry close the bar. Don't serve any more now till afterward."

"I was just going to get Joe a snifter of calvados to go with his cigar."

"Please," she said. "Joe won't mind postponing it."

I have not been asked, but I do not mind.

"O.K.," Bill says. "You know what you're doing, I guess. Did you get anything to eat? I kept looking around for you."

"I'll get something later. As soon as people seem to be through, Jerry can start arranging the chairs. I went over it with him this afternoon."

"Check," says Bill. A smile, puzzled, protective, and fond, follows her back to the musician's table. "Bothers her," Bill says. "She's got her heart set on something great. Old Arnold had better be good."

We are silent, stuffed. I commune with my cigar, looking sleepily around this movie set where the standard of everything is excess. Somewhere down deep in my surfeited interior I conduct a little private argument with my client and conscience, Murthi. He is bitter. He thinks it is immoral to fill your stomach. In India, he tells me, the only well-fed people are money-changers and landlords, grinders of the faces of the poor. But these people, I try to tell him, grind no poor. They are not money-changers or landlords. They are the rich, or semi-rich, of a rich country, not the rich of a poor one. Their duty to society is not by any means ignored; they do not salve their own consciences with a temple stuck with pieces of colored glass. They give to causes they respect, and many of them give a great deal. And they don't put on a feast like this because they want to show off, or even because they are themselves gluttonous. They do it because they think their guests will enjoy it; they do it to introduce a struggling young artist. And anyway, why should good eating be immoral?

You pay nothing for it, Murthi says. It is too easy. It does not come after hard times and starvation, but after plenty. It is nothing but self-indulgence. It smothers the spiritual life. In the midst of plenty, that is the time to fast.

I am too full to argue with him. I feel as if I might lift into the air and float away, and the whole unreal patio with me, bearing its umbrella of artificial moonlight and its tables and people and glass-fronted cabaña, its piano and its Artist, high above the crass valley.

It is like a *New Yorker* cartoon, and me with my turned-up Muslim slippers and baggy pants, one of the Peninsula pashas on a magic carpet of the latest model, complete with indirect lighting, swimming pool, Muzak, and all modern conveniences.

All? Nothing forgotten? My feet insist on my notice. I stoop on the sly and feel the cement. Sure enough, the magic carpet has radiant heating too.

V

KAMINSKI IS BOOTED AND SPURRED and ready to ride. The audience is braced between the cabaña and the pool. The moonlight is turned off. The air is cool and damp, but the pavement underfoot radiates its faint expensive warmth. Inside, one light above the piano shines on Kaminski's white jacket as he sits fiddling with the knobs, adjusting the bench. The shadow of the piano's open wing falls across his head. The Degas has become a Rembrandt.

On a lounge sofa between Sue and Ruth, old Joe Allston, very much overfed, is borne up like a fly on meringue. Bill has creaked away somewhere. A partition has slid across the barbecue, and from behind it, during pauses in the hum of talk, comes the sound of a busy electric dishwasher.

"Are people too comfortable, do you think?" Sue asks. "Would it have been better to put out undertaker's chairs?"

I assure her that she has the gratitude of every over-burdened pelvis in the house. "There is no such thing as *too* comfortable," I say, "any more than there is such a thing as a large drink of whiskey."

Her hands pick at things on her dress and are held still. Her laugh fades away in a giggle.

I say, "What's he going to play?" and quite loudly she bursts out, "I don't know! He wouldn't tell me!" One or two shadowy heads turn. Kaminski stares out into the dusk from his bench, and the shadow wipes all the features off his face.

We are sitting well back, close to the edge of the pool. "How did you manage to get him to play after all?" Ruth murmurs.

It is as improbable to see the sneering curl of Sue's lip as it would be to see an ugly scowl on her face. "I *crawled!*" she says.

The cushions sigh as Ruth eases back into them. But I am sitting where I can watch Sue's face, and I am not so easily satisfied. "Why?" I ask.

"Because he's a great artist."

"Oh." After a moment I let myself back among the cushions with Ruth. "I hope he is," I say, and at least for the moment I mean it.

The eyeless mask of Kaminski's face turns again. Even when he speaks he does not seem to have lips. "For my first number I play three Chopin Nocturnes. I play these as suitable to the occasion, and especially for Mrs. Casement."

Beside me I can feel Sue shrink. I have a feeling, though it is too dark to see, that she has flushed red. While the murmur rising from the audience says How nice, handsome gesture, what a nice compliment, she looks at her hands.

At the piano, Kaminski kneads his knuckles, staring at the empty music rack. When he has held his pose of communing with his *Geist* long enough for the silence to spread to the far edges of the audience, but not long enough so that any barbarian starts talking again, he drops into the music with a little skip and a trill. It is well timed and well executed. Without knowing it, probably, Sue takes hold of my hand. She is like a high school girl who shuts her eyes while the hero plunges from the two-yard line. Did he make it? Oh, did he go over?

The cabaña acts like a shell; the slightest pianissimo comes out feathery but clear, and Kaminski's meaty hands are very deft. Behind us the faint gurgle and suck of the pool's filter system is a watery night sound under the Chopin.

God spare me from ever being called a critic or even a judge of music—even a listener. Like most people, I think I can tell a dub from a competent hand, and it is plain at once that Kaminski is competent. The shades of competence are another thing. They are where the Soul comes in, and I look with suspicion on those who wear their souls outside. I am not capable in any case of judging Kaminski's soul. Maybe it is such a soul as swoons into the world only once in a hundred years. Maybe, again, it is such a G.G. soul as I have seen on Madison Avenue and elsewhere in my time.

But I think I can smell a rat, even in music, if it is dead enough, and as Kaminski finishes one nocturne and chills into abashed silence those who have mistakenly started to applaud too soon, and pounds into the second with big chords, I think I begin to smell a rat here. Do I imagine it, or is he burlesquing these nocturnes? Is he contemptuous of them because they are sentimental, because they are nineteenth century, because they don't strain his keyboard technique enough, or because he knows Sue adores them? And is he clever enough and dirty enough to dedicate them to her as an insult?

It is hard to say. By the third one it is even harder, because he has played them all with great precision even while he gives them a lot of bravura. I wish I could ask Ruth what she thinks, because her ear for music and her nose for rats are both better than mine. But there is no chance, and so I am still nursing the private impression that Kaminski is hoaxing the philistines when I am called on to join in the applause, which is loud, long, and sincere. If the philistines have been hoaxed, they are not aware of the fact. Beside me, Sue wears her hands out; she is radiant. "Oh, didn't he play them *beautifully?* They loved it, didn't they? I told you, *nobody* can play Chopin the way Arnold can."

In the second row of lounge chairs the musical crowd, satisfactorily applauding, bend heads each to other. Mr. Ackerman's big droopy face lifts solemnly against the light. Kaminski, after his bow, has seated himself again and waits while the clapping splatters away and the talk dies down again and a plane, winking its red and white wing lights, drones on down and blinks out among the stars over Black Mountain. Finally he says, "I play next the Bach Chaconne, transcribed for piano by Busoni."

"What is it?" Sue says. "Should I know it?"

Over Sue's head Ruth gives me one of her raccoon looks. I am delighted; I rouse myself. This time my lie detector is going to be a little more searching, because I have heard a dozen great pianists play the Chaconne, and I own every recording ever made, probably. Every time I catch a competent amateur at a piano I beg it out of him. In my opinion, which I have already disparaged, it is only the greatest piece of music ever written, a great big massive controlled piece of mind. If Kaminski can play the Chaconne and play it well, I will forgive him and his bad manners and his tantrums and the Polish soul he put into Chopin. It takes more than Polish soul to play the Chaconne. It takes everything a good man has, and a lot of good men don't have enough.

Maybe Kaminski does have enough. He states those big sober themes, as they say in music-appreciation circles, with, as they also say, authority. The great chords begin to pile up. Imagine anyone writing that thing in the first place for the violin. As usual, it begins to destroy me. Kaminski is great, he's tremendous, he is tearing into this and bringing it out by the double handful. A success, a triumph. Listen to it roll and pour, and not one trace, not a whisker, of Polish soul. This is the language you might use in justifying your life to God.

As when, in the San Francisco Cow Palace, loudspeakers announce the draft horse competition, and sixteen great Percherons trot with high action and ponderous foot into the arena, brass-harnessed, plume-bridled, swelling with power, drawing the rumbling brewery wagon lightly, Regal Pale; ton-heavy but light-footed they come, the thud of their hoofs in the tanbark like the marching of platoons, and above them the driver spider-braced, intent, transmits through the fan of lines his slightest command; lightly he guides them, powerfully and surely they bring their proud necks, their plumed heads, their round and dappled haunches, the blue and gold wagon Regal Pale— sixteen prides guided by one will, sixteen great strengths respondent and united: so the great chords of Bach roll forth from under the hands of Arnold Kaminski.

And as, half-trained or self-willed, the near leader may break, turn counter to his driver's command, and in an instant all that proud unanimity is a snarl of tangled traces and fouled lines and broken step and cross purposes and desperate remedies, so at a crucial instant fails the cunning of Kaminski. A butch, a fat, naked, staring discord.

To do him credit, he retrieves it instantly, it is past and perhaps not even noticed by many. But he has lost me, and when I have recovered from the momentary disappointment I am cynically amused. The boy took on something too big for him. A little later he almost gets me back, in that brief lyrical passage that is like a spring in a country of cliffs, but he never does quite recover the command he started with, and I know now how to take him.

When he finishes there is impressed silence, followed by loud admiration. This has been, after all—Allston *dicens*—the most magnificent piece of music ever written, and it ought to be applauded. But it has licked Kaminski in a spot or two, and he can't help knowing it and knowing that the musicians present know it. As he stands up to take a bow, his face, thrust up into the light, acquires features, a mask of slashes and slots and knobs, greenish and shadowed. He looks like a rather bruised corpse, and he bows as if greeting his worst enemy. In the quiet as the applause finally dies out I hear the gurgle of the pool's drain and catch a thin aseptic whiff of chlorine, a counterwhiff of cigar smoke and perfume.

Says Sue in my ear, tensely. "What did I tell you?"

"For my last number," Kaminski's thick voice is saying, "I play the Piano Pieces of Arnold Schoenberg, Opus Nineteen."

I have had Schoenberg and his followers explained to me, even urged upon me, several times, generally by arty people who catch me with my flank exposed at a cocktail party. They tell me that these noises are supposed, among other things, to produce *tension*. Tension is a great word among the tone-row musicians. God bless them, they are good at it. It astonishes me anew, as Kaminski begins, that sounds like these can come out of a piano. They can only be recovered from through bed rest and steam baths, maybe shock therapy.

For no amount of argument can convince me that this music does not hurt the ears. And though I am prepared to admit that by long listening a man might accustom himself to it, I do not think this proves much. Human beings can adjust to anything, practically; it is a resilient race. We can put up with the rule of kings, presidents, priests, dictators, generals, communes, and committees; we learn to tolerate diets of raw fish, octopus, snails, unborn ducklings, clay, the bleeding hearts of enemies, our own dung; we learn to listen without screaming to the sounds of samisens, Korean harps, veenas, steam whistles, gongs, and Calypso singers; we adjust bravely to whole-tone, half-tone, or quarter-tone scales, to long skirts and short skirts, crew cuts and perukes, muttonchops and dundrearies and Van Dykes and naked chins, castles and paper houses and *barastis* and bomb shelters. The survival of the race depends upon its infinite adaptability. We can get used to anything in time, and even perhaps develop a perverted taste for it. But *why?* The day has not come when I choose to try adapting to Schoenberg. Schoenberg hurts my ears.

He hurts some other ears, too. The audience that has swooned at the Chopin and been respectful before the Bach is systematically cut to ribbons by the saw edges of the Piano Pieces. I begin to wonder all over again if Kaminski may have planned this program with perverse cunning: throw the philistines the Chopin, giving it all the *Schmalz* it will stand; then stun them with the Bach (only the Bach was too much for him); then trample them contemptuously underfoot with the Schoenberg, trusting that their ignorance will be impressed by this wrenched and tortured din even while they writhe under it. A good joke. But then what is he after? It is his own career that is at stake, he is the one who stands to benefit if the musicians' corner is impressed. Does he mean to say the hell with it on these terms, or am I reading into a not-quite-good-enough pianist a lot of ambiguities that don't exist in him?

It slowly dawns on me, while I grit my teeth to keep from howling like a dog, that Kaminski *means* this Schoenberg. He gives it the full treatment; he visibly wrestles with the Ineffable. Impossible to tell whether he hits the right notes or the wrong ones—probably Schoenberg himself couldn't tell. Wrong ones better, maybe—more tension. But Kaminski is concentrating as if the music ties him into bundles of raw nerves. For perhaps a second there is a blessed relief, a little thread of something almost a melody, and then the catfight again. Language of expressionism, tension and space, yes. Put yourself in the thumbscrew and any sort of release is blessed. Suite for nutmeg grater, cactus, and strings. A garland of loose ends.

He is putting himself into it devotionally; he *is* Schoenberg. I recall a picture of the composer on some record envelope—intense staring eyes, bald crown, temples with a cameo of raised veins, cheeks bitten in, mouth grim and bitter, unbearable pain. Arnold Schoenberg, Destroyer and Preserver. Mouthful of fire and can neither swallow nor spit.

In the cone of light under which Kaminski tortures himself and us, I see a bright quick drop fall from the end of his nose. Sweat or hay fever? Soul or allergy? Whatever it is, no one can say he isn't trying.

The piano stops with a noise like a hiccup or a death rattle. Three or four people laugh. Kaminski sits still. The audience waits, not to be caught offside. This might be merely space, there might be some more tension coming. But Kaminski is definitely through. Applause begins, with the over-enthusiastic sound of duty in it, and it dies quickly except in the musical row, where the accompanist is clapping persistently.

Sue is clapping her hands in intense slow strokes under her chin. "Isn't that something?" she says. "That's one thing he's been working on a lot. I just don't see how anybody plays it at all—all those minor ninths and major sevenths, and no key signature at all."

"Or *why* anybody plays it," I am compelled to say. But when her hands start another flurry I join in. Kaminski sits, spiritually exhausted, bending his head. Encore, encore. For Sue's sake, try. My arms begin to grow tired, and still he sits there. A full minute after my impertinent question, her hands still going, Sue says, "I admit *I* don't understand that kind of music, but because I'm ignorant is no reason to throw it away."

So I am rebuked. She is a noble and innocent woman, and will stoop to beg Kaminski and leave a door open for Schoenberg, all for the disinterested love of art. Well, God bless her. It's almost over, and she can probably feel that it was a success. Maybe she can even think of it as a triumph. Later, when nothing has come of all her effort and expense, she can console herself with a belief that there is a conspiracy among established musicians to pound the fingers of drowning genius off the gunwale.

"Well, anyway, *he's* terrific," I say like a forktongued liar. "Marvelous." Rewarded by all the gratitude she puts into her smile, I sit back for the encore that is finally forthcoming. And what does Kaminski play? Some number of Charles Ives, almost as mad as the Schoenberg.

Probably there might have been enough politeness among us to urge a second encore, but Kaminski cuts us off by leaving the piano.

Matches flare, smoke drifts upward, the moonlight dawns again, Bill Casement appears from somewhere, and a discreet white coat crosses from the barbecue end of the cabaña and opens the folding panels of the bar.

VI

IT SEEMS THAT QUITE A NUMBER of times during the evening I am condemned to have Sue at me with tense questions. She is as bad as a Princeton boy with a manuscript: *Have I got it? Is it any good? Can I be a writer?* "What do you think?" Sue says now. "Am I wrong?"

"He's a good pianist."

Her impatience is close to magnificent. For a second she is Tallulah. "Good! Good heavens, I know that. But does he have a chance? Has he got so *much* talent they can't deny him? They say only about one young pianist in a hundred..."

"You can't make your chances," I say. "That's mostly luck."

"I'll be his luck," she says.

The crowd is rising and drifting inside. Trapped on the lounge, I lean back and notice that over our heads, marbled by the lights, white mist has begun to boil on some unfelt wind. The air is chilly and wet; the fog has come in. Ruth stands up, shivering her shoulders to cover the significant look she is giving me. I stand up with her. So does Sue, but Sue doesn't let me go.

"If you're his luck, then he has a chance," I say, and am rewarded by one of her smiles, so confident and proud that I am stricken with remorse, and add, "But it's an awful skinny little chance. Any young pianist would probably be better off if he made up his mind straight off to be a local musician instead of trying for a concert career."

"But the concert career is what he *wants*. It's what he's been preparing for all his life."

"Sure. That's what they all want. Then they eat their hearts out because they miss, and when you look at it, what is it they've missed? A chance to ride a dreary circuit and play for the local Master Minds and Artists series and perform in the Art Barn of every jerk town in America. It might be better if they stayed home and organized chamber groups and taught the young and appeared once a year as soloist with the local little symphony."

"Joe, dear," Sue says, "can you imagine Arnold teaching grubby little unwilling kids to play little Mozart sonatas for PTA meetings?"

She could not have found a quicker way to adjust my thermostat upward. It is true that I can't imagine Kaminski doing any such thing as teaching the young, but that is a commentary on Kaminski, not on the young. Besides, I am the defender, self-appointed, of the good American middle-class small-town and suburban way of life, and I get almighty sick of Americans who enjoy all its benefits but can't find a good word to say for it. An American may be defined as a man who won't take his own side in an argument. "Is Arnold *above* Mozart?" I ask. "For that matter, is he above the PTA?"

She stares at me to see if I'm serious. "Now you're being cute," she says, and blinks her eyes like a fond idiot and rushes inside to join the group around Kaminski. I note that Kaminski now has a highball in his hand. The Artist is only mortal, after all. If we wait, we may even see him condescend to a sandwich.

"Shall we get out of this?" I ask Ruth.

"Not yet."

"Why not?"

"Manners," she says. "You wouldn't understand, lamb. But let's go inside. It's cold out here."

It is, even with the radiant-heated magic carpet. The patio is deserted already. The air above boils with white. Between the abandoned chairs and empty lawn the transparent green-blue pool fumes with underwater light as if it opened down into hell. Once inside and looking out, I have a feeling of being marooned in a space ship. Any minute now frogmen will land their saucers on the patio or rise in diving helmets and snorkels from the pool.

Inside there are no frogmen, only Kaminski, talking with his hands, putting his glass on a tray and accepting another. The white head of the critic is humorously and skeptically bent, listening. The dour accompanist, the velvet-coated Mr. Budapest, the solid Ackermans, Sue, three or four unknowns, the little piano teacher, make a close and voluble group. Kaminski pauses amid laughter; evidently these others don't find him as hard to take as I do. As if he feels my thoughts, he looks across his hearers at Ruth and me, and Ruth raises her hands beside her head and makes pretty applauding motions. Manners. I am compelled to do the same, not so prettily.

Sam Shields goes past us, winks sadly, leaving. His wife is crippled and does not go out, so that he is always among the first to leave a party. This time he has five or six others for company, filing past Bill and being handshook at the door. To us now comes Annie Williamson, robust dame, and inquires in her fight-announcer's voice why we don't join the Hunt. They have fourteen members now, and enough permissions so that they can put hurdles on fences and get a run of almost fourteen miles. Of course we're not too old. Come on...Herman Dyer will still take a three-bar gate, and he's five years older than God. Or maybe we'd like the job of riding ahead dragging a scent or a dead rabbit. Make me Master of the Hunt, any office I want. Only come.

"Annie," I tell her sadly, "I am an old, infirm, pathetic figure. I have retired to these hills only to complete my memoirs, and riding a horse might cut them untimely short. Even art, such as tonight, can hardly make me leave my own humble hearth any more."

"What's the matter?" she says. "Didn't you like it? I thought it was swell. The last one was kind of yowly, but he played it fine."

"Sure I liked it," I say. "I thought it was real artistic."

"You're a philistine," Annie says. "An old cynical philistine. I'd hate to read your memoirs."

"You couldn't finish them," I say. "There isn't a horse or a beagle in them anywhere."

"A terribly limited old man," she says, and squeezes Ruth's arm and goes off shaking her head and chuckling. She circles the Kaminski crowd, interrupts something he is saying. I see her mouth going: Thank you, enjoyed it very much, blah blah. She first, and now a dozen others, neighbors and unknowns...so much...envy Sue the chance to hear you every day...luck to you...great treat. Some more effusive than others, but all respectful. Kaminski can sneer at his overfed alcoholic audience, but it has listened dutifully, and has applauded louder than it sometimes felt like doing, and has stilled its laughter in embarrassment when it didn't understand. If he had played nothing but Chopin they would have enjoyed him more, but he would have to be even more arrogant and superior and cross-grained than he is to alienate their good will and sour their wonderful good nature. Luck to you...And mean it. Would buy tickets, if necessary.

"Madame," I say to my noiseless wife, "art is troublesome and life is long. Can't we go home?"

For answer she steers me by the arm into the musical circle. Except for four people talking over something confidential in a corner, and the white coats moving around hopefully with unclaimed highballs on their trays, the musical circle now includes the whole company. Kaminski, we find, is still doing most of the talking. His subject is—guess what? The Artist. Specifically, the Artist in America.

I claim one of the spare highballs in self-defense. I know the substance of this lecture in advance, much of it from Murthi. And if Kaminski quotes Baudelaire about the great gaslighted Barbarity that killed Poe, I will disembowel him.

The lecture does not pursue its expected course more than a few minutes, and it is done with more grace and humor than I would have thought Kaminski had in him. A couple of highballs have humanized his soul. Mainly he talks, and without too obvious self-pity, about the difficulties of a musical career: twenty years or so of nothing but practice, practice, practice; the teachers in Boston and New York and Rome; the tyranny of the piano (I can't be away from a piano a single day without losing ground. On the train, and even in an automobile, I carry around a practice keyboard to run exercises on). It is (with a rueful mouth) a rough profession to get established in. He wonders sometimes why one doesn't instead take the Civil Service examinations. (Laughter.) But it is understandable, Kaminski says, why the trapdoor should be closed over the heads of young musicians. Established performers, and recording companies and agencies clinging to what they know is profitable, are naturally either jealous of competition or afraid to risk anything on new music or new men. (That charming little Ives that I used for an encore, for instance, has practically never been played, though it was composed almost fifty years ago.)

The case of Kaminski is (with a shrug) nothing unique. The critic and the Ackermans know how it goes. And of course, there is the problem of finding audiences. Whom shall one play for? Good audiences so few and so small, in spite of all the talk about the educational effect of radio and recordings. People who really know and love good music available only in the large cities or—with a flick of his dark eyes at Sue—in a few places such as this. Oh, he is full of charm. The little music teacher bridles. But generally, Kaminski says, there is only the sham audience with sham values, and the whole concert stage which is the only certain way of reaching audiences one can respect is dominated by two or three agencies interested only in dollars.

"Shyme, shyme," says old Joe Allston from the edge of the circle, and draws a startled half-smile from his neighbors and a second's ironic stare from Kaminski.

"What, a defender of agents in the crowd?" the critic says, turning his white head.

"Literary only," I say. "And ex, not current. But a bona fide paid-up member of the Agents' Protective Association, the only bulwark between the Artist and the poor farm."

"Are agents so *necessary?*" Sue says. "Isn't it possible to break in somehow without putting yourself in the clutches of one of them?"

"Clutches!" I say. "Consider my feelings."

Ruth gives me an absolutely expressionless, pleasant look in which I read some future unpleasantness, but what the hell, shall a man keep quiet while his lifework is trampled on?

"Would you admit," says Kaminski with his tight dogfish smile, "that an agent without an artist is a vine without an oak?"

The little music teacher brings her hands together. Her eyes are snapping and her little pointed chin, pebbled like the Pope's Nose of a plucked turkey, quivers. Oh, if she were defending the cause of music and art against such commercial attacks, she would...She is listening, comprehending, participating, right in the midst of things. Kaminski turns to her and actually winks. As a tray passes behind him he reaches back and takes a third highball. Joe Allston collars one too. The benevolent critic pokes his finger at old Joe and says encouragingly, "How about it, Agents' Protective Association? Can you stand alone?"

"I don't like the figure," I say. "I don't feel like a vine without an oak. I feel like a Seeing Eye dog without a blind man."

This brings on a shower of protests and laughter, and Sue says, "Joe, if you're going to stick up for agents you'll have to tell us how to beat the game. How could an agent help Arnold, say, get a hearing and get started?"

"Any good agency will get him an audition, any time."

"Yes, along with a thousand others."

"No, by himself."

"And having had it, what does he get out of it?" murmurs Mr. Ackerman. He has winesap cheeks and white, white hair, but his expression is not benevolent like the critic's, mainly because his whole face has come loose, and sags—big loose lips, big drooping nose, a forehead that hangs in folds over his eyebrows. He reminds me of a worried little science-fiction writer I used to know who developed what his doctor called "lack of muscle tone," so that his nose wouldn't even hold up his glasses. It was as if he had been half disintegrated by one of his ray guns. Mr. Ackerman's voice sags like his face; he looks at me with reddish eyes above hound-dog lower lids.

They all obviously enjoy yapping at me. Here is the Enemy, the Commercial Evil Genius that destroys Art. This kind of thing exhilarates me, I'm afraid.

"That's not the agent's fault," I say. "It's a simple matter of supply and demand. A hundred good young pianists come to New York every year all pumped full of hope. They are courteously greeted and auditioned by the agents, who take on anyone they can. Agents arrange concerts, including Town Hall and Carnegie Hall concerts, for some of them, and they paper the hall and invite and inveigle the critics and clip the reviews, and if the miracle happens and some young man gets noticed in some special way, they book him on a circuit. But if ninety-nine of those young pianists slink out of New York with a few pallid clippings and no rave notices and no bookings, that isn't the agents' fault."

"Then whose fault is it?" cries Sue. "There are millions of people who would be thrilled to hear someone like Arnold play. Why can't they? There seems to be a stone wall between."

"Overproduction," murmurs old Devil's-Advocate Allston, and sips his insolent bourbon.

Mr. Ackerman's face lifts with a visible effort its sagging folds; the critic looks ironical and skeptical; Kaminski watches me over his glass with big shining liquid eyes. His pitted skin is no longer pale, but has acquired a dark, purplish flush. He seems to nurse some secret amusing knowledge. The music teacher at his elbow twists her mouth, very incensed and impatient at old commercial Allston. Her mouth opens for impetuous words, closes again. Her pebbled chin quivers.

"Overproduction, sure," I say again. "If it happened in the automobile industry you'd blame it on the management, or the government, or on classical capitalist economics, or creeping socialism. But it's in music, and so you want to blame it on the poor agent. An agent is only a dealer. He isn't to blame if the factory makes too many cars. All he can do is sell the ones he can."

"I'm afraid Mr. Allston is pulling our leg," the critic says. "Art isn't quite a matter of production lines. Genius can't be predicted and machined like a Chevrolet, do you think, Mr. Casement?"

He catches Bill by surprise. Evidently he is one of those who like to direct and control conversations, pulling in the hangers-on. But his question is no kindness to Bill, who strangles and waves an arm. "Don't ask me! I don't know a thing about it." Even after the spotlight has left him, he stands pulling his lower lip, looking around over his hand, and chuckling meaninglessly when he catches anyone's eye.

"So you don't think a New York concert does any good," Sue says—pushing, pushing. After all, she held this clambake to bring us all together and now she has what she wanted—patrons and critics and agents in a cluster—and she is going to find out everything. "If they don't do any good, why bother?"

"Why indeed?" I say, and then I see that I have carried it too far, for Sue's face puckers unhappily, and she insists, "But Joe..."

The critic observes, "They may not do much good, but nothing can be done *without* one."

"So for the exceptional ones they *do* do some good."

"For the occasional exception they may do everything," the critic says. "Someone like William Kapell, who was killed in a plane crash just a few miles from here. But Kapell was a *very* notable exception."

I cannot read Kaminski—it is being made increasingly clear to me that one of my causes of irritation at him is precisely that I don't know what goes on inside him—but I can read Sue Casement without bifocals, and the look she throws at Kaminski says two things: One is that here, just five feet from her, is another Notable Exception as notable as Kapell. The other is that since Kapell has been killed on the brink of a brilliant career, he has obviously left a vacancy.

"A lot of young pianists can't afford it, I expect," she says—hopefully, I think.

The critic spreads his hands. "Town Hall about fifteen hundred, Carnegie two thousand. Still, a lot of them find it somewhere. It's a lot of money to put on the turn of a card."

Determination and resolve, or muscular contractions that I interpret in these terms, harden in Sue's rosy face. "Is it hard to arrange?"

I can't resist. "Any good agent will take care of it for you," I say. She throws me a smile: you old devil, you.

"But no one can count on one single thing's coming from it," the critic says, and he looks kindly upon both Sue and her protégé. I respect this benevolent old creature in spite of his profession. He is trying to warn them.

Not being one of these socially clairvoyant people, I would not feel extraordinarily at home in a Virginia Woolf novel. But I get a glimpse, for the most fragmentary moment, of an extreme complexity pressing in upon us. There is of course Ruth emanating silent disapproval of her husband's big argumentative mouth, and there is Sue, radiant and resolute, smiling promises at Kaminski. There is Kaminski with his deer eyes wide and innocent, his mouth indifferently half smiling—a pure enigma to me, unidentifiable. And there are the critic, ruminating kindly and perhaps with friendly sorrow his own private doubts, and Ackerman incognito behind the heavy folds of his face, and Mrs. Ackerman, who looks as if she would like nothing better than to get off her aching feet and start home, and the music teacher bristling with excitement and stimulation, saying to Kaminski, "But *imagine* getting up on the stage at Carnegie Hall with Virgil Thomson and Olin Downes and everybody there...." Also there is Bill Casement with his long creased face that looks as overworked as Gary Cooper trying to register an emotion. What emotion? Maybe he is kissing two thousand dollars good-bye, and wondering if he is glad to see it go. Maybe he is proud of his wife, who has the initiative and the culture to do all this of this evening. Maybe he is contemplating the people in his cabaña and thinking what funny things can happen to a man's home.

So only one thing is clear. Sue will stake Kaminski to a New York concert. I don't know why that depresses me. It has been clear all along that that is exactly what she has wanted to do. My depression may come from Kaminski's indifference. I would like to see the stinker get his chance and goof it good.

An improbable opening appears low down in the droops and folds of Mr. Ackerman's face, and he yawns. "Darling," his wife says at once, "we have a long drive back to the city."

In a moment the circle has begun to melt and disintegrate. Sue is accosted with gratitude from three sides. The accompanist and the velvet-coated Mr. Budapest stay with Kaminski to say earnest friendly things: I want you to come up and meet...He will be interested that you have appeared with...of course they will have heard of you...I should think something of Hovhaness'...yes...excellent. Why not?

Since the discussion took his career out of his hands, Kaminski has said nothing. He bows, he smiles, but his face has gone remote; the half-sneer of repose has come back into it. He is a Hyperborean, beyond everybody. All this nonsense about careers bores him. Why do the heathen rage furiously together? Beyond question, he is one of the greatest bargains I have ever seen bought.

Also, as he turns and shakes hands with Mr. Budapest and recalls himself for the tiresomeness of good nights, I observe that perhaps what I took for snootiness is paralysis. He does not believe in alcohol, which is drunk only by pigs, but I have seen him take four highballs in twenty minutes, and Bill Casement's bartenders have been taught not to spare the Old Granddad.

VII

WHILE THE OTHER LADIES ARE ABSENT getting their coats, Kaminski holds collapse off at arm's length and plays games of solemn jocularity with the homely little music teacher. He leans carefully and whispers in her ear something that makes her flush and laugh and shake her head, protesting. "Eh?" he cries. "Isn't it so?" With his feet crossed he leans close, rocking his ankles. Out of the corner of the music teacher's eye goes an astonishingly cool flickering look, alert to see if anyone is watching her here, *tête-à-tête* with the maestro. All she sees is old Joe Allston, the commercial fellow. Her neck stiffens, her eyes are abruptly glazed, her face is carefree and without guile as she turns indifferently back. Old Allston is about as popular as limburger on the newlyweds' exhaust manifold. He hates us Youth. The Anti-Christ.

"You can joke," she says to Kaminski, "but I'm serious, really I am. We know we aren't very wonderful, but we aren't so bad, either, so there. We've got a very original name: The Chamber Society. And if you don't watch out, I *will* sign you up to play with us sometime. So don't say anything you don't mean!"

"I never say anything I don't mean," Kaminski grins. "I'd love to play with you. All ladies, are you?"

"All except the cello. He's a math teacher at the high school."

"Repulsive," Kaminski murmurs. The teacher giggles, swings sideways, sees me still there, nails me to the wall with a venomous look. Snoop! Why don't I move? But I am much too interested to move.

"Three ladies and one gentleman," Kaminski says, smiling broadly and leaning over her so far he overbalances and staggers. "A Mormon. Are the other ladies all like you?"

Because I know that none of this will sound credible when I report it to Ruth, I strain for every word of this adolescent drooling. I see the music teacher, a little hesitant, vibrate a look at Kaminski's face and then, just a little desperately, towards the group of men by the door. Kaminski is greatly amused by something. "I tell you what you should do," he says. "You reorganize yourself into the Bed-chamber Society. Let the Mormon have the other two, and you and I will play together. Any time."

He has enunciated this unkind crudity very plainly, so plainly that at fifteen feet I cannot possibly have misheard. The little teacher does not look up from her abstract or panicky study of certain chair legs. Her incomplete little face goes slowly scarlet, her pebbled chin is stiff. That little cold venomous glance whips up to me and is taken back again. If I were not there, she would probably run for her life. As it is, she is tempted into pretending that nothing has been said. She is like Harold Lloyd in one of those old comedies, making vivacious and desperate chatter to a girl, while behind the draperies or under the tablecloth his accidentally snagged pants unravel or his seams burst or his buttons one by one give up the ghost. Sooner or later the draperies will be thrown open by the butler, or someone's belt buckle will catch the tablecloth and drag it to the floor, and there will be Harold in his hairy shanks, his Paris garters. Oh Lord. I am not quite able to take myself away from there.

Kaminski leans over her, catches himself by putting a hand on her shoulder, says something else close to her red-hot ear. That does it. She squirms sideways, shakes him off, and darts past the ladies just returning from the cloakroom. Kaminski, not so egg-eyed as I expect to see him, looks at me with a smile almost too wide for his mouth, and winks. He could not be more pleased if he had just pulled the legs off a live squirrel. But the music teacher, darting past me, has given me quite another sort of look. There is a dead-white spot in the center of each cheek, and her eyes burn into mine with pure hatred. That is what I get for being an innocent bystander and witnessing her humiliation.

For a few seconds Kaminski stands ironically smiling into thin air; he wears a tasting expression. Then he motions to one of the Japanese at the bar, and the Japanese scoops ice cubes into a glass.

It is time for us to get away from there. The elegant cabaña smells and looks like Ciro's at nine o'clock of a Sunday morning. Outside, the pool lights are off, but the air swirls and swims, dizzy with moonlighted fog. The sliding doors are part way open for departing guests. Sue comes and catches Kaminski by the arm, holding his sleeve with both hands in a too friendly, too sisterly pose. They stand in the doorway with the mist blowing beyond them.

"Now please do come and see me," Ackerman says. "One never knows. I would like to introduce you. Perhaps some evening, a little group at my home."

"Good luck," says the critic. "I shall hope before long to write pleasant comments after your name."

"Ah, *vunderful*," says Mr. Budapest, "you were *vunderful*! I have so enjoyed it. And if you should write to Signor Vitelli, my greetings. It has been many years."

"Not at all, not at all," says Bill Casement. "Happy to have you."

"It was so good of you all to come," Sue says. "You don't know how...or rather, you do, all of you do. You've been generous to come and help. I'm sure it will work out for him somehow, he has such great talent. And when you're as ignorant as I am...I hope when you're down this way you won't hesitate...Good-bye, good-bye, good-bye."

The women pull June fur coats around them, their figures blur in the mist and are invisible beyond the Mondrian gate. But now comes the music teacher with a bone in her teeth, poor thing, grimly polite, breathless. She looks neither to left nor right past Sue's face: Good night. A pleasant time. You have a very beautiful place. Thank you. And gone.

Her haste is startling to Sue, who likes to linger warmly on farewells, standing with arms hugged around herself in lighted doorways. Kaminski toasts the departing tweed with a silent glass. The figure hurries through the gate, one shoulder thrust ahead, the coat thrown cape-wise over her shoulders. Almost she scuttles. From beyond the gate she casts back one terrible glance, and is swallowed in the fog.

"Why, I wonder what's the matter with her?" Sue says. "Didn't she act odd?"

Bill motions us in and slides the glass door shut. With his back against the door Kaminski studies the ice cubes which remain from his fifth highball. All of a sudden he is as gloomy as a raincloud. "I'm the matter with her," he says. "I insulted her."

"You *what?*"

"Insulted her. I made indecent propositions."

"Oh, Arnold!" Sue says with a laugh. "Come on!"

"It's true," Arnold says. "Ask the agent, there. I whispered four-letter words in her ear."

She stares at him steadily. "And if you did," she says, "in heaven's name *why* did you?"

"Akh!" Kaminski says. "Such a dried-up little old maid as that, so full of ignorance and enthusiasm. How could I avoid insulting her? She is the sort of person who invites indecent exposure." There is a moment of quiet in which we hear the sound of a car pulling out of the drive. "How could I help insulting her?" Kaminski shouts. "If I didn't insult people like that I couldn't keep my self-respect." Nobody replies to this. "That is why nobody likes me," he says, and looks around for a white coat but the white coats are all gone. Automatically Sue takes his empty glass from him.

Ruth says, quite loudly for her, "Sue, we must go. It was a lovely party. And Mr. Kaminski, I thought you played beautifully."

His flat stare challenges her. "I was terrible," he says. "Ackerman and those others will tell you. They are saying right now in their car how bad it was. The way I played, they will think I am fit for high school assemblies or Miss Spinster's chamber society. I am all finished around here. Nothing will come of any of this. I have muffed it again."

"Finished?" Sue cries. "Arnold, you've just begun."

"Finished," he says. "All done."

"Oh, what if you did insult Miss What's-her-name," Sue says. "You can go and apologize tomorrow. It's your playing that's important, and you played so beautifully...."

Bill Casement, by the door jamb, rubs one cheek, pulling his mouth down and then up again. He gives me a significant look; I half expect him to twirl a finger beside his head. "Well, good night," I say. "I'm tired, and I imagine you all are."

Bill slides the door open a couple of feet, but Sue pays no attention to me. She is staring angrily at Kaminski. "How can you *talk* that way? You did beautifully—ask anybody who heard you. This is only the first step, and you got by it just—just wonderfully! I told you I'd back you, and I will."

I have never observed anyone chewing his tongue, but that is what Kaminski is doing now, munching away, and his purple cheeks working. His face has begun to degenerate above the black and white formality of jacket and pleated shirt and rigid black tie. "You're incurably kind," he says thickly—whether in irony or not I can't tell. He spits out his tongue and says more plainly, "You like me, I know that. You're the only one. Nobody else. Nobody ever did. This is the way it was in Hollywood too. Did you know I was in Hollywood a while? I had a job playing for the soundtrack of a Charles Boyer movie. So what did I do? I quarreled with the director and he got somebody else."

With a resolute move, Ruth and I get out of the door. Pinpricks of fog are in our faces. From inside, Sue says efficiently, "Arnold, you've had one too many. It was a great success, really it was."

"Every time, I fail," wails Kaminski. His Mephisto airs have been melted and dissolved away; he is just a sloppy drunk with a crying jag on. His eyes beg pity and his mouth is slack and his hands paw at Sue. She holds him off by one thick wrist. "Every time," he says, and his eyes are on her now with a sudden drunken alertness. "Every time. You know why? I *want* to fail. I work like a dog for twenty years so I'll have the supreme pleasure of failing. Never knew anybody like that, did you? I'm very cunning. I plan it in advance. I fool myself right up to the last minute, and then the time comes and I know how cunningly I've been planning it all the time. I've been a failure all my life."

I am inclined to agree with him, but I am old and tired and fed up. I would also bet that he is well on his way to being an alcoholic, this anti-food-and-drink Artist. He has the proper self-pity. If you don't feel sorry for yourself in something like this you can't justify the bottle that cures and damns you. This Kaminski is one of those who drink for the hangover; he sins for the sweet torture of self-blame and confession. A crying jag is as good a way of holding the stage as playing the piano or bad manners.

Now he is angry again. "Why should a man have to scramble and crawl for a chance to play the soundtrack in a Boyer picture? That is how the artist is appreciated in this country. He plays offstage while a ham actor fakes for the camera. Why should I put up with that?

If I'm an artist, I'm an artist. I would rather play the organ in some neon cocktail bar than do this behind-the-scenes faking."

"Of course," Sue says. "And tomorrow we can talk about how you're going to go ahead and be the artist you want to be. You can have the career you want, if you're willing to work hard—oh, so hard! But you have to have *faith* in yourself, Arnold! You have to have confidence that nothing on earth can stop you, and then it can't."

"Faith," says Kaminski. "Confidence!" He weaves on his feet, and his head rolls, and for a second I hope he has passed out so we can tote him off to bed. But he gets himself straightened up and under control again, showing a degree of co-ordination that makes me wonder all anew whether he is really as drunk as he seems or if he is putting on some fantastic act.

And then I find him looking out of the open door with his mouth set in a mean little line. "*You* don't like me," he says. "You disliked me the minute you met me, and you've been watching me all night. You want to know why?"

"Not particularly," I say. "You'd better get to bed, and in the morning we can all be friends again."

"You're no friend of mine," says Kaminski, and Sue exclaims, "Arnold!" but Kaminski wags his head and repeats, "No frien' of mine, and I'll tell you why. You saw I was a fake. Looked right through me, didn' you? Smart man, can't be fooled just because somebody can play the piano. When did you decide I wasn't a Pole, eh? Tell me tha'."

I lift my shoulders. But it is true, now that I have had my attention called to it, that the slight unplaceable accent that was present earlier in the evening is gone. Now, even drunk and chewing his tongue, he talks a good deal like...

"Well, what is the accent?" I ask. "South Boston?"

"Seè, wha' I tell you?" he cries, and swings on Sue so that she has to turn with him and brace herself to hold him up. Her face puckers with effort, or possibly disgust, and now for the first time she is looking at Bill as a wife looks towards her husband when she needs to be got out of trouble. "See?" Kaminski shouts. "Wasn't fooled. You all were, but he wasn'. Regnize Blue Hill Avenue in a minute."

Again he drags himself up straight, holding his meaty hand close below his nose and studying it. "I'm a Pole from Egypt," he says. "Suffered a lot, been through Hell, made me diff'cult and queer. Eh?" He swings his eye around us, this preposterous scene-stealer; he holds us with his glittering eye. "Le' me tell you. Never been near Egypt, don't even know where Poland is on the map. My mother was not made into soap; she runs a copper and brass shop down by the North Station. So you wonner why people detes' me. Know why? I'm a fake, isn't an hones' thing about me. You jus' le' me go to Hell my own way, I'm good at it. I can lie my way in, and if I want I can lie my way out again. And what do you think of that?"

Bill Casement is the most good-natured of men, soft with his wife and over-generous with his friends and more tolerant of all sorts of difference, even Kaminski's sort, than you would expect. But I watch him now, while Kaminski is falling all over Sue, and Sue is making half-disgusted efforts to prop him up, and I realize that Bill did not make his money scuffing his feet and pulling his cheek in embarrassment at soirées. Underneath the good-natured husband is a man of force, and in about one more minute he is due to light on Kaminski like the hammer of God.

Even while I think it, Bill reaches over and yanks him up and holds him by one arm. "All right," he says. "Now you've spilled it all. Let's go to bed."

"You too," Kaminski says. "You all hate me. You'll all wash your hands of me now. Well, why not? That Carnegie Hall promise, that won't hold when you know what kin' of person I am, eh? You'll all turn into enemies now."

"Is that what you *want*, Arnold?" Sue says bitterly. She looks ready to burst into tears.

"Tol' you I wanted to fail," he says—and even now, so help me, even out of his sodden and doughy wreckage, there looks that bright, mean, calculating little gleam of intelligence.

Bill says, "The only enemy you've got around here is your own mouth."

"My God!" Kaminski cries loudly. Either the fog has condensed on his face or he is sweating. I remember the bright drop from his nose while he struggled with the Piano Pieces. "My God," he says again, almost wearily. He hangs, surprisingly frail, from Bill's clutch; it is easy to forget, looking at his too-big head and his meaty hands, that he is really scrawny. "I'll tell you something else," he says. "You don't know right now whether what I've tol' you is true or if it isn'. Not even the smart one there. You don't know but what I've been telling you all this for some crazy reason of my own. Why would I? Does it make sense?" He drops his voice and peers around, grinning. "Maybe he's crazy. *C'est dérangé.*"

"Come on," Bill says. He lifts Kaminski and starts him along, but Kaminski kicks loose and staggers and almost falls among the chairs in the foggy patio, and now what has been impossible becomes outrageous, becomes a vulgar burlesque—and I use the word vulgar deliberately, knowing who it is that speaks.

"Don't you worry about me!" Kaminski shouts, and kicks a chair over. "Don't you worry about a starving kike pianist from Blue Hill Avenue. Maybe I grew up in Egypt and maybe I didn't, but I can still play the piano. I can play the God damn keys off a piano."

He comes back closer, facing Sue with a chairback in his hands, bracing himself on it. "Don't worry," he says. "I can see you worrying, but don't worry. I'll be out of your damned little gardener's cottage in the morning, and thank you very much for nothing. Will that satisfy you?" With a jerk he throws the chair aside and it falls and clatters.

Bill Casement takes one step in Kaminski's direction, and the outrageous turns instantly into slapstick. The pianist squeaks like a mouse, turns and runs for his life. Behind a remoter chair he stops to show his teeth, but when Bill starts for him again he turns once more and runs. For a moment he hangs in mid-air, his legs going like a cat's held over water, and then he is in the pool. The splash comes up ghostly into the moonlight and the fog, and falls back again.

* * *

MAYBE HE CAN'T SWIM. Maybe in his squeaking terror of what he has stirred up he has forgotten that the pool is there. Maybe he is so far gone that he doesn't even know he has fallen in. And maybe, on the other hand, he literally intends to drown himself.

If he does, he successfully fails in that too. By the time Bill has run to flip on the underwater lights the white coat is down under, and Kaminski is not struggling at all. While the women scream, Bill jumps into the water, and here he comes wading towards the shallow end dragging Kaminski under his arm. He hauls him up the corner steps and dangles him, shaking the water out of him, and Kaminski's arms drag on the tile and his feet hang limp.

"Oh my God," Sue whispers, "is he dead?"

Bill looks disgusted. After all, Kaminski couldn't have been in the pool more than a minute altogether. As Bill lowers him on to the warm pavement and straightens him out with his face turned sideways on his arm, Kaminski shudders and coughs. His hands make tense, meaty grabs at the concrete. The majordomo, Jerry, pops out of the kitchen end of the cabaña in his undershirt, takes one look, and pops back in again. In a moment he comes running with a blanket.

Kaminski is not seriously in need of a blanket. For the first time that evening, he is not seriously in need of an audience, either. We stay only long enough to see that Bill and Jerry have everything under control, and then we get away. Sue walks us to the gate, but it is impossible to say anything to her. She looks at us once so hurt and humiliated and ashamed that I feel like going back and strangling Kaminski for keeps where he lies gagging on the patio floor, and then we are alone in the surrealist fog-swept spaces of the parking area. In the car we sit for a minute or two letting the motor warm, while the windshield wipers make half-circles of clarity on the glass.

"I wonder what..." Ruth begins, but I put my hand over her mouth.

"Please. I am an old tired philistine who has had all he can stand. Don't even speculate on what's biting him, or why he acts the way he does. I've already given him more attention than I can justify."

As soon as I take my hand away, Ruth says softly, "The horrible part is, he played awfully well."

We are moving now out the fog-shrouded drive between curving rows of young pines. "What?" I say. "Did you think so?"

"Oh yes. Didn't you?"

"He hit a big blooper in the Chaconne."

"That could happen to anybody, especially somebody young and nervous. But the interpretation—didn't you hear how he put himself into first the one and then the other, and how the whole quality changed, and how really authoritative he was in all of them? Some pianists can only play Mozart, or Beethoven, or Brahms. He can play anybody, and play him well. That's what Mr. Arpad said, too."

"Who's Mr. Arpad?"

"The one that accompanies singers."

"He thought he was good?"

"He told me he had come down expecting only another pianist, but he thought Kaminski had a real chance."

Tall eucalyptus trees are suddenly ghostly upreaching, the lights shine on their naked white trunks, the rails of a fence. I ease around a turn in second gear. "Well, all right," I say in intense irritation. "All right, he was good. But then why in the hell would he..."

And there we are back on it. Why would he? What made him? Was he lying at first, lying later, or lying all the time? And what is more important to me just then, where in God's name does he belong? What can the Sue Casements do for the Arnold Kaminskis, and where do the Bills come in, and what function, if any, is served by the contented, beagle-running, rabbit-chasing, patio-building, barbecuing exurbanites on their hundred hills? How shall a nest of robins deal with a cuckoo chick? And how should a cuckoo chick, which has no natural home except the one he usurps, behave himself in a robin's nest? And what if the cuckoo is sensitive, or Spiritual, or insecure? Christ.

Lights come at us, at first dim and then furry and enormous, the car behind them vaguely half seen, glimpsed and gone, and then the seethe of white again. I never saw the fog thicker; the whole cloudy blanket of the Pacific has poured over the Coast Range and blotted us out. I creep at ten miles an hour, peering for the proper turn-off on these unmarked country lanes.

The bridge planks rumble under us as I grope into our own lane. Half a mile more. Up there, the house will be staring blindly into cottonwool; my study below the terrace will be swallowed in fog; the oak tree where I do my birdwatching will have no limbs, no shade, no birds. Leaning to see beyond the switching wiper blades, I start up the last steep pitch, past the glaring-white gate, and on, tilting steeply, with the brown bank just off one fender and the gully's treetops fingering the fog like seaweed on the left. All blind, all difficult and blind. I taste the stale bourbon in my mouth and know myself for a frivolous old man.

In the morning, probably, the unidentifiable bird, towhee or whatever he is, will come around for another bout against the plate glass, hypnotized by the insane hostility of his double. I tell myself that if he wakes me again at dawn tomorrow with his flapping and pecking I will borrow a shotgun and scatter his feathers over my whole six acres.

Of course I will not. I know what I will do. I will watch the fool thing as long as I can stand it, and ruminate on the insanities of men and birds, and try to convince myself that as a local idiocy, an individual aberration, this behavior is not significant. And then when I cannot put up with the sight of this towhee any longer I will retire to my study and sit looking out of the window into the quiet shade of the oak, where nuthatches are brownly and pertly content with the bugs in their home bark. But even down there I may sometimes hear the banging and thrashing of this dismal towhee trying to fight his way past himself into the living-room of the main house.

We coast into the garage, come to a cushioned stop, look at each other.

"Tired?" Ruth whispers.

Her pet coon face glimmers in the dim light of the dash. Her eyes seem to be searching mine with a kind of anxiety. I notice that tired lines are showing around her mouth and eyes, and I am filled with gratitude for the forty years during which she has stood between me and myself.

"I don't know," I say, and kiss her and lean back. "I don't know whether I'm tired, or sad, or confused. Or maybe just irritated that they don't give you enough time in a single life to figure anything out."

Sources

"Literary By Accident" from *Utah Libraries*, Volume 18, Number 2, Fall 1975, Utah Library Association: Salt Lake City, UT, p. 7–21. Delivered at the Utah Library Association Convention March 1975. Copyright © 1975 by Wallace Stegner. Reprinted by permission of the Estate of Wallace Stegner.

"The Rediscovery of America: 1946" from *The Sound of Mountain Water*, Doubleday & Company: Garden City, New York, 1969, p. 44–76. Copyright © 1946, 1947, 1949, 1950, 1952, 1958, 1959, 1961, 1963, 1965, 1966, 1967, 1969 by Wallace Stegner. Reprinted by permission of the Estate of Wallace Stegner.

"Why I Like the West" from *Marking the Sparrow's Fall*, edited with a preface by Page Stegner, Henry Holt and Company: New York, 1998, p. 96–105. Copyright © 1948, 1950, 1957, 1958, 1961, 1962, 1966, 1969, 1975, 1980, 1981, 1983, 1985, 1987, 1990, 1992 by the Estate of Wallace Stegner. Reprinted by permission of the Estate of Wallace Stegner.

"The West Coast: Region with a View" from *One Way to Spell Man*, Doubleday & Company: Garden City, New York, 1982, p. 99–108. Copyright © 1959 by Wallace Stegner. Reprinted by permission of the Estate of Wallace Stegner.

"Comments for the Committee for Green Foothills' 25th Anniversary" delivered to the Committee for Green Foothills May 9, 1987. Copyright © 2008 by the Estate of Wallace Stegner. Reprinted by permission of the Estate of Wallace Stegner.

"Striking the Rock" from *The American West as Living Space*, The University of Michigan Press: Ann Arbor, 1987, p. 29–60. Copyright © 1987 by Wallace Stegner. Delivered as one of the Cook Lectures in the School of Law at the University of Michigan, October 29, 1986 and first published as "The Spoiling of the American West" in the *Michigan Quarterly Review*, Spring 1987, p. 293–310. Reprinted by permission of the University of Michigan Press.

Excerpt from *Beyond the Hundredth Meridian*, Houghton Mifflin Company: Boston, 1962, p. 96–110. Copyright © 1953, 1954 by Wallace Stegner. Reprinted by permission of the Estate of Wallace Stegner.

"How Do I Know What I Think Till I See What I Say" from *All the Little Live Things*, The Viking Press: New York, 1967, p. 3–12. Copyright © 1967 by Wallace Stegner. Reprinted by permission of the Estate of Wallace Stegner.

Excerpt from *Angle of Repose*, Doubleday: New York, 1971, p. 3–17. Copyright © 1971 by Wallace Stegner. Used by permission of Doubleday, a division of Random House, Inc.

A CALIFORNIA LEGACY BOOK

Santa Clara University and Heyday Books are pleased to publish the California Legacy series, vibrant and relevant writings drawn from California's past and present.

Santa Clara University—founded in 1851 on the site of the eighth of California's original twenty-one missions—is the oldest institution of higher learning in the state. A Jesuit institution, it is particularly aware of its contribution to California's cultural heritage and its responsibility to preserve and celebrate that heritage.

Heyday Books, founded in 1974, specializes in critically acclaimed books on California literature, history, natural history, and ethnic studies.

Books in the California Legacy series appear as anthologies, single author collections, reprints of important books, and original works. Taken together, these volumes bring readers a new perspective on California's cultural life, a perspective that honors diversity and finds great pleasure in the eloquence of human expression.

Series editor: Terry Beers
Publisher: Malcolm Margolin

Advisory committee: Stephen Becker, William Deverell, Charles Faulhaber, David Fine, Steven Gilbar, Ron Hansen, Gerald Haslam, Robert Hass, Jack Hicks, Timothy Hodson, James Houston, Jeanne Wakatsuki Houston, Maxine Hong Kingston, Frank LaPena, Ursula K. Le Guin, Jeff Lustig, Ishmael Reed, Alan Rosenus, Robert Senkewicz, Gary Snyder, Kevin Starr, Richard Walker, Alice Waters, Jennifer Watts, Al Young.

Thanks to the English Department at Santa Clara University and to Regis McKenna for their support of the California Legacy series.

If you would like to be added to the California Legacy mailing list, please send your name, address, phone number, and email address to:
California Legacy Project
English Department
Santa Clara University
Santa Clara, CA 95053

For more on California Legacy titles, events, or other information, please visit www.californialegacy.org.

Other California Legacy Books

Califauna: A Literary Field Guide
Edited by Terry Beers and Emily Elrod

Dawson's Avian Kingdom: Selected Writings by William Leon Dawson
Edited by Anna Neher

Death Valley in '49
William Lewis Manly

Eldorado: Adventures in the Path of Empire
Bayard Taylor

Essential Mary Austin
Edited with an Introduction by Kevin Hearle

Essential Muir
Edited with an Introduction by Fred D. White

Fool's Paradise: A Carey McWilliams Reader
Foreword by Wilson Carey McWilliams

Mark Twain's San Francisco
Edited with a New Introduction by Bernard Taper

A Separate Star: Selected Writings of Helen Hunt Jackson
Edited with an Introduction by Michelle Burnham

The Shirley Letters: From the California Mines, 1851-1852
Louise Amelia Knapp Smith Clappe

Spring Salmon, Hurry to Me!: The Seasons of Native California
Edited by Margaret Dubin and Kim Hogeland

Unfolding Beauty: Celebrating California's Landscapes
Edited with an Introduction by Terry Beers

Unsettling the West: Eliza Farnham and Georgiana Bruce Kirby
in Frontier California   *JoAnn Levy*

HEYDAY INSTITUTE

Since its founding in 1974, Heyday Books has occupied a unique niche in the publishing world, specializing in books that foster an understanding of the history, literature, art, environment, social issues, and culture of California and the West. We are a 501(c)(3) nonprofit organization based in Berkeley, California, serving a wide range of people and audiences.

We are grateful for the generous funding we've received for our publications and programs during the past year from foundations and more than three hundred and fifty individual donors. Major supporters include:

Anonymous; Audubon California; BayTree Fund; B.C.W. Trust III; S. D. Bechtel, Jr. Foundation; Fred & Jean Berensmeier; Joan Berman; Book Club of California; Butler Koshland Fund; California State Automobile Association; California State Coastal Conservancy; California State Library; Candelaria Fund; Columbia Foundation; Community Futures Collective; Compton Foundation, Inc.; Malcolm Cravens Foundation; Lawrence Crooks; Judith & Brad Croul; Laura Cunningham; David Elliott; Federated Indians of Graton Rancheria; Fleishhacker Foundation; Wallace Alexander Gerbode Foundation; Richard & Rhoda Goldman Fund; Marion E. Greene; Evelyn & Walter Haas, Jr. Fund; Walter & Elise Haas Fund; Charlene C. Harvey; Leanne Hinton; James Irvine Foundation; Matthew Kelleher; Marty & Pamela Krasney; Guy Lampard & Suzanne Badenhoop; LEF Foundation; Robert Levitt; Dolores Zohrab Liebmann Fund; Michael McCone; National Endowment for the Arts; National Park Service; Philanthropic Ventures Foundation; Alan Rosenus; Mrs. Paul Sampsell; Deborah Sanchez; San Francisco Foundation; William Saroyan Foundation; Melissa T. Scanlon; Seaver Institute; Contee Seely; Sandy Cold Shapero; Skirball Foundation; Stanford University; Orin Starn; Swinerton Family Fund; Thendara Foundation; Susan Swig Watkins; Tom White; Harold & Alma White Memorial Fund; and Dean Witter Foundation.

For more information about Heyday Institute, our publications and programs, please visit our website at www.heydaybooks.com.

About the Editor

Page Stegner was born in Salt Lake City, Utah, in 1937. He attended Stanford University, where he received his B.A. in History in 1959 and his Ph.D. in American Literature in 1964. From 1967 to 1995 he was Professor of American Literature and Director of the Creative Writing Program at the University of California, Santa Cruz, retiring early in 1995 to devote full time to writing. He currently lives with his wife, novelist Lynn Stegner, and his 19-year-old daughter, Allison (when she is not in attendance at Stanford) in Santa Fe, New Mexico.

He has been the recipient of a National Endowment for the Arts Fellowship (1979-80), a National Endowment for the Humanities Fellowship (1980-81), and a Guggenheim Fellowship (1981-82).

He is the author of *The Edge* (Dial Press, 1969); *Hawks and Harriers* (Dial Press, 1972); *Sportscar Menopause* (Atlantic/Little Brown, 1977); *Escape i nto Aesthetics* (Dial Press, 1968); *Nabokov's Congeries* (Viking Press, 1970); *American Places* (with Wallace Stegner and Eliot Porter, E.P. Dutton, 1981); *Islands of the West* (with Frans Lanting, Sierra Club Books, 1985); *Outposts of Eden* (Sierra Club Books, 1989); *Grand Canyon, The Great Abyss* (Harper Collins, 1995); *Winning the Wild West: The Epic Saga of the Opening of the American West: 1800-1899.* (Simon and Schuster, 2002); and he has been a frequent contributor over the past thirty-five years to numerous publications, including *Harper's, Atlantic, Esquire, Audubon, Outside, Sierra, Wilderness, New York Review of Books, New West, Los Angeles Times, Arizona Highways, National Parks, Geo, McCall's,* and *Mademoiselle*. He has recently edited *The Selected Letters of Wallace Stegner* (Shoemaker and Hoard, 2007) and completed a fourth collection of essays, *Adios Amigos: Tales of Sustenance and Purification in the American West* (Shoemaker and Hoard, 2008).